MERCURY BOYS

MERCURY BOYS

CHANDRA PRASAD

SOHO
TEEN

Published in the United States by Soho Teen
an imprint of Soho Press, Inc.
227 W 17th Street
New York, NY 10011

Library of Congress Cataloging-in-Publication Data

Prasad, Chandra, author.
Mercury Boys / Chandra Prasad.

ISBN 978-1-64129-265-8
eISBN 978-1-64129-266-5

1. Supernatural—Fiction. 2. Secret societies—Fiction.
3. Friendship—Fiction. 4. Racially mixed people—Fiction.
5.Moving, Household—Fiction.
LCC PZ7.1.P697 Mer 2021 | DDC [Fic]—dc23
LC record available at https://lccn.loc.gov/2020055361

Robert Cornelius image restoration:
Tetyana Dyachenko/digitartgallery.com

Interior design by Janine Agro, Soho Press, Inc.

Printed in the United States of America

10 9 8 7 6 5 4 3 2 1

To my readers—
Don't believe the naysayers.
You can do it.

"Mercury acts in the body through oppositions. It is both poison and medicine, both solid and liquid, both gravity and flight."
—RICHARD M. SWIDERSKI, *QUICKSILVER: A HISTORY OF THE USE, LORE AND EFFECTS OF MERCURY*

"Love is like quicksilver in the hand. Leave the fingers open and it stays. Clutch it and it darts away."
—DOROTHY PARKER

"There is a young gentleman of this city, by the name of Robert Cornelius, one of the firm of the well known house of Cornelius, Son & Co., who has more genius than he yet supposes himself to possess."
—*GODEY'S LADY'S BOOK*

FROM THE HOWARD AND ALICE STEERKEMP DAGUERREOTYPES COLLECTION

Name: Robert Cornelius

Born: 1809

Died: 1893

Profession: Chemist, Pioneer of Photography

Primary Place of Residence: Philadelphia, PA

Name: Samuel Pendleton

Born: 1834

Died: 1855

Profession: Poet

Primary Place of Residence: England

NAME: *Emery Westervelt*

BORN: *n/a*

DIED: *n/a*

PROFESSION: *Union Soldier*

PRIMARY PLACE OF
RESIDENCE: *Ipswich,
Massachusetts*

NAME: *Mack*

BORN: *n/a*

DIED: *n/a*

PROFESSION: *Pickpocket*

PRIMARY PLACE
OF RESIDENCE:
New York City

NAME: *Cassie*

BORN: *n/a*

DIED: *n/a*

PROFESSION: *Teacher*

PRIMARY PLACE OF
RESIDENCE: *New York*

CHAPTER ONE

Obsessions usually begin in a fiery cauldron of anger, jealousy, love, or revenge, but Saskia Brown's started in an ordinary high school classroom with bored students and a scuffed linoleum floor.

The class was Early American Innovation and Ingenuity. She'd decided to take it because it sounded hopeful and exciting, and also because it was Pass/Fail. Only last week she and her father had left Arizona and driven thirty-seven hours to Coventon, Connecticut. Though they were mostly settled into their new home, she still felt discombobulated. Better not to overload herself at school, she figured. Better to start slow. Next year, when she had the lay of the land, she could take some AP classes and really push herself.

Besides, there was only a month left in the school year. She hadn't even wanted to start at Coventon High so close to summertime. But her dad had insisted.

"Better to keep busy," he'd said.

To Saskia, it sounded like the same advice he probably gave himself. *Keep your mind occupied. Don't think about Mom.*

The teacher, Mr. Nash, wasn't young, but he acted like he was . . . in a good way. He jumped from topic to topic at a pace that made her head spin. He got excited when he talked, gesturing with his hands, occasionally pumping his fists in the air. His job hadn't made him jaded and cynical like other teachers his age.

The last assignment of the year was to study little-known American pioneers. Mr. Nash had the kids draw names out of a hat. Saskia got a guy named Robert Cornelius. She'd never heard of him. Now she had less than two weeks to research and write a ten-page report and prepare a fifteen-minute oral presentation on him. Back at her old school, giving a presentation wouldn't have been a problem. She'd been outgoing. Extroverted. But here, all she wanted to do was blend in.

No, strike that—all she wanted to do was fade into the background.

Because faded is exactly how I feel, she thought.

Sitting back down, she shoved the scrap of paper aside. She glanced at her bland gray T-shirt and bare, chewed-down fingernails. In her old town, she'd worn black and silver nail polish. She'd had a pair of jeans that she'd splashed with colored paint, Jackson Pollock–style. Sometimes she'd scrawl words she liked on her T-shirts: *agnostic, sensory overload, Rasputin, continental drift, abacus, ambrosia, mercenary.* Back then, she hadn't been afraid to stand out. Not that she'd been super popular. But she'd been fine with that. Fine with being herself: the girl who watched too many old movies; who had a tendency to daydream; whose big, curly, uncontrollable hair seemed to have a mind of its own. The one no one could quite pigeonhole. ("Is she Black?" "Nah, her dad's white." "Yeah, but her mom's not.")

Those days seemed liked ancient history now. They had even before the move.

After word of her mom's affair leaked out, lots of her so-called friends abandoned her, gossiped behind her back. They'd called her mom a cradle snatcher. And Saskia couldn't deny it. Her fifty-year-old mother was seeing a twenty-four-year-old. Gross. Since Saskia had left Arizona, not a single one of her friends had called or texted to make sure she was okay. Not even her best friend, Heather. That hurt a lot. It upset her almost as much her mom's infidelity.

Heather had been unpredictable, maybe even reckless, but Saskia had adored her. The bottom line was that Heather knew how to have fun—and Saskia had fun with her. During one memorable sleepover, they'd made White Russians at Heather's house on the down-low after her parents had gone to sleep. There hadn't been any milk, so they'd used cream. *Small sips*, Heather had said encouragingly, when Saskia admitted she'd never tried alcohol before. She remembered vomiting as quietly as possible, her stomach churning, hoping the noise wouldn't wake up Heather's parents. She remembered laughing so hard her ribs hurt.

But she also remembered the final text Heather had sent her. Last minute, her supposed best friend had canceled their plans to hang out. Again. Heather had blamed a sore throat, but Saskia had seen her at school that very day, and she'd seemed fine: lively, a little hyper, very Heather-ish. So it was pretty obvious she was blowing Saskia off.

It would have been better if Heather had just come out and said it: *"I don't want to be your friend anymore. Your family is hella embarrassing."*

Better to rip off the Band-Aid all at once, Saskia thought now.

During free period she went to the library and googled "Robert Cornelius" on her laptop. She scanned the entries and picked up some basic info. Cornelius was a pioneer in early photography. He'd worked with photos known as daguerreotypes. His family owned a prosperous gas and lighting company. He had expertise in chemistry and metallurgy. Metallurgy? She made a mental note to look that up later, as well as "daguerreotypes."

She clicked on "images," not expecting much, but getting an eyeful. The same grainy, black-and-white photo appeared over and over again. "Robert Cornelius: Self-Portrait," the captions read. Here was a striking young man with an intense, arresting stare. His arms were crossed defiantly. The collar of his dark coat was turned up. He looked, frankly, like a nineteenth-century badass.

She heard a whistle from behind.

Whipping around, she saw Lila Defensor, her new friend—scratch that, her *only* friend—at Coventon High. Lila was small, not even five feet. Fun-sized, she called herself. Her freckles, hair, and eyes were all the exact same color of dark amber, a synchronicity that was offset by the bright earrings and headbands she usually wore.

Saskia had gravitated toward Lila the second she'd seen her. Walking near each other in a hallway, they had rolled their eyes in tandem at a girl leaning against her locker, pouting and preening as she took selfies. "That's a serious commitment to self-absorption," Lila had whispered to Saskia, who'd known at that moment that she and Lila were like two Twix bars in the same wrapper.

Like Saskia, Lila had little patience for shallow people. But unlike Saskia, Lila radiated confidence and self-possession. Even her sassy cherry-red glasses screamed smart and quirky rather than socially inept. The fact that Lila had a part-time job at Western Connecticut State and got to hang around college students only added to her coolness quotient.

"He's not bad for a dead guy," Lila said, gazing at Robert Cornelius. "He *is* dead, right?"

"Yeah, he's gotta be. This is from, like, the 1800s."

"Who is he?" Lila leaned closer to Saskia's screen.

Saskia told her what little she knew, adding, "I guess that photo's the first self-portrait ever taken."

Lila stared unblinking for several seconds, her eyes both lively and contemplative. Suddenly her face lit up in recognition. "Wait a minute; I've seen this photo before! It's in the library where I work."

"Seriously?"

"Yeah, Western Connecticut has an archive of thousands of old photos: tintypes, Carte de Visites, Cabinet Cards, cyanotypes, ambrotypes, daguerreotypes. It's, like, the second biggest in the country."

"Random."

"Completely. That's got to be a daguerreotype, right?"

Saskia was impressed. "It is. How'd you know . . . and what the heck is a daguerreotype?"

"I've been working at the archive a year now, so I've had to

learn out of necessity. Don't want to get fired, right? Daguerreotypes were made on sheets of copper plated with a coat of silver.
Photography back then was complicated."

Lila dropped her backpack on the floor with a *thunk* and
slumped into a seat. The unzipped pack revealed a trove of thick,
heavy books. Saskia didn't know how she hauled them all around.
"What did you do," Saskia asked, "take the college library with
you?"

"Pretty much."

"Ever hear of a Kindle?"

"I'm old-school," Lila said. "I like the smell of old paper and
dust." She took a book out and sniffed the binding.

Saskia laughed. "Weirdo."

Lila didn't react. She was gazing at the screen again, a pensive
look on her face. "Hey, I hate to break this to you, but I just realized something. By taking this picture, Cornelius basically invented
the selfie."

"Oh my god, you're right!"

Saskia and Lila looked at each other and burst out laughing.
When they'd regained their composure, Lila said, "I could show
you the photo in the archive, if you want . . ."

"You could smuggle me in?"

"Don't you want to see the actual daguerreotype?"

Saskia nodded. "Yeah, of course, but I don't want to get you in
trouble."

"I like to live on the edge," Lila joked. She pulled out a Western
Connecticut State employee ID card she kept dangling on a chain
around her neck. "For real, it's no problem; I've got access. And the
security guard there—Rich—he loves me."

"And you're absolutely sure this guy Cornelius is there?"

Both girls again looked at the image on the smudged screen
of Saskia's laptop. They felt the weight of the man's stare. Saskia
sensed he was almost challenging her.

"I'm sure," Lila replied, adjusting her vivid ikat headband. "I
never forget a pretty face."

. . .

For the rest of the day Saskia couldn't get Robert Cornelius out of her head. He kept coming back to her like a song on repeat, only instead of lyrics buzzing in her brain, she saw his daguerreotype.

She couldn't wait to go with Lila to the archives, not just because she'd get to see his image firsthand, but also because she hadn't been out with a friend in a long time. A really long time. She had a feeling hanging out with Lila would be a good change of pace. Besides, what high school girl *didn't* want to hang out at a college?

After last period, Saskia went to her locker to gather her homework. She tried not to tense up when the girl with the neighboring locker, Paige Sampras, appeared beside her. In her brief time at Coventon High School, Saskia had learned a few things: avoid the girls' restroom across from the auditorium—it was *always* gross; sit in the back of Mr. Gionni's class because he had dog food breath; befriend Paige Sampras if you wanted to look cool.

At Saskia's old school, there had been the usual queen bees: cheerleader types who wielded their gleaming popularity like lightsabers. But Paige seemed different. For one thing, she was accomplished: top ten in their class, editor of the school's literary magazine, captain of the swim team. Plus, she was nice. Sunny, with an easy charm. Even though she could have gotten away with being a snob, she acted pleasant to everybody.

Saskia stared at her out of the corner of her eye. She searched for a zit, a mole, some sign of mortal imperfection.

Nothing.

"What do you think of school so far?" Paige asked, turning to her with a smile.

Saskia's cheeks warmed. She felt like she were staring into the eyes of a celebrity or something. "I don't know."

"It takes a while to settle in, I guess."

Under Paige's gaze, she felt self-conscious. She liked her body just fine, but her clothes were beyond boring: baggy shorts and that terrible gray T-shirt. Talk about faded. Meanwhile, Paige looked great in a black tank dress that drew attention to her waist, which was small like Vivien Leigh's in *Gone with the Wind*. Saskia thought that she should stop watching so many old movies.

"Hey, I meant to say this before, but if you ever want to hang out," Paige said, "let me know. I can introduce you to some people, maybe show you 'round town."

Saskia's face felt as if it were on fire. "Th-thanks," she stuttered. "That would be great."

She smiled at Paige, but Paige's attention had shifted. A boy had stopped by to talk. "Hey," he said to Paige.

Paige slammed her locker door a little harder than she needed to. "Hey, yourself."

"How've you been?"

"Josh, have you met Saskia?" Paige asked, avoiding the question.

If Saskia had been nervous before, now she was full-on panicked. She didn't know if Josh recognized her, but she more than recognized him. He was in her Early American Innovation and Ingenuity class. He sat a couple of rows in front of her: a brooding, quiet, detached, mesmerizing boy. Today Saskia had caught him shuffling a deck of cards until Mr. Nash had confiscated them.

We haven't met, Saskia wanted to say, *but in my daydreams you play an Asian Jim Stark in* Rebel Without a Cause. *I'm your girlfriend, a brown Natalie Wood, like when she played an improbable Puerto Rican in* West Side Story.

"Nah, I don't think so," he replied, causing Saskia to wince.

"Well, consider this your official introduction," Paige said. "Josh McClane, meet Saskia Brown. Saskia Brown, meet Josh McClane."

Josh saluted her without much interest, then looked away. "Did you hear that Ethan's planning a party?" The question was clearly meant for Paige. "You going?"

Paige blew back a wisp of hair. "I doubt it."

"Why not?"

"Better things to do, I guess." She turned again to Saskia, who wished she had one iota of Paige's game. "Are you going, Saskia?" she asked.

"Um, I don't know yet." The truth was, Saskia didn't know who Ethan was.

Josh leaned on Paige's locker door, bending his head close to hers. "I was hoping you'd be there," he murmured.

"Well, don't get your hopes up."

Suddenly Saskia felt like a fly on the wall. A very awkward fly.

"We'll talk later?" he asked.

"Maybe," Paige said.

He straightened up. His inky-dark eyes grew sulky. "See you later, then, I guess."

Saskia watched him shuffle away in his Chuck Taylors, backpack flung over his shoulder. Restless and tortured, just like Jim Stark.

"Do you guys have a history or something?" she blurted, surprised the words had come out of her mouth.

Luckily Paige chuckled. "History's the right word. Ancient history."

"I think he's still into you."

"Nah, he's just nostalgic."

Saskia looked in the direction he'd gone. He rounded a corner, disappearing from view. "Why'd you break up?"

"God, I don't know. We're like a freakin' Taylor Swift song. Always on and off."

Saskia deposited the last of her books into her backpack and shut the locker door. "Someday you can tell me the story."

"Sure," Paige replied. "Someday when we have, like, a hundred hours to kill."

Saskia sat in the middle of her bed, pillows all around, and stared at her laptop. She had read half of the twenty or so Robert Cornelius entries sprinkled on Google, and was hungry for more. Each tidbit was like opening a door into Cornelius's world—a world so different from her own, before Wi-Fi and TV, social media and cell phones. A simpler world, maybe, but Saskia wasn't so sure when she stared at Cornelius's self-portrait. Something about his expression— the ardent, appraising eyes—made her think there had been nothing simple at all about his life.

She'd learned his basic biography. He was the son of Christian Cornelius, a Dutch immigrant in Philadelphia. As a boy he'd gone to private school. From there, he'd worked for his father, mastering many skills, included silver-plating. He became so adept at silver-plating, in fact, that the Smithsonian Institute hired him for jobs. Eventually, he developed an interest in daguerreotypes. Between 1839 and 1843, he partnered with a chemist, Paul Beck Goddard, and operated two photography studios. Yet he decided to give up photography shortly thereafter, and abruptly went back to running the family's prosperous gas and lighting company.

As for his personal life, Cornelius had married a woman named Harriet Comely in 1832. They'd had eight children together, five daughters and three sons. Cornelius had lived to the age of eighty-four. Of all the daguerreotypes he'd made in his lifetime, only a handful still existed.

Online, Saskia waded through old newspaper articles, encyclo-pedia entries, and chemistry texts. She read about his home city, Philadelphia, and what it had been like during his lifetime. But she still had questions about Cornelius's life. She wanted to know why he'd given up photography. Was it because he'd made more money in lighting? Or had he grown tired of his studios? None of the sources said.

She stared again at his face, trying to tease out an answer from his expression. But he was inscrutable. A little like Josh McClane.

At six thirty, hunger pangs drove her out of her room and into the kitchen. She microwaved a Healthy Choice frozen meal—there were about fifty of them stacked in the freezer—and joined her father in the small adjoining living room. She usually tried to stay out of there. The carpet stank of cat pee. Saskia wouldn't have been surprised if the previous owner had been a crazy cat lady.

"I'm not sure I like this," she said after the first bite.

"Which one is it?"

"Spicy Caribbean Chicken. Too much pineapple."

"Oh, I like that one. Leave it for me."

"Hey, Dad, can you get more of the Chicken Alfredo Florentine?" She'd been living on those for the past week, and they still tasted pretty good. Cereal boxes and Healthy Choice meals were the extent of their culinary choices now. Saskia's mother had been the chef in the family.

"Sure."

"Which episode is this?" Saskia pointed her fork at the TV.

Lately her father had taken to watching *Gilmore Girls*, an old show about a young single mother and her only daughter who had moved to a small Connecticut town. The daughter was witty, pretty, and polished. Her mother was the sassy owner of a bed-and-breakfast. Cleverly they bantered their way through life against the background of bucolic New England scenery.

For some unknown reason, her father couldn't get enough of the show. He'd watched every episode at least once. Saskia was almost sure they'd moved to Coventon because of that. She suspected she and her father were stand-ins for the main characters, Rory and Lorelei, only less charming, attractive, and well adjusted. Instead of owning a big bed-and-breakfast, they owned a ranch that reeked of cat piss. Instead of a mother-and-daughter team, they were father and daughter—two peas in the same dysfunctional pod.

"The one where Rory goes for a joyride on a yacht with her new boyfriend."

"I didn't realize she was such a rebel," observed Saskia.

"I know. It's completely out of character."

"What happens next?"

"In some other episode, she has to do three hundred hours of community service," her father replied.

"Serves her right."

"I disagree. That punishment's a little extreme. Other than this one crime, she's a pretty good kid."

"Come on. What if *I* went for a joyride on a yacht?"

Her father turned to her. "Depends. How big is the yacht?"

His cell phone rang. He reached for it on the coffee table, amid a clutter of newspapers, empty coffee cups, and MCAT review books. Her father was a nurse, but he had hopes of someday going to medical school.

"Hello, Emefa," he said, hitting PAUSE on the show.

Saskia made a face.

Her father and mother exchanged curt, awkward pleasantries. Then he cupped the mouthpiece and asked, "Are you home?"

Saskia shook her head.

"You should be home," he whispered.

"I don't want to talk to her," she whispered back.

"She's your mother."

"*You* don't want to talk to her."

"That's different; she's not my wife anymore. She'll *always* be your mother."

Saskia frowned. Her father frowned. He said Saskia was in the shower and would call her mother back. Then he hung up and exhaled.

"What does she want?" Saskia demanded.

"She wonders what you want for your birthday."

"She hasn't asked me that since I was eight years old."

"Well, she's asking now."

"She's bribing me. Trying to buy my forgiveness."

"That's an interesting interpretation, Sask. Maybe she just wants to be nice because she loves you. And because she misses you."

Her father pushed aside some of the mess on the coffee table to make room for his feet.

All of their belongings, table included, were new and cheap. When he wasn't studying, working, or watching *Gilmore Girls*, her father was assembling IKEA furniture. At all hours, Saskia could find him on the floor puzzling over assembly instructions. She'd suggested buying furniture at a consignment shop or Goodwill, but her father didn't want anything "old or used."

Or attached to memories. To other people's happiness and heartache.

Saskia stared at the frozen screen, at Lorelei and Rory sitting in Luke's Diner, smiling over their cheeseburgers. What her father wanted, really, was a fresh start. A clean slate. But he was an adult; he should know better. Even Saskia knew better, and she was a kid. There was no such thing as a real do-over. People carried their emotional baggage with them until the very end.

"Dad, do you ever feel like we maybe made a mistake . . . moving here?"

"No," he said firmly, scratching his stubbly face. Lately, no matter what time it was, he always had a five-o'clock shadow. "It was the right decision. We're just in a transitional period. And transitional periods are tough."

"You sound like a self-help guide."

"Where do you think I got the wording? Listen, in a few months, we'll feel like we were made for Coventon."

"I hope so."

Saskia started to straighten up the coffee table, but stopped when she found an ashtray underneath a copy of the Sunday *New York Times*. She'd caught him smoking a couple times outside, too. Until they'd moved here, she'd never once seen him with a cigarette. She wondered if he'd smoked in the past, or if this was a new thing. A new bad habit to go with their new bad life.

"Hey, Dad," she announced, "I'm going out tonight."

"You are?" He looked a little apprehensive, but his voice was encouraging.

"Yeah, out with a friend. Her name's Lila. I met her in school."

"See, honey, I told you you'd make friends here."

"I said *a* friend. Singular."

"Well, that's a start. A good start! What's the mission—studying or girl talk?"

Saskia ate another forkful of Spicy Caribbean Chicken, even though her stomach protested. "I don't know. Both?"

"Well, have fun. I mean it. Try to let go of some of your worry and just . . . live."

"Oh god, Dad, talk about self-help wording . . ."

He waved his hand toward the TV. "It's this," he griped. "Too much estrogen."

"You're the one who watches it!"

"I know, I know. Hey, my shift starts in two hours—I won't be home when you get back."

"Drink some coffee," she told him.

"Don't worry, I'm living on it. These irregular shifts are killing me."

CHAPTER TWO

Fifteen minutes later, her teeth brushed to get the taste of pineapple out of her mouth, Saskia climbed into Lila's car—a big old Buick that had seen better days. The front fender tilted to one side, and dings and dents bruised the body. The interior wasn't much better, but a car was a car. At least Saskia was out of the house and going somewhere.

"Ready to meet Robert Cornelius?" Lila asked.

"He's just Cornelius to me."

Lila looked at her quizzically.

Saskia shrugged. "He looks more like a Cornelius than a Robert, don't you think? I mean, he's definitely not a *Bob*."

"Whatever you say."

Lila put her foot on the gas, and the car lurched forward. She told Saskia how she'd bought the Buick last year with money earned from her library gig. "It's a clunker, yes, but at least I've got some freedom. It's *torture* being around my brothers and sisters all day."

"How'd you get your job?"

"My mom works at Western Connecticut State."

"She's a professor?"

"No, she works in the cafeteria. She's been there ever since my dad walked out. Fifteen years now. She's one of the serving ladies."

Saskia appreciated how Lila didn't mince words. "Does she like it there?"

Lila gave her a cryptic smile. "She has a lot of friends. She knows everyone—even the president of the college. She asked him about a part-time job for me while she was serving him mac and cheese."

"Seriously?"

"Seriously. My pay grade's good, too. I think the president has a soft spot for older Latinas—or for mac and cheese."

"Do you work a lot?"

"Yeah, but I don't mind. It's quiet. Sometimes I do my homework there. Anyway, it's mostly grunt work: answering emails, making calls, scanning. I've become an expert at retrieving and returning daguerreotypes. They're fragile, so we have to be really careful."

"Will you keep your job over the summer?"

"Hell, yeah. I hope to score more hours, too."

"I probably shouldn't ask this, but are there any other jobs available?"

Lila glanced at her and stuck out her bottom lip. "No, sorry. My department's not hiring."

"I have no idea what I'm gonna do this summer," Saskia said, as much to herself as to Lila. "I'm kind of dreading it—all that free time."

"I hate free time, too. Because it means babysitting all my brothers and sisters."

"How many do you have?"

"Five, all younger. They're like a pack of wolves."

"I'm an only child."

"Lucky!"

"Hey, what's this?" Saskia asked after a few moments. She examined an insect charm dangling from the rearview mirror.

"That? A dragonfly."

"It's really pretty." It was. Sleek and silver, with four paper-thin, filigree wings, the dragonfly was both elegant and lifelike.

"Thanks. My grandmother gave it to me before she died. She was the best. She was, like, the one person who was always there for me. Always rooting for me."

"When did she pass?"

"Last year. Springtime. Right when the crocuses came out—those were her favorite flowers. I think she waited to see them before dying."

Saskia fingered the charm. "Why a dragonfly?"

"Well, there's a story behind it." Lila glanced at her sheepishly. "You wanna hear it?"

"Sure."

Lila cleared her throat. She gripped the wheel a little tighter, her eyes on the road. "Okay, so, it's kind of a fable. There was this pond, and at the very bottom lived a bunch of water bugs. Every once in a while one of them would get the urge to swim up. It would get to the top and climb onto a lily pad. Then it would transform into a beautiful dragonfly. The dragonfly would want to tell the others what had happened. But it couldn't. Because it couldn't go back into the water. All it could do was buzz above the surface. And when the other water bugs looked up, they didn't recognize their old friend because it looked so different." She hesitated for a moment, her brow furrowed, as if she were unsure of whether to continue.

"That's sad in a way," Saskia said quietly.

Lila shrugged. "In a way," she echoed. "The meaning, I guess, is that you can't communicate after certain lines are crossed—like the line between the living and the dead. But just because someone's dead doesn't mean they're really gone. They're just in a different place." She sighed.

"Sad but beautiful, too," Saskia added, and meant it.

"My grandmother gave me that charm so I wouldn't forget her, but you know, she didn't need to. I still think about her every day."

"Do you think it's true? That when people die, they're still . . . somewhere?"

"Personally?" Lila shook her head. "I don't know. My family's Catholic. They believe in heaven, hell, angels playing harps—the whole shebang. Me? I'm a realist. Much as I loved my grandma, sometimes I think death's the end. Finito." She took one hand off the wheel and pretended to slash her throat with her finger. Then she flicked the turn signal. "So I guess we're lucky, right? We made it here alive."

Western Connecticut State's campus was a maze of stately buildings, statues, benches, and square patches of lawn bisected by brick paths. Walking beside Lila, Saskia felt a little starstruck by the college students scurrying past: the girls all seemed worldly and glamorous; the boys looked like handsome extras from the CW network.

There had to be some magic that happened between high school and college, Saskia reasoned. It was almost like a fairy godmother waved a wand and made all the geeky, gawky high schoolers turn into Cinderellas and Prince Charmings when they finished senior year.

By the time the two of them reached the library, Saskia felt downright intimidated. The place reminded her of the White House: huge white columns preceding a massive white edifice. She hunched her shoulders and hid behind her hair as they walked inside. Lila flashed her ID at a guard sitting behind a desk. He nodded, and Lila led Saskia through a vast, air-conditioned foyer. From behind, Saskia couldn't help but notice Lila's body language. Her posture was bold, her stride assertive. She obviously felt at home. This was her place, where she belonged. Saskia envied that feeling. She could barely remember it.

There were wide stone corridors on three sides, and a circulation area a hundred yards in. The girls proceeded down a corridor and several narrow hallways and up one escalator before arriving at a door marked THE HOWARD AND ALICE STEERKEMP DAGUERREOTYPES COLLECTION in glinting bronze letters.

"Who the heck are Howard and Alice Steerkemp?" Saskia whispered.

"Filthy rich alums," Lila muttered, pressing her ID card against a sensor. The door unlocked with a metallic *click*.

Inside, the girls were greeted by a man with thick black glasses and a perfectly bald head. He had a faint coffee stain down the middle of his "Campus Security" shirt, and his name tag read RICH. "I had a bunch of good jokes and no one to tell them to," he said to Lila. "What took you so long?"

"Tell me one now," she replied.

He tapped his head. "Can't remember any. You gotta be here when the lightning strikes, you know?"

"Sorry, lost opportunity."

"You got that right." He frowned at Saskia. "Who've you brought?"

"My friend Saskia. She wants to see the daguerreotypes."

Saskia swallowed and forced a smile, tucking a coil of hair behind her ears. "Hello."

He gave her a curt nod and turned his attention back to Lila. "Now, you know Marlene's back, right?"

"What? She said she was coming back Monday."

"She must've changed her mind."

"Is she here now?" asked Lila.

"Nah. She stepped out, probably fifteen minutes ago. Maybe gone for the night. Maybe not."

Lila shot Saskia a nervous look. "No one's supposed to be here after hours except for my boss, Marlene, and Rich. But since Marlene's usually gone, and Rich doesn't mind, sometimes I come anyway."

He chuckled. "I don't mind? I stick out my neck every time you come in here at night." He turned to Saskia, his expression softening. "She comes all the time. 'Why?' I ask her. 'You're young—get out there. Grab life by the horns. Don't end up like me, a relic of the past.' You know I still have VHS tapes and a Blockbuster card?"

Confused, Saskia shook her head.

"You know I come because I like the company," Lila said.

"Yeah, yeah." He groaned. "Go on, then. Go on and do your thing. I'll keep a lookout."

"Don't let her know I'm here."

"Do I ever?"

Lila scurried past him, tugging Saskia behind her.

"He's funny," Saskia whispered.

"He is that."

"What's his story?"

Lila shrugged. "He's one of those people who missed the train to adulthood, I guess. He lives in his mother's basement and pays her rent."

"Oh."

"Maybe he's onto something, though."

"What do you mean?"

Lila let go and slowed down. "Like, not that I want to live in my mother's basement, but I'm not sure I want to get married and have kids. You know, go the conventional route."

Saskia looked at her to make sure she was serious. She was.

A moment later Lila paused in front of a large wooden door. "You ready?"

The Howard and Alice Steerkemp Daguerreotypes Collection room was a stark, sterile-feeling place with identical filing cabinets on three sides. The cabinets were very tall, reaching well above Saskia's and Lila's heads, and the drawers were wide and flat. Lila pointed out a series of numbers and letters on each one: the department's classification system.

"This room is temperature controlled—always sixty-eight degrees," Lila said matter-of-factly. "And low humidity. Daguerreotypes don't like damp or extreme temperatures."

She pulled open a drawer and selected a white box. "All the photos are in acid-free containers," she continued, "'cause acid causes decay."

Inside was a tattered leather case, roughly six by eight inches. It had been ornate once, with a series of gold flourishes and curlicues around the edges, but was now scuffed and tattered. Lila fingered it gently, then lifted the cover, revealing the image of a woman with a ponderous expression. Her hair was parted down the middle and pulled back severely. She wore heavy earrings and a brooch on her high-collared blouse. Her hands were neatly crossed in her lap. The black-and-white image seemed to capture the essence of the woman without the distraction of color.

Lila showed Saskia how a preserver, glass, and mat were all mounted over the daguerreotype to protect it and keep it in place. "You can tell the age of the daguerreotype by the texture and shape of the mat, and by the type of case and preserver," she said.

"By the clothing and hairstyles, too," Saskia observed.

Lila smiled at her. "Right. I've learned that the super proper-puritan look—like this lady is wearing—means the picture was probably made in the 1840s. The more fancy styles mean the picture was made later." She handed the daguerreotype to Saskia for a closer look. The image had a mirror effect, depending on the angle at which it was held. Correctly guessing what Saskia was thinking, Lila said, "Remember I told you daguerreotypes are made on silver? Those silver plates are basically mirrors. That's why they're reflective. Sometimes daguerreotypes were called 'mirrors with a memory.'"

For the first time, Saskia realized something that should have been obvious all along: her new friend was a full-fledged, unabashed, all-in daguerreotype nerd. Saskia liked her all the more for that. "Nice," she replied, moving the image. "How are daguerreotypes made, exactly?"

"I only know the basics. There are eight steps involved: polishing the plate, coating it . . . ." Lila took the daguerreotype out of Saskia's hand and put it down. "Come on. I want to show you something."

She led Saskia into an adjoining room. It had a couple of tables with stools, and shelves cluttered with tools, equipment, and supplies. There was a long counter with a deep sink on one side. In a corner, a few ancient-looking cameras stood on tripods.

"This is the workshop," Lila said. She showed Saskia several wooden tools that were scattered on a table. "This is a plate box. And this one's a buffing stick. I don't know the rest. These were the things used to make daguerreotypes."

"I thought Western Connecticut State collects daguerreotypes. It makes them, too?"

"Sometimes. My boss, Marlene, likes to experiment. Mostly this room is used for repair, though. We have to clean a lot of the images we get. They come in damaged. Sometimes the pictures are so faded we can't even make out what they are."

Lila crossed the room to the sink. Motioning to a shelf above it, she showed Saskia an assortment of bottles and tins and decanters labeled iodine, bromine, sodium thiosulfate, gold chloride, mercury, and more. "Here are all the chemicals used in the daguerreotype process."

"No wonder my guy Cornelius had to be good at chemistry."

Saskia watched as Lila took a glass bottle marked MERCURY from the shelf. She grimaced. Saskia associated mercury with thermometers and old paint. With fish that pregnant women shouldn't eat. With the bad stuff they used to put in vaccines. The word *toxic* came to mind. She wondered what Lila was planning to do.

"Mercury has to be stored in glass because it reacts to other metals," Lila said casually. She tipped the container and poured a few drops right onto the countertop. The drops moved as if they were alive, little beads of silvery water that bobbed and jiggled. "Did you know mercury's the only metal that's liquid at room temperature?"

Saskia shook her head nervously.

Lila bent over the droplets and blew on them like birthday candles. They slunk a few inches across the counter.

"My uncle played with mercury as a kid. He used it in school, in science class," Lila continued. "The teacher let the kids touch it."

"That was a bad idea," Saskia said.

"I don't know. My uncle turned out fine, no damage done." Lila touched one of the quivering beads with her index finger.

Saskia flinched. "Don't do that," she blurted out. "It's poisonous."

"Not really," Lila said in a calm voice. "I mean, yes, technically mercury is poison. But one little touch isn't gonna do anything. Did you know people used to take it on purpose? President Lincoln used to take little blue mercury pills every day called 'blue mass.' Doctors said it helped with depression."

Saskia chewed a fingernail. She was anxious but now also curious. "Seriously?"

"Yeah."

"Okay, fine, but we don't have to touch mercury *now*."

"Relax, Sask. We're already exposed to tons of chemicals every day—in our food and water, on our lawns, in the air. All the adults have turned this planet into a toxic waste dump. Plus, we live near Arrivo, the worst chemical company in the state!"

Even though Lila was being too cavalier, Saskia suspected she was right. It seemed like every time Saskia read the news, there was another massive oil spill in the ocean, another fracking accident, another pesticide that caused cancer. Previous generations had already polluted the planet, endangering everyone; a little mercury wasn't going to make much of a difference. With her mangled fingernail, Saskia gingerly brushed one of the blobs. It jiggled like Jell-O. She recoiled.

"What did it do? Bite?" Lila joked.

Frowning, Saskia tried again. This time she pushed two beads together. They coalesced into a single bubble. She didn't want to admit it, but it was fun to join all the beads into one big blob, then divide them again. Almost like a game.

"If you'd told me I'd be playing with mercury tonight, I never would have believed you," she said.

"And just think—we haven't even gotten to the main event!"

"Cornelius?"

"Who else?"

Lila pushed the beads back into their bottle and led Saskia to a sink to wash their hands, and then the girls headed to the Collection room. After returning the daguerreotype of the puritanical woman, Lila retrieved the one they'd come for. She gingerly handed it to Saskia with a little smile.

Saskia stared at the image, losing herself in it. In person, Robert Cornelius's image was different from the versions she had seen online. It was lighter, more vivid and vibrant. The man himself seemed younger—closer to twenty than to thirty. There was another difference, too, although it took Saskia several moments to put her finger on it. Onscreen, Cornelius's expression had seemed willful, but here it was slightly questioning. Almost as if he were asking the answer to a question that eluded him.

"He's dreamy, all right," Lila said.

"Is it weird that I feel jealous of his wife?" Saskia asked. "His *dead* wife?"

"Do you really need to ask that?"

Saskia giggled. She held the daguerreotype at an angle, observing its mirror quality. She looked for clues—clues to what Robert Cornelius might have been thinking. She slipped the picture out of its case and turned it over. The back read: "The first light Picture ever taken. 1839."

Saskia shook her head. "Amazing," she murmured.

After a minute or two, Lila began to shift on her feet. Saskia looked up. Her friend was clearly fidgety.

"It's getting late," Lila said. "And Marlene wouldn't appreciate seeing us here, believe me." She reached for the image. "Don't worry, you'll see your boyfriend again. We'll come back another time."

"I have a better idea. I'll take him home," Saskia said, clutching the daguerreotype to her chest.

With lightning speed, Lila plucked it away. "Maybe mercury *does* make people crazy," she muttered.

Saskia swallowed. Strangely, she felt as if she were being deprived of something that was rightfully hers. "You promise we'll come back?"

Lila put her right hand over her heart. "Swear on my grandmother's grave."

Back home, Saskia clicked off the TV and dumped the remaining Spicy Caribbean Chicken into the garbage. From what she could tell, her father hadn't touched it. On the kitchen counter she found a note. *Don't forget to call your mom. She wants to hear from you TONIGHT!*

Saskia crumpled it up and threw it away.

Upstairs, remembering the mercury, she scrubbed her hands with soap and warm water.

Then she washed her face, noticing with a groan two new pimples on her forehead. She tried to get through her homework but was preoccupied with thoughts of Cornelius and daguerreotypes.

By the time she shut down her laptop, the alarm clock read 12:45. With a sigh, she slumped onto her bed. She didn't even change her clothes or take off her shoes. She just fell asleep.

Saskia

Saskia was lingering outside a shop and gazing at the sign above the door, which read in florid, old-timey script: CORNELIUS & CO.

It was a gray day, with low-lying clouds and a sense of imminent rain. She wasn't scared of getting wet, but something told her she should enter the shop. When she opened the door, she was surprised by the light. It came at her from all directions—bright and yellow and warm. The interior was such a contrast to the bleak day that she squinted, momentarily overcome, as if she were staring at the sun.

Cornelius & Co. could have lit all of Philadelphia. The huge, high-ceilinged store was crowded with sconces, candelabras, and more lamps than she could possibly count. But the most light came from the ceiling. Dozens of chandeliers, adorned with prisms, threw off dazzling refracted light. Saskia felt like she was in the most glorious ballroom in the world.

She wandered, trying to take everything in. The shop filled her senses. She touched elegantly cut crystal, veined marble, cool cast iron. She breathed in the fishy smell of whale oil, the tang of tobacco, and the undercurrent of something else. Cinnamon? No, peppermint.

There were only two other people in the store: a couple of men behind a counter. Their voices echoed faintly, muted and distorted. She tried to make out what they were saying as she studied the chiseled faces of bronze statues: Benjamin Franklin, Andrew Jackson, Daniel Boone. These were scattered amid the lights, a motley cast of frozen characters.

She moved closer to the counter. As she approached, the men remained oblivious to her, lost in conversation. She couldn't see the face of the younger one, whose back was to her, but she could tell the older man was upset. His body language was stiff, his expression annoyed.

"I'm skeptical about the whole proposition," he complained.

"I'm not," the younger man replied. He was tall and lean, with a head of dark, unkempt hair. "These new lamps are the future. I'm confident of that. In fact, I've already applied for a patent."

"Ha! That's only habit. You apply for a patent every other day."

"And why shouldn't I? You heard the bookkeeper: our sales increased fifty percent this year. We ought to be capitalizing on our growth."

"Our growth is exactly why we shouldn't change. Our customers like what we offer."

"It's our job to inform them of their options. If they knew they could light lamps with cheaper fuel, they would."

The older man, who was heavyset, leaned his considerable girth against the counter. "No proper lady or gentleman wants to put kitchen grease and lard into their lamps."

"Whale oil is getting too expensive. You can't argue that."

"No, I suppose I can't."

"If my new lamp will save them money, they'll come around to using lard."

The older man sighed. "What's it called? Your newfangled contraption?"

"The solar lamp."

The younger man reached down and retrieved something from below. At that moment, Saskia caught a glimpse of his profile. Robert Cornelius, without a doubt. She had to remember to breathe.

"See here," he said, holding up a lamp. "This is one of two models I made. It's not so bad, is it?"

Saskia thought it was quite pretty. The glass shade of the lamp was embellished with a flower pattern. Wide at the bottom and tapered on the top, it featured dangling spear-point prisms.

"Why, it's the same as an astral lamp!" the older man exclaimed.

"It's the *sister* of an astral lamp. Same shape, but I've modified the font. It now accommodates lard—solid or liquid."

The portly man took the lamp and examined it carefully, harrumphing under his breath. He admitted, finally, that it wasn't terrible.

When he went to place it on the counter, he noticed Saskia. She felt the pressure of his gaze as he looked her up and down. His outright assessment made her clench up inside. She was always uncomfortable when men appraised her, although in this instance, he seemed more bewildered than lecherous.

But Robert Cornelius was a gentleman. He opened the flip door on the counter and came out to greet her, bowing slightly. "Good afternoon, miss. How may I help you?"

He was more expressive than in the daguerreotype. The corners of his mouth were turned up: a whisper of a smile. His eyebrow was cocked. Was he mocking her? No, Saskia decided, he was only trying to understand her. But what was it about her that confused him?

She glanced down, and that was when she realized her error. The men were wearing fancy suits—old-fashioned suits with waistcoats and cravats and watch chains. The older man sported a top hat. Saskia, meanwhile, was sporting the same T-shirt and shorts she'd been wearing all day. She must have looked ridiculous, not to mention inappropriate and immodest. They probably thought she was insane.

But that wasn't the only troubling thing. She remembered that Cornelius had lived from 1809 to 1893. Slavery had been a reality of American life at that time—a bloody, brutal, unconscionable reality, but one that many white Americans accepted as normal, even necessary. Saskia knew that Pennsylvania, a Northern state, had emancipated the vast majority of its slaves by the mid-1800s, but that didn't meant its white residents would welcome someone like her. Though she had no idea what Cornelius's personal opinions were on Black people or abolition, she had to assume the worst. Acknowledging the long ugly shadow slavery cast on American history, both past and present, she'd be stupid not to keep her guard up. It was dangerous for her to be here—a mixed-race girl alone in his shop.

He took a step toward her. His expression had gone from bemused to concerned. The older man, meanwhile, looked increasingly contemptuous. Though she registered his sneer, she chose not to show it

"Pardon me, miss," Cornelius said, "but you seem . . . lost."

His eyes were warm, but even so, she wrapped her arms around herself. Goose bumps had risen on her skin. She didn't know what to do or what to say. The only thing she was sure of was that she didn't belong. The past was the past, and she had no business being in it. No business at all.

"I'm sorry," she whispered, meeting his eyes. She turned on her heels and dashed for the exit.

Only when the door had shut behind her could she catch her breath. It was raining now. She lifted her face to the falling droplets. She felt them, one by one, cool bits of comfort on her hot face.

CHAPTER THREE

S askia woke up, still in her bed. She was drenched. Not just her face, but her hair and clothes. Everything soaked through. *From the rain?* she wondered. *But that's impossible.*

Her heart was beating so hard she could feel it hammering against her chest. She couldn't recall ever remembering a dream in such detail. Such exquisite and alarming detail. If she shut her eyes, she could still see the lamps and statues. She could still smell the noxious odor of burning whale oil. She had memorized the exact color of Robert Cornelius's eyes: green-gray, like the New Haven Harbor.

She tasted a bead of liquid that rolled off a lock of her hair. It was salty. She was covered in sweat, not rainwater.

It was only a dream, she told herself.

Suddenly, she realized the dream might have been a result of the mercury. Maybe she'd hallucinated. Panicking, she grabbed her cell phone off her nightstand and looked up the symptoms of mercury poisoning. Concentration and attention problems, anxiety, agitation, impaired motor function, tremors, slurred speech, *hallucinations.* There it was.

Growing more worried by the second, she texted Lila.

S: had weirdest dream. EVER. met Cornelius. woke up sweaty. mercury poisoning?!

She waited for Lila to text her back, to reassure her, but the minutes ticked by until a whole hour had passed. Lila must be asleep, of course. All reasonable people were asleep, Saskia told herself. She got up, trying not to make too much noise, and changed her sheets. After a quick shower, she wiped off the condensation from the mirror so she could look at her face. She saw worried eyes with smudges underneath, the two new pimples like a little pair of red eyes. She gave herself a pep talk, saying that everything was okay.

But she'd said the same thing to herself over and over these past few months. And the truth was, everything wasn't okay. Barely anything was.

Back in bed, she couldn't stop thinking about Cornelius. Much as the dream had freaked her out, she would have liked to see him again. Those eyes, silvered with light, were hard to get out of her head.

She didn't know how long it took for her to fall asleep again, but when next she awoke, it was morning. She punched the snooze button on her alarm clock several times before sitting up. When she was finally lucid, she checked her clothes. Dry. She tried to conjure the details of the dream again and found that they were still fresh.

Yawning, she reached for her cell phone. Lila had texted her back finally.

L: U WERE NOT POISONED! was probably a fever dream

A fever dream? What was that? Saskia would have to find out, but not now. She was late.

On the ride to school, Saskia gazed sleepily out the window. She felt dazed and inert, still half caught in the fever dream or whatever it was. The early morning sun did nothing to rouse her. Clearly, she was spending way too much time on Cornelius.

She hoped to catch Lila at her locker, or between periods, but didn't see her until lunch. By then she was so eager to hear what Lila had to say, she couldn't think about anything else. She practically ran to the cafeteria.

Lila took a seat across from her at what had become their usual table. Saskia watched her tear into a slice of pepperoni pizza. "Spill," she said.

"Aren't you going to eat?"

Saskia hadn't had time to pack a lunch, and she'd forgotten to bring any money. No matter. She wasn't hungry for food, just for information.

Lack of appetite: another symptom of mercury poisoning?

"So . . . a fever dream—what is it?" Saskia asked.

Lila swallowed. "It's exactly what it sounds like. A dream caused by a fever. An intense, crazy dream."

"But I didn't have a fever."

"You texted you woke up sweaty. That must be because your fever broke. It's happened to me before."

"You've had a fever dream?"

Lila nodded and took a sip of chocolate milk.

"You don't think the dream had anything to do with the mercury?"

"It's just a coincidence."

Saskia shot her a disbelieving look.

"Look, I know how you feel," Lila continued. "Fever dreams can be freaky—and scary."

"But it wasn't scary. The end was the only bad part. The rest was kind of . . . nice."

Saskia explained about the lights in the store and the way Cornelius had come out to greet her. Lila listened carefully, poking at her fruit cup. Saskia noticed she didn't like pineapple, either.

"Here's what I think," Lila said. "I think you're stressed. Maybe a little sick, too—thus the fever. The dream was your body's way of letting go of some of that."

"Lila . . ."

"Seriously. You need to chill. You're fixating on Robert Cornelius because something else is bothering you. Something you don't want to deal with."

"What are you, a psychiatrist?"

"That's what I want to be," Lila replied.

"Okay, Dr. Defensor. You think my problem is stress. But just pretend it isn't. Isn't it possible that the mercury did it? I read it can be absorbed through the skin."

"I touched it more than you did, and I'm fine."

"Different people react in different ways."

"You're reaching."

Saskia closed her eyes. When she opened them again, she asked the question she really wanted to ask. "There's a third possibility. For the dream, I mean. Maybe somehow—and I know it sounds crazy—maybe I really did meet Robert Cornelius."

Lila snorted.

"No, really," Saskia insisted. "I'm not saying it happened. I'm just saying it *might* have happened."

"You *might* have met his ghost?"

"No, not his ghost. Him. I might have met him. Somehow."

"So you visited the nineteenth century in your sleep?"

Saskia shook her head. "I know it sounds wacko."

"You need to get out more. That's all there is to it. This weekend, I'll take you out. Maybe that will make you forget about Robert Cornelius."

Saskia looked down at the table. Graffiti was scribbled on the laminate surface: *Tanya loves Marcus. Mr. Havensack sucks. Beware P and S. The Patriots are #1! Coventon is for loosers!*

"Lila?" she asked.

"Yeah?"

"Can I ask you for a favor?"

"Depends."

"Can we go back to the library? Tonight? I want to see the daguerreotype one last time."

"I don't think that's a good idea."

"Just one more time, I swear."

"You're fixating."

"I need closure."

"You need closure," Lila repeated, adjusting her red glasses. "That's good. Very good. When I open my psychiatry practice, you can be my partner."

• • •

Saskia had to beg—by text and phone and email—but Lila finally relented.

"If it were anyone but you, I wouldn't do it," Lila said. She glanced at Saskia with uncharacteristic bashfulness.

"Thanks. I owe you."

Both girls agreed 9 P.M. would be the best time. They would get their homework finished, then head to the library. Saskia imagined Lila tucked away somewhere in her crowded, noisy house, diligently working out problems for her AP science classes. Saskia, meanwhile, wasted hours reading up on daguerreotypes, chemical elements, the history of mercury, and American life in the second half of the nineteenth century.

This is a Pass/Fail class. This is a Pass/Fail class. This is a Pass/ Fail class.

She had no excuse. Lila was right: she *was* fixating.

When Lila came at nine sharp, Saskia still hadn't finished up her other work. She was too giddy and revved up to care, though.

"Better pray Marlene's not there," Lila said when they got into the car.

"I keep picturing her as this big ugly dragon. Breathing fire."

"Put her in a navy suit and pantyhose, and you're not far off."

When they got to the Howard and Alice Steerkemp Daguerreotypes Collection, Rich eyed Saskia apprehensively. "Again?" he asked Lila.

"The gorgon's not here, right?"

"Doesn't mean she's not gonna show up."

Lila avoided his gaze. "We'll take our chances."

Inside the Collection room, Lila walked a fine line between nervous and paranoid.

"If Marlene suddenly walks in, you're a student, not a friend. Understand?"

"I go to college here?" Saskia asked.

"Yes."

"Score. Can I pick whatever major I want?"

Lila ignored the question and handed over Cornelius's daguerreotype. She chewed on her nails as Saskia lifted the tattered cover.

Arms crossed over his chest, Robert Cornelius stared at the girls, and they stared back. Once again, Saskia was struck by the urgency of his gaze. She still had the sense he was trying to convey something, a question or an answer, an idea that was just out of reach. She held the image at various angles. Different versions of Cornelius, some shadowy and vague, others bathed in light. Different versions of the same man, depending on the perspective. She lifted the glass cover, hoping to feel things she couldn't see, but Lila reached out to stop her.

"Don't smudge it. I wouldn't put it past Marlene to check for fingerprints."

It was more painful this time to give the daguerreotype back. Saskia actually grimaced when Lila slid it back into its box. "My project is due next week," she said. "That's only a few days away."

Still holding the box, Lila glanced at her.

"I'm getting a lot of information online. But Wikipedia is nothing like the real thing. The primary source."

"What are you getting at?"

"I know I asked before. And I know you could get in trouble. But please, *please* let me take the picture home. Just for a few days. Until my report's done. I swear I'll give it back." Saskia clasped her hands into a tight knot.

"You cannot ask me this."

"I know. I'm sorry! But . . . I am. I'm asking you this."

"It's stress. I'm telling you, you need to stop thinking about Cornelius."

"You don't understand," Saskia said. "So much has happened lately. It's been hard: new school, new town. My dad's been having a rough time, and my mom's driving me insane, even though she's twenty-five hundred miles away. You are literally my only friend here. The photo—well, it's like an escape . . . a little vacation from real life."

She paused, feeling a twinge of shame. Or maybe it was guilt. She knew she shouldn't lay on this sob story. It wasn't fair to Lila. But she wasn't lying, either.

"Everyone has problems," Lila replied.

"Sure, but not everyone's mom is dating a twenty-four-year-old substitute teacher."

"Really?"

"Oh, it gets better. She met him while he was teaching at *my* high school. She picked him up like freakin' Mrs. Robinson."

"Who's Mrs. Robinson?"

"You know, from *The Graduate*? The movie?"

Lila shrugged. "Never heard of it."

"Doesn't matter. The point is, she's twice his age. It's nauseating."

Lila was quiet for several seconds. Staring at Saskia, she seemed to weigh her options. "I can't believe I'm doing this," she said at last, her expression softening. "Seriously, I could get in big trouble. *Huge*."

"I'll be so, so careful with it."

"You'd better be."

"And I'll return it the minute I'm done . . ."

"The second."

"Promise. As soon as my presentation's over."

"Crap. Okay." Lila put the daguerreotype in Saskia's hand and returned the empty box to the cabinet. "Hide it in your shorts, and don't say a word."

"Lila, you're the best!"

In response, Lila gave her a sidelong look, a warning not to screw up. "Follow me," she ordered.

Saskia knew they had to pass two checkpoints: Rich and the guard at the library exit. She figured passing Rich would be a breeze; he wasn't apt to hold anything against Lila.

But maybe their worry showed—on their faces or in their body language. His brow knitted when they said they were leaving. "Short visit tonight," he remarked.

"We still have to finish one of our assignments," said Lila.

Saskia watched her friend fidget with the drawstring cord of her hoodie. Saskia wanted to grab her hand and keep it still.

"What's wrong?" Rich asked.

"What?"

"You look like somebody stole your candy bar."

"I'm just tired," Lila muttered.

"You girls haven't been up to anything, have ya?"

Lila kept on fidgeting. She glanced meaningfully at Saskia. Saskia ignored her and explained, "We're in exam period. It's nerve-racking. If we get a bad grade, our GPAs drop, and then no college, no job, no future. Basically, this week determines the rest of our lives . . ."

"Uh-huh." Rich didn't sound the least bit convinced.

"We're borrowing one," Lila piped suddenly. "One daguerreo-type."

Saskia stared at her in disbelief.

"I'll bring it back in a little bit," Lila went on. "This is just a loan. I know Marlene would be pissed, but what's the harm? I'll be careful. We'll make sure—"

"Why you looking for trouble?" Rich interrupted, rubbing his temples.

"We're not looking for trouble," Saskia replied.

His eyes darted between the two girls, settling on Lila. "*You* know better than this."

She hung her head, becoming a little smaller. "It's just this once."

"I don't hear you. I don't see you."

Lila looked like she wanted to say more, but Saskia pulled on her hand, practically dragging her through the turns and twists of the library. Somewhere along the way, Lila recovered her wits. By the time they got to the guard, she was calm again. They opened their bags for him to inspect. He looked through the contents briskly, then waved them through.

Outside, in the warm early summer air, Saskia felt light and free, happier than she'd been in weeks. She wanted to share her joy, but Lila's expression was grim.

"I couldn't lie to him," she said.

"That's obvious."

"I put him in a bad position."

Saskia exhaled. "No, *I* put him in a bad position. And I put you in one, too. But it's going to be fine. Like you said, it's a loan. Nobody's gonna get caught."

She was trying to reassure Lila, but she wasn't having much success. Lila's attention had shifted to the sky. It was a clear night, and a few stars sparkled, like Marilyn Monroe's diamonds in *Some Like It Hot*. But Saskia could tell Lila wasn't looking at those. Her friend was gazing at the college bell tower, the highest point of the campus skyline. Saskia looked at it, too, thinking that the spire at the top looked sharp enough to draw blood.

CHAPTER FOUR

When Saskia got into bed, she held the daguerreotype against her chest. The old dream still played in her memory. She had no trouble conjuring Robert Cornelius's face, his voice, his searching eyes. She hoped if she fell asleep with him on her mind, he'd be in another dream.

She wanted to be back in the lighting store. She wanted a second chance to talk to him. This time, she swore, she wouldn't stammer or run away. She'd stand tall and straight, like she used to, and ask him about his inventions, his discoveries, his life. Everything.

But morning came, and when she awoke, she knew she hadn't seen him. Disappointment washed over her, followed by jolting anxiety. It occurred to her she might never see him again. She could take the daguerreotype to bed every night, but there was no guarantee Cornelius would ever reappear. She couldn't just will it to happen. Pulling the daguerreotype from between the sheets, she stared at it for a moment. She wished she weren't so attached—

"Fifteen-minute warning," her father yelled through the door.

Ugh. The dreaded fifteen-minute warning. Saskia hated trying to shower, brush her teeth, dress, eat breakfast, find her backpack, and get out the door in such a short time. But she hated the sound of the bus driver honking even more. With a groan, she climbed out of bed, wishing she could delay her depressing reality a little longer.

. . .

In class Saskia felt tired, dazed, and slightly nauseous. She didn't bother trying to concentrate on what her teachers were saying. She was lost in her own thoughts, all of which seemed to involve Cornelius. She tried to get the original dream out of her head, but it was persistent, monopolizing, inescapable.

She would give anything for a second dream if only to shut out the first.

In English Literature, the teacher, Mrs. Jude, went around collecting the latest assignment: a two-pager on truth and justice in *Pride and Prejudice*. Saskia hadn't even started it yet. It was just one more thing she'd neglected.

"Not an auspicious start for you, Miss Brown," Mrs. Jude commented.

Saskia ducked her head and stared at the ikat pattern on Mrs. Jude's dress. Back in Arizona, Saskia would have gladly written the paper. She'd always done her homework on time and to the best of her ability.

Lately, though, she couldn't remember why she'd cared so much. She knew she was in a downward spiral, but she didn't care about that, either. She was descending willingly.

Saskia took the daguerreotype to bed again that night. Same routine: daguerreotype close to her body, mind orbiting Robert Cornelius like a satellite. Revved up and nervous, she popped a Benadryl. She figured the sooner she got to sleep, the better her chances of seeing him. But once again, morning yielded no reward.

As the days passed, she moved through life increasingly desperate and distracted. More homework piled up. More teachers made disparaging remarks. Besides Lila and her dad, Saskia pretty much ignored everyone, including her mom. Especially her mom. Saskia disregarded the half dozen messages her mom had left.

But she couldn't disregard her father when he finally confronted her in the kitchen.

"Call her now," he said sternly, handing her his cell phone. "Before she flies up here and yells at us in person."

Saskia grimaced. There were only so many excuses she could make. Her father could be tough when he wanted to be.

After the fourth ring, it seemed like her call would go to voice-mail. A stroke of luck. But her mother answered on the fifth. "Sweetheart, I've missed you so much. Where have you been?"

Saskia tried to ignore the nauseous feeling that had lately become habitual. "Connecticut."

"You know what I meant. Why haven't you called me back?"

"I've been busy, Ma."

"How's school? What's it like there? Is it anywhere as hot there as it is here?"

Saskia had always hated her mother's rapid-fire questions, a spill-over from her job as a litigation attorney. Saskia also hated the way her mother masked seriousness with a chirpy voice. "The weather's fine."

"Saskia, please, would it kill you to elaborate?"

She paused. "I don't know what you want me to say. How great it is here? Okay, it's great. The birds are singing. The sun is shining. Sometimes the whole town breaks into song."

"Saskia . . ." She could hear her mother's exasperation. "Listen to me. Nothing is set in stone. You can come back to Arizona, you know. Ralph and I would love it if you lived with us."

"Ralph and you would love it," Saskia echoed.

"Yes."

"But I wouldn't love it. I wouldn't love living with *Ralph*."

Her mother sighed. "Look, this is hard—it's hard for everyone—but you have to at least *try*. This is reality now. Ralph is in my life. And yes, it will take some getting used to. But I think you'll come to see it's for the best."

"Funny, that's what I was just telling Dad. That it's for the best." She glanced at her father and rolled her eyes.

He wagged his finger. *Be good*, he mouthed.

"Saskia, please try to understand," her mother said. "I deserve happiness, too."

"Well you've definitely prioritized *that*."

"I know you just got there, but it's not too late. You can still come back to your friends. Your life. I spoke with your principal. You're welcome anytime."

"How about Ralph? Did the principal welcome him back?"

"Saskia, Ralph's an adult. A consenting adult in a relationship with another consenting adult. He never had a problem professionally."

"Or so you think."

Her mother's breathing became a little ragged, like she were scaling a cliff. One false step, and she'd plummet. Saskia felt bad, but not bad enough to play nice.

"Saskia . . . I love you."

Saskia clenched her jaw and tried to keep the tears from flowing. Above all, she didn't want to cry in front of her father.

"I never . . . planned for this to happen," her mother continued.

"Mom . . ."

"If I could do it all over again, I wouldn't be so evasive. I'd let you know what was happening every step of the way. But I can't go back. What's done is done. So you're going to have to come to terms with it."

It wasn't what her mother had said that riled Saskia. It was what she *hadn't* said. She hadn't said, "If I could do it all over again, I wouldn't have had the affair. I'd choose you and your father over Ralph." Saskia burned with the desire to point this out, but she didn't. There were so many accusations she wanted to make. *You're a cheater. He's practically a kid; you're the reason this family's broken.*

But she kept her mouth shut. Why stomp on something that was already shattered? What was the point?

"What did she say?" her father asked when she hung up.

"She wants me to move back—with her and Ralph."

Her father snickered uncomfortably. "So they're shacking up?"

"People don't say that anymore, Dad."

"Forgive me. They're living together?"

"I guess." Saskia turned away, unable to stomach the pain he was trying to hide.

"That was fast."

When she didn't reply, he pretended to busy himself by cleaning the kitchen counter. It was spotless. "You think you'll go?" he asked.

She was aware that she could hurt her father, too. Both of her parents had become as vulnerable as newborn kittens.

Saskia moved the wastebasket so her father could throw away the imaginary crumbs he'd collected. "I'm not going to live with Mom," she told him. "I like being an only child."

After a few days Saskia's mother gave up on phone calls and started texting. Saskia didn't mind. It was easy to ignore those, too. Almost as easy as it was to obsess over Cornelius.

Practice makes perfect, she thought.

But she couldn't block out the manila envelope that arrived a couple days later by certified mail from Arizona. As soon as she saw that it was from her mother's law office, she knew what it was. Divorce papers. She tore open the envelope and felt her stomach tighten.

Once her father signed, it would be official. But was he ready to? It wasn't like he was coping well. His five-o'clock shadow was morphing into a fledgling beard—not a good look. She'd found more cigarettes, too, a whole pack stashed under a hand towel in the bathroom.

Would the papers push him over the edge?

Since he was working a double shift, she had plenty of time to decide how to break the news. She could leave the envelope on the kitchen table, the first thing he'd see when he came home. Or she could toss it into the trash, pretend it had never arrived. Better yet, she could send it back to her mother with a Post-it note. *Screw you, Ma. You, too, Ralph.*

In the end, she shoved it under some newspapers on the coffee table. She figured her father would find it eventually. Or maybe it would get buried in the recycling.

She wanted to curl up in bed but willed herself to work on the *Pride and Prejudice* paper. She hadn't abandoned her old self entirely. It was a struggle to fill up the first page. She was too distracted and antsy. Two hours in, she blew up the font, changed the spacing from double to triple, and called it a day.

Saskia wondered which was worse: turning in a terrible paper or not turning one in at all. But what did it matter? There was only one class at school that still captured her attention: Early American Innovation and Ingenuity. Specifically, the Robert Cornelius assignment. Funny, she'd had no trouble writing *that* ten-page paper. In fact, she had stopped herself at fifteen. She no longer felt shy about the oral presentation, either. Maybe because thinking about Cornelius allowed her to ignore the rest of her messy life.

On the day of the presentation, she felt nervous but also ready. She had her facts down pat. She'd read so much about Robert Cornelius, she was pretty sure she knew more about him than anyone else in her school, maybe even anyone else in the state of Connecticut. Though her hands shook when Mr. Nash called her name, she approached the front of the classroom with her head held high.

I've got this, she thought.

She delivered the speech pretty much as she'd rehearsed it, without even glancing at her notes. When her allotted fifteen minutes passed, she found she had more to say and continued on with details about Cornelius's life and times. After a while, Mr. Nash caught her eye. He tapped an imaginary wristwatch.

"One more thing?" she said.

She knew she shouldn't, but she couldn't resist. She retrieved the daguerreotype from her backpack. Holding it up, she told everyone what it was and how it had been made.

Mr. Nash seemed to perk up. He asked to see the daguerreotype up close. Then he suggested Saskia take it around the room so that everyone could see it. When she reached Josh McClane, her confidence waned. It was the way he looked at her, like she was an easy target.

"That really him?" he asked. He held another deck of cards in his hands. It probably wouldn't be long before Mr. Nash confiscated that one, too.

"Yeah, that's him," she said, a defensive edge to her voice.

"Where'd you get it?"

She chose to ignore the instigative gleam in his eye and started to move on to the next kid.

"You swipe it?" he persisted.

"What?"

"You heard me."

She straightened her shoulders and sized him up. Maybe *she* was an easy target, but she wasn't about to let Cornelius be. "I don't know what you mean."

"So you did." His eyes crinkled impishly at the corners. "Hey, it's okay with me. I'm not gonna judge."

"Is that it, Saskia?" Mr. Nash asked.

Grateful, she turned to him and nodded.

"Well done. Take note, everyone. This is what it means to go above and beyond."

She smiled, pleased that she'd aced the presentation, but wishing Mr. Nash hadn't put her on the spot. Compliments made her uncomfortable. She never knew what to do with them: accept them, and you seemed smug; disregard them, and you seemed ungrateful.

Returning the daguerreotype to her backpack, she glanced back at Josh to see if he were still appraising her. She wasn't sure if she felt relieved or sorry that he wasn't. All she knew for certain was that he might have figured out her secret a little too easily. Either she was an open book, or he was far more shrewd and observant than his distracted card playing suggested.

When she got home, she found her father asleep in the living room. She opened the windows to air it out. The smell of cat piss was *not* fading. Then she checked under the newspapers on the coffee table. The divorce papers were still in the same place, untouched. Unnoticed.

Later on, when her father had woken up and they'd eaten another bland microwaved dinner, Lila called. She wanted to know if Saskia was up for the party.

"What party?"

"Ethan's party. Come on, we talked about it."

"We did?"

"Yeah, we did. So you in?"

Saskia sighed. She did recall the conversation. She also remembered how Josh had asked Paige if she were going to be there. "I guess."

"What do you mean, you guess? What else do you have going on? Another date with the daguerreotype?"

Saskia groaned. "Okay, fine, I'm in."

"Good. I'll pick you up at eight. Hey, and don't take this the wrong way, but can you not wear gray?"

"Got it. No gray. What about black?"

"Jeez, don't get too crazy on me."

When Saskia hung up, her father gave her an inquisitive look but didn't ask any questions. Maybe he was just glad she was going out like a normal teenager.

She retreated to her room and poked through the sparse, drab contents of her closet. Truth be told, she would have preferred to stay in. Nestling in bed with the picture of Cornelius now felt like a comforting ritual. Something to look forward to. The party, on the other hand, inspired only dread.

She kept flipping through hangers, not sure what she was looking for. Not sure she even had it. No gray, Lila had said. And Saskia knew why. Gray meant forgotten and forgettable, ashes and dust. It meant dreary skies, old age, crumbling tombstones, the daguerreotype of someone who had died lifetimes ago. Most of all, gray meant depressing.

CHAPTER FIVE

The day her father resolved to take her to Connecticut was the day she'd thrown away most of her clothes. Online, she'd helped her father pick a U-Haul attachment for the car. They'd both decided smaller was better. They'd pack minimally, just the basics, and leave most of their old things behind. It was part of her father's "fresh start" philosophy.

She gave her betta fish, Marrakesh, back to the pet store, bowl and all. Her father posted his exercise equipment on Craigslist. They carted boxes of clothes to Big Brothers Big Sisters. Goodwill came to pick up books, kitchen items, old electronics, and most of their furniture.

The clutter of life, her father had said. *Who needs it?*

Her bed had been the last thing left in her old room in Arizona. It looked like a lone island surrounded by hardwood floor. And Saskia, marooned on top.

To be honest, she was happy to be marooned. All the curious stares and conspiratorial whispers at school had left her exhausted. She'd stopped checking her social media accounts weeks ago and refused to post anything new. She wouldn't give the trolls anything more to feast on. She felt like Hester Prynne with a big letter on her chest. Only she had an "S," not an "A." An "S" for "sucker." That's what she was. A sucker for trusting her mother, for failing to see what was happening right in front of her face. A sucker for being at the same school, and sometimes in the very same room, as Ralph.

Saskia was deeply ashamed that she and her friends had ever called him "the cute sub." What had they been thinking? After news of the affair got out, she could no longer stand the look of him. Everything about him was heinous: his hawkish nose and stupid smile; his nasal voice and giddy, puppy-dog walk. Several times she'd thought about tripping him in the hallway.

When she thought back to those last days in Arizona, she was glad to be gone. Glad to be somewhere—anywhere—else. Even Coventon, though it sounded like a place where witches vacationed. She even kind of liked the new house: a small ranch, everything on one floor. But Saskia knew that no matter how far away you moved, you could never really escape your past, which was why she wasn't entirely surprised to find a piece of her old life in her closet. A little red skirt hanging at the very back.

Frowning, she held it at arm's length. She remembered how Heather had said it was "too loud" and "fake glam," like Saskia "was trying too hard." Then again, her former best friend hadn't liked to be outshone. But Lila wasn't like that; Saskia was pretty sure she'd approve.

Wiggling into the skirt, Saskia wondered what the party would be like. In Arizona, she'd only been to one "real" party: keg in the corner, cigarette and pot smoke swirling in the air. Saskia remembered being intimidated and wanting to leave long before a drunk Heather was ready to. Hopefully tonight wouldn't be so hard-core.

Getting into the Buick, Saskia was promptly enveloped in a cloud of perfume. It was sweet and spicy, like orange blossoms mixed with hot sauce. The scent suited Lila perfectly. She was wearing lipstick, too, and glittery nail polish. Saskia self-consciously adjusted the collar of her shirt, so her bra strap didn't show.

"Does Ethan throw a lot of parties?" she asked as they began to drive.

"One or two a year, when the stars align," Lila replied.

"Which stars are we talking about?"

"Well, Ethan's parents have to be out of town, and Ethan's brother's got to be home from college. He's the one who buys the beer. When those things come together, the parties are epic."

Saskia nodded and looked out the window, watching the shadowy landscape coast by. She wondered if she would fit in at an "epic" party in Coventon. She doubted it. She was more like Joan Fontaine in Alfred Hitchcock's *Laura*, unsophisticated, naive, and in way over her head.

"I like your skirt," said Lila, glancing at her. "You know, you should wear red more often. Sometimes it seems like you're living in a black-and-white movie."

You don't know the half of it, Saskia thought. "Ethan's brother sounds cool. I don't know many guys who would buy beer for their little brothers."

"Those two are close—and kind of the same. Both top of the charts in smarts and dorkitude."

"Where does the brother go to college?"

"MIT." Lila turned up the radio full blast. "I love this song," she yelled, bopping her head along to the lyrics of a propulsive chart topper about raising the roof, then burning down the house.

"What does he study?"

"What?"

"WHAT DOES ETHAN'S BROTHER STUDY?"

But Saskia couldn't hear the answer. Aerospace? Aerodynamics? Aero-something. It was impossible to understand Lila over the thick, booming bass.

They arrived a few minutes later. Lila parallel-parked into a tight spot in front of what must have been the party house. It was impressive—big and brick, with an expansive front lawn and wraparound porch. It occurred to Saskia that Lila had passed a railroad crossing sign a few minutes ago. Heck, the old saying must be true: Ethan lived on the right side of the tracks.

"Just so you know, I'm only having one beer," Lila said as she slid out of her seat. "Designated driver. I've got to protect my passengers."

"Thanks," Saskia said appreciatively. Her dad would be pleased, too. He was always warning her about drunk driving. He'd made it clear that if she ever needed a ride, day or night, he'd be there, no questions asked. But she'd never needed to take him up on his offer, and she didn't want to tonight.

Ethan himself opened the front door to greet them. He was tall, with dimples and a toothy smile. Saskia didn't register the dorkitude, but she'd take Lila's word for it. Ushering the girls inside, he led them past luxe brocade furniture, lacquered surfaces, oriental rugs, a grand piano. Stuff that most certainly was not from IKEA.

The party was in the basement, a shame since the basement was not like the rest of the house. Though large, it was stark and industrial, with pull-chain ceiling lights, concrete walls, and metal shelving. It was probably a hipsters' paradise, but Saskia had never liked windowless places. Besides, it was a little claustrophobic. There were a lot of people jammed together—sixty or more. Saskia recognized some faces from school, but knew hardly any names. Almost immediately she wished she were home. What she wouldn't give to be watching an old movie right now, microwave popcorn in hand.

Ethan offered her a cup of beer. "Just one thing," he said. "If you need the bathroom, use the one down here. Upstairs is off-limits, 'kay?"

She nodded. Before she knew it, he was off to attend to other arrivals.

She sipped her beer gingerly. She didn't particularly like the taste or smell—it reminded her a little bit of B.O.—and tried to listen to Lila. The music wasn't as loud in here as it had been in the car, but it still made conversation difficult. When Lila introduced her to a couple of girls, Saskia had trouble catching their names. Then again, maybe the confusion had less to do with the music and more to do with her nerves. Maybe she was too anxious to focus. Again. She wished she hadn't worn the red skirt. She felt like a stop sign.

Sometimes Saskia had trouble wrapping her mind around how much she'd changed since the affair.

When she finished her drink, Lila handed over her own cup. It was still full. Saskia downed it as quickly as she could. *Liquid courage*, she thought. Right now she could use all the courage she could get. Her fingers were literally trembling.

Fortunately, the second beer seemed to help. Some of her worry lifted. She began to feel lighter, less stuck in her own head. The smoky atmosphere of the basement seemed to enhance her buzz.

Lila, meanwhile, was on a natural high: giggling, cracking jokes, making the people around them laugh. She grabbed Saskia's arm, pointed to a guy in a fedora, and said something about remembering him from nursery school. "I've gotta go talk to him. He was my first friend—like, *ever*."

A sober Saskia would've felt worried when Lila disappeared, wiggling through a clog of people. But a buzzed Saskia went to find the keg for a refill. She waited in line until it was her turn, then took the hose and pressed the button attached to the spigot. Nothing. She wondered if she was doing it wrong. She probably was.

"You have to pump it first," a female voice said from behind.

"What?"

"Pump it."

The girl came forward and reached for the black ball attached to a metal straw atop the keg. She pumped the ball up and down several times. Then she took Saskia's cup, held it at an angle, and pressed the button. Beer streamed out in a golden arc.

"Thanks," Saskia said, taking back the cup.

"No problem."

"You've done this before."

"Once or twice."

"I'm Saskia," she said, with effort. The girl looked down at her and smiled. She was very tall, NBA-player tall, with frizzy red hair, white skin, and squished features that were concentrated at the center of her face as if by pushed by a centripetal force. Saskia couldn't decide if she were very beautiful or very ugly.

"You're new, right?" the girl asked.

"Right." Saskia wiped beer foam off her upper lip. "I am, officially, the new girl."

"Well, I am officially Adrienne. And this"—Adrienne made a ta-da flourish with her hand—"is what kids in Coventon do on Friday nights. I'm sorry to say it doesn't get much better."

"That's all right. It's already better than where I'm from."

"Where's that?"

"Arizona."

Adrienne's squinty eyes widened. "Oh my god, you're so lucky. I hear Arizona is *beautiful*."

"Some of it is. I can't get used to all the green here. I'm used to the desert."

A girl in a cheerleading uniform stopped by to peck Adrienne on the cheek and to squeal something in her ear. When she'd gone, Adrienne rolled her eyes. "Ugh. I can't stand that girl. The cheerleaders didn't even have a game today. She's just wearing her uniform so guys will look at her butt. Hey, you're not a cheerleader, are you?"

Saskia stifled a laugh. "Nope. Just the new girl."

"What are you into? Any clubs or sports?"

Saskia shrugged. In her old life, she'd been a joiner. She'd been on the student council, played soccer, and written articles for the school newspaper. But she had no idea what she'd do in Coventon, if anything.

"Next fall you should go out for the drama club," Adrienne said. "Our stage productions are *savage*. Last year, when this girl Aniyah Buckley graduated, she went straight to Broadway. I don't blame her. I'd skip college, too, for a part in *Hamilton*."

"I'm not much of an actress."

"Oh, that's okay. You can work backstage."

Saskia shrugged again.

Out of the corner of her eye, she suddenly caught sight of Josh. He was standing on the outskirts of the party, slouching against a wall. He seemed to be fiddling with a deck of cards again. A couple of girls were standing nearby, watching.

Groupies, Saskia thought.

Maybe it was the alcohol, or maybe she felt confrontational after his comments on the day of her presentation. Whatever it was, she surprised herself by telling Adrienne she had to go. There was someone she needed to talk to.

"Sure. It was good to meet you!" Adrienne replied with a smile.

"You, too!" Saskia said, slipping away.

Josh was wearing jeans that were ripped at the knee and frayed at the hem. His black T-shirt read: YOUTH IN ASIA. A girly headband, black with hot pink stripes, made his hair stick out around his head like flower petals. On someone else the headband would have been stupid. But it fit Josh to a T.

From several feet away, Saskia watched him do a bunch of tricks: shuffling with one hand, forming a rainbow in the air as he tossed the cards from one hand to the other. He was good. Vegas good. Not that she'd ever been to Vegas.

"Hey, Saskia Brown's in the house," he said, not taking his eyes off the cards. She was startled he remembered her name.

Emboldened, she slipped in front of the fangirls. It felt strange to look directly at his face, no more staring at his back. She decided he was more Paul Newman than James Dean. A young Paul Newman in *The Long, Hot Summer*, more rake than rebel. She took another sip from the cup and noticed that the noises in the room sounded comfortably muffled, all the voices blending into a pleasant thrum.

"Pick one," he said to her, fanning out the cards. She admired his fingers—long and honey-colored, with square nails. "Look at it, but don't show it to me."

Taking another sip, she drew one.

"You know what it is?" he asked.

"Yes."

"Don't show it to me and slide it back anywhere you like."

She did, a smile playing at the corner of her mouth.

He shuffled the deck, making crisp, snapping sounds. When he smiled back at her, she felt herself flush.

"I know the trick. You put my card in your pocket," she said.

"Nope. You can check."

Under other circumstances she would have balked. But she'd had enough beer that her hands didn't hesitate to search each pocket of his jeans, front and back.

"Just some loose change and a box of Tic Tacs," she said, taking out the latter. "Wintergreen—unusual choice. I'm an orange fan myself." She put back the Tic Tacs a little more slowly than she needed to and added, "All right—you're clean."

"Told you."

"Can I shuffle the cards? To keep you honest?"

"Go ahead."

She took the deck, divided it, and clumsily mashed one half into the other. When she was little, she and her father used to play Go Fish and War, but that was about the extent of her experience with cards. She handed back the deck.

"We good?" he asked.

Saskia wasn't sure. When he looked into her eyes, she worried he was reading her all over again.

He chose a card and held it up. The one she'd picked: the nine of spades.

"Not bad."

"It's just a way to kill time. Same as this party."

"Is that what you think we're doing—killing time?"

"What do you think?"

"I have no idea," she said honestly.

Josh grabbed her beer and took a sip. "What do you think of Coventon so far?"

"It's . . . it's different."

"Why do you say that?"

Because no one's whispering behind my back anymore. Because Ralph is twenty-five hundred miles away. Because you're the only boy I've talked to since being here.

"It's different than where I'm from."

"And where's that, Rikers Island?"

"What?"

"I'm talking 'bout that stolen photo. The one you brought to school."

She grabbed back the beer. "It's called a daguerreotype. And you've got an active imagination. Overactive."

"So it's not stolen?"

"It's *borrowed*."

"Gotcha."

"Change of subject," she insisted.

"All right—how about you tell me where you're from?"

"Guess."

He rubbed his chin for effect and took a long, hard look at her face. "Kansas," he said finally.

"Kansas! Really?"

"I was thinking *Wizard of Oz*. Dorothy and all that. You kind of remind me of her."

"What?!"

"Something about your voice."

"Definitely overactive," she said.

"So were you a juvenile delinquent in Kansas, too?"

"Arizona."

"Whatever, Arizona."

"Wishful thinking."

She went quiet after that, having run out of clever things to say. It wasn't easy to maintain a conversation when the room was beginning to tilt and spin on an axis.

"So what now?" she asked.

"What do you mean?"

"What do we do? You wanna build a house of cards?"

It came out of nowhere, the question. A total non sequitur. Maybe, like her father, she'd watched too many episodes of *Gilmore Girls*.

"Seriously?" Josh asked.

"Yeah."

"Okay, I guess," he replied. To her surprise, he took her by the elbow and led her through the crowd. One of the fawning girls gave her a dirty look.

"Where are we going?"

"Upstairs. I can't hear myself think anymore."

"We can't go upstairs."

"Why not?"

"Ethan said."

"Nah, Ethan's good. He won't mind."

"But he . . ."

"Listen, I've known Ethan my whole life. I've lived down the street from him for the last three years. Him and his brother will be Windexing the crap out of every room in this house once the party's over. They're OCD. Us going upstairs isn't going to make any difference."

"All right," she agreed, though she felt guilty.

He wove through the crowd, tugging her along. It occurred to her that she hadn't seen Lila in a while. She should tell her friend what was happening, how she was about to disappear upstairs with a guy. But she didn't know where Lila was, and there was no way she was going to pull away from Josh's grip.

Because what if he changes his mind?

From the back his black hair looked ragged and uneven. Rock star hair. She wondered if he'd cut it himself before the party. They proceeded up the stairs. The last person she saw was the tall red-head, Adrienne. Saskia smiled and waved. Adrienne waved back blithely.

A potential friend? Saskia wondered.

Josh knew his way around the house like he'd been there a million times. He led her through a family room, a fancy kitchen with lots of granite and stainless steel, and down a long hall. They ended up in a bedroom, a destination that made her at once petrified and giddy. It wasn't much of a room, not compared to the rest of the house, just beige walls and basic furniture: a decorative desk in a corner and a couple of charcoal sketches of city street scenes on the walls.

Guest room, she decided.

Josh plopped down on the bed and lay on his back. His shirt rode up a little, revealing a taut stomach and a smeary, amateur-looking tattoo. He fished the cards out of his pocket and placed them beside him.

Saskia stood one foot inside the room, one foot out, wishing she had more experience with boys. What was going through his mind right now? Had he picked a bedroom on purpose? She wanted to think he was going to make a move. Party, bedroom, boy, girl. The equation was complete. Wasn't kissing next?

But the truth was, Josh looked kind of sleepy. He rubbed his eyes and even stifled a yawn. "We doing this or not?" he asked.

Did he mean making the card house or making out? She didn't have the courage to ask.

"Guess we should build it on the floor," he continued, gathering his sprawled-out limbs. "Flat surface and all." He got down on the ground and sat crisscross-applesauce, like a little kid.

We doing this or not?

They were building the card house, after all. Saskia sat down beside him and propped one card carefully against another. Soon they were taking turns drawing cards from the pile.

"Hey, why'd you think I stole that daguerreotype?" she asked him.

"You just seem like that kind of person. You know, wayward."

She shook her head. *"Wayward?"*

"Okay, okay. I was just messing with you."

"Thanks a lot," she replied drolly, laying a card against his.

"So did your parents move here for work?"

"Not quite."

"I assume everyone who comes to Coventon is coming for work."

"Why?"

"The plant—Arrivo. You know, out on Whallen Avenue."

"Oh yeah, I've heard of it. It's bad news, right?"

Her father had first told her about Arrivo before the move. It was the chemical arm of a big pharmaceutical company. It had been charged with quite a few wastewater discharge violations, which was how her father had found out about it. Google "Coventon," and at least a dozen news stories about Arrivo popped up. All of them talked about industrial waste spills and pollution lawsuits.

When her father had hunted for a place to live in town, he'd tried to steer clear of Arrivo. Still, they'd ended up closer to it than he would have liked. Real estate prices were simply too high in the better parts of town. On the right side of the tracks. Here.

Josh chuckled. "Everyone in town worries about it, but I'm glad it's here. My mom's a quality engineer there. She makes four times what she used to. I work there, too, on the weekends. All I do is shuffle papers, but the money's great."

"Don't you worry? My dad said there are all these chemicals that cause cancer."

"Maybe they do. But hey, we're all gonna die sometime, right?"

"That's a cavalier way to look at it."

"It's the truth."

"But why does Coventon allow the plant to be there when it knows it's dangerous?"

Josh looked at Saskia like she'd been born yesterday. "For the jobs, obviously. The money."

She sniffed. "Money's not everything."

"Says someone who's never worried about money."

"Please!" she cried indignantly. "You don't know anything about me."

He paused, card midair, and searched her face. "You're right, I don't. Tell me something."

His voice was disarmingly sincere, and Saskia's annoyance drained away. Maybe it was the beer coursing through her veins, but she decided to confide in him. "My parents are getting divorced."

As soon as she said it, she regretted it. She probably sounded pathetic. He probably thought she was a train wreck.

"Shit," he said. "Sorry."

"It's why me and my dad moved. We couldn't stand being there anymore."

"In the same house as your mom?"

"In the same town. It was so humiliating. My mom got together with a substitute teacher from my school."

"You're joking."

"I wish. I mean, if she were going to whore around, couldn't she have picked another school district?"

Smiling ruefully, Josh took off his headband and raked his fingers through his mussed hair. "That is screwed up."

"My dad and I—we *had* to move. He got a job in New Haven, at the hospital. And my mom, she didn't put up a fight. I think she was relieved when we left."

"Listen, you get used to it," he said. "Divorce. It's not so bad after a while. You get used to splitting your holidays and checking in with two parents all the time. You get used to feeling . . ." He hesitated. "Fractured."

"So your parents are divorced?"

"Oh yeah, happened when I was younger. They hate each other."

"And you live with your mother?"

"Yep."

The revelation that Josh and she were in similar circumstances surprised Saskia. She hadn't thought they would have much in common, except that he looked possibly mixed-race like she was.

"Which one of your parents is Asian?" she asked, taking a chance.

He looked amused by the question. "My mother. She's Japanese."

"Why'd she keep your dad's last name if she hates him so much?"

"Funny you'd ask. She once said his name's the only decent thing about him. Plus, her maiden name is Honda. It sucked to be asked about cars all the time."

He tried, unsuccessfully, to prop up another card. One bad play, and the whole house toppled down. It lay in a sad, flat heap. They stared at it a few seconds, then began rebuilding.

"Do you see your dad much?" she asked.

"Nah, not really. What about you? Plan to see your mom anytime soon?"

"Not if I can help it."

"Word."

A silence ensued. Normally dead air made Saskia nervous. But this pause felt welcome, even tranquil.

They took their time propping up the cards again. She didn't know how long it took, but eventually they used the whole deck. With three tilting stories, the house was nothing if not precarious. Saskia tried not to move or breathe very hard.

Josh stretched his gangly arms over his head. She noticed another tattoo on his left bicep. A scaly green dragon, but benign, more Puff than Smaug. He said, "I haven't done that since I was a little kid."

She felt as rickety as the house, her whole life did, and yet she couldn't hold back. Before she knew it, the words came gushing out. "When do you get used to it—divorce? I mean, how long does it take? Do all the bad feelings really heal, or do they just scab over? Because I'm the kind of person who picks at scabs over and over. So basically that means I'll never forgive my mom. And if I never forgive her, I'll be one of those screwed-up adults who's always in therapy—or worse. I don't want to be an alcoholic or run a meth lab. I just want to be . . . normal."

She squeezed her eyes shut, wondering if he'd be able—or willing—to wade through the flood.

Way to play it cool, Saskia.

When she opened them again, she was relieved to see that Josh was looking at her with something like kindness. He scooted over, deftly maneuvering his long legs around the house of cards, and put his arm around her. His touch felt generous.

Her head fell onto his chest. She didn't want him to see her face. Now, on top of everything else, she was crying.

Could this be any more mortifying?

As she choked on her own sobs, he rubbed her shoulders. She felt grateful that he was being nice to her. Someone like Josh, some-one so good-looking, didn't need to be nice. He didn't need to be decent. He could get away with anything really, the same way as Paige.

"All the shit you're feeling—it fades. It really does," he said softly.

But that word, *fades*, caused a fresh burst of tears. She couldn't get her emotions under control. She hadn't cried much since her parents had broken up, a fact that worried her father, and this was why. Once she started, she couldn't stop. She hated herself for letting it all out now, in front of Josh, of all people. He must think she was a real piece of work. That she'd moved to Coventon from Crazy Town.

His hands moved from her shoulders to her back. His touch radiated heat, which spread like wildfire through her body. She shuddered. It was a fight or flight moment. She could leave, fleeing the embarrassment she'd brought upon herself. Or she could stay and risk being even more embarrassed.

She lifted her head and looked at him. Somehow, his eyes were intense and aloof at the same time. She liked the way they were dark in the middle, light at the edges, like an eclipse. She liked the Cupid's bow of his lips. He was almost—but not quite—too beautiful to touch.

Taking a breath, she wrapped her arms around his neck and kissed him, mouth open, skin wet with tears. Her face was probably a swollen mess, but she didn't care.

The next thing she knew she'd climbed on top of him, straddling him, kissing him even more deeply. He was holding on to her and kissing her too, but she knew—even then, through the blur of alcohol and emotion—that he didn't feel what she did. He wasn't vulnerable or insecure.

She ran her fingernails up and down his back, lightly at first, then hard. Breaking skin? He pushed her back with a jolting roughness, looked her in the eye like he was trying to decide something.

"I just . . . I like you," she said.

Please like me back.

She couldn't read his face, but it didn't matter. She'd already made her decision. Made it on shame and adrenaline, desire and urgency. She unbuttoned his jeans and pulled down the zipper. As they stretched out on the floor, the house of cards came down again. This time, no one made any effort to rebuild it.

"Are you sure this is okay?" he asked.

"Yeah," she said, trying to revel in the moment and ignore an ugly little doubt in the back of her mind.

It won't be okay later.

He lay down, letting her do the work. She didn't quite know what she was doing, but she could improvise. Come to think of it, she'd been improvising ever since she'd arrived at Coventon.

CHAPTER SIX

When Ethan walked into the room, he had a spray bottle of Fantastik—not Windex—in his hand. He wore an apron, too. A flowery number with ruffles. Saskia might have laughed if she weren't so mortified.

"Are you serious right now?" he asked.

Somehow she and Josh had ended up on the bed. They were on top of a rumpled quilt. Josh didn't have his jeans on, and Saskia's skirt was twisted around her waist. Flushed with embarrassment, she scrambled to pull it down.

Clearly the party was over. The heavy thud of bass no longer pounded up through the floorboards. No more muffled laughter or voices, either. She had a headache, a bitter taste in her mouth, and the sense that things had gone wrong, very wrong, although how or when she didn't know. She wondered what time it was, if Lila was still here or if she and Josh were the last ones.

"Sorry, man," Josh said. Without looking at her, he got up.

"I told you not to come up upstairs," chided Ethan, the nozzle of the Fantastik bottle aimed at Josh's head.

"I know, I know. We just . . ." Josh said.

"And now on top of everything else, I gotta wash the bedding. Damn."

Saskia put her hands over her face. She wished she could teleport herself back home.

"I'll help you clean up?" Josh offered.

Ethan shook his head. "No, just get outta here. Scat."

Josh slunk out of the room. Not knowing what to do, Saskia shambled out behind him, head down, sure that her hair looked tangled and feral. The house was quiet and still. But the lights were on, and she caught sight of another boy—an older, taller version of Ethan—wiping down the kitchen counter.

"Come on," Josh whispered, finally acknowledging her. "This way." She let herself be led once again. "You gotta ride?" he asked her when they were outside.

She looked around, not seeing Lila's car. "I don't know."

It all depended on where Lila was, probably home by now. Saskia wondered if she should call her dad, then remembered that she'd left her cell in the Buick. She couldn't bear the thought of asking Josh if she could use his, or of asking *anything* of Ethan.

She decided walking wouldn't be so bad. Her shoes were comfortable. The fresh air might sober her up. She wasn't sure of the way, but she'd figure it out. Eventually.

"You need a ride or not?" Josh sounded petulant, put out.

The night air felt humid and warm, and the sky was that hazy kind of color that looked like old lace. If she'd heard anything other than reluctance in his voice, even common courtesy, she would have accepted.

"Don't worry about me," she said.

Two seconds later he was jogging briskly up the street, a long, lean shadow with flopping hair. Exhaling, she looked right and left, trying to get her bearings. She had no idea which way to walk. She'd always been lousy with directions, and Coventon was still so new. All she knew for certain was that home was a good five miles away, at least.

She was still in the same place, trying to pick—right or left?— when she heard footsteps, and a figure emerged from the shadows. It was Josh, jogging back. Maybe he'd be a gentleman and insist on driving her home. He stopped in front her, breathless.

Neither spoke. It was probably only two seconds, but to Saskia it felt like two years.

"Listen, I like you, too," he said.

"You do?"

"Yeah. You seem like a cool girl—I mean, from what I know."

She tried to look into his eyes, but they were averted.

"You'd probably make a great girlfriend, too," he continued. "But the thing is, I'm not looking for a relationship. Not right now. I'm not in that headspace, know what I mean?"

She nodded.

"It's, like, the timing—not you."

"The timing," she echoed, her stomach churning.

"I hope you don't think I'm some kind of . . ."

Ass?

"Jerk," he continued.

"I don't think anything."

"I'm just looking for something short-term. Something . . . loose."

Loose, like you think I am?

"I'm not looking for anything serious, either. I mean, I just got here!"

She didn't sound particularly convincing to her own ears. Then again, at least she wasn't crying. It was a step in the right direction.

"I just don't want you to think I'm that guy. That jerk that never calls back."

You said it, not me.

"I don't think anything," she repeated.

"So we're good?" He was finally looking at her. Damn, she wished those eyes weren't so extraordinary.

"We're good."

"All right." He leaned in for a hug. She gave him a pat on the back. "I'll see ya, Saskia."

When he sprinted off again, she took the headband out of her pocket. She knew she shouldn't have, but she'd swiped it. A keepsake. Memento. She thumbed it gently for a moment, then stretched

it as far as she could, to its breaking point. When it snapped, she
tossed it to the curb.

She decided to walk the opposite way as Josh. God forbid he think she
was following him. Saskia Brown: wayward stalker, she thought
sarcastically. She'd made it a few blocks when she realized a car was
following her. Freaked out, she froze. What kind of driver sidled
up to a lone girl in the middle of the night? Someone on the Most
Wanted list, that was who. She got ready to run. But then she recognized the vehicle.

A second later Lila herself leaned over to open the passenger-side
door. "Get in," she ordered.

"I'm sorry," Saskia said.

"You should be."

Inside the car, Saskia gnawed nervously on her nails. She wasn't
sure what more to say. She wasn't even sure Lila would tolerate any
excuses. Cocooned in the dark interior, they fell silent.

The car's clock read 3:17. Saskia had never stayed out so late
before. She found her phone wedged between the seat cushions and
responded to her father's three million texts. The last one indicated
he was about to call the police.

> S: be home soon, dad! sorry!!!!! everything 👍 . we had a
> flat. AAA on its way

> F: Where are you? I'll pick you up!

She ignored his response and looked out the window. Lila drove
slowly, below the speed limit. Despite the hour, she evidently was in
no rush to get home. Nor was Saskia. While her father didn't ask a
lot of questions, he'd want to know what had happened. She didn't
want to lie to him. But she didn't want to tell him the truth either.

As the miles ticked by, her hand trailed out the window. She
wasn't quite sure where Lila was going, and she didn't quite care.

"So you're really not going to say anything?" Lila asked finally.

"I don't know what to say."

"What happened back at Ethan's?"

Saskia wished she'd had more time to think it through, every-thing, every word and action, from the moment she and Josh had flirted in the basement till Ethan had found them in the bedroom. It was like she'd fallen in love and broken up all in a matter of hours, her emotions running the gamut from anticipation to exhilaration to anger to shame. And now all she had to show for it was a broken headband. Actually, she didn't even have that.

"You didn't have to drive around looking for me," she said.

"Yeah, I *did*. You can't just roam around in the dark."

"I thought Coventon was safe."

Lila sighed and adjusted the old telephone book she was sitting on. She was so short she needed a boost to look over the dash. "There are crazy people everywhere—even Coventon."

She slowed down in front of a McDonald's, then turned into the drive-through.

"You're hungry?" Saskia asked.

"Very."

Lila paused a full minute before the lit-up menu, then ordered like it was her last meal: two Double Cheeseburgers and Chicken McNuggets. "Want something?" she asked Saskia.

"Yeah, might as well. Fries. Small—no, large."

When they got their bag of food, Lila found a parking spot and cut the engine. Saskia bit into a French fry and breathed a sigh of relief. She felt suddenly safer, like the darkness and cozy warmth inside the car somehow insulated her from the embarrassment and anguish outside of it. Like she and Lila were untouchable. *Some-times girls can create secret, safe havens for themselves*, she thought. *Sometimes they have to.*

Rustling through the bag, Lila found a packet of salt. She ripped it open and deposited the contents into her mouth.

"I've never seen anyone do that," Saskia said, shaking her head. "You're gonna get high blood pressure."

Lila ground salt between her teeth. "I probably already have it."

"But you wanna be a doctor! Why are you doing something so unhealthy?"

"Everyone has their vices."

"I guess."

"Hey, is your dad gonna be mad?"

"I told him we had a flat."

"Interesting."

"Yeah, so if he asks," Saskia said, "AAA came and fixed it."

"Okay."

"Will your mom be mad?"

"No. I don't have a curfew."

"Really?"

Lila took a bite of burger and chewed thoughtfully. "My mom figures she doesn't need to worry about me. I'm on the honor roll. The president of Western Connecticut State said I'm eligible for a scholarship if I keep up my GPA and continue with my job. I'm her golden child." She reached over to take a few of Saskia's fries.

Saskia handed over another packet of salt. "You must have the fastest metabolism," she remarked. Seeing Lila stuff herself, she couldn't help but think of Lorelei and Rory, the Gilmore girls, who guzzled down junk food but had no body fat. It was a Hollywood illusion—the idea that you could eat whatever you wanted and still fit into size-two jeans. But in Lila's case, maybe it was true.

"Not really. I just don't care about my weight." Lila glanced sidelong at Saskia. "So what happened at the party?"

Saskia turned to look out the window. Then she took a deep breath and let the story pour out, every detail, even the embarrassing brush-off in front of Ethan's house. "I guess it was nothing—to him," she finished.

"Was it something to you?"

"I don't know."

"Well, how did you expect him to act—after?"

"I don't know," Saskia repeated. "I thought maybe hooking up could be the beginning of something."

"Like a relationship?"

She shrugged uncomfortably.

"Saskia, don't you know that guys will do anything to get into your pants? When they're hooking up, they're not thinking about relationships."

"I guess I'm kind of ignorant about stuff like that," Saskia admitted, cringing. "Have you ever hooked up with a guy and regretted it?"

"Me? No."

"Why?"

"Various reasons."

"Name one."

"Well, I don't want to get stuck with a kid, for one," Lila said. "No way I'm going to end up like my mother."

"So no sex until marriage?"

"No sex until after med school. Until I'm financially secure."

"God, listen to you. You sound so responsible."

Lila shrugged. "Someone has to be. But it's not like I'm perfect. I have issues like everyone else."

"Do you think Josh has issues?"

"Sure. His girlfriend, for one."

Saskia turned to Lila so fast she got whiplash. "But Josh is single."

"*Technically* single. You're new—you don't know the history. He and Paige are always on and off."

"I thought they were broken up."

"They're never *really* broken up."

"Oh." Over the course of the night, Saskia had felt like a loser and a reject. Now she felt like a backstabber, too. Not that she was close to Paige—she barely knew her—but still.

"Yeah, they're thick as thieves," Lila continued. "It's been that way since elementary school. In second grade he used to like My Little Pony just because she did. They would play sparkly horses every day at recess, swear to god."

"Why are they 'on and off'?" she asked.

"Who knows? They're tormented. Star-crossed. Like Romeo and Juliet without the suicide."

"God, I'm so embarrassed."

"Why?"

"You know why."

"Hey, what's done is done. And it's not like Paige ever has to know."

Saskia smiled ruefully. Just knowing Lila understood made her feel a little better.

As they finished up their food, her phone beeped. Another harried text from her father, probably, or maybe her mother checking in. Then again, why would her mother think about her in the middle of the night? She was probably cuddling in bed with *Ralph*. Saskia tossed the cell into the back seat.

"Listen," Lila said, "from now on if we're at a party or whatever, we tell each other what's going on. Everything. No secrets. Deal?"

She stuck out her hand to shake on it.

Saskia thought, *This must be what growing up is all about: discovering that people aren't always what they seem. Realizing that someone you've loved your whole life doesn't love you back, and that the bond you have with a new friend is a hundred times stronger than the frayed and unraveling one you left behind.*

She took Lila's hand in her own and held it fast. She felt almost shy meeting Lila's eyes. "Deal," she replied.

Back at home Saskia tried to keep her story simple. Her father was pacing the kitchen, his brow furrowed into deep ridges, a mug of coffee in his hand. She sat at the kitchen table chewing gum and hoping that her breath didn't smell like beer.

"Why did it take the AAA person so long to come?" her father asked.

"Actually, he came pretty quick, but he had a hard time. He said he needed a special tool."

"What kind of special tool?"

Simple, she reminded herself. "Like a socket wrench?" She was surprised she could remember the name of any wrench. She still got flat-head and Phillips screwdrivers mixed up.

Her father looked at her skeptically. "He didn't have a socket wrench?"

"Not the right one, I guess."

"Lila must have special tires if they require special tools."

"I guess."

"She must," her father insisted, "if it took hours to replace *one*." Saskia nodded noncommittally.

"And how was the party?"

"Good, Dad."

"A lot of kids you know from school?"

"Yeah, a few."

"And you had a good time?"

"Uh-huh."

"You hung out mostly with Lila?"

"Mostly. Lila and a couple other girls."

Her father stopped pacing and stared at the floor. She wondered if he was thinking what she was: he sounded like her mother. The breakneck questions were all too familiar. Or maybe he knew she was lying and wondering whether he ought to confront her or let it go. Then again, maybe he was just glad she was home safe.

She kept chewing her gum, trying not to fidget.

Finally he sighed. "We should probably head to bed," he said. The tone of his voice had shifted from dubious and concerned to tired and defeated. "My shift starts in three hours. Do you want me to wake you up before I go?"

"Lord, no."

"So you'll be on your own tomorrow. Don't skip breakfast, okay?"

"I won't."

"And don't forget to call or text me if you go out."

"Okay."

"Good night, then," he said, kissing her on top of her head. "You sure you don't have anything else to tell me?"

"Good night, Dad."

Alone in her room, Saskia felt like an anvil had been lifted off her shoulders.

Lying down, she clasped the daguerreotype to her chest. But she was restless; there was something she couldn't get off her mind. She ran through the night she'd seen Cornelius, as she had so many times before, but this time she backtracked. She reexamined the whole evening from beginning to end: eating dinner with her father while watching *Gilmore Girls*; driving with Lila and listening to the story behind the dragonfly; venturing for the first time into the Howard and Alice Steerkemp Daguerreotypes Collection; learning the steps required to make daguerreotypes; marveling at how liquid mercury seemed to respond to her touch, almost like it were a living organism . . .

At that moment, Saskia knew. Mercury was the variable she'd forgotten. She'd been able to see Cornelius that first time because she'd touched mercury beforehand. Mercury, the only liquid metal known to man, as reflective as daguerreotypes themselves, which Lila had called "mirrors with a memory." Cornelius and mercury were inextricably connected. Of course.

Saskia quietly slipped out of bed and crept down to the basement, where there were still a couple of boxes her father hadn't unpacked. They contained an assortment of medical instruments, including some old-fashioned mercury thermometers. These were made of glass and had little bulbs at the end. Nowadays no one used them, but her father had held on to them during the purging. He'd always been protective of old medical paraphernalia. Saskia assumed it had something to do with his dream of going to med school.

She took a thermometer and a medicine dropper and tiptoed to the bathroom. Over the sink, she snapped the thermometer in half and carefully spilled the drops of mercury into a paper cup. They looked just as they had in the development room: beads of liquid silver. With the dropper, she squeezed one of the beads into her palm. Rolling it about, she watched, mesmerized, as it snaked and danced over the lines of her skin. After a few moments she let the drop slip from her palm into the cup. She put the cup under her bed, then scrubbed her hands with soap and hot water until her skin burned. The cringeworthy memory of what had happened with Josh kept resurfacing again and again, but she tried her best to push it back down.

What's done is done, Lila had said, and she was right.

Her headache finally gone, Saskia lay down again, still dressed, her shoes hanging over the footboard. The daguerreotype was now a familiar weight atop her chest. When she closed her eyes, she felt different, optimistic, as if by chance she'd guessed right.

Saskia

The light was more blinding this time, spilling all around Saskia with a radiance that made her eyes water. Above her shone the biggest chandelier she'd ever seen, a regal chandelier that could easily have hung in Versailles or Buckingham Palace. A thousand brilliant crystal prisms, like diamond teardrops, dripped from it.

She was looking down, her eyes averted from the light, when she heard his voice again.

"Pardon me, but weren't you here before?"

When Saskia raised her face, she smiled. It was a relief to see Cornelius in person again at last. A relief to see his eyes. She'd looked too long at his image, frozen and still.

"I was," she replied. When she realized she was holding the daguerreotype taken with her from the present, she quickly put it behind her back.

"Are you looking for a particular item? We've just stocked a new high-grade lamp called a solar lamp. It's remarkably efficient and economical. Would you like me to show it to you?"

She took a breath. "No, actually. I'm not looking for a lamp."

On a dime his expression changed from solicitous to confused.

"I was looking for you," she added.

"Do we know each other?"

"We do, in a way."

Saskia had no idea how to explain the mercury and the dreams. She doubted her story would make sense. There was a good chance he would think she was a basket case. Then again, she had to try. This might be her last chance to see him. There was no guarantee she'd have a third opportunity.

"This is going to sound strange—really strange. But I come

from somewhere you've never been. I'm a student there, and I've been learning about important people from the past. People who invented things that changed the world. People like you."

At this, Cornelius rubbed his chin.

"I've been studying all the things you've done," she continued. "You're a chemist and an expert in metals. You discovered a way to develop daguerreotypes more quickly by adding bromine to iodine. You took a picture of yourself, and on the back you wrote, 'The first light Picture ever taken. 1839.'"

He shook his head, his eyes flashing with something like anger. Saskia flinched. Did he believe her? Would he throw her out of his store?

"How do you know about my personal affairs?" His voice was low, impatient.

"I . . . I told you. I come from a different place. Well, it's not just a different place. It's actually a different time." Saskia struggled to meet his eyes. She tried to keep her voice steady. "From the future."

"Criminy! Clearly you've looked through my personal effects."

"I didn't, I swear." She put her hand over her heart, which was quickening.

"Why are you here? What is it you want from me, money? Are you some kind of charlatan?"

"No! All I wanted to do was meet you. I wanted to know how it's possible that we're here in the same place."

"Is this a joke?"

She gathered her courage. "I wanted to know how we can be in the same place . . . when you died over a hundred years ago."

He drew a sharp breath. "Young lady, if you do not leave right now, I'll summon the police. I have half a mind to bring you to the station myself."

"No! Please, you've got it all wrong. I didn't come to extort you, or taunt you, or do anything bad. I just came here to talk, that's all. To talk about this."

She revealed the daguerreotype from behind her back. When he saw it, his face colored. Confusion and indignation filled his eyes. "You stole it."

"It was in a library archive in Connecticut."

Angrily, he grabbed her by the arm and pulled her into a room off the counter area. She was shaking when he shut the door behind them. It was clear that he was stronger, and that she was vulnerable, too vulnerable. Instinctively, she looked for another door, a window, some means of escape. She saw nothing. She wondered suddenly if she'd made the worst mistake of her life.

Sternly, Cornelius directed her to sit in one of the two chairs flanking a large, cluttered desk. Her eyes frantically scanned the room. It was cramped and dominated by the desk, whose surface was hidden by reams of paper: sketches, drawings, diagrams, and notes scrawled every which way. More papers were pinned helterskelter to the walls and in stacks on the floor. Saskia saw the word *patent* printed over and over again.

"Stay where you are," Cornelius ordered. Not knowing what to do, Saskia obeyed.

He took a key from his pocket, then went behind the desk and knelt down. Saskia heard the click of a lock and the squeak of a drawer being opened. She heard him breathing as he riffled through whatever was inside. She was breathing hard, too. The air in the room felt stagnant and oppressive.

He took something out and stared at it for several moments before slumping into the chair beside Saskia's.

Cautiously, she took a peek at what he held: another daguerreotype—an exact replica of the one she had. Without a word, they held up the pictures side by side.

He has to believe me now. There were no copying machines in the 1800s.

"I'm sorry I touched you so roughly," Cornelius said. "It's not my way."

"Don't do it again," Saskia replied tersely. "I was only telling the truth."

"You're right to be angry," he replied.

Saskia kept her chin up, on the defensive.

They continued holding up the pictures, their eyes locked on the identical images, trying to make sense of them.

"I knew there was something peculiar about you. I knew it when you came into the store the first time," he said.

"What was *peculiar*?"

"Your clothes. Your appearance."

She thought he meant the color of her skin. She knew the lighting store couldn't have many—if any—Black customers. Philadelphia may have been progressive compared to many other American cities at this time. There was a robust Black population engaged in political, economic, and cultural life; America's first independent Black organization, the Free African Society, had started here; and an abolitionist newspaper, *The Liberator*, had been popular. But even so, racism and violence had flourished in this city, too. She'd be wise to keep her wits about her.

"In particular, your shoes," Cornelius said, glancing down. Saskia was taken aback. "I've never seen anything like them. I thought you were a foreigner."

"I guess I am . . . a foreigner."

He pointed at a sketch pinned high on the wall, nearly lost in the collage of paper. She was shocked to see a drawing of her sneakers—accurate right down to the Adidas logo. He must have sketched it right after she'd left.

"There are no shoestrings, buckles, or buttons," he remarked. "I've been wondering how they stay on."

"Velcro."

"Velcro?"

She leaned down and showed him the two sides of the Velcro straps, how they could be pressed together or separated.

He looked nothing less than dazzled. "You invented this?"

"No." She laughed, softening.

"This *Velcro*—it's brilliant. It could revolutionize the way shoes—and many other things—are made."

"Um, I think it already has. In fact, I think Velcro is used by astronauts."

"What?"

"Astronauts. You know, guys in space."

Saskia realized even as she was speaking that "guys in space" would sound as bizarre to him as "watermelons on a trampoline." She tried to break it down. "So in modern time, *my* time, travel into space is possible. People have landed on the moon. We've sent rovers to Mars—you know, the red planet. And we've put things in space to learn more: satellites, robots, telescopes . . ."

Cornelius stared at her, unblinking. If she were trying to sound crazy, she realized she was succeeding brilliantly. She struggled to look convincing as he sat back, mystified. Clearly he was having trouble grasping everything she was saying. Everything her presence suggested. She could almost see the wheels in his head turning.

"How did you arrive here?" he asked. "By carriage?"

She suppressed a laugh. "There aren't many carriages where I'm from."

"And you got this daguerreotype—of me—in an archive . . . from the future?"

She nodded. "*Your* future. My present."

"I—I don't understand."

"It's hard for me to understand, too."

"What is your name, miss?"

"Saskia Brown."

"Miss Brown, I've never in my life heard a tale like this, except in storybooks."

At that, Saskia threw her remaining caution to the wind. She told him how it had all started with Mr. Nash's assignment and her trip with Lila to the library. She told him every detail, minus the fact that she couldn't stop thinking about him. She had to save a little bit of pride, after all.

As she spoke, she was acutely aware of how preposterous all of it sounded. But neither she nor Cornelius could ignore the proof: the identical daguerreotypes in their hands.

"So maybe truth *is* stranger than fiction?" she finished.

Cornelius looked lost in thought. He idly twisted a ring on his left hand. His wedding ring, she realized. Though she knew he'd married in 1832, she couldn't help but feel a jolt of disappointment and jealousy.

"When you were in the library, in the development room, you say you touched mercury?" he asked finally.

"Yes, and then I touched it again a little while ago."

There was a new fervor in his eye. "Did you ingest it?"

"You mean, eat it?" She balked. "Of course not."

"Not even a little?"

"No."

"But you did have exposure." It was a statement, not a question. She nodded.

"Then maybe your presence here is not as strange as I thought."

He got up abruptly and paced what little empty floor space there was. He was so tall that the hanging lamp above his head nearly brushed his hair. His self-possession reminded her of Henry Fonda in *Twelve Angry Men*. She tried not to stare at him, but then found herself gazing at the daguerreotype and had to look away from that, too.

"In my life I've worked with mercury a great deal," Cornelius said. "It started when I learned fire-gilding."

"Fire-gilding?"

"Yes. It's an ancient process, hundreds of years old. It entails applying silver, gold, or copper to a base metal. You need mercury to do this. For example, an amalgam of mercury and gold can be applied to bronze. When the surface is heated, the gold bonds to the bronze, and the mercury is driven off."

"Driven off?"

"Yes, it vaporizes." He snapped his fingers. "Disappears."

He stopped pacing and stared at the wall. "It's rather magical, watching a metal vanish as if it never existed. While fire-gilding, I became addicted to that sight."

"Physically addicted?"

He smiled. "Mentally. I became addicted to the lure of mercury, and I'm not the first. Mercury's the most fascinating of the elements. Beautiful. Mysterious. Dangerous. It's enchanted man for ages."

"Why?"

"Because throughout history man has believed mercury can do just about anything: cure yellow fever, conjure spells, enhance fertility, inspire enlightenment, guarantee immortality, bring about alchemy . . ."

"Do *you* believe mercury is magical?"

"I believe mercury has secrets." Cornelius glanced at Saskia sheepishly, the expression of a boy caught with his hand in a cookie jar. "And I've always hoped I'd be the one to unlock them."

"What do you think mercury can do?"

His voice dropped to a conspiratorial whisper. "Although I lack proof, I suspect mercury played a role in your presence here. There are traces of mercury on the daguerreotype you're holding. Perhaps those traces, when combined with the liquid mercury you touched in the library archive, somehow catalyzed an extreme reaction. A remarkable reaction."

"You mean, like time travel?"

"Well . . . yes."

Saskia eyed him skeptically.

"I'll admit it does sound far-fetched."

"Is there any way to prove it?"

"No. But there is a certain method to my madness. Mercury conducts electricity extremely well at cold temperatures. The lower the temperature, the better the conductivity. It's my belief that, at one hundred degrees below zero Fahrenheit, electricity would run infinitely through mercury wire. It would encounter no resistance whatsoever."

Saskia shook her head. "I don't understand."

"Miss Brown, have you ever ridden a bicycle?"

"Of course."

"Good. Now picture yourself riding a bicycle down a hill. It would pick up speed, wouldn't it? But after a while, if you didn't pedal, it would slow down and eventually stop. With mercury in an extremely cold state, your experience would be different. Even if you didn't pedal, your bike would continue on and on for thousands of miles. You'd keep going. Forever."

"I still don't get it."

"If electricity can travel infinitely through space, then isn't it possible that a human being could travel infinitely through time?"

"You think this happened to me?" she asked incredulously. "That mercury somehow . . . moved me through time?"

"I do . . . perhaps."

"But the mercury I touched wasn't super cold."

"Yes, well, that's true. I'll admit I don't have all the answers. Just the knowledge that mercury can act as a radical stimulus."

Saskia let that settle for a moment. She, too, believed that physical contact with mercury had played a part in her presence here. But hearing Cornelius talk about a perpetually moving bike made her realize just how ludicrous that sounded.

"It's just a theory," he admitted. "But science has many unknowns. We chemists discover new things all the time—even new elements, the very basis of matter! Any man who thinks he knows everything is a fool."

"Any man . . . or woman."

He smiled. "Yes," he agreed. "Or woman."

"It sounds like you experiment with mercury a lot. Do you think you're still 'addicted' to it?"

At that, his mood seemed to darken. He sighed deeply. "Not long ago I experimented with mercury every day, for hours, sometimes deep into the night. Until one day when something quite scary happened."

He took a seat again and leaned toward her, his face flushed. "There's a reason I've returned to the lighting shop full-time."

"Isn't it your family business?"

"Yes, but what drew me back to this place was not family. It was fear."

Saskia's stomach dropped. Looking into his eyes was like looking into a well bottom, an abyss. She wanted to comfort him but resisted the urge to put her hand on his.

"Miss Brown, you mustn't repeat what I'm about to tell you. I haven't told another soul."

"I won't," she promised.

"I've made scores of daguerreotypes. One was of an old man: Jack Wickett. He walked into one of my shops wanting a portrait—some record of his life beyond a birth and death certificate."

"Well, it's natural to want to be remembered, isn't it?"

Another soft smile appeared on Cornelius's lips. "Yes, Miss Brown. In any case, I made Mr. Wickett's daguerreotype, and he was very pleased with it. He said he'd come back in a few days to pay, but never did. I sent a bill to his home. No response came. So I ventured to his residence. His wife met me at the door and handed me the daguerreotype. She said it had been timely. Mr. Wickett had died."

"Oh no. What did you do with his daguerreotype?"

"I returned it to his widow. I couldn't ask for payment—it wouldn't have been right under such circumstances."

Saskia nodded.

"To be honest, I didn't think much of Mr. Wickett's passing," Cornelius continued. "He was old and hadn't appeared in good health. But that same night, after learning of his death, I had a terrible dream. Jack Wickett found me here in this shop. He asked me to follow him. I didn't want to, but I obliged. We walked a long time, down narrow streets I didn't recognize. The air became dark and very hot. I realized he was taking me to a bad place."

"Why didn't you run?"

"I didn't feel I was in control."

"What happened next?"

"The streets pitched. We began to descend. Down, down, down we went. I felt as if we were walking into the very bowels of the earth. And Mr. Wickett—he looked at me with eyes that spoke of blood, misery, and evil."

"He was taking you to hell," she whispered.

"Perhaps."

"Why?"

"Perhaps he wanted company?"

Her eyes widened.

"It was only a dream," he continued, "but it felt astonishingly real. A nightmare come to life."

She realized that her hand had settled on his, after all. She removed it abruptly.

"You mustn't touch mercury anymore," he warned. "There is something about it—when combined with the right circumstances and the elements of photography—that yields unpredictable results. Magical, but menacing results. When I saw John Wickett, I trod somewhere forbidden. Somewhere humans are not meant to go."

A sudden knock on the door made Saskia's heart jump. It was the heavyset man, the one Cornelius had spoken with at the counter during her first visit. He said Cornelius's name. The sound of his voice made her stomach curdle. She closed her eyes.

CHAPTER SEVEN

Saskia's eyes flew open. She found herself back in her room, still in bed, the daguerreotype clenched in her hands. Her ears were ringing. Her face felt hot—she was sure it was flushed. She remembered how she'd touched Cornelius's hand and how she'd felt—embarrassed, but thrilled, too. Already she yearned to see him again, to hear the gravity of his voice and see him leap from the dull confines of the photo into the drenching light of his shop.

Cornelius had warned her not to touch mercury again. But now that she knew where it could take her, she wouldn't be able to resist.

The remaining days of school passed in a blur. None of the kids wanted to be there. You could see it in their faces. Even the teachers seemed distracted, disoriented, disinterested. An early summer heat wave coupled with a lack of air-conditioning made being inside unbearable. The hallways and classrooms sweltered. Everyone trudged around with dead eyes and damp clothes.

Every time Saskia saw Josh in Mr. Nash's class, her skin turned to gooseflesh. She desperately wished to speak with him and at the same time prayed he would vanish from the face of the earth. She wanted him to want her and at the same time hoped her own feelings would cool into apathy. But when she saw Josh's devil-may-care expression each day in class, she realized he was experiencing zero aftereffects. In fact, the only time he showed any emotion was when Mr. Nash confiscated his cards—again.

His frown then gave her a bittersweet sliver of satisfaction.

"Water under the bridge, Saskia," Lila kept reminding her. "You're too good for him anyway."

Saskia appreciated Lila's pep talks. But she didn't appreciate what always came next.

"The presentation's over, Sask," Lila would conclude gently, but urgently. "It's time."

Saskia knew this. She also knew that Lila had jeopardized her job by letting Saskia take the daguerreotype in the first place. But she couldn't bring herself to give it back. Before, she'd wanted it. Now she needed it. After all, she couldn't travel to Cornelius without both mercury and the daguerreotype. There was only one route to the lighting shop.

Over the next few days, she developed a routine that seemed to work. First, she dropped a little mercury into her palm. Then, rolling the beads around, she returned them to the bottle, took the daguerreotype, and got into bed. Most of the time this ritual bought her a ticket to the past. With each visit, she grew closer to Cornelius.

One day she told him about her daily life, and he listened in wide-eyed amazement as she explained what a laptop, television, and microwave were. She needed several visits to adequately describe the Internet. He, in turn, showed her hundreds of drawings and sketches—all ideas for new contraptions, inventions, machines, even new chemical compounds. She loved the way his eyes gleamed when he shared his ideas and the excited, almost manic way he raked his fingers through his mad scientist hair.

Unfortunately, Lila didn't want to hear about Cornelius or his ideas. She maintained that Saskia's trips to the past were fake. Fabricated. Fever dreams. Delusions.

"You have an unconscious desire for escapism," she kept telling Saskia.

"All I'm hearing is 'Blah, blah, blah, Miss Freud.'"

"Girl, you're in *deep*."

• • •

The last day of school was the hottest day on record. Even the principal walked around in a sleeveless blouse that looked suspiciously like a tank top. Saskia's own shorts and T-shirt were the usual drab variety. As she stood next to Paige at their lockers, she felt like a sparrow next to a peacock.

The girls smiled at each other. Not for the first time, Saskia considered coming clean about Ethan's party. Paige was always so nice to her, and how had Saskia repaid her? By hooking up with her boyfriend—or ex-boyfriend. Whatever Josh was to Paige, Saskia knew that she'd made a questionable decision that night. She didn't think of herself as someone who would break the girl code. But she had. And now, not only did she feel guilty, she also felt too ashamed to admit her wrongdoing. *Maybe*, she thought, *what happened at Ethan's party will always be a secret.*

"What are you doing this summer?" Paige asked brightly.

Truth be told, the question was a source of great worry. Saskia wanted a job. She feared being bored, restless, rudderless. With too much time on her hands, she suspected her outsize interest in Cornelius would morph into full-fledged obsession. Plus, it wouldn't hurt to make money. There were more and more bills piling up on the coffee table, above the divorce papers her father still hadn't read.

"I haven't decided yet," she said. "What about you?"

"I might lifeguard at the town pool," Paige replied. "I did that last year. But I want to try something different. Shake things up a little. Know what I mean?"

Saskia nodded.

"Hey, I meant to ask you something," Paige continued, playing with a shiny lock of hair. "Do you want to come over tonight? To hang out?"

Saskia was stunned, flattered, and nervous all at once, but fought not to show it. "Sure. Sounds fun," she said after a moment. Her voice sounded surprisingly mellow.

Paige whipped out her phone to get Saskia's number, so Saskia did the same. She couldn't help but notice that even Paige's phone was pretty: robin's-egg blue. The color of Tiffany's boxes. Saskia's had a cracked screen.

How's that for symbolism?

"It'll just be a couple of us," Paige said. "Totally low-key."

"Great. Would you mind if I brought a friend?"

For a split second Paige looked unsure, maybe even slightly put out. But she recovered so quickly, Saskia couldn't be sure. "Of course! The more the merrier."

Paige's house, like Ethan's, was on the right side of the tracks. Lila laughed uncomfortably as she parked her car on the street between two BMWs.

"One of these things is not like the other . . ." she sang in a childish voice inflected with sarcasm.

"Is that from *Little Einsteins*?" asked Saskia.

"Sesame Street," Lila said. "Old school."

For a few seconds, the girls stood on the sidewalk and just gaped. Paige's house was three oversized stories of immaculate white brick. The front lawn was beautifully landscaped with sloping stone walls, a manicured garden, and a huge tree with hanging branches. A willow? An elm? Saskia wasn't sure; there weren't any trees like that in Arizona. There was also a fountain of a naked mermaid, water spewing from a metal conch she was holding.

"Are you kidding me?" Lila said. "A freaking fountain?"

Saskia looked down at her olive-colored jumpsuit; it was a definite step up from her usual T-shirt and shorts combo. But now she wondered if she should have worn a ball gown or something. She'd suggested Lila dress up a little, too, but her friend had been defiant in her choice of frayed cut-offs.

"I know what you're thinking," Lila said, noting Saskia's grimace. "And you were right. This is like a freaking wedding venue."

"Never mind," said Saskia, pulling on her arm. "Just hurry up."

The girls walked up a bluestone path to the door. They wiped their feet on the clean welcome mat—*Who has a clean welcome mat?* thought Saskia—and pressed the doorbell.

Paige answered immediately, looking perfect as usual. Saskia found solace in the fact that she was wearing shorts. "I'm so glad you could make it. Hi, Lila!" she gushed, ushering them in.

"Hey," Lila replied tentatively.

"Thanks for the invite," Saskia said. She hoped the soles of her old Adidas weren't too gross. The inside of Paige's house was spotless.

"Anytime. The others are in the den. Come on."

It seemed to Saskia that Paige's den was the same square footage as her own whole house. It had a cathedral ceiling, built-in cabinets, and a gargantuan glass wall with a sweeping view of the backyard, where Saskia could make out the vague blue shimmer of a swimming pool. The furniture and rugs were serene and pale: white, cream, eggshell, ecru. Saskia wished she could go back to the welcome mat and wipe her feet again.

The best part of the den, though, was the wall of books opposite the glass wall. There had to be a few thousand titles lined up, row after row, all the way to the ceiling. It was like having a whole library at your fingertips.

"Those are Paige's," a girl said. She was sitting cross-legged on an ottoman. She wore a funky bohemian dress and a long necklace of wooden beads that clacked when she moved. Her pale blond hair was twisted up in two braids atop her head, milkmaid style. She looked like she'd just stumbled out of Coachella. "She's read every book. Twice. She's a closet nerd."

"Wrong. I'm an out-and-proud nerd," Paige replied, wagging a finger at the girl. "Lila and Saskia, this is my sister, Sara Beth." Sara Beth smiled, but didn't get up.

There was another girl, too. The tall redhead from Ethan's party, Adrienne. She waved at Saskia giddily from the couch.

Paige did the introductions, but they weren't really necessary. With the exception of Sara Beth, everyone knew one another.

"Are you the older or younger sister?" Lila asked Sara Beth. Saskia couldn't tell, either. Sara Beth wore so much makeup, her age was a mystery.

"Irish twin," she replied. "We're eleven months apart."

"I'm older," Paige said.

"Why don't you go to Coventon High?" asked Lila.

"I go to Fulton Academy."

"Never heard of it."

Sara Beth stared at her icily. "It's a school for the arts in Hartford."

"Very prestigious and selective," Paige added.

"Hartford—that's a long commute," remarked Lila, unimpressed.

"It's worth it." Sara Beth sniffed. "I'm learning what I need to, not a bunch of stuff I'll never use."

"Uh-huh," Lila replied.

"Excuse me," Paige broke in, "but I have an announcement to make. Ladies, we're officially done with school." She held up a bottle of champagne. "It's time to celebrate!"

Saskia and Lila glanced at each other.

Sara Beth asked, "How long are the 'rents out for tonight?"

"Till midnight, at least. They're at the Sullivans'," Paige replied.

"Oh, the *Sullivans*."

"Who are the Sullivans?" asked Saskia.

"Old hippies trying to relive their youth by partying too much," said Paige.

"It's sad. But what's more sad is the husband's toupee. It's like roadkill on his head," added Sara Beth.

Saskia giggled.

"The Sullivans and our parents are clearly having a midlife crisis," Sara Beth elaborated. "They smoke pot, listen to old music, and pretend they're at Woodstock."

Paige smiled at her. "Then why aren't you there?"

"Shut up!"

Paige stuck out her tongue. Then she handed both the bottle and a corkscrew to Sara Beth. Saskia had a feeling they'd done this before, perhaps many times.

"Your parents won't find out?" Lila asked.

"After coming back from the Sullivans'?" Paige said. "They'll be so sloshed they'll think they drank the champagne themselves."

Paige took out five goblets from a cabinet. These were expensive-looking: ruby-red crystal with thick stems and gold flourishes.

"To the end of school!" Sara Beth said, as the cork popped off and a stream of champagne spewed into the air.

"And the beginning of summer!" Paige yelled, laughing. "It's about damn time."

Sara Beth poured out the champagne. Saskia took a small sip, remembering apprehensively all the beer she'd drunk at Ethan's party. Then again, Josh, not the alcohol, had been the most toxic aspect of that night. As the girls did more and more toasts—to one another, to new friends, to the Sullivans, to Mr. Sullivan's toupee—she started to relax. After sip number five or six, she realized why people drank champagne. It made you feel all fizzy inside, lighter than air.

All too soon, the bottle was empty, and Paige went looking for another. Judging from the size of the family liquor cabinet, they'd never run out. Sara Beth left for a few minutes and returned with a bowl of popcorn. Greedily, the girls grabbed handfuls.

"Let's play a game," Sara Beth suggested, in between bites.

"Okay with me," said Paige, nodding at her sister.

"Me, too," added Adrienne.

Saskia forced a smile. She wasn't sure what the sisters had in store.

"Everyone in a circle," Sara Beth ordered. "Oh, and we need candles . . ."

"For what?" asked Adrienne.

"Ambience. Speaking of which, we need incense, too."

Paige ran to fetch both. Saskia wondered what kind of game could possibly require a certain kind of *ambience*.

Five minutes later, the den was dark except for the flicker of tea lights and a soft, ghostly glow entering through the glass wall. Saskia thought the room smelled, not unpleasantly, like a spice cabinet. Whether it was the ambience Sara Beth had insisted upon or the champagne settling in her stomach, Saskia decided that her nervousness was baseless. In fact, if anything, she should be excited about the prospect of making new friends.

"So what's the game?" Lila asked, after the girls sat in a circle on the floor. Her original glass of champagne, still full, rested by her side.

"Truth or dare?" said Adrienne.

"That's so elementary school," Sara Beth complained. "How about just truth?"

"I already know your secrets," Paige replied.

"Yeah, but you don't know theirs."

"True, true, true." Paige rubbed her hands together and looked at Saskia and Lila mischievously.

Giggling nervously, Saskia gulped down the rest of her glass. She tried to remember if it was her second refill or her third. Then again, who was counting?

"Don't get too excited," Lila warned the sisters. "We're pretty boring."

"Speak for yourself," said Saskia, still giggling.

The game started slowly but grew more interesting as the questions became more personal. *Who do you consider your best friend? Would you die for her? If you could trade places with any kid at school, who would you choose? If you could commit any crime, what would it be? Who do you want to kiss? How far have you gone?*

Saskia was surprised to learn that Adrienne, Paige, and Sara Beth were not virgins. Back in Arizona, none of her friends had had sex yet, except for Heather. But Heather was the first of their gang at everything, or at least everything involving controversy. Many of Saskia's other friends hadn't even had their first kiss yet.

Clearly the girls in Coventon were more in Heather's league. Adrienne had lost her virginity a few months ago to some guy named Benjamin. Paige had been fifteen when she'd "experimented" with Josh. And Sara Beth? She'd been fifteen, too—only her first time was with a camp counselor who was several years older.

Saskia felt hopelessly naïve in comparison. When Sara Beth looked at her and said, "Your turn," she wanted to flee. She waved off the question.

"Fine—if you're too shy about that, then at least tell us the last time you kissed someone," Sara Beth persisted.

The correct answer was Josh. But Saskia was not so drunk that she'd admit it. "I pass."

"You can't *pass*."

"Ask me something else, then."

Sara Beth rolled her eyes. In the candlelight, her winged eyeliner and red lipstick made her look like a movie star, a classic screen siren like Brigitte Bardot. "God. At least tell us the last bad thing you did," she said irritably.

Saskia glanced at Lila, who gave her a noncommittal look. "The last bad thing?" she repeated. "I guess it's that I stole something. Well, borrowed it—long-term."

"This better not be a library book," Sara Beth muttered.

"No."

"So what was it?"

"A daguerreotype."

"A duh-garro-what?"

"It's an old photograph. Like, from the 1800s."

Paige looked like she was about to yawn.

"But it's just not just any old photograph," Saskia insisted. "It's got power."

"What kind of power?" Sara Beth said, pronouncing the word *power* like she was sucking on a lemon.

Saskia glanced at Lila, who shrugged. Her friend still didn't believe her meetings with Cornelius were real.

"Okay, let me explain," Saskia said. "I was studying this guy, Robert Cornelius, for a class. He's really fascinating. An inventor. Pioneer. Lighting entrepreneur. Kind of hot, too," she added bashfully. "Anyhow, Lila mentioned that her library actually has a daguerreotype of him, and I wanted to see it. So we went to where she works and took out the picture. We touched liquid mercury, too, just randomly; it's one of the chemicals used to make daguerreotypes. Afterward, when I got home and fell asleep, something weird happened. Really weird. I was able to enter Cornelius's lighting shop. I saw everything in detail—individual crystals in the chandeliers, shiny bronze statues . . . I could smell things, too: cigar smoke and peppermint and whale oil. It was as if I was standing right there. I've never had a dream so realistic."

"So what happened next?" Paige asked, no longer looking bored.

Saskia took a deep breath. "I saw him—Cornelius. He was talking to an older guy, a colleague or something. He was talking about a new lamp he'd invented, a solar lamp, and how it was gonna change the world. Later on, after I woke up, I googled 'solar lamp' and realized it was the exact same thing Cornelius had been holding. But before that night, I'd never even heard of a solar lamp, so there was no way I could have dreamed about it! Same with smelling whale oil—I've never smelled it in my life, and yet I did that night. I'm sure of it."

"Interesting . . ." Paige said, grabbing a handful of popcorn. "Go on."

"Well, I actually talked to him—Cornelius. I heard his exact voice; it's low and kind of gravelly. I saw every little detail of his old-fashioned suit. We talked, but only for a minute. I woke up after that, and I realized—I *knew*—that what had just happened was no dream. It was like, well, an alternate reality."

By now she had the full attention of Paige, Sara Beth, and Adrienne. They began to pepper her with questions.

Sara Beth pulled out her phone and googled Cornelius's image. "He's cute," she remarked. "A little old, though."

"Not very," said Saskia. "He looks younger in person—and in color."

Paige giggled, causing Saskia to laugh, too. She was thrilled that the girls were interested. She hadn't expected them to believe her, much less to care.

"Do you consider this guy your boyfriend?" Adrienne wanted to know.

"Like, my dead boyfriend?" Saskia asked flatly.

Sara Beth squealed excitedly. "Oh my god, your *dead boyfriend*. That's the best kind of boyfriend! Think about it: he can never cheat, or lie, or be jealous, or . . ."

". . . Have sex," Paige added dryly.

"I don't know. Maybe it's possible," Saskia said, blushing.

Sara Beth took a swig from one of the champagne bottles. "I love this idea: a secret dead boyfriend."

"It's kind of morbid and twisted, but I like it, too," Paige admitted.

"Do you see Cornelius every night?" Adrienne asked Saskia.

"Almost. I need to touch liquid mercury first and then hold the daguerreotype. But then, somehow . . . it just happens."

"Let me ask you something," Paige said, snatching the champagne bottle from her sister. "Is it even remotely possible that you're dreaming—like, even one percent possible?"

Saskia sighed. She desperately wanted them to believe her. "Listen, I couldn't make this up on my own. When I go to that other place, it's so detailed. So *exact*. Sometimes it feels more real than my real life."

"So you're *sure* it's actually happening?"

"Yes."

"Are you still interested in regular guys now that you've met Cornelius?" Paige asked.

"Regular guys—like, living guys?"

"Yeah, like guys at school."

Saskia, uneasy, looked down. "I—I guess not."

"Can you take us there?" Sara Beth asked breathlessly. "To the library? I wanna see these daguero—whatevers."

"Can't. Be. Done," Lila retorted, rapping her knuckles on the floor with each word for emphasis. "What Saskia left out is that no one besides employees are supposed to be there."

"But you snuck *her* in," Sara Beth said, pointing at Saskia.

"She's one person. You're three."

"Come on. I wanna see if there are other guys like Cornelius for us."

"You realize these are photographs . . ."

"Not just any photographs," Sara Beth corrected. "*Magic* photographs."

Lila stared at her confrontationally, then turned to Paige, looking for an ally.

"I have to admit, I want to see the daguerreotypes, too," Paige said.

Sara Beth put her hands together and begged, "Please, Lila!"

"I can't help you," Lila said firmly.

Saskia realized something in that moment. Seeing the sisters' fervor, their desire for something out of reach, she felt a pang of satisfaction. Surprisingly, she had something that they didn't. She knew she was being petty, but still, she relished the power.

"Can you convince Lila?" Paige whispered, looking at her.

Saskia laughed, thinking, *I can try.*

CHAPTER EIGHT

On the ride home, Saskia still felt tipsy. She leaned her head against the headrest and closed her eyes. The motion of the car made her feel like she was flying, winging through space, heading to parts unknown.

It had been a perfect evening, the best time she'd had since arriving in Coventon. She'd felt as if she belonged, laughing and acting silly with a bunch of friends. Not that Lila wasn't great. She was. But there was something about a group—all of them together, hanging out, Paige, Sara Beth, and Adrienne—that made Saskia forget about Josh and her mom, that made her feel normal again . . . or almost normal.

"Hey," Saskia said, the buzz of alcohol a low humming in her brain. "What did you think about tonight?"

"I don't know."

"Really?" Saskia had assumed Lila felt like she did—euphoric.

"Yeah, those girls just live in a different world. Their own world."

"You mean, 'cause they're so rich?"

"That's part of it."

"What's the other part?"

"I can't put my finger on any one thing," Lila said. "The drinking, Sara Beth and her camp counselor, that stuff about their parents, all of it—it just feels *off*."

"Well, I had a great time."

Lila looked at her askance. "Okay, I guess."

"Not everyone makes a great first impression," Saskia said, wishing Lila hadn't put a damper on her mood.

"You did."

Saskia did a double take. "I did?"

"Yeah; why else do you think I'm hanging out with you?"

"Should I be flattered or annoyed?" asked Saskia, laughing.

"You decide."

"Um, after all that champagne, I can't decide *anything*."

Lila laughed, too, but she looked a little nervous. "Okay, Miss Brown, that's my cue to get you home."

Less than twenty-four hours later, in a parking lot on the campus of Western State Connecticut, the tables had turned. Lila was now the one who couldn't make up her mind. "I still can't believe we're here. I'm such a sucker."

"You're not," Saskia insisted.

"I am."

"We can still turn around . . ." Saskia said unconvincingly.

"You'll kill me if we do."

"I will."

Lila resignedly turned off the Buick's ignition and switched off the headlights. "Remind me why I'm doing this?"

"Because you're a nice person," said Saskia.

Lila shook her head. "I'm not that nice."

"Because you're generous?"

"Nope. I'm just a sucker."

"Hey," Saskia said, grabbing Lila's wrist excitedly. "Look, they're here!"

But Lila couldn't have missed the sisters' midnight-blue Mercedes as it slid smoothly into the parking spot beside her battered Buick. The two cars were an automotive version of *Beauty and the Beast*.

"Wonderful," she murmured cynically.

All the girls exited the cars and giddily followed Lila. Strolling through the college walkways, Saskia felt a palpable excitement. The air seemed charged. Twilight had turned the sky into a candy confection of orange, yellow, and pink. It was the kind of sky you only saw once or twice a year. The kind of sky under which anything could happen.

Inside the library, Lila told them that her boss, Marlene, was at a work conference. She wasn't expected back until tomorrow. Saskia knew Rich would be there, of course. But she also knew Lila could count on Rich not to rat them out.

"What's going on?" he asked Lila when all five of them appeared. "Are you multiplying?"

"Rich, these are my friends. You remember Saskia, and this is Paige, Sara Beth, and Adrienne."

Paige and Adrienne beamed. Sara Beth curtsied.

Rich gave them a tight, cautious look. Addressing Lila, he said, "You realize this is not a sorority house."

"Really?" Lila said. "I could have sworn . . ."

"Jesus. You're a good kid, and I like you. But not enough to get my ass handed to me."

"Marlene would never touch your ass."

"It's true, but you don't need to rub it in."

"She's still in Boston, right?"

"She's been known to come back early. You know that." Rich stared pointedly at Lila.

"Listen," Lila said, "if she does come back—*not that she will*— I'll take the fall. Promise."

"It's not like I'll be off the hook. What kind of security guard lets in"—he paused to count with his finger—"*five* teenage girls?"

"Is there anything we can do," Sara Beth interjected, "to make you feel better?" She leaned forward, smiling coyly and giving Rich a look that was at once sweet and provocative. Saskia wondered where she'd learned to act like that, so mature, so sassy and brazen, like Rita Hayworth in *Gilda*.

Rich looked at her blankly.

"Something that maybe would make you feel better," Sara Beth persisted.

Rich shook his head. He looked away from Sara Beth like she was a nuclear bomb about to detonate, and again addressed Lila. "Assuming Marlene doesn't come back, and assuming you girls aren't gonna burn this place down, and assuming this is a one-time deal and you never speak of it ever in your lifetimes, I'll let you in. Once."

"Richard Anderson, I owe you," Lila told him. Ruefully, he waved them through, ignoring the kiss Sara Beth blew in his direction.

Saskia didn't feel as nervous as she had the first time she'd set foot in the Howard and Alice Steerkemp Daguerreotypes Collection room. Though it had the same clinical atmosphere, she was no longer cowed by the starkness, or by the immense filing cabinets. She'd been here with Lila two times now; it was familiar, their territory.

Lila explained how daguerreotypes were stored and arranged, and the parts of each one, including the case, mat, glass, and preserver. She showed everyone how to handle them—gently, cautiously. The girls listened, but Saskia knew they'd rather bypass the specifics and get straight to searching. They all wanted their own Cornelius.

Reluctantly, Lila set them loose. The girls were quiet and subdued as they sifted through the images. Paige did so methodically, row by row, careful not to skip any. Sara Beth proceeded randomly, picking out specimens willy-nilly. And Adrienne had stopped searching altogether. She was gazing—transfixed—at the very first daguerreotype she'd selected.

"He's the one," she said to no one in particular.

"Who is?" Paige asked, gathering her hair in a loose ponytail.

"This guy."

Paige stood next to her and examined the image in Adrienne's hands. "Is there any information about him?" she asked.

"No."

"That's what the Internet's for," Sara Beth piped up. She was still sorting, her lips pursed in concentration.

"There's no name. Nothing," said Adrienne.

"But you can see he's in uniform," said Paige. "He's a soldier."

Adrienne peered closer, squinting. "Oh . . . right."

"Had to be the Civil War," added Saskia, gazing at the man. "Daguerreotypes were popular then."

"So the question is," asked Paige, "was he fighting for the North or the South?"

"I wonder if he died in battle," said Adrienne, her voice both exhilarated and horrified.

The girls were silent for a moment, and then Paige said, "Guys were different then, weren't they? More mature, more worldly. They wanted to make a mark, take a stand. They risked their lives for what they believed in. What do guys do now? Play video games and chase girls. There's no comparison."

"That's true," Adrienne agreed. "You know, this was the very first daguerreotype I picked. It's almost like fate that I found it, don't you think?"

"It was meant to be," Lila said sarcastically. "Obviously."

"Don't make fun of me! Isn't that why we're here—to pick one? A boy? Well, this one's my choice."

"Oh no. I let you come so you could *look* at the daguerreotypes, not *claim* them."

"But I have a feeling about this one," Adrienne insisted. "A gut feeling. Did you feel that way about Cornelius, Saskia?"

Both Lila and Adrienne stared at her expectantly. Saskia shrugged, knowing she couldn't please both of them.

"It doesn't matter," Adrienne continued. "There are some things you just can't explain. I don't know why I feel a connection with this guy, but I do."

Saskia saw that Adrienne was clutching the daguerreotype with the same tenacity that she sometimes clutched Cornelius's.

"That's two out of five," Paige said.

"What?" Lila asked.

"Looks like two of us have found dead boyfriends, and three of us are still looking."

Saskia listened for sarcasm in Paige's voice. She looked for a hint of a smirk on Paige's lips. But there was only sincerity. Saskia didn't know how or when or why, but the idea of finding a dead boyfriend seemed to have gone from a tongue-in-cheek proposition to real aspiration.

"You're really looking for someone?" she asked Paige.

"I wouldn't be against it. I mean, if what you said is true—that we can really meet these guys—then maybe we should try."

"But I don't know if everyone can do it."

"Why not?"

Saskia struggled to find the right words. "I don't understand how it works. I think I understand the method: the mercury and all that, but I don't get the logistics of it. All I know is that once I'm sleeping, I'm able to see Cornelius. I'm transported, somehow, to his time and place."

"If you can do it, then I'm sure the rest of us can."

"I hope so."

"It's *got* to work," Paige said firmly. "I'm ready for a change. Yesterday Josh called me—he wanted to see me again. And I thought, *Do I really want to get back together with him for the billionth time?* It's the same roller coaster ride. He wants me back, and then he changes his mind. I can't keep doing it. Isn't there a quote? 'Insanity is doing the same thing over and over again, but expecting different results.' That's me and Josh."

"Hallelujah!" said Sara Beth. "My lectures are finally sinking in."

Paige ignored her and said to Saskia, "So how do I do it? I pick a photo and you show me how to meet him?"

"I . . . I guess so."

"The moment has to be unforgettable," Adrienne interjected. "Like how I clicked with this boy."

"You mean, how you clicked with his *picture*," Lila said irritably.

"Whatever. The point is, you have to feel a connection. You

have to feel it here and here." Adrienne touched her heart and her head dramatically.

"I think I'm gonna throw up," said Lila.

"That's only because you haven't found the right person."

"And I'm not going to," Lila retorted. "You guys can do this raise-the-dead, hocus-pocus voodoo crap all you want, but I'm not getting involved."

"You already are," Paige told her. "You're here, aren't you? You let us in. That means some part of you must believe."

Saskia expected another sassy reply, but Lila seemed all out of sarcasm. "Just hurry up," she admonished. "We can't spend all night here. Rich has to lock up."

Paige nodded. "You heard her. Let's get moving," she urged. "Our Forever Boyfriends are waiting."

Forever Boyfriends?

Again, Saskia listened for a joking tone, a touch of irony. But as Paige resumed sorting through the daguerreotypes, her brow furrowed in concentration, Saskia realized she was a hundred percent sincere.

Did this mean Paige was finally over Josh? Was this her way of officially moving on? Saskia hoped so. She was tired of feeling simultaneously guilty for having hooked up with Josh and resentful that Paige had the ability to ditch him as effortlessly as he'd ditched Saskia.

Paige had finally met her match.

His name was Samuel Pendleton. At least, that was what was written on the back of the photo.

"Samuel Pendleton?" Sara Beth sniffed dismissively. "That sounds so blah."

"Shut up," Paige replied, her eyes still glued to the daguerreotype. It was in near-perfect condition, unlike the off-center, faded self-portrait of Cornelius. Samuel's hand rested atop a book, and he was holding a quill pen. Dressed like a dandy, he had smooth skin and thick hair styled in a pompadour. He looked lost in reverie, like he was pondering a sunset.

"He's the *definition* of vanilla," complained Sara Beth.

"Maybe, but he's cute. He looks like he's creative. Artistic."

"Well, I found someone, too," Sara Beth said, gazing at her own daguerreotype. "I like his smile—like he just robbed a bank and got away with it." When she waved the picture in the air, the girls gathered close to take a look. Saskia had to admit she liked the man's roguish smile, too.

Two things set Sara Beth's daguerreotype apart from the rest. First, the photo had color. Hints of it, at least. The man's cheeks and lips were pale pink, his skin vaguely beige. Saskia wondered what technique had been used to make the daguerreotype more lifelike. The second thing was what had drawn Sara Beth to it in the first place: the man's smile. In the archive most of the people looked contemplative, serious, even dour. Sure, there were hints of liveliness: a gleam in the eye, a turn of the lip. But it was clear to Saskia that photographers in the mid-1800s had never said, "Smile! Say cheese!"

"I like his clothes," said Sara Beth. "Check out the top hat. He's rocking it like Lincoln." She removed the photo despite Lila's admonishments and turned it over to examine the back. "There's nothing, no name or date." She smiled impishly. "But I'll get to the bottom of the mystery."

"Well, I guess that's four of us," said Adrienne. "What about you, Lila? You're the last one."

Lila shook her head, looking like she'd had enough. "I'm not a part of this."

"But you know we're going to borrow the photos, right?" Paige said.

Lila frowned at Saskia. "I don't approve," she said. "I don't approve *at all*."

"Come on, Lila," Saskia begged. "Please?"

Lila stared at the floor for several seconds; she looked torn, like she was having an argument with herself. Finally she rolled her eyes. "Oh God. *Fine.* Hide the pictures in your clothes. Carefully! Security only checks backpacks."

As the three girls giggled and slid the daguerreotypes into their shorts and down their tops, Saskia pulled Lila aside. "I forgot to tell you . . . we need to take more mercury," she said. "I have a little, but not enough for everybody."

Lila stared at her incredulously. "You realize I'm *this close* to losing my job, right?"

"This whole thing won't work without mercury."

"When is this going to end?"

But Saskia couldn't answer that.

Lila shook her head and stomped off. A minute later, she returned and handed a bottle of mercury to Saskia.

"Thank—"

"Just don't ask me for anything else, okay? It's beginning to feel like you're taking advantage."

Saskia tightened the lid and slipped the bottle into her bra, painfully aware that Lila was right.

Lila was the last person to leave the Collection room. But Saskia noticed something just after her friend flicked out the lights and closed the door behind her, something that made her feel a little better. It was the glint of a white box hidden in the waistband of Lila's cutoffs.

"Any collateral damage I need to know about?" Rich asked the girls on their way out.

"Of course not," Lila replied.

"No floods, fires, car accidents?"

Lila shook her head.

"Did you borrow more pictures?"

Of course not, Saskia wanted Lila to repeat. Instead, Lila looked at Rich guiltily. "Only a few," she replied.

"Seriously?"

"I know I said it wouldn't happen again, but this really is the last time. Promise."

"Okay, a) when you break a promise and then promise again, no one believes you. And b) for the life of me, I can't understand why you'd want those pictures. Are they popular on the black market or something?"

"Rich," Lila began, "it's hard to explain."

"Try me."

She cleared her throat, but nothing came out. Meanwhile, Saskia wiped her sweaty palms on her shorts and waited for Sara Beth to try to flirt her way out of this one.

"What Lila didn't tell you," Paige said, "is we're working on a project."

Rich appraised her for several seconds before responding. "I might be old, yes. But I'm not dumb. School is out."

"Oh, the project isn't for school. It's for independent study."

He stared at Paige skeptically, but she continued. "Because all of us like photography, we formed a club. We're tracing photographic history from the early 1800s to now. We've done a lot of research on tintypes, ambrotypes, cyanotypes, and especially daguerreotypes, and Lila suggested maybe it would be a good idea to look at them up close."

"Can't you look at them up close *in* the library?"

"We could, but it's not the same. We want to look at them in natural light. We want to study them under a microscope. We want to take pictures of the pictures."

"Why are you so interested in daguerreotypes?"

Paige gave him a bright, winsome smile. "Easy! This is learning for ourselves, not our teachers. I've wanted to study photography since I was seven. I saw a Diane Arbus exhibit at the MET: *Portraits in Parks*. I'll never forget it. A little boy with an innocent face and a toy hand grenade. A young guy with his wife, her hair in an awesome beehive, like Amy Winehouse. It made me fall in love with photography, at the power of pictures, how they can be transportive. Sublime. These daguerreotypes . . . they're like catnip to me."

Damn, she's good, thought Saskia.

Rich cleared his throat. "Can't say I share your

enthusiasm—especially about Amy Winehouse's hairstyle. But I guess if you're going to have a hobby, daguerreotypes are better than, say, collecting Hummels or old dolls. Those are just creepy."

"Do you have any hobbies, Rich?" Paige asked.

"Oh no—this is about you, not me."

"But if you did have an outside interest, something you feel passionate about, maybe you'd understand . . ."

Saskia could tell that Rich wanted to nod. He wanted to agree and maybe even open up to her. There was just something about Paige. Everyone felt it. She was like a star with gravitational pull. Saskia, too, wondered if Rich had a hobby and what it might be. Collecting comic books, Legos, Magic cards, action figures? Something that hinted of immaturity, a stunted adulthood? Something he was too embarrassed to admit?

"All right, what can I say?" he replied, clearing his throat. "You ladies do what you need to do. You obviously have something important you're working on." He turned to Lila. "But remember: everything needs to be returned in the same condition. I'm holding *you* accountable. Understand?"

Paige answered for her. "Perfectly," she said, still smiling.

Outside the library, Saskia felt jubilant. There was the relief of not getting caught, and then there was the thrill of the plunder. And though Saskia couldn't say it aloud, there was also happiness in knowing Lila was all in, too—even if she was keeping it secret. In the shadows the girls took out their daguerreotypes. The young men looked different outside of the confines of the library. More accessible. More real.

"I definitely made the right choice," Adrienne gushed. She reminded Saskia of a starstruck boy band fan.

"I think we all did," Paige responded. She put her arm around Saskia's shoulders and gave her a playful squeeze.

Saskia smiled, feeling high on friendship, romantic possibilities, and the promise of an exciting summer. "You know," she continued, "what you said to Rich about having a club isn't exactly a lie. We *are* all interested in photography . . ."

"I think our interest is more *specific*," Sara Beth said.

"Right. We're specifically interested in photos of cute boys."

"Not all of us," Lila said disdainfully.

Saskia expected Paige to glower at Lila. Instead, she ignored her and said, "I think we should call our club the Dead Boyfriends Club."

Sara Beth snorted. "The Dead Boyfriends Club? We can do better than *that*."

"Hunks from the Crypt?" Paige said.

"Studs Six Feet Under?" Sara Beth responded.

"History's Hotties?"

"Drop Dead Gorgeous?"

"Dead Dudes and the Girls Who Love Them?"

The sisters went on and on until Lila complained, "This is the shallowest conversation I've ever heard. I mean, you're basically objectifying dead guys. It's weird *and* morbid."

"How is objectifying dead guys in old pictures any different from objectifying living guys on Instagram or Snapchat?" said Paige. "I mean, yes, we're being shallow. But all modern social media is basically shallow, so you can't say what we're doing now is any worse."

"She has a point," Saskia said to Lila.

"Look, whatever we intend to call these guys, the question remains," said Sara Beth. "Are we really gonna do this?" She took out a tarnished silver compact and reapplied her blood-orange lipstick.

Lana Turner, not Brigitte Bardot, thought Saskia.

"Sure we are," Paige replied. "Are you in, Saskia?"

"I've got the mercury," Saskia replied, fishing out the bottle from her bra.

"Perfect," Paige said.

"Mercury for our Mercury Boys," Adrienne said in a singsong voice.

"Hey, what about that?" Paige asked. "The Mercury Boys Club?"

All the girls except for Lila beamed.

"It works," Sara Beth said.

Saskia thought so, too. The Mercury Boys Club suggested excitement, allure, mystery, even magic—all the things that came to mind when she thought about Cornelius.

"So we are really gonna do this," said Adrienne breathlessly. And this time it wasn't a question.

Paige turned to Saskia. "Okay, let's get down to business. Tell us exactly how this works."

Saskia

The weather in Philadelphia happened to be the same as in Coventon. Meaning it was hot. But here, at least, a constant breeze subdued the bright sun. Saskia and Cornelius loitered in front of the lighting shop. It was the first time they'd met outside the store, and they were both a little discomfited at being out in public.

Saskia gazed at the hand-painted street signs, trying to get her bearings. In researching Cornelius, she had studied some old maps of Philadelphia. In theory, she understood its gridded pattern, how numbered streets ran counter to major streets like Locust, Spruce, Arch, and Walnut. Cornelius and Co. was located on Eighth Street between Market and Chestnut, smack-dab in the heart of the city.

Looking beyond the signs to examples of bustling city life, she was acutely aware that she was now in the past. Women wore modest dresses with full skirts and puffed sleeves all the way to their wrists. Some of the dresses were bright and ornate, with ruffles and bows; others were plain and rough-hewn, made of only the most serviceable material. Saskia saw feathered bonnets, cloth shoes, gloves, hair coaxed into corkscrew curls. Like the women's clothes, the men's varied by economic status. The most extravagant included overcoats with back tails, tapered trousers, wide neck scarves tied in soft bows, standing collars, and tall silk hats.

Saskia felt as if she were at a costume party.

She also felt terribly exposed. Just about everybody who walked by cast a disapproving eye on her T-shirt and shorts.

Acknowledging her discomfort, Cornelius took off his overcoat and offered it to her. She accepted it gratefully. She swam in it, and it would probably make her sweat, but at least she was covered. They began to walk, albeit several feet apart. Saskia understood that he was wary of being seen with her. Even this, a simple stroll, could be misinterpreted.

They didn't speak for several minutes, but the silence didn't bother Saskia any. She focused on her surroundings. The sidewalks were swept clean and shielded from the sun by white awnings supported by simple wood beams. Here and there, children played marbles and rolled hoops. A boy in knicker pants whistled, offering them a penny newspaper. Cornelius bought two and handed one to her. She tucked it under her arm as she watched horse-drawn carriages and men on horseback travel along the street. The clapping of hooves filled her ears.

Cornelius began to point out buildings: the five-story United States Hotel, Garrett and Eastwick Locomotive works, the railroad depot, a tavern, an inn.

"And that . . . that is where I made the daguerreotype," he said, gesturing toward a nondescript stretch of sidewalk.

"The daguerreotype of yourself?"

He nodded.

"I've been meaning to ask: how did you make it?"

"It wasn't difficult. I removed the lens cap, ran as quickly as I could into the frame, and stood still as a stone."

"For how long?"

"Oh, maybe five minutes."

He turned and smiled at her. They had an easy rapport now, a familiarity that sometimes felt a few degrees warmer than friendship.

"How did you become interested in photography in the first place?"

"That's simple. Back when I did silver-plating, a man named Joseph Saxton approached me. He asked me to make a plate for his daguerreotype of Central High School. That's here in Philadelphia. The more he talked about photography, the more interested I became.

"Saxton is an inventor, too," he continued. "We make a fine pair! The both of us are mad as hatters. All we want to do is bring our imaginings to life."

Saskia watched him wink at a little girl sitting on granite steps, sky-blue ribbons in her hair, chin in her hands. "But what I really want to know is," Saskia asked, "where did you get the courage to try something new?"

"I took a deep breath and jumped."

She shook her head dolefully. "You're braver than me."

"Nonsense! You're here, aren't you? You took a risk, though you couldn't predict the outcome. That's the very definition of bravery."

"But I'm not brave in my regular life."

Without planning to, she found herself telling him about her parents' separation, and how challenging it was adjusting to a new town and new people.

"May I be so bold as to make a suggestion?"

She nodded.

"Perhaps you can try looking upon failure as a good, not an evil. We all fail before we succeed. Consider my example," he said, smiling ruefully. "I have invented hundreds of things. Yet almost all of them have failed. They don't work. Or the patent office rejects them. And still I persist."

"Doesn't all that rejection make you want to give up?"

He crossed his arms. She realized he'd assumed the exact same stance as in the daguerreotype. "On the contrary. It makes me want to keep trying! Failure is merely a necessary catalyst, propelling us ever closer to success."

"'Failure is merely a necessary catalyst, propelling us ever closer to success,'" she repeated slowly, committing it to memory.

"Besides, what's the alternative? Being idle? Giving up? Then you'll never stand a chance."

"A chance at what?"

"At becoming your best self."

She smiled. "Have you always been so philosophical, Mr. Cornelius?"

He winked at her the same way he'd winked at the little girl.

As they continued walking, she noticed they were closer. Their sleeves nearly brushed.

"What is it *you* want, Miss Brown?" he asked.

"You mean, in life? I—I don't know. Most of the time, I feel like I'm just drifting along, aimless."

"What about the rest of the time?"

"Well, every so often I feel like I'm on to something—that it's within my reach, if I could only figure out what it is."

"Well, when you do find it, I hope you'll come back to tell me about it. I suspect it will be very special."

Under Cornelius's heavy coat, Saskia flushed. "There is something else I've been wanting to ask you," she ventured.

"Don't hesitate. Go on."

"Well, what I've been wanting to ask is . . . what we're doing—right now—do you think it's real? I mean, that it's really happening? Do you think it's replacing what already occurred? Are we rewriting history?" She sighed. "I'm not even sure I'm making sense."

He was silent for several moments before answering. "You make perfect sense. I've been thinking about the very same questions. If in fact I've already lived, as you say, and my story is already known, then your presence here in the past is a very serious matter. Without knowing it, you could inadvertently steer me from my predetermined course. Even a word or action could have major consequences."

"Right," she said. "The butterfly effect."

"What is that?"

"It's this physics theory that says even minor things can trigger major events. Like, for example, a butterfly flapping its wings in one place could lead to a hurricane in another."

"I don't know if a butterfly could single-handedly cause that. I'm a chemist, not a physicist. But I do know that any chain of events is subject to change when a new stimulus is introduced. A person suddenly thrust into another time and place could surely change the trajectory of lives."

"Do you think I'm altering what is supposed to be?"

"I don't know. Maybe this *is* what is supposed to be. Maybe you were always destined to be here. It could be that the course of my

life *depends* upon your intervention. But there's no way to know."
He shook his head. "Before meeting you, I never supposed that
humans could travel through time the same as they travel between
points in space."

She glanced at him, studying his long, bristly sideburns, the hair
on his chin. It was so easy to talk with him that she sometimes forgot he was a decade older.

"Maybe I'm here to introduce you to Velcro," she joked, trying
to lighten the mood.

He laughed but soon resumed a more serious expression. "I
could never take credit for something that's not mine. There's an
honor code among inventors."

"But the guy who invented Velcro would never know!"

"That's beside the point."

"If I were you, there would be things I'd want to know.
Aren't you curious about what happens in your life? I could tell
you . . ."

"No," Cornelius said firmly. "I don't want to tamper with fate.
I like to think that such things are in God's hands."

"If they're only in God's hands, then what does that make me?"

He stopped in his tracks and gazed at her earnestly. "His mes-
senger, perhaps? An angel?"

Saskia was too embarrassed to respond.

Looking around, she noticed that they'd walked beyond the city
proper. She'd been so focused on their conversation she hadn't realized. Here on the outskirts of Philadelphia, the streets were dirty
and littered with garbage. There were many animals, some roaming
free, others in filthy pens. The stench of manure was strong. Fine
architecture had given way to narrow row houses and rundown
tenements. The people had changed, too. So many of them looked
skinny and forlorn, clothed in tattered rags. Saskia's heart especially ached for the children.

"It's not safe here," he whispered. "Disease has swelled. Small-
pox, cholera, and tuberculosis. In the summer it's always worse. My
father says the Germans are responsible. He won't let immigrants

into our store even though he is one. But I don't believe the Germans are to blame. I don't believe anyone is."

She nodded mutely. There was no way to observe so much hardship without feeling despair.

"We'd better head back," he said, touching her arm lightly. "We've gone too far."

CHAPTER NINE

S askia felt all around her sheets. As she searched, she became increasingly frantic. It must be here: the copy of the paper Cornelius had bought for her. *The Philadelphia Inquirer*, issue June 18, 1840. If she could find it, then she would have hard evidence. A crisp paper without a single tear or yellow page from 1840—nobody would be able to deny it. *She* wouldn't be able to deny it.

But it was nowhere to be found. Not in her bed or on the floor. Somehow she hadn't been able to bring it back with her. She didn't understand why she could bring things to the past—like the daguerreotype—but not bring them forward. It seemed unfair. And puzzling. Then again, just about all of this was puzzling.

At least she still had the memory of her walk with Cornelius. It lingered at the edge of her consciousness. She was sure that was what it was—the authentic memory of a perceptible reality rather than the unreliable memory of a dream.

Saskia spent the morning watching the tail end of *Gaslight*—she loved when Ingrid Bergman got revenge on her deranged husband—and searching for a summer job. Online, she scrolled through two dozen positions in and around Coventon. Most she wasn't qualified for. Most were year-round, not summer work. She knew she ought to approach local businesses directly. She should put on a nice outfit, walk into pizza places and grocery stores, and apply in person. But the thought of going door-to-door, a résumé in hand, terrified her.

Despite what Cornelius had said, she didn't feel brave.

At noon she gave up and went into the kitchen to have lunch. Another goddamn Healthy Choice frozen meal. Her father had stocked up on Chicken Alfredo Florentine, at least, but even that had grown old.

Afterward, she went for a walk. She made it two blocks under a sweltering sun before turning around and heading back, dejected and sweaty, to air-conditioning.

For the thousandth time that day, she found herself thinking about Cornelius. She wished she could conjure him right now. She wished she could bring him into her life, her *real* life. She was sick of seeing him only in her sleep . . .

Suddenly, her phone buzzed with a text from Paige.

P: all I can say is sam's PERFECT. i'm blown away

S: what happened?!

P: what didn't happen? i feel like i've known him for years & we only just met. Can't stop thinking about him. maybe I'm under a spell?

S: maybe. tell me more

P: tell u everything tonight. Every juicy detail

S: how juicy

P: u won't be disappointed. I'm falling fast. 8 pm - Ok?

S: c u then

When Lila picked her up that night, Saskia was already waiting at the front door. Her dad barely had a chance to say goodbye before she jumped into the car.

Saskia immediately started to talk about her newest dream, but stopped when Lila shook her head. "What? You still don't believe me?"

"It's not just that. I'm getting sick and tired of the whole daguerreotype obsession."

They drove in silence for a few minutes. Saskia debated whether or not to call Lila out, to tell her what she'd seen. After all, if Lila owned up to the fact that she'd taken a daguerreotype, too, then she would also have to admit that she was at least a little bit invested in the Mercury Boys Club.

But Lila remained quiet. And Saskia didn't press for more. As tempted as she was, she knew it wasn't fair. Lila would confess in her own time, on her own terms. Besides, the truth was, Saskia was ashamed of demanding so much of Lila. She needed to give a little, too.

The front door of Paige's house was wide open. Saskia and Lila let themselves inside and found the other girls in the kitchen, drinking again. Vodka this time. Sara Beth was squeezing limes with a fancy crystal juicer that was probably worth more than Lila's car. Adrienne and Paige were sitting with their bare feet propped up on the kitchen table, painting their toenails and sipping from glass tumblers. Saskia glanced enviously at their mile-long legs.

"Hi, ladies!" Paige called. "We're having a little nightcap. Want one?"

"Neat or on the rocks?" Sara Beth asked.

Saskia, not knowing the difference, replied, "Either, I guess."

Sara Beth smiled and poured Grey Goose into a big tumbler. "And you?" she asked Lila. When Lila shook her head, Sara Beth added, "Oh, I forgot. You're a *good* girl."

"Where are your parents tonight?" Saskia asked the sisters.

"At a concert," Paige replied.

"They go out more than we do," added Sara Beth.

"I feel like we should give *them* a curfew."

"Yeah, but who wants them home early?"

"Or at all."

"Did they go out with those neighbors again?" asked Saskia.

"The Sullivans?" Paige said. "Of course. Where the Sullivans go, they go."

Paige set down her glass, examined the seashell-pink polish on her toenails, and straightened up. "Okay, enough with the small talk. Let's get down to business. As most of you know, I met Samuel last night."

"I've been waiting for this story!" exclaimed Adrienne.

Sara Beth rolled her eyes. "Can I leave? I've already heard it three times."

"No, stay," insisted Paige. "It's important that we all know what's happening. We're in this together."

"Fine," said Sara Beth. "But can we at least go somewhere? Bonding in the kitchen makes me feel like we're at a Tupperware party."

"Where do you want to go?" asked Paige.

Sara Beth's eyes lit up suddenly. "I have the best freaking idea!"

She dashed out of the room, excited as a little kid on Christmas. Minutes later she returned with an overstuffed beach bag. The girls followed her outside to the front yard, which struck Saskia as even more grandiose than the first time she'd seen it. In the darkness, the oversized fountain glowed. A series of spotlights illuminated it from all sides. At the center stood the mermaid, whose large stone boobs and water-slick surface made her look practically pornographic. The conch shell in her hand had a bright green patina. A burbling stream of water splashed out of the conch's mouth down to a rock basin as big as a hot tub.

"Someone put a scarf around Meryl Streep's neck last weekend," Sara Beth said.

Saskia giggled and shook her head. "I have no idea what you're talking about."

"Meryl Streep—that's the name of the mermaid. Or at least what Paige and I call her."

"Why?"

"Because she's so dramatic. Obviously."

"Someone put a scarf on the fountain's mermaid?" Saskia said.

"Yep. Knotted it so tight that the housekeeper had to cut it off with scissors."

Housekeeper? Saskia almost asked out loud, but she bit her tongue. It really was a different world on this side of the tracks. She wondered, grimly, if the housekeeper was Black. "Where did you get that fountain, anyway?"

"My dad had it custom made. The stone's from a quarry in Italy. Some poor dude spent a year carving it. It's probably worth more than a college education." Sara Beth giggled. "My dad has a thing for mermaids."

Saskia tried not to let her astonishment show.

Sara Beth kept walking, leading the girls past the fountain to the enormous tree. "Behold the Tree of Terror," she said, with a flourish of her hand.

"We're not toddlers anymore," Paige replied. "It's a weeping beech."

Whatever its name, the tree was indeed scary. Shaped vaguely like an umbrella, it was almost as tall as the sisters' house. Its branches cascaded down like long green ropes, the ends touching the ground. Together, the branches and leaves created such a dense canopy that there was no way to see what lay behind.

"Come on," Sara Beth said, flicking on a flashlight. She parted a cluster of branches with her hand.

"We're going in there?" asked Adrienne.

"Yup."

"I liked the kitchen better."

"Paige and I used to hang out here when we were little. It'll be fun."

"But," Adrienne said, "what if something's under there? An animal . . . or something worse?"

"Don't be a baby. *We* haven't spotted a psychotic, ax-wielding rapist yet," chided Sara Beth, disappearing behind the leafy curtain. Paige went next, followed tentatively by Adrienne.

"Be my guest," said Lila apprehensively, motioning for Saskia to proceed.

"You're coming, right?" Despite the moonlight and generous outdoor lighting in the Sampras yard, Saskia could barely see. She wished she had Sara Beth's flashlight.

"Yeah, against my better judgment," Lila replied.

It was very dark under the canopy. Not pitch-black, horror-movie scary, Saskia thought, but close. She was relieved when Sara Beth's flashlight swept the interior, proving they were quite alone.

Fishing through the bag, Sara Beth took out a cigarette lighter and a dozen small votive candles. She and Paige lit them and placed them in a large circle on the ground. The soft, flickering light had a transforming effect. Saskia could see now that the interior looked more like a kids' clubhouse than an evil lair. There were even old toys strewn about: Barbies and a dilapidated plastic play kitchen, its parts dirty and cobwebbed. Two lawn chairs lay moldering near the trunk of the tree. The ground under the canopy was a combination of loamy soil and moss.

"Perfect," Sara Beth said, looking around.

Saskia wasn't sure *perfect* was the right word. She picked up a one-armed Barbie. The blond hair had been hacked off. Saskia could imagine the sisters playing hairdresser—and butcher—as kids.

Paige motioned for them to sit within the ring of candles. Sara Beth retrieved the bottle of vodka from the beach bag and passed it around. Saskia sipped tentatively. Since meeting the sisters, she'd drunk a lot. But she wasn't yet used to the taste of alcohol, or the feel of it, warm and rousing in her belly, relaxing and distortive in her head.

"Let's go 'round and tell each other what happened with our Mercury Boys," said Paige. "Should I go first?"

"Yes!" exclaimed Adrienne, giggling. "The suspense is killing me."

"Okay," Paige said. "Well, the first thing I remember after falling asleep is being in a meadow. A huge meadow. I didn't know how I got there or what I was supposed to be doing. But there were people, and they invited me to sit with them on a big checkered picnic blanket. Samuel was there, and the others looked about his age.

College age. They were dressed differently. Kind of conservatively. The girls had on long skirts and blouses. One had a polka-dot scarf in her hair. The boys wore pants and blazers, even though it was hot. I could tell I was in England because everyone had an accent. They sounded so proper. So *posh*."

"What happened?" Adrienne pressed.

"Be quiet and keep listening," Paige said, smiling mysteriously. "It gets better."

Paige

Sitting on the checkered picnic blanket beside Samuel, the meadow around her stretching as far as the eye could see, Paige was suddenly aware that she was the center of attention. Her back tensed, but her face remained placid.

"You must be one of Delilah's chums," said a girl with loose, sandy-colored braids.

Paige nodded brightly. She wondered who Delilah was.

"What's your name?" asked the girl.

"Paige."

"Are you about to go for a swim, Paige?"

Paige knew what she was getting at—her frayed cut-offs weren't exactly nineteenth century–friendly. Still, the girl didn't have to call her out on it. "Maybe."

"Your bathing costume's quite daring," the girl continued.

"This?" Paige said, smiling and stretching out her athletic legs confidently. "This is just every day. My bathing costume's *much* more revealing."

The girl glowered.

"Delilah's chums are always bright lights, aren't they?" Samuel said. "Where are you coming from?"

"America, obviously," the girl interjected. She stared at Paige coldly. "Your accent gives you away."

"I wasn't trying to hide it." Paige looked pointedly at Samuel. "And where are all of you from? Around here?"

He shook his head. "None of us lives in Cranleigh. We're all on holiday."

"Delighted to be away from our studies!" added a petite, black-haired girl.

"I think we all ought to properly introduce ourselves to our new American friend," Samuel said. "You made quite an entrance. I swear you materialized out of nowhere like the divine Lampetia."

"Lampetia?" Paige asked.

"A nymph in Greek mythology. The daughter of Helius and Neaera. Born to shine."

Paige laughed. "I don't know about that."

"Well, I make no claim to divine lineage. I'm Sam Pendleton. Just plain Sam."

"Good to meet you," she said. "I don't know why, but you look a little familiar." He studied her face for a moment, making up for a lack of mutual recognition with a warm smile.

The others introduced themselves one by one. There were three boys and four girls in total: Sam, Sylvia, Iris, Adeline, John, Clara, and William.

"Can we finally begin?" Adeline, the snarky girl, complained.

"Sure. What are you guys up to?" Paige asked.

"This is our daily meeting of the New Transcendentalists Society. We have it every morning—usually right here."

"This is our kind of church," added William, gesturing to the vast expanse of wildflowers and long grass, which swayed in the breeze.

Paige's eyes widened. Back in the eighth grade, she'd studied the Transcendentalists: Ralph Waldo Emerson, Nathaniel Hawthorne, Walt Whitman, Margaret Fuller. She vaguely remembered reading *Walden*: a book about a guy living in the middle of nature in a cabin he'd built himself. But she didn't know anything about the *new* Transcendentalists.

"Who wants to read first?" asked Adeline.

"Shouldn't we start off with Henry?" said Iris, who seemed to Paige to have more freckles on her face than there were stars in the sky.

"Shouldn't everything start off with him?" joked Sam.

"Indeed!" remarked John.

"I've got something," said Iris. She stood up and smoothed out her voluminous silk dress. Trimmed with so much white lace, it reminded Paige of a tablecloth or a really big doily. Iris began reciting out of a little notebook.

All things are current found
On earthly ground,
Spirits and elements
Have their descents.

Night and day, year on year,
High and low, far and near,
These are our own aspects,
These are our own regrets.

Ye gods of the shore,
Who abide evermore,
I see you far headland,
Stretching on either hand;

I hear the sweet evening sounds
From your undecaying grounds;
Cheat me no more with time,
Take me to your clime.

After a pause, Sam said, "Remarkable. What's that one called?"
"'All Things Are Current Found.'"
"Henry never disappoints, does he?"
Something clicked in Paige's head. She realized only then that they were talking about Henry David Thoreau, the author of *Walden*.
"Thanks for that, Iris," Adeline said. "Now then, I hereby call the New Transcendentalists meeting to order."
"Hear, hear!" said John.
"Who wants to read her own poem? Any volunteers? Paige?"
Normally, Paige prided herself on being able to improvise in any

situation. But making up a decent Transcendental poem on the spot was asking a little much, even for her.

Sensing her hesitation, Sam cleared his throat. "I'll go," he said, jumping to his feet. For the first time Paige was able to really look at him, and she liked what she saw: jovial eyes; raked-up hair; a long, lithe body; and cat-quick reflexes.

As for his poem, it barely registered. She tried to understand it. She really did. But it was purple and florid, stuffed with so much imagery she couldn't keep track of it all. When he'd finished, she had no idea what it had been about.

"Thoughts?" he asked hopefully.

There were a few seconds of silence.

"I enjoyed the alliteration at the beginning," said Adeline finally.

"And the part where lions and zebras gather for the eclipse," said Sylvia, the black-haired girl. "That was extraordinary."

"Quite," added Adeline. "I think Henry would approve."

Paige had to resist rolling her eyes. She knew precisely what these girls were doing: complimenting Samuel's second-rate poem in the hopes that he would reward them with attention.

"And you, Paige?" he asked her.

"Me?"

"Yes. What are your thoughts?"

She took a deep breath. "Well, honestly, I think you could have used an editor. It was a little . . . over-the-top."

Frowning slightly, he ran his fingers through his hair, raking it up still higher.

"I mean, don't get me wrong," she added. "There's potential there." This wasn't entirely true, but she had to say something nice.

"Perhaps you're right about an editor. I do have a tendency to go on."

"And on," joked John.

"It's always better to write too much than too little," Paige said. This wasn't entirely true, either, but she didn't want to discourage him. "I can have a look at it later if you want. I'm pretty good at pruning."

He smiled gratefully. "Splendid!"

From the corner of her eye, Paige saw Adeline frown.

More people read their work, and more people critiqued. Most of the feedback was overly charitable, in Paige's opinion. She stopped listening for quality and instead listened for themes. She started to recognize some that she'd learned when studying Transcendentalism: beauty and truth in nature, resistance to established ideology, self-reliance as the key to a fulfilling life.

Over the next hour or so, bits and pieces of her eighth-grade unit on Emerson and Thoreau came rushing back to her. *Do not go where the path may lead.*

"*Go instead where there is no path and leave a trail,*" she said under her breath.

"Pardon?" Sam asked.

"Oh, nothing."

"You Americans are quite mysterious."

"Sammy, to you, every pretty girl is mysterious," said John. Adeline poked him in the ribs. Paige realized that no matter what the century, some girls would always vie for the best-looking boy. Fortunately, she tended to win such competitions.

"Paige, what do you reckon of the new Transcendentalists?" John asked her.

"To be honest, I'm a little bored."

That made him laugh out loud.

"Delilah really does pick some gems," Sam said, sharing in the laughter.

"Where is she, anyway?" Paige asked, picking a blade of grass.

John mockingly made the sign of the cross. "I'm afraid her grandfather was just laid to rest in his eternity box."

"She's in town for his funeral," Sam explained. "She didn't tell you?"

Paige shrugged. "Is she very sad?"

"Sad? Hardly. The old codger didn't leave her an inheritance. Left it to a lushy cousin instead."

"Oh."

"But Delilah will survive. Her parents already bequeathed her their estate. The one in Winchester. Have you visited?"

"Not yet."

"It's grand," said Sylvia. "Twice as big as my father's, and twice as nice."

Paige nodded as if she knew a lot about bequeathed estates. "Have you come into your inheritance?" she asked Sam.

"Two more years," he lamented. "You?"

"One," she lied.

"Good girl," he cheered.

"Not to change the subject," Paige said, "but Adeline mentioned bathing costumes . . ."

"And?"

"And I wouldn't mind going for a dip."

"I assume Delilah told you about Mirror Lake," said Sam.

She prayed he would stop mentioning Delilah, whoever she was. How much longer before the group realized Paige and this girl were complete strangers?

"Yes, Mirror Lake," she said. "It's nice, right?"

"Glorious. The sand beneath is silvery as the moon."

"Shame about its real name, though," said John.

"Mirror Lake is actually George's Hole. A travesty of a title," Sam explained, shaking his head.

Paige got to her feet and offered him her hand. "Well, come on," she said.

He looked at her in confusion.

"It's time to go," she said. "Mirror Lake awaits our arrival."

His uncertainty transformed into mirth as he accepted her offer, taking her hand and kicking off his shoes.

"But the meeting isn't over yet," Adeline complained. Paige caught a hint of desperation in her voice.

"For us it is," she said cheerfully.

"Wait, I'll join you."

"Sorry, you can't. We're going 'where there is no path,' and there's only room for two."

Adeline scowled as they strode off.

Paige found George's Hole a lot less poetic than its nickname. The water was murky, and the sand at the bottom seemed like ordinary brown mud to her. Still, she was game for a swim, and giggled when Sam stripped down to his underwear: a large, woolly onesie that was as endearing as it was ridiculous. She watched him take a wild running leap into the water.

"Come on in!" he clamored. "Let's baptize you into the New Transcendentalists Society!"

"Please don't tell me you really do that."

"No, but maybe we should."

"Is the water cold?"

"Warm as summer rain falling on a hot tin roof. Wait—too 'over-the-top'?"

"Yes."

"Do you write a lot of poetry, Paige?"

"Nope. I prefer prose. Fiction."

"Where do you study? Trinity?"

"Is that where all of you study?"

"Most of us. I'm about to finish, though. It's my last year."

She put her toes in the water. "What'll you do after?"

At that, a shadow seemed to descend on Sam's carefree mood. "Lord Alfred Tennyson is looking for a pupil. A protégé," he said thoughtfully. "There are only a few fellows in the running."

"And you're one?"

He nodded, waist-deep in the water. "I sent him my best poems. That's how he'll decide. He'll assess our work and look for the bloke with the most talent."

"You really want this, don't you?"

"I've admired Lord Tennyson since I was a boy. He's England's greatest living poet. The *world's* greatest living poet. His opinion is the *only* opinion."

Paige walked into deeper water. She hated that she could barely see the bottom, imagining all kinds of creepy-crawlies, but she kept going. "It's dangerous to put so much stock in one person," she told him.

"But Tennyson's not an ordinary person. He's more like . . . God."

"So become an atheist."

Samuel shook his head. "Why do you say that? You don't think he'll like my work?"

"I'm not concerned with him. I'm concerned with you. It's stupid to put all your eggs in one basket. You need to diversify."

"Diversify?" he repeated.

"Yeah, it's this American way of saying you need other options. A backup plan. A Plan B." She waded in farther, till she was up to her hips.

"Criminy. Maybe you're right. Maybe you're not a nymph, but a sage?"

"I'm whatever you want me to be," she replied cheekily. Then she gathered her courage and dove underwater, into the unseen.

CHAPTER TEN

"And then I woke up," Paige said.

Saskia watched her tremble at the memory and couldn't help but shiver herself.

"Confused—but excited, too," Paige finished. "I was back in bed, like it never even happened. The only proof I had was the fact that I was soaking wet."

"Are you sure if was from the lake water?" Saskia asked, remembering when sweat, not rain, had dampened her clothes after she'd first met Cornelius.

"Well, yeah, of course," Paige replied briskly.

"Were you scared?" Adrienne asked.

"I was . . . but more than anything, I felt strange. Off-balance. Like I had one foot in this world and one foot somewhere else."

"I wonder if you really were on the other side," said Sara Beth. Her voice was quiet. She sounded as if she were talking to herself.

"The other side of what?" asked Adrienne.

Paige rolled her eyes. "You know what. The other side of life. Death."

Maybe Saskia should have felt scared, but she didn't. She felt relieved. The field of wildflowers. The new Transcendentalists. Lord Tennyson. The sweat that Saskia was sure Paige had mistaken for lake water. All of these intimate details convinced her that Paige wasn't making this up. Paige couldn't have pulled such a story out of thin air, or even Wikipedia. No, just like Saskia, she had some-how crossed a divide, switching between two different centuries and two different realms.

Saskia looked at the other girls, wondering about their reactions. Adrienne looked tense and fearful, like Paige's story had unnerved her. Saskia wondered what part of the tale had scared her. Lila was attempting a poker face, but Saskia knew her well enough by now to realize she was hiding something. But what was it? Maybe she'd met her dead boyfriend, but was determined to continue playing the role of unbeliever. And Sara Beth? Paige's sister looked lost in thought as she fiddled with a decapitated Barbie a little too aggressively.

"Who's next?" asked Paige.

"I'm not sure I can go after you," Adrienne said. "My story will sound . . . what's the word?"

"Anticlimactic?" said Paige.

Adrienne nodded. "Yeah, that."

"Just go for it," Saskia said encouragingly. "This isn't a competition."

Adrienne smiled shyly at her. "Fine, okay. So I did the routine just like you told us, Saskia. I held the picture of my Mercury Boy and ran my fingers over it. I thought about him really hard. Then I put some mercury in my palm and rolled it around. That was a little freaky." She fidgeted, fingers lacing and unlacing again and again. "I had trouble falling asleep. Nerves, I guess. After about an hour, I must have nodded off. The next thing I knew, I was somewhere else. Outside. But it wasn't a nice meadow with wildflowers." She glanced nervously at Paige. "This place, my place . . . well, it was like something out of a nightmare."

Adrienne

Her sandals half sank as she squished through the mud. The heels and sunny yellow canvas quickly turned brown. It would have made sense to stop walking, to turn back, but Adrienne couldn't. She felt inexplicably propelled, even magnetized, toward the camp in the distance: several tents and a barn.

The tents were set up helter-skelter. They reminded her of the ones she'd built as a child: white sheets draped over sticks. Crude structures. A woman, oblivious to her presence, ducked into one, coming out a moment later with what looked like a pair of scissors. Adrienne cringed at the sight of her old-fashioned dress. In the heat, Adrienne wondered how the woman could stand the high neck, long sleeves, and dirt-grazing skirt.

The woman scurried away. Adrienne continued forward, but cautiously. She smelled something foul. Blood, sweat, urine, rot, sickness—these were the things the odor reminded her of. She stepped over a thin streambed, alarmed to see that the trickle of water ran pink. "It's not blood. It's not blood," she whispered to herself. But she suspected that it was. Panic lodged in her throat like a stone. Dread filled her body like a toxic fog. What was she about to walk into?

Again, she thought about turning back. Again, she couldn't. She knew she would end up at the camp no matter what. She didn't know why, but the destination felt inevitable. Predetermined.

Suddenly Adrienne stopped short—nearly stumbling into a long trench in the earth. Nervously, she wondered if it had been built for cover. Was this a war zone? But when she peered down, all she saw was excrement. The trench, about six feet deep, was a latrine— a latrine even more crude than the tents. Hovering over its foul contents were flies, their metallic green bodies glinting bright in the sun. Adrienne tried to cover her ears as well as her nose. The insects' buzzing nauseated her almost as much as the stench.

Gingerly, she walked around the trench to the first tent, pausing when she heard crying and whimpering. Someone in pain. She tiptoed around the periphery, not wanting to know what was happening inside. Whatever was going on behind those flimsy sheets sounded like the soundtrack to a horror movie.

Near the barn, she saw a long table. She gazed at scraps of food on scuffed metal plates: the skin of a baked potato, eggshells, a gristly strip of gray meat, half a biscuit. The leftovers, spoiling in the sun, crawled with more fat green flies. As for the table itself, it was nothing but sticks and boards nailed into submission. There were no chairs, just crates and barrels. Like everything else in this godforsaken place, the furniture looked makeshift and shoddy.

Finally she reached the derelict barn. The whole thing tilted to the side, like a tired beast on the brink of collapse. Adrienne lingered by the half-open door, not realizing at first what was beside it: a bloody pile that caused her nausea to reach a crescendo. She bent over and threw up all over the front of her shirt. Wiping her mouth, she screwed her eyes shut. Maybe she'd been mistaken. Maybe her eyes had deceived her. She counted to three, then commanded herself to look at the pile again.

Alas, she hadn't been wrong. The pile was comprised of body parts: arms, hands, feet, legs, fingers, toes. These parts were clearly human, but they weren't normal. The skin was grayish-black, or sickly yellow, or too bloody to see. Some limbs were lumpy, bloated, and disproportioned; others were mangled; still others skeletally thin. All of them were grotesque. Judging by the ragged edges of skin and bone, Adrienne figured they'd been sawed off—and sloppily, at that. Like the food, they were rotting in the sun.

She vomited again, but this time only bile, putrid and vinegar sharp, came out.

Head throbbing and heart pounding, she opened the barn door

the rest of the way. It creaked on one hinge. Inside, the odor was worse than by the latrine. She put her hand over her mouth and scanned the room, glad that there was nothing left in her stomach to purge. Inside were about a dozen men. Injured men. Men in agony. Some lay on rough-hewn cots, elevated a few inches off the ground. Others rested on dirty mats, or bare earth. The men were mostly young—even as young as she was—and closer to death than to life. They must've been the ones making the noises she'd heard. And no wonder. Their wounds were gruesome: gashes, ripped-up flesh, limbs half-hanging from sheets of skin.

She was frozen, immobilized by horror. The only thing she could move was her eyes. And these she wanted to close.

Finally someone took hold of her arm. A woman. The same woman she'd seen before. In the same awful dress, confining as a nun's habit. The woman was maybe Adrienne's mother's age, maybe older. It was hard to tell. Grime and exhaustion overwhelmed her face.

"Another volunteer," the woman said. It wasn't a question.

Adrienne stared at her.

"Good," the woman continued. "We're short. Eliza caught dysentery." Her mouth flattened into a grim line when she saw Adrienne's soiled shirt.

Before Adrienne knew it, the woman was pulling her toward the back of the barn. Adrienne let herself be led, listening to the swish of the woman's skirt. Some of the injured men looked at her. But most were too dazed to notice anything.

Abruptly the woman stopped. A bloodstained table stood before her. On the ground, knives, scalpels, and a small handsaw soaked in a metal bucket of water. Pink water.

"I'm—I'm not a volunteer," Adrienne stuttered, staring at the bucket and remembering the streambed.

"Well, you're here, aren't you?"

Adrienne looked at her blankly.

Frowning, the woman looked her up and down in a no-nonsense way. "Well, you're filthy—and you're dressed like a public woman.

Certainly you're not up to the standards of a Union nurse. But I
need an extra set of hands, so you'll have to do."

Before Adrienne could argue, a man entered from the back door
of the barn. Adrienne caught glimpses of a wool suit underneath
his blood-spattered apron. The man bowed curtly at the nurse and
glanced curiously at Adrienne.

"Another volunteer," the woman told him.

"Just one, Nurse?"

"That's all we have."

The man showed no interest in further discussing the matter.
Adrienne watched him remove the wet saw from the bucket and
wipe the blade on his soiled apron. "This will be my third amputation of the day," he complained.

"Mine, too," the nurse muttered under her breath.

Adrienne began to feel dizzy. "I can't help with an amputation,"
she whined, her voice small and brittle.

"You will," the surgeon replied. "You're a sturdy girl. Tall as a
chimney, too."

"I wouldn't know what to do . . ."

"We are all doing what we didn't think we could."

The nurse looked at her sternly. "You'll hold him down and
keep him down. We've run out of chloroform and ether, so
you've got to be strong about it. Some men take the pain better
than others."

"What if I can't?"

"Enough," the nurse snapped. "It's not you who's losing an arm
today."

Adrienne shrank as much as a six-foot girl could. She watched
the surgeon take off his wire-rimmed spectacles and attempt, unsuccessfully, to clean the lenses on his grimy apron. She watched him
dip a stained sponge into the bucket and squeeze out the excess
water. From a plush-lined case, he removed a dirty scalpel and
wiped that, too, on his apron. Adrienne was appalled. She couldn't
believe any surgeon could care so little about cleanliness.

"He's in a tent," the nurse said.

"Let's bring him in," the man replied, glancing with annoyance at Adrienne. She wondered what she'd done wrong.

They disappeared, returning a minute later with an injured man. His head hung low. His arms were slung around the doctor's and nurse's shoulders, and he leaned so heavily on them that they sagged under his weight. Adrienne couldn't take her eyes off the blood that soaked his sleeve, crusted over the shiny brass buttons of his jacket, and almost obscured his face.

His face.

It was him, she realized. The boy in the daguerreotype. The boy with the needle-sharp stare and cleft chin. Her boy.

After the surgeon and nurse laid him down, the surgeon gave Adrienne another reproachful look, guilting her into helping. But Adrienne's hands were shaking. Now that she'd seen the boy's face, she couldn't look away from it. Under the blood, it was white as the belly of a fish. His eyelids flagged. He seemed to be stuck in an unbearable purgatory between consciousness, sleep, and death.

"Miss," the nurse said sharply. Adrienne moved without thinking, her hands suddenly on his body as she adjusted him on the table. Her muscles tensed. The nurse hacked off his bloody sleeve with a pair of scissors. The surgeon examined the large wound on the boy's arm. It was a dreadful sight, but Adrienne thought the surgeon's grubby fingers were just as bad.

To her horror, he soon plunged those same fingers deep inside the wound. The boy began to writhe and shriek. Grasping him firmly, Adrienne and the nurse held him down.

"Shouldn't you wash your hands?" Adrienne cried out.

"What?" the surgeon replied. He probed distractedly.

"Wash your hands!"

The nurse glared at her, but she didn't care. She thought about her mother in the phlebotomy lab, about the strict rules that all the clinicians followed: frequent hand-washing with soap and warm water, disposable gloves, special containers for contaminated items, frequently bleached floors and countertops, nonstop Purell, face masks when necessary. Never in a million years would her mother think of touching a patient's open wound with her bare hands.

At last the surgeon extracted something. A bullet, Adrienne observed. A large, conical bullet with grooves on one side. He wiped this, too, on his apron.

"Another Minié ball," the nurse murmured.

The surgeon nodded. "Shattered the humerus. Tore the tissue and muscle, too."

"Here, give it to me."

The doctor handed the bullet to the nurse. She dropped it with a *clink* into a large glass jar beneath the table. A jar filled with identical bullets, Adrienne saw. The nurse turned her attention back to the young man on the table, whose body had gone still.

Adrienne shivered, fearing the worst. "Is he alive?" she whispered.

"Of course he is," the nurse snapped. To the doctor, she asked, "Whiskey?"

"Not in this case," the doctor said. "Better to save it for someone who's worse off."

Adrienne couldn't imagine anyone worse off than the boy in front of her.

"Take his shoulders," the surgeon instructed her. "Press down hard. The pain will be bad."

"Like hell on earth," added the nurse.

"This whole place is hell on earth. God save us."

Sweating, nauseated, and as close as she'd ever been to fainting, Adrienne did as told. She stood over the boy's head and clamped her hands firmly on his shoulders. Briefly, she gazed at his pallid face, admiring the contour of his jaw, the shape of his lips. The nurse twisted a soiled white tourniquet tightly around the boy's upper arm. Adrienne averted her eyes. When she looked again, a bright, ruby-red spurt of blood shot up like a geyser.

The doctor had made his first incision.

Adrienne winced, but did not let go. She watched the surgeon make several more cuts. Deep cuts, right to the bone. The boy jerked and flailed, but miraculously, did not rouse.

The surgeon put down the scalpel and took the saw from the bloody bucket.

"No!" Adrienne exclaimed.

"Hush!" the nurse rebuked.

"You have to use clean water! Don't you have clean water?"

"Stop it. Have you no sense, girl?"

Adrienne wanted to ask the nurse and surgeon the same question. Unfortunately, it was too late to argue. Already, she heard the terrible sound of the saw grinding against bone.

More blood spurted. A tremendous amount of blood. It ran in sticky scarlet rivulets off the table, puddling on the ground. Before she knew it, the boy was a madman: screaming, thrashing, buckling, struggling with all his might to resist. His eyes were the petrified eyes of a man being tortured—which was exactly the case, Adrienne thought. A sharp splinter of bone ricocheted off her hand. The nurse's scornful scolding added to the noise. Adrienne pushed him back down. Using all her weight, she leaned onto him, pinning him to the table. In his current state, he was no match for her strength. Little by little, he gave up protesting. Little by little, he seemed to give up on life.

"Stay with me," she whispered. Her face was inches from his. His delirious eyes found hers. She had stared at his daguerreotype a hundred times, but black-and-white photography only revealed so much. It hadn't revealed, for instance, that his eyes were palest green, like grass seedlings in early spring. It didn't reveal that they were kind eyes. She bent closer, until her lips brushed his ear. He would be all right, she promised. He would get better, she would stay by his side, and the pain would go away. She stroked his hair, which was matted with dirt and dried blood.

With almost casual disregard, the surgeon tossed the boy's arm out an open window. Using a piece of string, the nurse tied off the blood-spraying artery. Then the surgeon used another tool from the bucket to buff the jagged edges of what was left of the boy's protruding bone. Finally, the nurse licked the end of a thread and teased it through a needle. The surgeon went to work sewing the loose flaps of skin back together into a stump, leaving a portion open.

"For the wound to drain," he told Adrienne as she gaped. When he was through, he took a step back, surveyed his work, and sighed. The whole process had taken no more than ten minutes.

"What now?" Adrienne croaked. She could hardly find her voice.

"Well, he made it this far," replied the nurse. "A quarter of them die once the limb is off. 'Course, we lose even more to surgical fever."

"Surgical fever?"

"It happens sometimes after the amputation. The men become all possessed-like. They get a fever so high they boil in it." The nurse sighed, too, and dipped her hands into that cesspool of a bucket. "Even worse, though, is hospital gangrene. That's truly the devil's work. A black blight spreads over the body, leaving a smell so bad it would drive a saint away."

This information only stoked Adrienne's fears.

"Any others, Nurse?" the surgeon asked.

"One more, but I doubt he'll last till dusk."

"Injuries?"

"Legs. Both of them."

"Give him two hours. If he's still alive, I'll do it," he replied briskly. He placed the scalpel, still wet with the boy's blood, back into its plush case. Then, without further ado, he disappeared the same way he'd come, out the back of the barn.

"You'll be staying, I presume?" the nurse asked Adrienne when he'd gone.

She could feel the nurse's stare grow heavier as she stroked the boy's face. "Yes."

The nurse cleared her throat. "A few rules, then. My name is Sally Reynolds. You are to refer to me as 'Miss Reynolds' or 'Nurse Reynolds.' As for attire, what you're wearing is prohibited. From now on, it's black or brown. No bright colors. No ornaments, bows, curls, jewelry, or hoops, either. We strive for modesty here."

Adrienne looked down at herself. "I don't have anything like that."

"Public women usually don't." Nurse Reynolds sniffed. "Well, Eliza left a second dress. It will be too short, of course—you are a tall one. But it should be serviceable. Air it out first, though, on account of the dysentery."

Adrienne's eyes widened.

"She's in the nurses' quarters—Eliza," Nurse Reynolds continued. "Follow the stream north. It will bring you to our cabin. We take turns sleeping and changing there. Mind you don't walk south. The fighting's still close."

Adrienne nodded, already worried she'd walk in the wrong direction.

"You never told me your name."

"Adrienne. Adrienne Arch."

"Well, Miss Arch, the work is tremendously hard, as you've witnessed. But you'll find it's not without fulfillment. Every hour of every day is a gift you are bestowing upon the Union. As for compensation, you'll receive forty cents a day plus rations and housing. Transportation to and from the camp is by foot, of course. All the horses have gone to our soldiers."

"Yeah, that makes sense." Adrienne gazed again at the boy, relieved to see his chest subtly rising and falling.

"When he wakes, he'll be frightened beyond belief. And in agony," Nurse Reynolds said. She didn't appear moved by this, although her tone was not uncharitable. The horrors of this place must have hardened her, Adrienne reasoned, or else she'd be heartbroken by now.

"I'll be there for him."

The nurse raised her chin. "Miss Arch, you must understand something: we nurses are like mothers and sisters. We care for the patients. But nurses and patients may not associate . . . socially."

Adrienne straightened her back. She realized suddenly that she was head and shoulders above Nurse Reynolds. She realized, too, that she was not quite as cowed by her. Nor was she quite as terrified by the extreme circumstances into which she'd been thrown. It was clear now why getting to the barn had felt so urgent. It was her fate to be here. To be with him. Whatever Nurse Reynolds had to say about it didn't matter much.

"In other words," Nurse Reynolds continued, "Union nurses and patients are forbidden to form close attachments."

But Adrienne had stopped listening. She was too busy thinking about the boy and wondering what she'd say to him when he woke up.

If he woke up.

CHAPTER ELEVEN

"Go on," said Paige eagerly.

"I can't," said Adrienne.

"Why?"

"Because that's it."

"No! Need. More. Info."

Adrienne looked down apologetically. "That's all I have."

"Well, what you have was crazy town," said Sara Beth. "And I mean that in the best way."

"Yeah, we need the next installment," said Paige. "Pronto."

"I need it, too," Adrienne admitted. "Because now I'm worried he didn't make it. Or maybe he never was there in the first place. I don't know! It's all so confusing. Was this in my head? Or did it actually happen?"

"What do you think?" Saskia asked.

Adrienne took a deep breath. "I'd say it was all a crazy dream, except that when I woke up, my arms ached. From holding him down! And I smelled like vomit. How could I make that stuff up?"

"You couldn't," said Paige.

"But now I have so many questions. Can I get back there—to wherever I was? And if I do make it back, could I get stuck? I'm scared I'll, like, be trapped in some other dimension. But I'm also scared I won't be." Adrienne went back to knotting and unknotting her fingers.

Paige and Sara Beth looked at her, and then exchanged a look of their own. Seeing them, Saskia suddenly wished she had a sister. Someone who could understand what she was thinking with just a glance.

"Don't try to analyze it," said Sara Beth. "Not everything in life makes sense."

Paige nodded emphatically. "But maybe there's a greater logic to it—something out of our reach. Maybe you were meant to meet that soldier! Maybe you were meant to be the one who helps him."

"Do you really think so?" Adrienne asked.

"I do," said Paige.

"That makes me feel a little better."

"Well, at least *someone*'s feeling a little better," said Sara Beth.

"What do you mean?" asked Adrienne, confused.

"Not to sound selfish or anything, but you, Saskia, and my sister met your Mercury Boys. Meanwhile, I tried, and nothing happened."

"Did you take all the steps—with the mercury and the daguerreotype?" Saskia asked.

"All of them."

"How long did you hold the mercury?"

"I don't know—ten seconds?"

"I hold it at least a minute."

"I didn't hold it that long," said Adrienne, "and it worked for me."

"I guess it's not an exact science," Saskia conceded.

"I'm still not sure if it's science at all," said Lila.

Paige shot Lila a contemptuous look. "Why are you so convinced you're right and the rest of us are wrong?"

"It's a little thing called common sense."

"I call it fear," said Paige curtly.

"I'm with my sister," said Sara Beth. "You're too scared to try something new, so you hide behind sarcasm."

"It's your shield."

"Your crutch."

"Your Achilles heel."

Lila's cheeks colored. The sisters had obviously gotten under her skin. "You guys really believe you went back in time and saw a bunch of guys who died in a different century? What did they do, rise from their graves? I mean, think about it!"

"Look, you haven't tried what we have," said Paige. "You don't even have a daguerreotype. So who are you to doubt us? You're all talk, no action."

Saskia expected Lila to one up Paige with a fierce, clever retort. Her friend wasn't one to back down. But for once Lila seemed all out of steam. The only thing she gave Paige was a stony look. The exchange seemed to alter the mood of the group, and even the night itself. Once again, the hideout started to feel like a bad place—or at least a place where bad things could happen.

Goose bumps rising on her skin, Saskia suddenly remembered a particularly horrible murder she'd once read about. The death of a teenage girl named Martha Moxley, who had also lived in Connecticut. She'd been found bludgeoned to death underneath a tree. Had it been a tree like this one?

"Guys, guys, please, let's get back to business," said Adrienne. "When's our next meeting?"

Paige took a deep breath and regrouped. "How about tomorrow. Same time, same place?"

"I'll be here," said Adrienne.

"What about you, Saskia?" asked Paige.

Sheepishly, Saskia glanced at Lila, her de facto ride.

"Yeah, we'll be here, too," Lila mumbled.

"Guess if it's my own yard I have to be there," added Sara Beth. "But I better meet my man before then, or there'll be trouble tomorrow."

She smiled slyly. Then, with a reptilian flick of pink tongue, she licked her fingertips and began to snuff out the candles. The blackness seemed to snuff out conversation, too. Saskia thought Sara Beth would turn on the flashlight, but she didn't. Blindly, the girls pushed aside branches and scrabbled out of the canopy.

When she emerged, discombobulated, Saskia wasn't sure which was darker: their new hideout or the world beyond.

An uncomfortable silence extended from the moment Saskia and Lila got into the car until they arrived at McDonald's. Saskia waited.

"The usual?" Lila asked, veering in the direction of the drive-through.

"Yup."

"So I thought about what Paige said."

Saskia held her breath nervously. "Yeah?"

"Don't get me wrong—I don't agree with her. But maybe she has a point. Maybe I'll give the mercury thing a try."

Finally, Saskia thought. She'd hoped that Lila had already tried to meet her boy, but better late than never.

"I still think she's kind of a bitch, though," added Lila.

Saskia ignored that. "Did you find a daguerreotype?" she asked, knowing full well the answer.

"I did."

"Can I see it?"

"I don't have it with me."

"It's at home?"

"Yeah."

"Tell me about him."

"I don't know what to say. He caught my eye." Lila laughed uncomfortably. "Oh god, that sounds so pathetic."

"No, it doesn't."

Lila ordered, paid the cashier, took the bag of food, and handed Saskia some fries. "I don't expect much to happen," she said finally, cramming an onion ring into her mouth.

"Don't knock it till you try it."

"Okay," Lila said, still chewing. "I'll knock it afterward."

Saskia ignored that, too. She was pretty sure her friend would come around.

• • •

At home, Saskia found her dad at the kitchen table, the divorce papers spread out in front of him. His jaw, clenched so tight his bones protruded, worried Saskia. But his eyes worried her more. They looked dull, like he was too spent to feel anything.

She hesitated—she had to quash the urge to flee to her room—then greeted him cautiously. Scanning the cupboard, she grabbed a box of cereal and poured herself a bowl. Then she took a seat across from him, hoping once again he wouldn't be able to smell the alcohol on her breath.

"Have you seen these? The envelope was open." He sounded more curious than accusing.

"Yeah," she said, not looking up from her Honey Nut Cheerios. She had no appetite; her stomach was still full of McDonald's. But spooning the cereal into her mouth gave her fidgety hands something to do while her dad stared at her expectantly.

"And?"

"And what?" she asked.

"What is your reaction to them?"

"Mom's a jerk."

"Saskia, there's no need for that."

"But it's true."

"It's not," he said firmly.

"Okay, whatever you say. What's *your* reaction?"

Her father scratched the hair on his chin, which was beginning to look more and more like a full-fledged beard. "I feel . . . like I should shave." Abruptly, he got up to fix himself a bowl of Honey Nut Cheerios, too. For several minutes they concentrated on chewing.

"This tastes better than I thought," he said finally.

"That's because you've been eating Healthy Choice for weeks. *Anything* would taste better."

"You've got a point."

Saskia got up and brought her bowl to the sink, where she poured the rest of the milk-soaked cereal down the garbage disposal. She let the loud, whirring noise go on longer than it needed to.

"Sask, we have to talk about it," her father said over the racket.
Her back to him, she flicked off the switch and rolled her eyes.
"Okay."

"Can you take a seat?"

She obeyed, but not without a sigh of resignation.

"Look, I knew this was coming," he said, studying her face.
"These papers aren't a surprise. I even met with a lawyer."

"You did?"

"Yeah, a guy here in Coventon."

"Are you glad?"

"About the papers? *Glad* isn't the word."

"Pissed?"

"Relieved."

"Are you happy for her?" She was surprised by how bitter the
question sounded.

"Look, I don't want to see her miserable. That wouldn't do anyone any good."

"Well, *I* want to see her miserable."

Her father shook his head. He looked so tired, like he could
sleep twenty hours straight if given the opportunity. "In another
year you won't say that."

"'In another year.' I don't understand why you're always thinking ahead! I don't want to be thinking about how I *will* feel or how
things *might* be. I want to think about now."

"That sounds wise."

"It does?"

"Yes—let's make some changes . . . immediately. I say we start
with food."

Biting her nails, she watched as her father got up and opened the
freezer. He gathered up every single Healthy Choice frozen meal in
his arms and dumped them unceremoniously into the trash. "Tomorrow," he said, "I pick up meat, produce, and good bread. Real food."

She gaped at him.

"I sense you're skeptical," he said.

"I've never seen you cook before."

"There's a first time for everything."

"I'll help you."

"I've never seen *you* cook before."

"I can look for easy recipes online."

"Okay," he agreed. "And if we screw up, I hear the Coventon diner's not too bad."

That night Saskia had trouble falling asleep. When she finally managed to drift off, it was two-thirty in the morning.

A couple hours later, she awoke groggy and disappointed, realizing straightaway that she had not seen Cornelius. She had no memory of seeing him. No memory of anything.

Lying on top of her sheets, she wrestled with anxiety. What if this was the beginning of the end? What if she never saw him again?

She tried to talk herself out of being pessimistic. Like she'd said to Sara Beth, the process of meeting the Mercury Boys was not an exact science. There were bound to be times when the usual routine didn't work for whatever reason, especially when no one knew how and why it worked in the first place. And yet she couldn't stop worrying that Cornelius would suddenly slip away. That prospect now scared her more than the divorce.

At six in the morning, still fighting a wave of worry, Saskia heard her phone buzz on her bedside table. Lila. She'd never called so early before.

"What's up?" asked Saskia.

"My grandmother was wrong."

"Too early. Don't understand."

"About the dragonfly story."

"Lila, you've gotta break this down. I'm still half asleep."

"I met my guy! I had a dream, and it was just like you said. It was beautiful, crazy, mesmerizing, there just aren't enough good adjectives . . ."

"That's great, but what does that have to do with your grandmother?"

"Don't you remember? My grandmother said that when someone dies, that's it. There's no seeing them ever again. But in my
dream, I not only saw my guy—we, like, vibed."

"Really?"

"Yeah, our connection felt totally real."

Saskia stood up and stretched out. She was awake now, awake
and all ears. "I'm glad," she told Lila. "Tell me everything."

"I'll tell you the whole thing tonight, okay? Today is crazy. I
promised to take my brothers and sisters to the water park. It's
going to be a *long* day."

"Can you tell me his name, at least?"

"Look, I'll tell you everything later. Promise."

"Fine. I can't wait. Paige is going to go nuts when she hears."

There came a long silence. Saskia thought she'd lost the connection, but then Lila's voice rang out crystal clear. "Sask, why does it
matter so much what Paige thinks?"

"It doesn't."

"It does to you."

"Well, I respect her opinion."

"Why?"

"Why are you asking me these questions?"

"Because I care, and I'm not sure she does."

"Maybe I don't need *you* to care so much."

"Look, forget it," Lila said tersely. "I'll see you later, okay?"

"Yeah, okay," Saskia replied. She fell back onto the bed, wondering what exactly they'd just argued about.

The day seemed never-ending. Saskia's father had already left for
his shift when she dragged herself to the kitchen. Even after coffee,
which she hated, her mind still felt cloudy. She ate some buttered
toast, then began looking for a job again.

But scanning through the listings was too much to bear, and by
10 A.M., she'd flipped on the TV. *All About Eve* was playing. Saskia
loved Bette Davis, how her huge, owlish eyes conveyed her every

emotion, even when she was perfectly silent. But Saskia couldn't concentrate; Cornelius and seeing the girls later that night were all she could think about.

By dusk, she was already waiting in her driveway for Lila to show up. The old car couldn't get there fast enough.

She and Lila made it to the Sampras house early. This time the front door was closed. They knocked repeatedly, but no one answered.

"Do you think they're out?" Lila asked.

Saskia shook her head. "Pretty sure we have the right time."

"Wouldn't it be funny if the parents answered?"

"They won't. The sisters are total latchkey kids."

"True."

"Let's go around," Saskia suggested finally. She was eager—maybe overeager—to see the other girls. Lila had told her a little about her own Mercury Boy in the car, but only enough to whet Saskia's appetite. Lila had said she'd tell the whole story once the group had gathered.

As they walked around the house, Saskia wondered if any alarms would blare. The Sampras property seemed like the kind of property that would have a state-of-the-art security system. But no alarms or warning lights went off. The only sound she and Lila heard as they made their way was splashing.

Paige, Sara Beth, and Adrienne were in the pool. The astonishing pool. Its opulent size, beautiful tile and stonework, and sheer glamour reminded her of the pool featured in *Sunset Boulevard*—minus the dead body, of course. In the center Sara Beth lounged on an inflatable shark. Though the sun was going down, she wore oversized sunglasses that matched her polka-dot halter top swimsuit. Old Hollywood, thought Saskia—definitely *Sunset Boulevard*. Underwater, Adrienne turned somersaults. Paige swam laps.

Seeing Saskia, she glided the length of the pool to greet her. "Hey! How long have you guys been here?"

"Not long," said Saskia.

"Wanna come in? It's really warm."

Saskia hesitated.

"I, for one, am done with water for the day," answered Lila.

"She took her brothers and sisters to a water park," Saskia explained.

"Why don't you come in, Sask?" Paige asked. "I've got, like, ten bikinis, if you want to borrow one."

Saskia laughed uncomfortably. "Not sure yours would fit me."

"What, you're, like, a size six, right? I'm a four."

Saskia bit her tongue. She wondered if Paige was being polite, or if she really didn't see the size difference between them. Saskia wasn't usually inhibited when it came to swimsuits. But in comparison to Sara Beth, Paige, and Adrienne, who were all super skinny, with no spare flesh to speak of, she couldn't help but feel self-conscious about her hourglass shape.

Eventually, all three girls got out of the pool and dried off, joking around and flicking their towels at one another. Sara Beth casually took off her bikini and slipped on a pair of shorts and a tank top. Saskia wondered if the neighbors had binoculars. When it came to nudity, she herself was more modest—and cautious. She'd never change in a friend's yard in front of other people. She wondered if Sara Beth would call her a prude if she knew.

I'm just being paranoid.

"Should we go under the tree again?" asked Adrienne.

"Yeah, definitely," replied Paige. "It feels like *our place* now."

"I'll get the candles," said Sara Beth.

Paige watched her sister make a beeline for the house. Then she put on a flimsy mesh cover-up and sidled up to Saskia. "See how she's glowing? Last night she met her guy. His name's Mack. She's into him, too. One night, and she's already calling him her Forever Boyfriend."

"No way . . ."

Paige put up her hands. "Swear. She's hooked. Whipped."

"Lila met her Mercury Boy, too," Saskia whispered back. She felt both gleefully conspiratorial and slightly guilty for spilling Lila's news.

"No!"

"Yes. I think she's hooked, too."

"This gets wilder by the day, doesn't it?"

Impulsively, Paige gave Saskia a soggy hug. Saskia squeezed back, feeling suddenly hopeful, like, despite the bad run she'd had in the last year, her luck was changing. It had to be. Somehow, in only a couple of weeks, Paige Sampras had gone from being a locker-side acquaintance to a real friend.

"Hey, everyone," Paige announced when the girls had congregated under the tree. "I have an idea."

"Always a bad sign," quipped Sara Beth.

"Be quiet!" Paige chided playfully. "So I'm sure you've heard of blood brothers. You know, guys cutting themselves and mixing their blood and swearing loyalty to each other? Well, I think we should do our own 'blood sisters' version."

"That sounds grisly. Besides, I hate blood," Sara Beth complained.

"Can't say I'm fond of it, either," said Saskia.

"Well, I guess our thing doesn't *have* to involve blood," replied Paige. "We can all swear on something else."

Saskia could see the wheels turning in her friend's head. Paige picked up a candle and watched a trail of molten wax slink down the side. For a few moments, she seemed mesmerized by the dancing flame. Then a grin spread across her face. She put down the candle and clasped her hands.

"Okay, gang. Joining a club requires an initiation, correct?" She didn't wait for an answer. "I feel like finally we're all invested in the Mercury Boys Club." She glanced pointedly at Lila, who looked away, embarrassed. "What we've discovered is a big deal—groundbreaking, actually. And the bond between us members is equally astonishing and groundbreaking. Maybe even sacred. So I propose we go through an initiation. An initiation that shows not only our loyalty to the club, but also to each other."

"What will it involve?" Saskia asked cautiously.

"Flesh and flame."

"Excuse me?"

"Here's how I see it. We'll each put a finger over this candle flame. As close as we can, for as long as we can. And while doing it, we'll repeat this phrase: 'My love for my Mercury Boy burns bright as fire.'"

Saskia blinked. Paige was kidding, wasn't she? Her proposal sounded ridiculous and brutal in equal parts. Then again, Paige rarely kidded around. Saskia studied her face; judging from Paige's solemn expression, she meant every word. Worse, Sara Beth and Adrienne were nodding in agreement.

"I'm not so sure about this," Saskia said, smiling nervously, her stomach turning.

"Come on. I wouldn't expect that kind of reaction from you," Paige replied. "You're our pioneer!"

"Besides," added Sara Beth, "this isn't exactly a sacrifice. If someone can't take a little burn, a little pain, then I'd have to question why she even deserves to be in the club."

"Very true," said Paige.

"Okay, okay," Saskia said defensively. "I get it."

"Why don't you go first? That way, you'll get it over with," Paige suggested.

"It won't be that bad—you'll see," added Sara Beth.

A fake smile was still pasted on Saskia's lips. She kept it there, unwilling to let the sisters see how scared she was.

"You know, I'm sure we could come up with a better initiation," said Lila, glancing at her. "One that won't involve an ambulance."

"No, it's fine," Saskia said, feigning enthusiasm. "I'll do it. No problem."

"Great," said Paige, placing the candle in front of Saskia. "Show us the way, pioneer."

Hesitantly, Saskia positioned her hand near the candle, then whipped her finger through the flame quickly.

"Really?" chided Sara Beth. "That's the best you can do?"

"Don't be hard on her!" said Paige, but then to Saskia added, "Remember, this is for Cornelius. The longer you hold it, the more he'll know you care."

Will he? Saskia wondered.

"And don't forget to say the line," Paige reminded her. "'My love for my Mercury Boy burns bright as fire.'"

Coming from Paige's mouth the second time, the phrase somehow didn't sound so crazy, or maybe it was just that Saskia could no longer think straight. She was too focused on the candle, on getting through this bizarre ordeal.

And there was something else—Saskia realized she didn't want to disappoint Paige. Though she had sowed the seeds for the Mercury Boys, it was Paige who had taken her strange discovery to new lengths, establishing this secret club and creating rituals for it. It was Paige who insisted that the girls were bonded now—sisters. Even before all of this happened, Saskia had admired Paige, but now she felt almost beholden to her.

Saskia bit her lip and put her finger over the flame. This time, she let it linger. The phrase came out of her mouth; she heard it, though she didn't remember deciding to say it. Funny how the pain didn't hit immediately. Whole seconds ticked by before she sniffed the sick odor of burning flesh. She tried to remain stoic, but tears filled her eyes.

"Saskia!" Lila admonished, pushing her hand out of the way of the flame. "What's gotten into you?"

Saskia gasped as Lila's words sunk in. Then, like sunlight through a magnifying glass, her attention narrowed into pinprick focus. Suddenly, all she could think about was the agony of the burn. All she could see was the grotesque yellow blister rapidly ballooning on her fingertip.

"Well done!" cheered Paige. "You are committed to this club, no doubt about it."

"I'll go get an ice pack," volunteered Sara Beth with uncharacteristic attentiveness.

"Get some Tylenol, too," said Lila. Gingerly, she took Saskia's hand and examined the blister. "What the hell? Why'd you do it for so long?"

Saskia shook her head.

"Because she kicks ass," said Paige. She gave Saskia a look of such tender admiration, Saskia felt a burst of pride despite herself.

"No one's gonna be able to top that performance," added Adrienne.

And it was true. When the other girls took their turns, none held their fingers over the lit wick for even half so long. None even got a blister. Saskia felt an odd sense of victory, like she'd won some kind of contest. A masochistic contest, but a contest, nonetheless. Her triumph, however, did not block out the pain, which continued to throb even after the Tylenol and ice.

At least she had Lila's story to look forward to. But Lila seemed more aloof now and even a little panicked, though her initiation had been easy. She demurred when the girls pressed her for details on her Mercury Boy, claiming she didn't feel ready to tell them yet; she had to be in the right state of mind, and all she felt now was tired and concerned about Saskia's burn.

Fortunately, Sara Beth came to the rescue, volunteering to explain how she'd met her Mercury Boy, Mack. She rubbed her hands together gleefully, and the girls hooted and hollered in anticipation, Saskia loudest of all.

Sara Beth

Sara Beth felt pulled as if by a great magnet to the enormous building in front of her. It seemed both majestic and magical—a vision of shiny glass and cast iron that stirred something deep and well rooted inside her. The stuff of her childhood imagination, before a volcanic eruption of teenage cynicism had covered it up.

She had seen more modern buildings—buildings so tall they pierced the clouds. But this one was more fascinating somehow. Like something out of a fairy tale or Roald Dahl's imagination. She liked the flags waving from its spires, the grand dome glistening at its center, the sunlight glinting off its countless windows, reflecting so much light that she wanted sunglasses.

"That's it," she heard someone say. "The Crystal Palace."

The Crystal Palace? How perfect, she thought.

She moved closer, trying to get a better look. Hundreds of people were flowing like a river in the same direction. Men and women. Children skipping and scampering in excitement. Tut-tutting mothers.

Sara Beth began to notice that people were leering at her. "What's your problem?" she demanded, giving one woman the stink eye.

The woman grabbed her umbrella a little tighter and turned away. Sara Beth saw that she wasn't holding an umbrella after all, but a parasol. A delicate parasol of lace and pale pink silk. How weird. Then again, all the people here were dressed strangely. The women wore bonnets and big, billowy skirts. The men wore old-fashioned double-breasted suits, their watch fobs swinging as they walked. Sara Beth felt like she'd landed in the middle of a Victorian play. Even the little girls were decked out in frilly white dresses.

Sara Beth shook her head. Why on earth would anyone dress grubby-fingered, snotty-nosed kids in *white*?

Nearing the Crystal Palace, she tried to shrug off a sense of displacement and confusion. Where was she? Who were these rude people who kept gaping at her? Normally she was good at brushing things off, but this time it was hard. Her heart raced and her head pounded as she spun around, trying to find something—anything—that looked familiar. Finally, she tugged on the sleeve of a passerby.

"Excuse me," she said. "Where am I?"

The man stopped abruptly. He was old, white haired, and slow moving. He leaned heavily on a curved cane with an embellished handle.

"Where am I?" she repeated anxiously.

"The Exhibition of the Industry of All Nations."

It sounded like gibberish, like too many prepositional phrases strung together.

"What?" she asked.

"New York City, young lady."

"Really?"

The man's rheumy eyes peered into hers with a combination of curiosity and reproach. With his free hand, he tapped the side of his head. "Some advice from an elder, if I may. Stay away from the dens, my dear. Opium melts the brain."

More confused than ever, Sara Beth watched the man lope away. Desperate for space, for a chance to think, she snaked her way out of the crowd. She tried to wrap her head around what the man had said. *New York City.* But how was that possible? The ground beneath her was bare earth, not asphalt. The skyline showed no skyscrapers, just a lot of small buildings and chimneys and trees and undeveloped land. Sara Beth spotted green fields and even roaming cows!

The only sign of urbanity, besides the Crystal Palace, was a slim wooden tower, triangular in shape, crosshatched with metal braces and culminating in a sharp steeple. Sara Beth had no idea what it was. Carriages, horses, and foot traffic trampled past in both directions, kicking up clouds of dust. On the corner, she spotted a sign.

Forty-Second Street.

Could it be?

She drew a deep breath and exhaled slowly. Then she smiled. Now she was beginning to understand. Now this mayhem was starting to make sense. She didn't recognize anything because she was in a different time. Around the 1850s, if she remembered Saskia correctly. That was when daguerreotypes had become fashionable. That was when the young man she'd chosen must have had his portrait made.

She remembered that "Rees & Co., Broadway" was stamped at the lower right section of the daguerreotype's brass mat. Before, that could have been any Broadway, in any town. But now it was clear Rees & Co. had been in New York City. The Big Apple. That was where she was going to meet him—whoever he was.

She shuddered, feeling just as Saskia said she would. Thrilled and terrified at the same time.

With a new sense of purpose, she strode back toward the Crystal Palace. She didn't know why, but she was sure she would spot him there. This time when people gawked at her, she smirked at them. *Stare all you want, losers. Soon you'll be pushing up daisies, but I'll still be alive.*

She elbowed her way to a ticket office at the building's entrance. The throngs were even thicker here, and more rude, but she rode a wave of people all the way through the door. She didn't stop to pay the fifty-cent admission fee. She couldn't. She didn't have anything in her pockets except lint. But she wasn't worried. She and Paige had done this kind of thing before, getting in for free. Concerts, clubs, bars—you name it. It was a matter of confidence. Act like you had every right to be somewhere, and people would think you did, especially if you were a pretty girl.

The main entranceway spilled into an airy glass atrium. The domed ceiling seemed a mile high. Even so, the sun beat heavily into the interior, giving the Crystal Palace the tropical, compressive feel of a greenhouse. Looking up, Sara Beth saw that there were two stories. Visitors on the second level peered down at her, their hands gripping a waist-high railing that wound ornately around the perimeter. Nearby, a man welcomed visitors, his voice booming through a megaphone. He was wearing a candy-cane-striped suit, reminding her of an old-fashioned carnival barker.

"Get your souvenirs hee-ah!" he cried. "Ashtrays, canes, medals for the gents. Thimbles, spoons, handkerchiefs for the ladies! Bring home a piece of history. A memento from the greatest collection of American ingenuity and invention ever assembled!"

Sara Beth wandered. The main room resembled a church's nave: huge and rectangular, replete with columns and arches. Its sides were sectioned off into open rooms, with items divided by subject matter and region. There were so many things to see, she soon felt overwhelmed trying to take it all in. She passed a gallery of fine paintings; a fire engine and schooner; rooms full of tapestries, sculptures, and busts. She browsed clocks, lamps, safes, safety pins, and a lighthouse lens. She admired a fountain that shot arcs of water into the air and a gun that looked like it belonged in Billy the Kid's holster. She saw more machines than she'd ever seen in her life—machines that sewed, printed, combed hair, carried water, sifted gold, made wood pulp, extracted teeth, washed dishes, and stirred ice cream. Most of them seemed primitive and quaint, things she might find in her great-grandmother's basement. But she realized from the astonished expressions of the people around her that these devices must have been extraordinary for their time.

"See the miracles of this age," she heard another carnival barker shout. "The height of modern technology!"

She scurried past a statue of Christ and his apostles. She and her sister had been raised as Protestants, but she didn't like to remember those long, boring hours in Sunday school. She'd always hated the idea of the Holy Trinity watching her every move, determining whether she was a better fit for heaven or hell. Given her penchant for trouble, it was already pretty clear where she was headed.

Finally, she passed a photography exhibit—ambrotypes, calotypes, cyanotypes, and—yes—even daguerreotypes. The only photography method that used mercury, Saskia had said. The only one that was *magical*.

Sara Beth expected to spot the man in her daguerreotype here, gazing at these same photographs. It was only fitting. She flitted through the people, anxious to find him. But he was nowhere to be seen. She continued to roam, growing increasingly worried. Perhaps her instincts had been wrong—perhaps he was nowhere near the Crystal Palace.

Just when she considered leaving, though, she spotted him. She should have known he'd be in the very center of the hubbub. Standing on a high podium of polished marble, beside a theatrical statue of George Washington on horseback, he looked larger than life. A crowd formed a semicircle around him. She couldn't believe she hadn't noticed him before.

She drew closer, watching him talk candidly, hands animated, smile megawatt bright. He was dressed exactly as he was in the daguerreotype: white shirt, old-fashioned bow tie, and elegant black suit, sharply cut and precisely pressed. His fingers fiddled with the bronze buttons on his velvet waistcoat. Briefly, he removed his shiny black top hat, revealing a head of equally shiny black hair. He looked expensive. Dapper. And very handsome.

Too handsome for his own good—or for mine, she thought.

She joined the crowd and jostled her way to the front. For a split second they locked eyes. Her heart lurched. He jumped down from the platform, landing with an easy grace. At first she thought he was walking over to her. Instead, he extended his hand to a child standing beside her.

"Would you like to be my partner for this next trick?" he asked the little girl. She nodded, her curly, beribboned hair bouncing.

The man peeked playfully into the child's ear and asked her why she was using it as a piggy bank. Hand on her mouth, she giggled. The crowd giggled, too. He showed his bare hands to the crowd, front and back, then proceeded to pull nickel after nickel out of the girl's ear. She turned red as he handed them to her in a glimmering silver stack.

"I'm sorry to tell you," he said somberly, "but there's more in there."

"More money?"

"No, I'm afraid."

This time the man pulled out a long red handkerchief. It seemed to go on and on, its every inch drawing more laughs. He had the crowd in the palm of his hand, this magician, this charming charlatan, and he knew it.

Dramatically, he peered into the girl's ear once more. His eyes grew comically wide. "Tell me, my dear, do you have a pet?"

The girl shook her head, suddenly serious.

"Are you sure?"

"Quite sure, sir."

"Well, I think she's about to get one," he told the crowd. Rubbing his fingers together, he took a deep breath. "Oh yes, it's trying to come out this very moment." His fingers touched the girl's ear. Sara Beth strained her eyes, looking for a sleight of hand, a secret revealed.

"It's stuck, I'm afraid," he said.

"What is?" asked the girl.

The man began to pull something out—something long and skinny. A piece of brown yarn, perhaps. He paused a moment, taking his time, making the crowd hungry. Suddenly the girl squealed. She stared in disbelief at what had emerged from her ear: not yarn, but a tail. The tail of a little mouse.

The man held the creature in his open hand. Its nose twitched. Its tiny eyes looked like black beads. "He's a cute little fella, isn't he?" he said to no one in particular. Much of the crowd roared with laughter; the rest looked aghast.

"Do you want to keep him?" he asked the girl.

She shook her head vigorously. Her blush deepened.

"But it's yours," he insisted. "He's been living in *your* ear, after all."

Letting out another squeal, the girl turned and ran into her mother's arms. The crowd tittered.

"All right, then," the man continued, faking resignation. "I suppose I'll take him home."

He removed his top hat and slipped the mouse gently inside. Then he gestured toward the girl, whose face was now buried in her mother's long skirt. "Let's have a hand for this little lady. She's a brave soul!"

The crowd applauded, clapping mixed with assorted hoots and hollers. Not wanting to lose momentum, he raised his top hat with a flourish, then slowly turned it upside down. Sara Beth gasped, sure the little mouse would fall out. Maybe it would even dash into the crowd. But nothing happened. The man showed that the hat was empty. The mouse had disappeared, or else it hadn't been there in the first place. Sara Beth smiled, impressed by the man's cleverness.

"If you've enjoyed the show, folks, feel free to *express* your appreciation," he said, putting his hat on the ground. A half dozen people stepped forward to pitch in coins. But the sound of tinkling metal didn't last. "Every little bit counts to a traveling man," he urged.

Too late, Sara Beth thought. The crowd had already begun to disperse, its attention scattering in a hundred directions. "I thought you'd do better," she said, approaching the man.

To her surprise, he ignored her.

"There are only a couple dollars in there," she continued. This time he followed her gaze to the handful of coins inside his hat.

"Not to worry, miss," he said dismissively. "This is just a hobby."

"If this is your hobby, what's your job?"

The man shook his head. Sara Beth was startled. She wasn't used to be disregarded, especially by men.

"Come on," she persisted. "You must do something important to afford a suit like that." And in fact, it looked even more expensive and well-tailored up close.

Sphinxlike, he met her eyes, refusing to give.

"You can tell me," she coaxed.

"Miss, I don't know you."

"But I know you."

His face showed confusion as well as irritation, and she realized with a jolt that her looks were likely the reason for his indifference. He probably had no idea what to make of her twenty-first-century outfit: T-shirt, shorts, and flip-flops. She must have looked like she'd run away from the circus. A freak.

"Rees & Company Gallery—isn't that where you had your photograph taken?" she asked, determined to win his interest. "At 289 Broadway?"

The man stared at her sharply, his expressive eyes issuing a stern rebuke. "How do you know that? Have you been following me? Are you one of Fat Mo's girls?"

"I have no idea who Fat Mo is," she replied, amused in spite of his anger.

"I don't believe you." Hastily, the man plucked the coins out of his hat, which he jammed onto his head. He suddenly looked like he was in a hurry. "Tell Mo he'll have his money. I need a few more days. He shouldn't have sent a woman to do his bidding."

"I told you, I don't know anyone named Mo. Never mind *Fat* Mo."

"You take me for a fool."

"You take *me* for a fool," Sara Beth countered.

"If you're not his acquaintance, why are you here?"

"Isn't it obvious? I'm trying to get your attention."

He cocked his head, seeming to assess her anew. "I saw the way you were studying me. What are you trying to learn, the tricks of my trade?"

"I still don't know what your trade is, remember?"

Obviously beginning to relax, he broke into a smile. "I don't know if I'd call it a trade."

"Why the big secret?"

As if making a decision, the man drew close to her, so close she could smell peppermint, tobacco, and talcum powder. "What I do isn't exactly honest."

She shrugged, murmuring, "Doesn't bother me."

"It's gotten me in trouble with the law—and with men like Fat Mo—more than once."

"So what is it—bribery, forgery, fraud, racketeering?"

"That's quite a list."

"Whatever it is, I'm sure it involves fooling people."

He gaped at her.

"Because if you can fool people so easily with your tricks," she continued, "why not use it to your advantage in real life?"

He laughed out loud. "You're very astute, miss."

"Maybe you're not that good, though," she said, gaining confidence. "You gave away so many nickels to that little girl—that's no way to run a business."

"I'm not in the habit of taking from children."

"Who are you in the habit of taking from?"

He leaned in even closer. She followed his gaze as he scanned the room. "There. Do you see her?" he whispered. "She's perfect."

"She's ancient," Sara Beth replied, dumbfounded by his choice: a heavyset old woman with a bonnet wrapped around her wizened face.

"Old is the best kind. They're slower—physically and sometimes mentally. And they want to trust, even if they know better. At a certain age, everyone is gullible."

"But why *her*?"

"See her clothes—how finely made? And her jewelry—there have to be twenty diamonds on that brooch."

"How can you tell?" she asked, squinting.

"Practice. Lots and lots of practice."

"So what is she, an easy mark? A sugar mama?" He looked at her quizzically. "How are you going to get that brooch?" she asked.

Again, he assessed her as if seeing her for the first time. "I see we have a similar way of viewing the world."

Sara Beth, feeling less like a member of a circus and more like herself, smiled. "Go on, then. Show me what you've got."

He clenched his jaw for a moment, deliberating, then seemed to decide.

"Wait here," he instructed.

CHAPTER TWELVE

"And?" Saskia demanded.

"And?" Sara Beth replied.

"What the heck happened?"

"I don't know! My darn alarm clock went off."

"You woke up?" Saskia asked disbelievingly.

"Yeah."

"Man, that *sucks*," Adrienne remarked.

"Tell me about it," Sara Beth replied with a dramatic sigh. "I would have liked to know what kind of criminal I'm dealing with."

Almost two weeks had passed since Sara Beth had shared her dream, and Saskia could now say for certain that she and the girls had settled into a new routine. A wonderful new routine. What had started as intermittent gatherings had morphed into nightly meetings—always at the sisters' house, and almost always under the tree. She looked forward to the meetings so much that the hours she wasn't with her new friends felt wasted—a necessary but unwanted prelude.

When she and her father had arrived in Coventon, Saskia had figured it would take at least a year before she felt like she belonged. She was even ready for the possibility of *never* belonging and finding her footing only after she left for college. After all, being a high schooler, no matter where you were, was like being a powder keg in a lightning storm.

Turned out, though, she'd been wrong. In just a few weeks, Saskia had not only found a great group of friends, friends who were cooler and more intrepid than even Heather, but she'd also found a sisterhood. Never before had she had such a close peer group: girls with whom she trusted her deepest secrets, girls who hung on her every word and vice versa. Even her father had noted that she was happier. "It's like a whole new Saskia," he'd said. "You've shed your moody, scaly teenage skin." And he was right—she had. The only person she was still salty around was her mother.

Sometimes Saskia thought back to the first time Paige had offered to hang out. That day by their lockers. Back then, Paige had been this perfect, popular girl on a pedestal; Saskia had felt privileged just speaking with her. Now Paige was one of her closest confidantes. And the best part was, Saskia wasn't the only who felt this way. At one of their meetings—this one in the Sampras den due to a rainstorm—Paige admitted she, too, loved the girls in the group.

"You know, I hope I don't sound stupid, but I never thought I'd have friends like you. I'm so . . . so grateful," Paige said.

Saskia felt moved by her sincerity.

Paige continued, "And our Mercury Boys—I never imagined they could be this amazing. We could go our whole lives and never meet guys like this, don't you think? They're cool, charismatic, charming . . ."

"Handsome. *Criminally* handsome," added Sara Beth, smirking.

"Smart," said Saskia.

"Perfect," piped up Adrienne.

"Exactly," finished Paige. "The only thing is, I feel protective of them. Know what I mean? God forbid word got out. What we have with these guys—it *has* to remain private. It's *ours*."

Saskia and the others nodded in unison.

"I've been thinking about this, the need for privacy, and have a proposition . . ."

"What?" Saskia asked curiously.

"I suggest we turn the Mercury Boys Club into a proper club. A secret club. With rules."

"What kind of rules?" asked Lila.

"Rules that make us accountable. Like how we can't talk about the Mercury Boys to other people. Ever. And how we can't date anyone else—that would be cheating."

"Isn't that a little much?"

"Not at all."

"Makes sense to me," said Saskia, glancing at Lila.

Paige beamed at her. "We owe you a big thanks, Saskia. I'm beyond thankful that these guys are in our lives. I feel like we won the lottery."

"Absolutely!" agreed Adrienne.

"We should do something. Something to celebrate," said Sara Beth.

"Another toast?" suggested Adrienne.

"No, bigger than that," insisted Sara Beth.

"What do you have in mind?" asked Paige.

"It's kind of a crazy idea . . ."

"It can't be crazier than what we've been doing in our dreams," Saskia replied.

"True. So here it is. Let's get tattoos. Mercury Boy Club tattoos."

Lila wrinkled her nose. "I'm not so sure about that."

"I think it's a fabulous idea!" said Paige, smiling ear to ear. "How about the letters MBC? Everyone in the club can get them wherever they want. The tattoo would prove membership. It would prove sisterhood and loyalty . . ."

"Aren't we underage?" interjected Adrienne.

"I'm sure we can convince somebody to do them," replied Paige confidently.

"With the right incentive," added Sara Beth.

"Oh Lord, I think I need a drink," Adrienne moaned, collapsing into giggles.

"Well, you're in luck," said Paige. "Our mother restocked the liquor cabinet this morning."

• • •

An hour later, the girls piled into Lila's car. The sisters, too drunk to take their Mercedes, were happy to let Lila drive. Saskia rode shotgun. The others crammed into the back.

"Dude, it smells like a deep fryer in here," Adrienne complained.

Sara Beth added, "Like year-old McDonald's."

"Nasty," said Paige. She passed a bottle of liquor to her sister, who took a swig.

"Seriously, you need to get this car detailed," said Sara Beth.

"What's 'detailed'?" asked Lila.

"Are you joking?"

"It's getting your car cleaned," said Paige. "Professionally."

"I can't even afford an oil change," Lila retorted.

Saskia squirmed, embarrassed by Lila's comment. She wished her friend would try a little harder to fit in.

"So where are we going?" asked Lila.

"To Never-Never Land," mused Adrienne, still giggly.

"For real."

"I don't know the address of the place, just the name," said Paige.

"What is it?"

"Graphic Content. It's somewhere in New Haven. Downtown."

Lila typed it into Google Maps on her phone. Luckily, the name was recognized, and they were soon on their way. Lila hopped on the highway and went directly into the fast lane, though her Buick topped out at 50 mph and groaned with mechanical exhaustion.

Saskia fiddled with the old radio until she found a song she liked—a catchy, feel-good confection of hard rap and bubblegum pop. Pure summer. She cranked up the volume and rolled down the window, savoring the moment.

Sara Beth rolled down her window, too, then half-climbed out of the car. Her head and torso sailed through the evening air as the car rumbled along. "Mercury Boys, we're coming for you!" she screamed into the night.

Paige yanked her back inside. Sara Beth toppled onto her sister, spilling booze on the back-seat upholstery.

"Maybe that will drown out the deep fryer smell!" she said. Adrienne dissolved into more laughter. Out of deference to Lila, Saskia tried to keep a straight face.

In New Haven the girls drove through Yale, staring at the buildings, passersby, a crowded outdoor concert on the town green. They passed a parade of impressive architecture—gothic cathedrals, a thicket of handsome brick dorms, a pretty stone chapel, ornate entryways, arches, and gates.

Then, as quickly as it had come, the campus faded away. It took only a mile to reach a seedier part of town: New Haven's version of the wrong side of the tracks: foreclosure signs, broken windows, liquor stores, and pawn shops. People stood around smoking and talking. Saskia couldn't help but notice a predominance of brown skin. She found herself praying no one in the car would make a racist comment. *Hey, lock the doors. Roll up the windows. You can't trust these people.* She didn't want to take on the responsibility of challenging her friends, of explaining how history's atrocities cast a long shadow on the present. But mostly, she didn't want them to follow up with, *Oh, but not you, Sask. You're different.*

She didn't think she could stomach that.

Lila spotted the neon sign: GRAPHIC CONTENT, in blinking lights. Purple and gaudy, it hung on a one-story building wedged between a row house and a gas station. Saskia stared nervously out the window, trying not to make eye contact with the men sitting on the stoop of the row house. They looked restless, bored, observant.

"Are those, like, meth heads?" asked Adrienne.

Oh god, here we go.

"Don't stereotype," said Paige, glancing at Saskia.

"Um, there's a reason stereotypes exist," Sara Beth replied. "It's 'cause they're usually true."

Saskia frowned as she watched Sara Beth get out of the car. Slamming the door shut, Sara Beth strode confidently toward the tattoo parlor. The men appraised her. She didn't blanch.

"Hurry up, bitches," she called to the other girls. "I don't have all night!"

The inside of Graphic Content was a lot like Saskia would have imagined: dim and a little dirty, with illustrations of tattoo designs and photographs of actual tattoos covering the walls. The air smelled thick and unpleasant: a medicinal odor with undercurrents of cigarette smoke and bodily fluids. In the center of the room sat a couple of black vinyl chairs, reclining and well worn, patched here and there with silver duct tape. Between the chairs was a large, shabby steel cabinet. The top housed a collection of needles, ink bottles, antiseptic, cotton balls in mason jars, and a couple of corded gadgets that looked like glue guns.

Tattoo machines, Saskia realized.

When the door shut behind the girls, a little bell chimed. A heavyset man entered the room through a doorway at the back. He took his time crossing the room, seeming neither pleased nor displeased to see them.

"What?" he asked.

"We're thinking of getting tattoos," Paige replied, unflustered. Saskia suddenly felt like she'd fallen into the deep end of a pool with bricks strapped to her feet.

"Yeah?" the man asked. "You got IDs?"

"We're of age."

The man snorted and smiled. His teeth were gnarly: yellow and crooked, with a big gap where one of the front teeth should have been. "I get that a lot. I still need IDs."

"We've got money."

"What kind of money? Milk money?"

"Cash," Paige replied, ignoring his condescension.

"Yo, Jimmy, these girls got *cash*," the guy called out sarcastically.

Another man, thinner and younger, emerged from the same doorway. Scratching his unkempt hair, he looked at first glance worthy of a second one. Saskia liked the razor-sharp contours of his face, how his blue eyes were pale and sharp as diamonds. She liked the fancy, colorful skull tattoos up and down his arms. Sugar skulls, she remembered they were called, something to do with Mexico and the Day of the Dead.

But upon closer inspection, Saskia realized there was something distinctly unhealthy about Jimmy. His skin looked clammy, like he'd been sweating, and he was way too skinny. Not hipster skinny, like a lot of boys her age, but sick skinny: cancer or drugs, a body gone haywire. Suddenly the angles of his face seemed more like the edges of his own skull trying to burst through.

He pulled at the bottom of his vintage Nirvana shirt and studied the girls one by one, stopping to linger on the sisters. "What? They want tattoos?"

"So they say," the heavyset guy replied.

"You girls in college?" Jimmy asked.

Sara Beth licked her lips and nodded.

"Oh yeah? Where?"

"Yale."

"What are you, freshmen?"

Again she nodded.

"So why're you here? It's summer."

"Getting a leg up on our studies," Sara Beth replied. She gave Jimmy a look that was like a promise. Saskia marveled at her hard-core flirting.

"Oh yeah?"

Jimmy's stare was like superglue, but to Saskia's surprise, Sara Beth was unruffled, even receptive.

He grinned, still pulling at his shirt like it was three sizes too small, even though he was swimming in it.

"We need consent forms for anyone under eighteen," the heavyset guy said. "You girls got parental consent?"

"We don't need it," Paige said. "Like I said, we're all of age."

"She ain't eighteen." He nodded at Lila, who, like Saskia, had positioned herself unobtrusively behind the others.

"She's a young eighteen."

"No consent forms, no service."

"Mike, don't be hasty, man," Jimmy chimed in. "Slow night tonight, anyway."

Mike exhaled audibly. He started to say something, but Jimmy cut him off. "What kind of tattoo you looking for?" he asked, the question clearly meant for Sara Beth.

"A cute one, somewhere special, maybe here, or here." Looking at Jimmy, she touched the place where her hipbone jutted out, then the inside of her thigh. "The letters MBC."

"Those your initials, sweetheart?"

"No," Paige interjected. "They're the initials of our friend. Mia Bree Coleman. She just passed away."

"Jesus, really?" Jimmy's face went the color of liver. "How?"

"Car accident. She was just walking on the sidewalk, minding her own business. Some idiot went right over the curb. Cracked her head wide open. By the time an ambulance came, she was already gone."

"That's terrible," Jimmy said.

"It was."

"What street did it happen on?"

"York."

"People drive like garbage in New Haven," said Mike. "I see it every day."

"You know what's even worse? The driver just drove off. It was a hit-and-run."

"Jesus," repeated Jimmy.

"Yeah, so we want to commemorate her," Paige said. "Because the rest of us are going on with our lives, and Mia's never gonna get that chance. She was robbed. High school graduation was, like, her last milestone."

"Hey, man, at least she got that," Mike said. Wearily, he set his body down on one of the black chairs. It made a sound like a softly hissing snake.

"So you understand why we need to do this?" Paige asked.

"Damn straight. I lost my younger brother when he was four. I'll never get over it."

"Was it a car accident, too?"

"Nah, leukemia."

"I'm so sorry."

He shook his head.

"Look," Paige ventured cautiously, "I don't know how much you charge for small tattoos. But we all want the same thing: Mia's initials. MBC. We heard through the grapevine you guys are the best, and we want the best for our friend. We want to remember her—forever."

"How small you want the letters?" Mike asked.

"Tiny." Paige used her fingers to show him the size.

"Maybe we can do it," Mike said, a little out of breath. "Maybe. For two hundred dollars apiece."

Saskia flinched; she had twelve dollars on her. Sara Beth and Paige exchanged looks.

"That's a little higher than we hoped," said Paige.

"That's what tattoos cost, darlin'. Good ones don't come cheap. You want cheap, you can find it. But then you'll get a crap job, and maybe an infection, too."

"But a thousand dollars total—that's, like, the cost of a year's worth of books."

"You're Yale girls? Come on, you got money."

"We're not all filthy rich, you know," said Sara Beth. "Some of us worked our asses off to get here on scholarship." She stretched her arms above her head. Saskia suspected she did it to flaunt her flat, tanned stomach.

"How 'bout we make a deal?" Paige said. "Negotiate."

Mike shook his head.

"What do you have in mind?" Jimmy asked gamely.

Sara Beth gave him a frisky little smile. "My sister and I spend five minutes alone with you, and you do all the tattoos for free."

"Both you and her?" Jimmy asked, glancing at Paige.

"Yeah."

"You're kidding me? Two smoking hot girls, a brunette and a blonde?"

"Man, calm the eff down. They're underage," Mike murmured from his perch.

Jimmy looked at him and shrugged.

"It's all you, Jimmy. I'm out." With effort, Mike hoisted himself out of the chair. "These girls could be bait, for all you know. Happened to Tribal Tattoo. 'Member the raid? J.J. got ten years. Feds took his weed, too."

"There's not going to be a raid," said Paige. "We've been honest with you from the beginning."

"Yeah, we're making you a fair offer," Sara Beth added. "More than fair. We can always go somewhere else . . ." She gazed at Jimmy, letting the words sink in.

"Okay, I'm in," he replied, clasping his hands together. "Five minutes in the backroom. You and her. You really sisters?"

"Yeah," Paige replied. "Five minutes and all five tattoos— right?"

"Right, baby. Whatever you want. The back room's this way." He gestured toward the hallway, which had a few closed doors, one being a restroom.

But Paige stood her ground and insisted Adrienne take the seat that Mike had vacated. The impression of his blocky body was still molded into the black vinyl.

"Tattoos first, payment after," she said.

"Yeah," finished Sara Beth. "That's the deal—take it or leave it."

"Take it," said Jimmy grudgingly, looking at the sisters with a combination of annoyance and wolfish interest.

The process didn't take as long as Saskia thought it would. Adrienne, Lila, and she all had theirs done first, and then the sisters asked them to step outside.

"Why?" Saskia asked Paige urgently.

"Tattoos in private places require *privacy*," she whispered back mysteriously.

Saskia didn't like the idea of leaving the building for anybody's sake, but she did as told, thinking that the private places Paige was referring to must be scandalous indeed if the normally uninhibited sisters didn't want their friends to see.

After all the tattoos were complete and the girls had reconvened, Jimmy told Paige and Sara Beth to meet him in the back room.

"Sure," said Sara Beth. Then she looked at her sister evenly. Saskia noticed that neither girl seemed scared or creeped out like she would be. They told Jimmy to give them a few minutes in the restroom "to get ready," and he agreed.

But only thirty seconds after they'd walked down the hallway and disappeared into the restroom, Saskia received a text from Paige instructing her, Lila, and Adrienne to sneak to the car as soon as Jimmy headed for the back room. Saskia was shocked, but she knew better than to question Paige.

Five minutes later, when Jimmy strolled down the hallway to see what was taking the sisters so long, she grabbed Lila's and Adrienne's hands and rushed them out the door. When they ran to Lila's car, they were shocked to see that Paige and Sara Beth were already there, crouching in a shadow.

"Unlock this thing and get us out of here," Paige instructed Lila calmly but forcefully. "*Now.*"

Lila fumbled with the keys, unlocked the Buick, and started the engine. Saskia worriedly stared at the door to Graphic Content, knowing any moment Jimmy would come bursting out.

Lila pulled out so fast the Buick scraped against the side of the car parked in front of it. Its wheels squealed as they raced down the street, the old engine rasping with effort. Paige and Sara Beth began laughing hard in the back seat, great big belly laughs, while Adrienne and Saskia glanced nervously through the back window.

"We're fine!" Paige assured them, her cheeks flushed. "Everything's fine."

"You Sampras girls are one hundred percent certifiably crazy AF," Lila said, ducking down another street.

And I love it, Saskia wanted to add, thrilled by their getaway.

Miles from the scene of the crime, the girls were still high from their madcap escape, periodically doubling over in laughter as they roamed the aisles of a Walgreens. They were looking for either Lubriderm or Aquaphor, which were good for tattoo aftercare, at least according to a website Adrienne had found. Saskia couldn't wait to remove the dressing Jimmy had secured with white medical tape. She was both excited and scared about what lay beneath.

She'd gotten her tattoo on her hip, a place she figured few would notice, except a boyfriend—if she ever found one—or maybe her pediatrician. She liked the way the tattoo had turned out: the letters so elegant, like calligraphy on a wedding invitation. But she was anxious, too. She worried she'd second-guess herself later and regret what she couldn't undo.

When the needle had first pricked her skin, she'd almost fled the chair. But she'd gone through with it in the end. The deciding factor wasn't alcohol or peer pressure. It was Cornelius. She liked the idea of committing to him in some way, even if he never found out about it.

Getting the tattoo had hurt—a lot. But she'd muscled through it, her hands curled into fists as the needle punctured her skin, buzzing like a dental drill. It was like getting stung by a wasp over and over again. Torture.

Now the tattoo felt like an open wound, which she supposed it was. Blood, pus, and little blobs of black ink soaked through the bandage. The pain was steady but tolerable now, not nearly as bad as the blister had been. She picked up a bottle of Tylenol as she and the girls headed for aisle nine: skin care.

"That was intense," said Sara Beth, linking arms with her sister. "But we pulled it off."

"We did," said Paige.

"You guys were like Bonnie and Clyde," Saskia told them admiringly.

"Who are they?" asked Sara Beth.

"Notorious outlaws," said Saskia. "Robbers during the Great Depression. There's an awesome movie about them with Warren Beatty and Faye Dunaway . . ."

Her voice trailed off when the girls displayed little interest in what she was saying.

No matter. Their reaction didn't detract from Saskia's confidence in the comparison or from her admiration for what the sisters had pulled off.

Lila dropped Saskia off last. They didn't make their usual run to McDonald's. Lila said she was too tired, and Saskia felt the same way. The trip to Graphic Content had exhausted them, mentally and physically. Saskia craved rest more than anything else, except of course time with Cornelius.

"I'm not gonna be able to sit for a week," Lila complained, braking in front of Saskia's house. The empty whiskey bottle rolled noisily on the floor of the back seat.

"Why the heck did you get it on your butt?" Saskia asked.

"I don't know. Seemed as good a place as any."

"You're gonna need to put a pillow on the phone book."

Lila laughed, sounding more lighthearted than usual. "I can't believe tonight actually happened. I can't believe we went through with it!"

Saskia couldn't believe it, either. Since arriving in Coventon, she'd spent a lot of time trying to forget certain things. But tonight she'd gone and done something that could never be forgotten. The tattoo would forever commemorate this particular moment in her life and the particular people she now called her closest friends: the other four members of the Mercury Boys Club.

"Text me when you wake up," she said, getting out and shutting the passenger-side door. After a moment, she stuck her head back through the open window. "And sweet dreams."

• • •

Saskia opened the front door quietly so as not to wake her father. She expected to find him passed out in front of the TV. Or maybe he was at work? She couldn't remember if he was on call. The last place she expected to find him was in the kitchen, cooking.

The delicious aroma of spiced meat filled the air. It was a familiar smell. Kyinkyinga, a shish kebab–like Ghanaian street food her mother liked to make. Saskia stood in the doorway, feeling a sudden wave of tenderness toward her father. He stood at the counter, his back to her, chopping something on a cutting board. She listened to the methodical *clack-clack* of the knife against wood, and smiled at how neatly he'd tied the apron strings behind his back. The scene filled her with such love, she almost started to cry.

"Shit!" he said, putting a stop to her reverie.

The knife clattered to the floor. Saskia winced. She knew at once he'd cut himself. She took a breath, ready to make herself known, but then she heard another sound, one that troubled her much more than his swearing. Her father was sobbing—the noise raw, guttural, heart-wrenching. Instinctively, she realized he wasn't reacting to the pain or the blood. Her father was used to those; he saw them every day on the job. No, it was the cut itself that had caused him to break down. Now that he'd been punctured, she suspected everything he'd pent up for so long was pouring out: anger, jealousy, disappointment, frustration, anguish. Every last evil in Pandora's box.

She wanted to run to him and give him a hug, but something held her back: the knowledge that he'd be embarrassed. She knew he wouldn't want her to see him like this, vulnerable and fragile, even emasculated. Nothing like the father he tried to be.

At a loss, she tiptoed to the bathroom. Inside, she locked the door. Carefully, she took off the dressing and examined her tattoo. It was hard to see the elegant script through the damage. Her skin was raised and irritated, scabby with dried pus, blood, and ink. She hoped the tattoo wouldn't end in regret.

In front of the mirror on the medicine cabinet, she stared at her face one feature at a time. Together, they looked like a series of disjointed parts. She wished, as she'd wished many times, that her dark eyes were not quite so far apart and her chin not so square. She wished the face staring back at her was as beautiful as Paige's.

She took two Tylenols and put a big Band-Aid over the tattoo. The website said it was okay to leave new tattoos uncovered after a few hours, but Saskia didn't want to get blood on her sheets. In bed, she went through the steps of the ritual—touching mercury and the daguerreotype—and tried her best to concentrate on Cornelius. Before long she drifted off.

But her last lucid thought had nothing to do with him. It had to do with her father.

What are the chances of us both bleeding at the same time, and how long till we heal?

Adrienne

After Adrienne had changed and returned to the barn, Nurse Reynolds cornered her. If the older woman had seemed exhausted when Adrienne had first met her, she looked now like she'd fallen off the edge of a precipice.

"I must get some rest. My feet are giving out," Nurse Reynolds said. She motioned to the men in various states of ill health. "You'll have to take care of them for an hour or two."

"Okay," Adrienne replied. She wasn't at all confident she could handle the situation, but she didn't really have a choice. She pulled at the hem of her dress, which barely covered her knees. It was dirty and musty, and stank of unwashed skin. She had shaken it outside the cabin for all of thirty seconds before putting it on. It had seemed wrong to worry about potentially getting sick when her Mercury Boy was fighting for his life.

"The young man whose arm was amputated . . ." Nurse Reynolds said, pausing to swipe back a loose tendril of hair. Adrienne felt her hackles go up. She didn't want another lecture on patient-nurse protocol.

"Yeah?"

"You'll want to keep an eye on him."

"Why?"

"He has a fever, a bad one."

Adrienne remembered what Nurse Reynolds had said, about how a patient could be boiled alive. A fresh terror seized her.

"Also, the patient who needed surgery—he just died," the nurse continued. "The doctor and I put him in one of the tents. In the morning he'll be carted away. He's lucky. At least he'll get a proper burial."

Adrienne wondered at the nurse's definition of lucky. Nurse Reynolds continued to talk, but her voice began to sound like white noise, a buzzy background secondary to Adrienne's rising panic. Her boy. A fever.

Before becoming a phlebotomist, her mother had studied to be an RN. Although she'd never earned her certification—the mental and financial cost of the divorce had put the kibosh on that—she'd come close. Adrienne still remembered how hard she'd studied: making flash cards, staying up till the early hours of the morning poring over books. Often, at breakfast, her mother would ask Adrienne to quiz her.

Adrienne still retained bits and pieces of information from those mornings. She remembered, for example, what a postoperative fever could mean: pneumonia, sepsis, infection. All horrible possibilities.

She left the nurse and headed swiftly toward the back of the barn, zigzagging around cots and injured men. When she reached the boy, what she saw made her even more concerned. Sweat dappled his face and soaked his hair. His breathing was ragged. His eyes were open, but they might as well have been shut for all the life in them.

Adrienne's mind raced. It worked faster and harder than she could remember it ever working before. What the boy needed, she knew, was antibiotics. But clearly they hadn't been invented yet. Christ, the doctor and nurse didn't even know the connection between cleanliness and germs. If they did, there wouldn't be dirty hands, bloody water buckets, filthy medical instruments, and food left out to rot. What medicine *was* available during the Civil War? She hadn't a clue. But she figured even if there were something that could effectively treat infection, it wouldn't be here, in this cruel joke of a camp. She wondered how many soldiers had died in field hospitals exactly like this one. Then again, maybe it was better not to know.

Taking the boy's hand in her own, she considered the options. An ice bath would bring down a fever, but she doubted refrigeration

was available yet, either. The best she could do was get cool water
from the stream. She'd get it near the cabin, where the water wasn't
tainted with blood. But first, she needed to take him out of the barn
and into fresh air. Squeezed in the same tight, airless quarters, the men
were no doubt infecting one another. They were infecting the nurses,
too. That was probably why Eliza had dysentery.

Adrienne took hold of the cot and dragged it toward the back
door of the barn. Sometimes she wished she were smaller, but not
now. She was grateful for her size and strength as she hauled the cot
outside, far away from the barn and the tents. She finally parked the
boy in the shade of a tree and held his hand a few minutes.

"I'll be right back," she said, wondering if he could hear her.

The sun was still beaming down, but the worst of the day's heat
was over. She found a bucket and jogged to the stream near the
cabin, wondering if Nurse Reynolds had returned and was resting
inside. If she spotted Adrienne, she'd be furious at her for leaving
the soldiers.

Adrienne filled the bucket and trudged back to camp, her arms
aching from the effort. Water sloshed sloppily over the rim. She left
the bucket near the boy, then entered the barn. It took her a few
minutes to find the bottle of alcohol hidden under the surgery table.
She found some sheets, too. Not clean, but cleaner than what he
had. Tucking these under her arm, she willed herself not to respond
to the cries of the other patients. Not yet.

When she reached the boy again, she gingerly tugged the dirty
sheet from underneath him. The mattress was made of straw, pieces
of which poked up sharply through the thin cover. She managed to
make the bed with the new sheet by rolling him to his side, gritting her teeth as she supported his weight with her already-fatigued
arms. Then she tore another sheet into thin strips with her fingers and teeth. The boy stared at her with such destitute eyes, she
couldn't meet them, or else she'd lose her nerve.

"I'm not gonna lie. It's gonna hurt," she whispered. Carefully,
she began to unwrap his stump. The look of it turned her stomach.
The sutured wound had turned nearly black. It looked like a dark

lightning bolt edged with clots of blood and yellow pus. She wondered if the blackness were a symptom of infection. A thick, foul-
smelling discharge dripped wetly from the hole the surgeon had left.
Trying not to gag, she uncorked the bottle of whiskey and poured it
over the stitches and hole. The boy cried out, and she nearly wept
for knowing that she was the cause of more pain.

"I'm sorry! It really will help, though."

Ever so slowly Adrienne cleaned around the discharge hole.
Then she rebandaged the stump. Finally, she pulled him into a sitting position and forced him to drink a cup of water. It took a long
time. By the time he'd finished, the sun had moved an inch closer
to the horizon.

"I have to help the other soldiers now," she whispered to him.
"But I'll come back soon. Rest." It was hard to leave him there all
alone, but she'd done what she could. No matter what happened,
she could take solace in that.

Back in the barn, she had to dig deep to carry on. Without even
realizing it, she'd started to feel like Nurse Reynolds: so exhausted
she could barely stand. Once again, Adrienne thanked her lucky
stars that she was strong and fit. If she weren't, she doubted she
would have made it through. She tried not to think about the fact
that she was single-handedly responsible for the lives of so many.
Instead she focused on the tasks at hand: changing bandages, securing a tourniquet, spoon-feeding an armless soldier, changing blood-
and urine-soaked sheets. She did what she could as quickly as she
could.

But when Nurse Reynolds returned, Adrienne felt more relieved
than in all her life. Hurrying outside, she checked on her boy, grateful that his breathing had improved. She gave him another cup of
water and brought him inside; night would be here soon. Then,
getting a second wind, she offered water to each and every man,
helping those who were unable to hold their cups.

"I need to go back to the stream near the cabin. We're out of
water," she told Nurse Reynolds.

"Get water from the stream here. It's much closer."

"Are you kidding me? That water's disgusting. Have you seen the blood?"

Nurse Reynolds stared at her coldly, but Adrienne wouldn't be deterred. She knew she was right—that time would prove her right. "We need to change the straw in all the mattresses," she continued. "And the laundry, there's so much of it. We have to deep-clean *everything*."

"Washing is done only on Monday, every other week."

"Yeah, and that's one of the reasons our patients are dying. This place is *filthy*."

Nurse Reynolds chose to ignore that. She tried to shut the barn door Adrienne had propped open with a rock, but Adrienne stood in front of it like a sentinel.

"What in heaven's name are you doing?" Nurse Reynolds demanded.

"The doors are going to stay open," Adrienne replied, crossing her arms. She was surprised by her own sass. But maybe she shouldn't have been. She was changing this summer. Everything was changing. "We need fresh air. Ventilation. The soldiers need it."

"I've never heard such nonsense."

"It's not *nonsense*. Good airflow, fresh water, clean clothes and sheets—that's Health Care 101."

The nurse assessed her with a combination of confusion, ire, and annoyance. "Now you listen to me, young lady. You have no right to speak to me in this manner. If you continue, I'll be forced to . . ."

"To what? Fire me? With all these men on your hands? You wouldn't dare."

The nurse pursed her lips. "There are other volunteers. And Eliza will recover, surely."

Adrienne wished suddenly that Paige were there. She would know how to negotiate with Nurse Reynolds. She would know how to twist her arm, flatter her, bribe her. To do whatever it took to get her on Adrienne's side. But Adrienne was on her own. Now that the nurse had called her bluff, she had no idea how to proceed.

Still protecting the open barn door, she realized her best bet might be humility.

"Nurse Reynolds," she began, "with your permission, I'd like to make a few changes around here. If you let me, I'll do whatever you need me to do, whenever you need me to do it. Promise." She uncrossed her arms. "Please?" she pleaded.

The nurse pursed her lips again. She took her time responding. Every second left Adrienne more on edge. There was a very real possibility that Nurse Reynolds would tell her to leave and never return.

"Open the barn doors if you must," she said finally. "And fetch the water upstream. But after that, I need you to do a different task."

"What?"

"You'll find a shovel behind the barn. Walk fifty paces from the tents and start digging. We need a new latrine."

Grimacing, Adrienne nodded. She understood that this was the best compromise she was going to get. At least for now.

She would be patient.

During the next few days, the boy's health greatly improved. His stump was healing rapidly. He was eating—not a lot, but some. His hellish fevers had ceased. He was even walking a little.

Best of all, he was talking. In bits and pieces, he told her Adrienne all about himself. His name was Emery Westervelt. He was nineteen years old and from Ipswich, Massachusetts. He was a printer's apprentice and wanted to own his own newspaper someday. He had a twin brother who had been killed weeks earlier by a short cannon called a Howitzer. Emery had been nearby when it happened. He told Adrienne how the Howitzer had looked brand-new, its smoking bronze tube still gleaming bright and beautiful as his brother fell in a heap to the ground.

Emery asked about her, too, but she hadn't been able to answer many of his questions. How could she? She needed time—and courage. Only then could she explain the odd circumstances that had brought them together, and what her real life was like.

On a routine visit, she ventured carefully through the barn, which was dark in the early evening hours. She walked toward his cot by the thin light of a kerosene lantern and saw that he was sleeping.

Though it was hard to tell through the murky light, Adrienne thought his color looked unusually good. She changed his bandage gingerly, not wanting to wake him. Almost no fluid drained from the stump now, and what little there was ran clear.

She wouldn't let herself feel relief—it was too soon for that. But she was cautiously optimistic. Before wrapping the stump in a new bandage, she poured another glug of alcohol over the healing stitches. This no longer caused him to recoil in pain, or even to awaken.

"What are you doing?" hissed a voice from behind her. She jumped when she saw an elongated shadow against the wall of the barn. Nurse Reynolds. Adrienne had thought she was sleeping. The older woman gaped at Adrienne. "So you're the one wasting it all! I thought it was the doctor tippling. We're down to a few drops," she groused.

Adrienne stepped away from the boy. "I'm not *wasting* it," she whispered. "It's an antiseptic. Haven't you noticed we haven't had a single infection this last week? It's because of this."

As she shook the corked bottle for emphasis, she realized the nurse was right: there was barely any alcohol left. With a long sigh, Adrienne rubbed her face. She hadn't glanced in a mirror for a while, but she was certain she looked awful. She was stressed out every minute of every hour at the field hospital. At the same time, when she wasn't there, she longed to be.

"Now I suppose you'll tell me about *germs* again?" the nurse asked. "Whatever your faults, you do have a gift for newfangled words."

Adrienne wanted to groan. She was too tired for another cynical lecture. Fortunately, Nurse Reynolds had softened since their first meeting, having realized that Adrienne, for all her idiosyncrasies and stubbornness, was an asset.

"We need more whiskey," Adrienne said. "Or else the infections will come back. It's really important."

"It's true that we haven't had a death this week," the nurse acknowledged. "You really think it's because of this *antiseptic* notion?"

Adrienne tried not to show her surprise. Normally Nurse Reynolds didn't take her seriously. "Yes! And the rags. There's a reason I boil them so much. We can't reuse the dirty ones till they've been sanitized." She nodded toward the nurse's soiled hands. "And those—you have to wash your hands really well, with plenty of soap, every time you handle a patient. Dirty hands spread disease."

Adrienne's own hands were peeling and calloused. She'd never realized how hard life had been before the advent of the washing machine. It was exhausting to spend a whole day washing clothes with nothing but a scrubbing board, boiling kettle, and boar-bristle brush.

"I suppose that's why we're running low on soap, too," the nurse mused. "Still, I'll admit the boys are doing better. I didn't believe you about the 'circulating air.' Or the clean sheets and water. But if our patients are healing, then maybe your notions aren't so queer after all."

Adrienne tried to keep from smiling.

"I have two more bottles of whiskey hidden in the cabin," the nurse continued. "You may use them."

"Oh, that's awesome!"

Nurse Reynolds stared at her curiously. "Miss Arch, where did you say you are from?"

"Oh, far. Really far, actually."

The nurse nodded, though she didn't look entirely satisfied with that answer.

Sometimes it was best to leave well enough alone. Especially in a place like this, where well enough was all you could ask for. "If you're hungry, Miss Arch, I left your rations in the cabin. I'll care for the men for the rest of the night if you return at dawn."

Adrienne thought about the food awaiting her. How the biscuits could double as paperweights. How the meat was all gristle and bone. Then she glanced back at her boy, who still slept soundly in the shadows. "No, thanks," she replied. "I'd rather stay."

CHAPTER THIRTEEN

"I'm not gonna name names," Paige said during another nightly meeting of the Mercury Boys Club. "But it has come to my attention that *someone* might have seen her ex-boyfriend recently." Her eyes scanned the girls, not settling on anybody in particular.

In the candlelight under the giant tree, Saskia shifted uncomfortably. Just a minute ago the members of the Mercury Boys Club had been laughing, talking about their itchy, still-healing tattoos. Paige had been poking fun at Jimmy, joking that he was probably still in the back room looking for her and her sister. Now her stare was icy—and the rest of the girls were trying to avoid it.

"Hold up. What are you saying?" Lila asked. Saskia looked at her with a mixture of wonder and concern. Paige didn't hold any power over Lila like she did over Saskia. It was like Lila's innate sensibleness and aversion to drama made her immune.

"What I'm saying is what I've said all along. We have to have rules. And we have to enforce them." Paige looked askance at Adrienne. "Otherwise, cheaters are gonna cheat."

Saskia was beginning to get a bad feeling. A very bad feeling. She was surprised by how quickly Paige's mood had shifted; she'd gone from friendly to accusatory in under a minute.

"All we did was get ice cream," Adrienne blubbered suddenly. "And we went so I could tell him about Emery!"

"You can never be friends with an ex," replied Paige. "It's impossible. I should know."

"But it was totally innocent. There was nothing romantic, nothing at all."

"Then why the need to meet with him?"

"I told you—to tell him about Emery. About how we're together now."

"There shouldn't be a need to explain that to an *ex*-boyfriend."

Adrienne scratched fretfully at the tattoo on her bicep. It just about leaped off her fair, freckly skin. "Well, Benjamin's sensitive, you know? I just wanted him to understand. He can be . . . emotional."

"You know he's still into you. So why go for ice cream? Why not just text him?" Paige demanded.

"You're leading him on," added Sara Beth.

"I'm not leading him on," said Adrienne.

"Getting ice cream with a boy is a *date*," said Paige.

Adrienne's bottom lip quivered. She looked close to tears. Saskia felt sorry for her—Paige was definitely going after her hard. Too hard. At the same time, Saskia could understand why Paige was so angry. As the de facto leader of their group, Paige needed to keep order and maintain discipline.

"But I didn't mean it to be!" Adrienne proclaimed. "Honest! Maybe he did think it was a date. And maybe I did make a mistake. But it's not like you've never made one before."

"Number one," Paige snapped, "we're talking about you, so stop trying to deflect blame. And number two, I haven't dated another guy since meeting Samuel, and I'm not going to."

"Okay, Miss Perfect."

Saskia was shocked—she had never heard Adrienne talk back to Paige before. She wouldn't have thought Adrienne had the nerve. In fact, if Saskia looked up to Paige, Adrienne practically worshipped her.

"So that's what you're going to do? Call me names? What are you, four?" Paige asked.

Adrienne flinched.

"Let's take a vote," Paige said, addressing the group. "Raise your hand if you think it's okay to have a boyfriend and still go out on a date with your ex-boyfriend."

Adrienne shook her head. "But that's not . . ."

"You just *admitted* he thought it was a date."

It was beginning to feel a little too hot and oppressive under the tree for Saskia's comfort. The dangling branches that encircled them suddenly felt constraining. She shifted uncomfortably, thinking that watching Paige and Adrienne go at it was a lot like watching Alfred Hitchcock's *Lifeboat* and waiting for the next poor soul to get thrown overboard.

"But you and Sara Beth almost hooked up with that tattoo guy. *Jimmy!*" Adrienne spat out the name like it had a bad taste. "How's that okay, but talking with Benjamin is not?"

Paige laughed. "You're so naive. Hooking up with that walking billboard for opioid addiction was never going to happen. We're way too smart for that."

"And frankly, I find the comparison between our situation and yours insulting," added Sara Beth.

"What I find even more insulting," said Paige to Adrienne, "is your ingratitude. We only pulled off that stunt so that *you* wouldn't have to pay for the tattoo. So that *you* could get it for free. Four hundred bucks is nothing for us."

Red-faced, Adrienne looked at Saskia imploringly, but Saskia didn't meet her eyes. She felt sorry for Adrienne, who just wasn't in the sisters' league in terms of smarts, savvy, or—as Paige had crudely pointed out—money. Paige's last comment was an especially low blow. The Sampras sisters were rich, yes, but their privilege didn't make them superior, especially considering that none of other girls could have afforded the tattoos.

Still, if Saskia were forced to pick a side, she would have picked Paige's. Paige was simply a better friend, and Saskia had more of an allegiance to her. Plus, she agreed with Paige on principle: Adrienne *had* broken the trust of their sisterhood by having another boyfriend.

Finally, there was another reason for Saskia to keep her mouth shut—one that she didn't really want to admit even to herself. Paige was beginning to scare her.

"Can we take this down a notch?" Lila asked calmly. "Adrienne made a mistake. She said she's sorry. Let it go."

Saskia took a deep breath. Thank god for Lila, honestly.

"I wish I could," Paige replied. "But if it happens once, it could happen again."

"So what do you want to do?" Lila asked impatiently.

"I told you: make rules," Paige replied. In a snap she jumped to her feet. Saskia half-expected her to kick Adrienne, but instead she exited the canopy.

Saskia exchanged a disbelieving look with Lila. *WTF just happened?*

Slowly, warily, the rest of the gang made their way out from under the tree. They found Paige inside the house, sitting on the floor of the den and typing on a laptop.

Judging by how quickly and decisively her fingers tapped the keyboard, Saskia could tell that Paige was sure of what she wanted to say. Maybe she'd already planned it out in her head.

Sara Beth sat down next to her. A wan and worried-looking Adrienne kept to the corner of the room. Saskia clenched Lila's arm as she watched Paige furiously pound the keys.

The Mercury Boys Club
OFFICIAL RULES OF MEMBERSHIP

1. Mercury Boys Club members must attend <u>all</u> meetings of the MBC.
2. Becoming a member of the MBC is a lifetime commitment.
3. MBC members must <u>pledge</u> their love and devotion to their Forever Boyfriends.
4. MBC members must visit their Forever Boyfriends at least once a week (preferably every night!!!).

5. MBC members must get the official MBC tattoo.
6. MBC members must obtain and share all necessities (mercury, etc.).
7. Membership to the MBC is top secret and must be kept <u>strictly confidential</u>. Revealing information about the MBC to outsiders is a PUNISHABLE OFFENSE.
8. Damaging or losing a Forever Boyfriend daguerreotype is a PUNISHABLE OFFENSE.
9. If a member wants to leave, the group must vote on the issue. Majority wins. It is a PUNISHABLE OFFENSE for an MBC member to leave the club without permission!!!
10. MBC members get to decide all forms of punishment!!!
11. If an MBC member wants to break up with her Forever Boyfriend, she must seek permission from the club.
12. MBC members must support their club sisters and help them remain HONEST.
13. MBC members must abstain from dates with boys other than their Forever Boyfriends.
14. When visiting their Forever Boyfriends, MBC members must wear APPROPRIATE CLOTHING.
15. MBC members will meet body and soul with their Forever Boyfriends in death!!!

Saskia felt faint. The little letters on Paige's screen were wiggling and dancing. She closed her eyes and took a deep breath. Some of the rules weren't surprising, while others were so hardcore and unexpected she got chills. Seeing them laid out and official made Saskia realize the significance of what they were doing. They made her feel both scared and proud, like she was embarking on a critical mission—a mission she wasn't entirely sure she could handle.

Saskia realized Lila, Paige, Sara Beth, and Adrienne were

connected to her now, emotionally and physically, bound exter-
nally by their shared tattoos and internally by their common
commitment to the Mercury Boys. The gravity of what they were
collectively experiencing—their sisterly bond, the boys they were
visiting, the fact that they knew a secret the rest of the world
didn't—all of it felt extremely important in light of the rules Paige
had written. Like nothing before mattered as much as what was
happening right now.

"Paige, you're going too far . . ." Lila said incredulously.

Paige appraised her for several seconds. "You're wrong. These
rules are exactly *far enough*."

"But we're sixteen," said Lila. "Do you honestly think we're
ready for a 'lifetime commitment'?"

Paige slowly removed her fingers from the keyboard. Again, she
waited a beat before answering. "Look, I'm not a very spiritual
person, but I believe that fate led us to our Forever Boyfriends. And
I believe we need to guard them."

"'MBC members will meet body and soul with their Forever
Boyfriends in death,'" Lila quoted. "*That* is going too far. We're
just teenagers!"

"When Samuel was alive, the average age of death was thirty-
nine. Back then, we'd probably be married by now, with kids. Sixteen is not that young."

Saskia found herself agreeing with Paige. She wished Lila would
stop having doubts. Couldn't she see that something momentous
was happening?

As if echoing her thoughts, Paige said, "Lila, you don't get how
big this. When we see our boys, we bend time. We bring them back
to life! It's like . . ."

"A miracle," said Sara Beth.

"Yes," agreed Paige.

But Lila's cautious expression made it clear she didn't necessarily
agree.

"The mercury and the way we see our boyfriends—it's like

nothing that's ever happened before," continued Paige. "If our secret got out, everything would be ruined. We'd get reporters, paparazzi, scientists swarming our houses!"

"The whole world would change!" added Sara Beth. "That's why we have to keep this on the down-low."

"Forever," Paige concluded.

"Well, I don't know if I'm ready for forever," answered Lila.

"Then walk away," Paige said evenly. "Right now. Because later it will be harder—I can promise you that."

Once again, Saskia found herself siding with Paige and fervently wishing Lila would, too.

"Maybe I should leave." Lila sighed. "I don't know."

At that, Saskia expected Paige to lose her patience entirely. Lila's skepticism was wearing even on Saskia.

Yet Paige's expression unexpectedly softened. "Look," she said, "you've been a valuable member of this club from the beginning, Lila. You've given us the daguerreotypes, the mercury, everything. So you above all should realize how much is at stake, and why it's so important that we safeguard it."

Lila looked surprised by Paige's plaintive tone. Maybe she was lowering her defenses, at least a little. "It is pretty mind-boggling," she admitted.

"I have a question," Adrienne peeped from her corner. "What if I change my mind? Because of how complicated everything is. Sometimes I worry. Like, what if Emery wants me to stay with him . . . in his century?"

"Like my sister said," Sara Beth replied, shaking her head, "if you have doubts, you should walk away now."

"No one's saying it'll be easy," said Paige. She straightened up and looked at the girls one by one, sizing them up. "And no one has all the answers. Life is ambiguous. But Sara Beth and I—we're a hundred percent committed to our Forever Boyfriends, no matter what. We're ready to fight for them. Is anyone else?"

"I am," Saskia said, raising her hand.

Lila swallowed. "You know what? It's crazy, but the way you put it makes me realize I'm ready to fight for my Forever Person too." Saskia squeezed her hand.

From her corner, Adrienne shuffled her feet. Her face was streaked with tears, and her eyes were pink and puffy. "I just want to say I'm sorry. I'm sorry for all the trouble I'm causing. And I want to be in the club if you'll let me." She looked dolefully at Paige.

"It's up to you, Adrienne," Paige said. "Can you commit to Emery, and Emery only?"

"I already have," she whispered.

Paige's expression shifted again. Beaming, she rose from the floor and gave Adrienne a hug. It seemed all was forgiven, especially when Saskia overheard Paige whisper into the wispy red cloud of Adrienne's hair, "I know you can do it."

"Can we drink, already?" Sara Beth asked, happily exasperated.

"Yes!" Adrienne and Paige replied at the same time.

In the kitchen Saskia found herself jiggling a sterling silver shaker, the name Sampras engraved on the side. She couldn't help wondering how much it cost—maybe more than all her new IKEA furniture combined.

Sara Beth ventured over and showed her how to make martinis, explaining that olive juice made them "dirty," while equal parts dry and sweet vermouth made them "perfect." There seemed no end to the adult knowledge the sisters possessed.

Saskia filled the martini glasses and then took one, admiring its long stem and wide, almost sensual mouth. Giggling, she raised it high, trying to keep the drink steady, while Paige and Sara Beth made toast after toast. Liquid sloshed over the top, rolling down her hand and wrist. She licked her skin, laughing dizzily, floating on excitement and adrenaline. Glancing at Lila, she could see that her friend was having a good time, too. It seemed Paige had finally managed to convert her.

Soon the tension of earlier that night felt long gone. Everyone was as giddy as when they'd trekked to the tattoo parlor, like life was one big joyride.

They stopped keeping track of how many drinks they'd had. Saskia's glass finally toppled over. She found some paper towels and tried to clean it up, but Paige admonished her, saying, "Why bother? The housekeeper will do it."

Saskia wiped up the mess, anyway. A housekeeper, engraved silver, a pool that probably cost more than her house—the wealth of the Sampras family and the sisters' nonchalant attitude toward it would never feel normal to Saskia, though she wouldn't admit that to Paige.

She turned to watch Sara Beth, who'd started doing impersonations. She had a gift for imitating quirks and mannerisms. *If she were at Coventon High*, Saskia thought, *she'd be in the drama club with Adrienne.*

"Do Paige! Do Paige!" clamored Lila.

Sara Beth acquiesced, stretching out her neck and cocking her head to the side exactly the way Paige did. She narrowed her eyes in a condescending, holier-than-thou, perfectly Paige-like way. Lila nearly lost it.

Paige rolled her eyes, but then said, "Can you guys come over here?" She was sitting on the floor again, laptop and drink in front of her. "I want to make this official."

"Make what official?" Saskia asked.

"Our club, silly girl."

"Now?" Lila asked, her voice a little slurred. "But Sara Beth is on a roll." Saskia couldn't be sure, but she suspected Lila had tipped a little gin into her glass of orange juice. Maybe Paige was changing her in more ways than one.

"We need to make this legal and binding," Paige insisted.

"What do you have in mind?" asked Saskia.

"This pledge," Paige said, pulling up a document. "We'll all sign it."

Saskia huddled next to Paige and began to read.

The Mercury Boys Club
OFFICIAL PLEDGE

Today, _____, I, _____, solemnly swear to take _____ as my Forever Boyfriend, my faithful companion and eternal love. In the presence of my fellow members, I make a commitment to be _____'s partner in good times and in bad, in joy and in sorrow, in life and in death. I promise to love him unconditionally, to honor and respect him, and to sacrifice myself for him, if need be. I swear to be a better girlfriend to my Forever Boyfriend than any other girl, living or dead.

"This is literally a marriage contract," opined Lila, wide-eyed.

Saskia found herself shivering. "Did you come up with this just now? On the spot?"

"Yup," Paige replied. "I felt inspired. It's okay?"

Okay wasn't the word for it. Saskia nodded, intimidated, enthralled, and terrified all at once.

Paige left to print out copies of the pledge, dimming the lights on her way out. When she returned, she brought a candle like the ones they'd been using under the giant tree. Solemnly, she placed it on the floor and lit the wick. Then she motioned for the girls to gather in a circle.

"Everybody hold hands," she instructed formally, taking Saskia's fingers. "Each of us will now recite the pledge." She'd placed copies in front of each of the girls. Saskia could barely make out the words through the scant light.

"We're really doing this?" Lila asked.

Saskia shushed her with a stern look.

"Who goes first?" Sara Beth asked.

Adrienne volunteered. Saskia suspected she was trying to compensate for her bad behavior earlier. She read the pledge slowly and uncertainly, struggling with the word *unconditionally* until Paige helped her pronounce it. When she was done, she looked at Paige searchingly.

"Please sign the pledge now," Paige said. "We will be your witnesses."

Gritting her teeth, Adrienne broke the circle of hands and signed. She slowly put down the pen.

"Congratulations," Paige said, her smile expansive and generous. "You, Adrienne Arch, are—now and forever—a member of the Mercury Boys Club."

Breaking out in grins, the girls clapped. Then, one by one, they followed in Adrienne's footsteps. When it was Saskia's turn, she tried to make her signature as fancy as possible, like John Hancock's on the Declaration of Independence. Privately, she thought that someday someone might study the pledge. Maybe it would be a historically significant document.

Paige was the last to sign. She read the pledge with a gravitas the other girls had lacked. Saskia noticed she didn't even need the sheet. She had it memorized.

After that, the mood in the room felt different. Saskia didn't know if the other girls sensed it, but she thought their bond had grown even stronger. They were galvanized, part of something none of them could have anticipated, part of a club that was surely the first and only one of its kind. Another delicious shiver ran down her spine.

Sara Beth turned toward her sister. "The 'rents will be back soon."

Paige nodded. "Yeah, we gotta wrap this up, MBC members. But before you head out, I've got something for you." Her expression turned impish. When she got up to open the liquor cabinet, Saskia wondered if there was ever a time when the Sampras girls didn't drink. Paige fished for something in the very back, her arm extended full-length. Saskia expected her to pull out another bottle, but instead she retrieved a small box. Inside were three sandwich-size baggies filled with pills, colorful as rainbow sprinkles. When Paige shook them, they rattled appealingly, like packets of Skittles.

"What are those for?" Adrienne asked.

"They're your party favors," Paige teased. "Sara Beth and I

went to the drugstore for more Aquaphor this morning. We bought, like, every sleep aid known to man: Unisom, Advil PM, melatonin pills, ZzzQuil, Benadryl, you name it. We even sprinkled in some Restoril. Took it from my mom. These bags will guarantee that we see our Mercury Boys without delay." She smiled mischievously and jangled the bags like maracas.

"But . . . there are so many," Adrienne said dubiously. "How do we know which ones to take?"

"They all work."

"Mix and match," added Sara Beth.

"Are you sure they're . . . safe?" Adrienne asked.

"Sure," said Paige. "They're just over-the-counter meds. Not prescription. Well, except for the Restoril."

Adrienne didn't look convinced.

"Girlfriend, if you want one hundred percent safe," added Sara Beth, "then this club ain't for you."

Adrienne became indignant. "I signed the pledge, didn't I?" She reached out and grabbed one of the baggies.

"Look at you, Red!" Paige exclaimed proudly.

Saskia, too, took a bag from Paige's hand—though she didn't really want to. The sheer number of pills was startling. Some had the names of the medicines minted in tiny letters; others were mysteriously blank. She had the same feeling she'd had when they'd arrived at the tattoo parlor, like she was treading water that was a little too deep, like maybe she'd drown if she weren't careful. At the same time, how thrilling that water felt, brisk and new and tingly on her skin.

"Now go home," Paige instructed, handing the last baggie to Lila. "Get into bed and visit your Forever Boyfriends. That's an order."

"Yes, ma'am," Adrienne replied, saluting her with a giggle.

Saskia was the last out the front door. But Paige grabbed her arm on the threshold. "Wait a second," she whispered urgently. "I want to tell you something."

The way Paige whispered made Saskia feel special. Privileged. She leaned close to her friend, eager to hear what she had to say.

"Sara Beth and I discovered something. We didn't want to tell you in front of the others. You know how Lila tends to freak out . . ." Paige murmured in Saskia's ear.

Saskia glanced behind her. The front walkway was clear. She was relieved that Lila was probably already waiting for her in the car.

"We figured out that if you take a drop of mercury," Paige continued, "your dreams change. They become, like, a hundred times more intense. More vivid. Like going from black-and-white to Technicolor."

Though the film analogy piqued Saskia's interest, she was scared of what Paige seemed to be suggesting. "Take a drop of mercury? You mean, swallow it?" she asked incredulously.

Paige nodded.

"But that's . . ."

"Dangerous."

"Not just dangerous. You could die."

Paige sighed. "Saskia, don't be paranoid."

"But the effects of ingestion are clear," Saskia said, squirming a little. "I've read about them, and they're bad. Terrible."

"You're wrong," Paige replied sternly. "The majority of the time liquid mercury passes right out of the body, no harm done. In fact, only .01 percent of ingested mercury even gets absorbed through the gastrointestinal tract. It's breathing in mercury *vapors* that causes real problems, but we don't do that."

"But what about all those things we get warned about? Mercury in fish, and paint, and dental fillings?"

Paige stared at her reproachfully. "That's *methyl* mercury, Saskia. What we're dealing with is elemental mercury, which is practically as safe as water."

Paige sounded so confident and knowledgeable Saskia didn't dare contradict her. Plus, Paige was right: Saskia wasn't sure what the different kinds of mercury were. But even though she was ignorant, she couldn't believe *any* mercury could be as safe as water.

"You don't have to do anything you're not comfortable with,"

Paige said, her irritation showing. "I just thought I'd tell you.
Because the feeling is amazing, and I want you to have it, too."

"I'll think about it," Saskia replied, trying to appease her friend.

"I mean, don't do me any favors."

"No, that's not what I meant . . ."

"Whatever, Saskia."

"I just feel a little scared."

Paige looked at her pityingly, which made Saskia feel even worse.
"Just do whatever you want," Paige replied flatly.

"Paige?"

"Yeah?"

"Nothing," Saskia murmured, not even sure what she'd been
planning to say, but knowing she'd let Paige down. She'd have to
find a way to redeem herself. "See you later."

"See you," Paige said, shutting the door so swiftly Saskia had to
take a step back to avoid getting hit. For a few seconds she stood
regretfully on the stoop. Then she remembered Lila and ran toward
her car. Having resolved not to mention her conversation with
Paige, she climbed into the passenger side.

"What was the holdup?" Lila asked, starting the ignition.

"Paige was going on and on about some kind of new wine she
and Sara Beth discovered."

"Those two are going to be in AA by the time they're twenty,"
Lila muttered.

"Tell me about it. Hey, I want to ask you something," Saskia
said.

"What?"

"Did you drink tonight?"

Lila shrugged noncommittally, but her cheeks reddened. "All
right, I had one. One. I'm still okay to be designated driver."

"I know you are," Saskia replied.

"What did you think of the baggies?"

"The pills? They're a little . . . much."

"Yeah, but I might take a couple."

"Really?"

"Sleep's been hard," Lila admitted. "I can't seem to relax when I'm feeling . . . up."

Saskia nodded. "Yeah, I hear you. I wish there was a way to guarantee it." Ruefully, she touched the dragonfly hanging from the mirror. "Maybe there is," she heard herself whisper.

Lila glanced at her sharply as she took the shortcut that led to McDonald's. "You mean, *die*?"

"I mean . . . not on purpose!"

Lila grimaced and shook her head. "Dying's *not* an option, Sask. Do I even need to stay that? We can't sacrifice our lives just because theirs are over."

"I know, I know. But . . . it's weird. I don't look at death the same way anymore. Now that I know it's not—permanent." As Lila drove, Saskia watched the dragonfly swing back and forth hypnotically, like a pendulum. She swallowed a lump in her throat.

"Hey, have you ever thought about taking a daguerreotype of yourself?" Lila asked shyly. "Sometimes I think we should, so that someone in the future will, like, maybe bring us back."

"I never thought about that."

"I do. I mean, how long do you think we'll be here? Not as long as we think . . ."

"How may I help you today?" The voice on the loudspeaker jolted the girls. Still lost in thought, Saskia waited for Lila to give their usual McDonald's order. Then Saskia handed her a five-dollar bill, the last in her wallet. She really needed a job. She really needed to get serious about looking for one.

They got their food, and Lila parked the car. Saskia looked at her friend sheepishly. "Hey, can I ask you something?" she said.

"Of course."

"Why don't you ever tell me about your Mercury Boy?"

"I don't know . . ."

"Come on, there's got to be a reason."

Lila shook her head, trying to dismiss the subject.

"And why won't you tell me his name? Is it, like, Elmo or Adolf or something?"

"No!"

"Is he ugly?"

"No!" Lila replied, laughing. "He's just . . . different."

"How?"

"Like . . . he's . . . I don't know . . ." Lila turned and looked out her window.

"What?"

"He's . . . not what you would expect."

Saskia waited.

"I knew I shouldn't have had a drink," Lila muttered to herself.

"Yeah, why did you? What made you change your mind?"

"Maybe I knew this was coming. This conversation. Alcohol's supposed to make you fearless, right?"

"Why would you need to be fearless?"

"Because I need to tell you something."

"You can tell me anything," Saskia said. "You *know* that."

"Okay," Lila said, taking off her glasses and wiping the lenses slowly. "Let's just say my tattoo's all wrong. Let's just say it should be MGC, not MBC."

Saskia frowned. She watched Lila put on her glasses again, unwrap a cheeseburger, and sprinkle salt on it.

"My Forever Boyfriend's a girl," Lila said finally. "Her name's Cassie."

"So . . . you're gay?"

"Yeah."

Saskia took a deep breath. It took a few moments for Lila's admission to sink in. She hadn't known her friend that long, but she'd thought she'd known her deeply, essentially, the way you knew a sibling. The fact that she hadn't known this core part of Lila was upsetting—partly because Saskia hadn't been savvy enough to figure it out before, partly because this new information clouded what she already knew of Lila, and partly—well, mostly—because Lila hadn't trusted her enough to tell her earlier.

"Why didn't you tell me?" Saskia demanded, surprised by the jagged accusation in her voice. She'd confided just about everything to Lila, but her friend had kept the biggest secret of her life to herself. Friendship wasn't friendship if it was one-sided. She'd learned that the hard way from Heather.

"I was scared," admitted Lila.

"But you're my best friend," Saskia replied, a little embarrassed to say it out loud. Yet now that she'd gone there, she might as well let it all out. "And besides, you promised, remember? You said, 'From now on, we tell each other what's going on. Everything.'"

"I remember."

"So why didn't you tell me *everything*?"

"Because it was complicated—and awkward."

Saskia shook her head in annoyance. "I don't understand."

"Okay, here it is: I liked you. In *that* way. When you came to Coventon, I had a crush. It's not easy to be best friends with someone you secretly want as your girlfriend."

"Oh." Saskia's cheeks warmed.

"I knew this would be awkward," Lila complained, rolling her eyes. "Don't get all weird on me, okay? Because I don't feel that way anymore. First of all, it's clear you're straight. And second of all, I like someone else—Cassie."

"Cassie?"

"Yeah, my Mercury Girl."

"Oh," Saskia repeated, feeling weird, just like Lila had predicted. "I just wish you'd told me before . . ."

"Well, this isn't really about you. It's about me. And I needed to do it in my own time."

Saskia nodded. "You're right."

"Listen, we're still the same people. And we're still gonna be best friends—I mean, assuming you still want to be."

"I do!"

"Good."

"Good." Saskia looked at Lila shyly. "So what happens now?"

"Hell if I know."

"Do you think you'll come out to other people?"

Lila exhaled audibly. "I don't know. It's not easy. I have no desire to wrap myself in a rainbow flag and parade down the school hall-ways with an LGBTQ sign."

"Come on, it doesn't have to be like that."

"Yeah, but it's still a big deal."

"Have you told anyone? Your family?"

"I'm out online. I have a bunch of friends there—a pretty good community."

"So is Cassie, like, your first girlfriend?"

Now it was Lila who blushed. "We're both new to this, but I've been really happy. Over-the-moon happy. And I'm way over you, in case you're wondering."

Embarrassed, Saskia waved her off. "What's this girl like?"

Lila reached over and opened the glove compartment. There in a manila envelope was the daguerreotype. Saskia studied it carefully. Cassie was a pretty girl with dark hair parted in the middle.

"She seems . . . sure of herself," Saskia said at last.

"Yeah, she's really confident."

"Is she out?"

Lila shook her head. "No way. Are you forgetting she lived in the 1800s? Like, *gay* still meant 'happy' then! And *queer* meant 'weird'!"

Saskia delicately put the daguerreotype back in the envelope and handed it to Lila. "I'm glad you showed me this."

"Me, too . . ."

"But you're still worried, aren't you?"

"Yeah."

"Don't—it'll be fine."

"But will *we* be fine?" asked Lila nervously.

"Yes. We will be fine, and we are fine. I don't have the energy to make another best friend."

Lila smiled. "Listen, please don't tell the other members of the club."

"Of course not."

"It's just . . . I'm not ready. And besides, who knows how they'd react?"

"Probably with more drinking, knowing Paige and Sara Beth."

Lila giggled. "It's late," she said after a beat. "Let's get you home." She started the engine. Saskia, thinking her friend looked relieved, leaned over to give her a hug.

Lila

In carriage after carriage they came. Some arrived on horseback. Others on foot. Dozens and dozens of women. Lila watched their gusseted, buttoned boots step tentatively on the dusty road. Some of their boots looked new. Others were well worn, the leather weathered and shabby.

The women walked to the front of Wesleyan Chapel: two unassuming stories of red brick. Staring at it, they wiped sweat from their faces with cotton handkerchiefs. Then they glanced at one another in curiosity, but also in silent allegiance.

Standing apart, Lila tried to count the women. She stopped at a hundred. There were too many to keep track of, and they were all roaming about. Some held small children by the hand. Some cuddled babies. There were a few men, too—including an African American man who looked familiar to Lila—but the women overpowered them in number and in excitement. Eagerly she wandered through the throngs, listening to clips of conversation.

"An army couldn't have kept me away!"

"They say it will last two days."

"I didn't tell my husband I was coming. Told him I was going to visit my sister in Baltimore."

"I told mine, and all he worried about was his supper!"

"I heard the organizers met at an abolitionist convention."

"I heard they're a couple of firebrands."

"If they can help raise my wages, I don't care who they are."

Talk was suddenly halted by a bustling woman making her way through the group, her long skirts swishing authoritatively. As she moved, the crowd parted for her. She cupped her hands to her mouth and called out, "Meeting's about to begin! Please enter the church!"

As the woman swept past Lila, her hair bounced in tight curls under a bonnet. She wore a brooch at her throat and a no-nonsense expression. Her voice carried so well, it wasn't long before people heeded her call and filed into the church. Lila let herself be carried along with the crowd.

Inside the chapel, the air felt thick and sultry. Lila found a place in a pew in between a woman who continually fanned herself and another whose hat was so big it brushed Lila's shoulder. She was lucky to have found a spot at all; the place was packed. The mood reminded her, oddly, of the mood before a rock concert. Electric. There was a pulse in the air she could almost feel, and a sense of anticipation that grew stronger by the second.

Finally, two women ascended the altar. One was the woman who had just ushered in the crowd. The other, thin and delicate looking, was a little older—probably in her forties. She wore a shawl over her long-sleeve dress. Just looking at her made Lila sweat. It had to be close to a hundred degrees inside, and she was willing to bet her library salary that deodorant hadn't been invented yet.

The younger woman stood behind the pulpit, flanked by the elder. Side by side, the women jogged something in Lila's memory. Again, she felt a strange sense of familiarity. But she couldn't put her finger on why. She hadn't met these women before, that much was certain.

"Welcome to the Seneca Falls Convention," the younger woman said, her voice forceful and resolute. Except for the lone howl of a baby, the room went quiet. "We are here today to discuss the social, civil, and religious condition and rights of women. My name is Elizabeth Cady Stanton, and this is Lucretia Mott."

Lila suddenly felt goose bumps. "Holy sh—" she murmured.

"Quiet!" came a stern rebuke from beside her. The hat lady frowned.

"Sorry!" Lila whispered.

Awestruck, she stared at the pulpit, trying to wrap her brain around the fact that two of the most famous women in American history were standing right in front of her. She'd read about

Elizabeth Cady Stanton. She'd written a report about her in sixth grade. And Seneca Falls—this was where it had all started. Women's liberation. The very first women's rights convention had been held right here. If not for this convention, women still might not be able to vote, to own property, to go on to higher education.

To be counted.

Breathe, Lila reminded herself. She had to pinch herself as she listened to Stanton read from the Declaration of Sentiments and Grievances. It was a treatise she had drafted, she said, using America's own Declaration of Independence as a template.

> We hold these truths to be self-evident; that all men and
> women are created equal; that they are endowed by their
> Creator with certain inalienable rights; that among these
> are life, liberty, and the pursuit of happiness . . .

Lila was in such a state of shock and reverie that she couldn't say why she turned her head suddenly. She didn't know why she glanced away from the famous speaker and toward the back of the chapel, where one more visitor filtered in: a girl with black hair parted in the middle and pulled back in the style of the times. She looked around nervously, and not finding a seat, sat right on the floor.

The girl hadn't made a peep. But Stanton halted her speech to address the girl. "You there, young lady," she said.

"Me?" the girl said, her cheeks flushed.

"Yes, you."

"I'm so sorry . . . I didn't mean to interrupt."

"Yes, well, never mind that. There's an empty spot in that pew, fourth row back. We don't want you sitting on the ground."

"Thank you, ma'am," the girl said, then hurried with a ducked head to the spot where she had been directed.

Stanton returned to her speech, and the audience forgot all about the girl. But Lila didn't. It was no coincidence that she'd observed the girl's entrance. Here now was Lila's flesh-and-blood Mercury Girl.

She wore a different dress, and her hair was different, too. But there was no mistaking her resemblance to the daguerreotype.

Focus, Lila told herself. *Focus.*

She turned back to Elizabeth Cady Stanton, who discussed the many injustices women were facing. She read all eighteen grievances and eleven resolutions in the Declaration of Sentiments and Grievances. Then she called upon the audience to demand equality, to organize, rally, and petition. Someone asked for the full declaration to be read again—paragraph by paragraph. This time women in the pews stood up to make suggestions. They threw off lifetimes of forced compliancy and embraced the revolutionary. The room grew ever hotter. Lila got worked up.

After more than three exhausting, exhilarating hours, the moderator finally called for a break. The group was to adjourn back in the church at two thirty.

Outside, dripping in sweat, Lila scanned the crowd until she spotted the girl. Cautiously, she followed her to the shade of an oak tree. Not surprisingly, others also sought shade. The spot was crowded. But somehow Lila felt like she and the girl were all alone.

Only a couple of yards separated them. Lila nervously wondered what to say. Fortunately, the girl addressed her first. "Do you want some water? It was awfully hot in there."

"Yes, thank you," Lila replied gratefully.

"Here, have some of my lunch, too. I always pack more than I can eat."

"Wow, that's so generous of you." Lila accepted a boiled egg and piece of corn bread. She tried to look the girl in the eye but peered at the ground instead.

"It was an incredible morning, wasn't it?"

"Magical," Lila agreed, cracking the egg and thumbing the shell. "I think it will be a big moment in history."

"Do you really think so?"

"I'm sure of it."

"My name's Cassie," the girl said. Lila took a deep breath and introduced herself, trying again to look at Cassie's face. She was rewarded for her second effort with a warm smile and the most luminous eyes she'd ever seen.

Cassie began to talk about the convention, about the individual grievances and resolutions. Lila tried to concentrate, but it was hard not to be distracted by the sound of Cassie's voice, the heart shape of her lips.

"Do you think the ninth resolution will pass?" Cassie asked.

"Which one is that?"

"Women's suffrage, of course."

"Yes, it'll pass. It has to."

"Someone told me Lucretia Mott herself doesn't think women should vote." Cassie wrinkled her nose in distaste. "But voting is everything, isn't it? It's power."

"And a voice," added Lila.

"And influence."

"Control."

"Equality."

"Independence."

Cassie laughed. "Maybe *you* should stand beside Mrs. Stanton."

"I think you'd be a better fit," Lila volleyed.

"I'm only a teacher," Cassie lamented. "And I don't have much power at all, sadly. There's a long list of things I can't do."

"Like what?"

"Well, I can't dress in bright colors, especially not red. I can't marry or go to ice cream stores. I can't wear fewer than two petticoats or forget to scrub the floor of the school every day. And I *can't*," she stressed, rolling her eyes, "wear a hemline shorter than two inches from the ground. The town rector made all these rules."

"That's crazy."

"I've been at the school for three years, and every year his list grows longer. I hate it. My job is to teach the children, not measure my hemline with a ruler."

"I couldn't agree more."

"Are you employed? Or married?" Cassie asked.

"Neither. I mean, I work a little in a library."

Cassie's eyes widened. "How wonderful! To be surrounded by books—what a dream."

Suddenly she moved closer and bent her head toward Lila's intimately. A new wave of heat coursed through Lila's body. "They're making fun of this convention," Cassie confided.

"Who is?"

"Everyone—at least in my town. They say we're miscreants. That we don't know our place."

"Don't worry," Lila said. "History will prove them wrong. Today is going to change everything."

Again, Cassie's gleaming eyes widened. "How can you be so sure?"

"I just have a feeling."

"Well, let's hope your feeling is right. Say, can I tell you something?"

Lila's heart seemed to stop mid-beat. "Anything."

"Just now I made a decision. I'm not going back to teaching."

"Really?"

"Yes. I've been thinking on it for a long time, but talking to you helped me make up my mind."

"What are you gonna do?"

"Go west. To San Francisco. My brother's out there."

"You're gonna stay with him?"

"No. He doesn't want me. He says California's no place for a lady." Cassie's voice dropped to a soft whisper. "Many of the women there work in brothels. They call themselves *entertainers*."

"Tell me that's not why you're going," Lila said.

Cassie raised her chin indignantly. "Of course not. I'm going for the gold. Why, just two months ago, my brother found a nugget worth two hundred dollars. Imagine that!"

Lila tried to imagine Cassie squatting in a streambed, a pickax in one hand, a pan in the other. She was wearing red. It wasn't hard to envision.

"I have it all planned in my mind," Cassie continued. "I've saved

up enough to go by ship. It will be a long journey around Cape
Horn, but I have a hearty constitution. I'm not one to take sick."

Lila had the sudden urge to ask, *Can I come, too?* But she
quashed it quickly. She'd only known Cassie for a matter of minutes, after all. She didn't want to scare her off. "Where will you
stay?"

Cassie shrugged. "Maybe in a boarding house. I'll find something. If I can survive twenty-six children, I can survive this. Besides,
I've always fancied myself lucky. My brother says that's all it takes
to find gold. Luck and patience."

"Would you write a letter to—?" Lila began.

"Look there!" Cassie interrupted. Lila followed Cassie's excited
gaze and saw the same distinguished-looking African American
man she'd glimpsed earlier. "It's Frederick Douglass, the famous
abolitionist! Did you know he supports our cause?"

So that's who it was, thought Lila. This day was bringing no end
of breathtaking revelations.

"We're all in the same boat, aren't we?" continued Cassie. "None
of us treated as people. All of us second-class. But look"—she gestured to the dozens and dozens of women all around them—"our
numbers are growing. We won't be second-class for long."

Lila, too, took in the throngs of excited freethinkers. She
glimpsed Elizabeth Cady Stanton again, talking animatedly, her
every word like the beat of a drum, inciting her supporters to reach
higher, to fight harder.

"A fire has been lit, don't you think?" Cassie said, taking Lila's
hand and squeezing it. Lila swore she could feel her Mercury Girl's
pulse through her soft skin.

"It's already a full-blown bonfire," she replied.

CHAPTER FOURTEEN

Saskia's father intercepted her while she was doing laundry. As she transferred a batch of dowdy gray and brown clothes from the washer to the dryer, he hovered nearby, awkwardly waiting for her to finish. In the past week they'd been passing like ships in the night. Her father would leave the house as she arrived, or vice versa. They'd exchanged maybe ten sentences, most of them being, "good night" or "see you later."

Saskia pushed the START button on the dryer, grateful for the white noise the machine created. She had a feeling her father wanted to have a talk—a talk she wasn't ready for.

"I don't have to go in until five," he told her.

Making a quick calculation, Saskia winced. Six hours. She and her father had six hours together. "*Gilmore Girls?*" she asked hopefully.

"Nah, let's do something active. I don't want to sit around."

"I'm tired," she said.

"Tired of doing what?"

Uh-oh, here it comes. You need to look for a job. You need to come home earlier. You need to be more responsible. You need to communicate with your mother.

"Let's go for a walk," he suggested.

"No, Dad. It's way too hot."

"Okay, somewhere with air-conditioning. The grocery store?"

Saskia sighed. It was as good a place as any. Besides, if her father wanted a heart-to-heart, it was better to have it in public. If need be, she could wriggle out of answering, act shy, embarrassed, or distracted.

"Fine," she agreed.

In the car, her father mentioned a surge in overdoses at the hospital. All kinds of people were being brought in. Adults abusing pain pills, teens gorging themselves on over-the-counter medicine. "The kids, they're looking for an easy high. We've seen a lot of dextromethorphan and pseudoephedrine abuse." He glanced at her nervously as he steered the car around a bend. "You're not into that, are you?"

"Of course not." Saskia looked away, thinking she needed to find a better place to hide the baggie of pills. Not that she was taking any, but her father would freak out if he suspected she was. Pills or no pills, she had to admit she was taking risks. Unnecessary risks.

Only last night, thinking about what Paige had said, she'd put a drop of mercury on her tongue, let it roll down her throat. She'd imagined it would taste like a dirty coin in her mouth, but that wasn't the case.

It had felt smooth and tasted bland. When she'd tilted back her head, how quickly it had slipped down her throat and into her stomach. Too fast for her to stop it.

"I had to ask." Her father paused. "You know, it's normal to want to experiment," he continued. "You'll hear about new things, things you'll want to try. And other kids will encourage you—push you, even."

"Dad, I've listened to about a hundred speeches on peer pressure and bullying. No one's *pushing* me."

"Don't be testy. This is just a conversation. I've noticed you've been more withdrawn lately. Every time I look for you, you're in your room." He paused. "Or off with those girls."

"You mean, my friends? You wanted me to make friends, remember?"

"Yes, but sometimes you get home in the middle of the night. Your hours are almost as bad as mine. That's not acceptable. I think maybe I've given you too long a leash. I have no idea what you've been up to or what's going on in your head."

Saskia fidgeted. "Nothing's wrong, Dad." After swallowing the mercury, she'd been up all night, paranoid with worried, sick with fear. So much for incredible dreams. She hadn't slept a wink. In the morning, she'd been grateful, though. Grateful to still be alive.

"Look, I don't want to fight. I realize you're still trying to process everything—the separation and the move and all that. But if there's more—if something, or someone, is bothering you—you can tell me. I'm not gonna punish you. I just want to *know*."

"Why?"

"Why?" her father snapped. He banged his hand, newly bandaged, on the steering wheel. "Because I'm your father. Because I was a kid once, too, believe it or not. Because I work at a hospital and see what happens when people make bad decisions. There are consequences, Sask, and they're not always pretty. A boy went into cardiac arrest yesterday after taking too much Advil. Advil!"

A morbid uneasiness settled over Saskia. She was feeling terrified about what that drop of mercury could do. Might have already done. She'd read online how it would feel to die by mercury. A prickly, pins-and-needles feeling in your mouth. The gradual disappearance of peripheral vision. The slurred words, shakes, and poor balance of a drunk. Add to that mood swings, difficulty breathing, and kidney failure, and you had yourself a full-fledged nightmare.

Staring out the car window, she was aware she was brooding obsessively, but she couldn't stop. Would that one drop be enough to kill her? What about the vaporized mercury she inhaled whenever she opened the vial? Suddenly, there was so much to worry about.

"I'm fine," she said, her hands in knots.

"From a diagnostic perspective, I disagree," her father retorted. "You've changed. You're sleeping a lot and less active. You've gotten thinner . . ."

She laughed in spite of herself. If only her dad took a good look at Paige, Sara Beth, and Adrienne.

He chuckled, too, unsure of what to make of her reaction. "Look, maybe everything is fine. Maybe this is normal. God knows I don't know what it's like to be a teenage girl. All I know is that it must be hard. So remember I'm here, okay? You are my first . . ." He paused. "You are my *only* priority."

Saskia kept staring out the window, watching everything zip by in a blur, an abstract collage of shapes and colors. Funny how ordinary things looked completely different when you were in motion. She couldn't help but wonder if the world really was blurry, and by standing still, people distorted its rightful appearance. For a fleeting moment, she debated telling her father about the daguerreotypes and the Mercury Boys, about her dreams, and the club. And Cornelius. How he'd changed her—expanded her mind, and maybe her heart, too. Ever since she'd visited the lighting store, reality had mutated. All the colors were suddenly bleeding through the lines. She couldn't find the boundaries anymore.

But to speak of Cornelius meant revealing secrets she'd promised to keep. It meant betraying Paige and the other girls. Why take that risk when her father might not understand? He was worried about her—that was what this car ride was all about. What if her admission made him so worried that he took away the daguerreotype and forbade her from seeing her friends?

And there was another reason to keep quiet. Maybe it was selfish, but she recognized that part of the reason Cornelius was so precious was his obscurity. If she shared him with her father, or any adult, she'd drag him into the light. And the truth was, she preferred him in the shadows. There, she could imagine what she liked. Her mind was free to fill in the question marks and blank spaces. In the darkness, Cornelius was all hers.

"We're here," her father said.

Saskia snapped to attention. Looking around, she saw that the car was parked, that the world was still again. In front of Shop Smart, rows of cars stood like soldiers at attention, and orphaned shopping carts waited on the steaming asphalt. People scurried to and fro. Lost, it seemed to Saskia. She looked at all that and put the idea of sharing to rest.

In the store, surrounded by people, Saskia felt better. She and her father scouted the aisles, leaving their previous conversation behind. With a grin, he brought up the Kyinkyinga, which he had burned. "If I'd just taken them off the indoor grill sooner . . ."

"They would have been good," she replied.

"And used more cayenne pepper. You can never use too much cayenne pepper."

"Uh, you can *definitely* use too much cayenne pepper."

"It was the wood skewers that burned. They say you're supposed to soak them first."

"Good to know."

"I didn't realize they could catch on fire so fast." Her father scratched his head and steered the cart around a display of baked beans. "Maybe we ought to invest in an outdoor grill."

"Next summer," she said, thinking the last thing they needed was another big bill.

Her period had started, and she said she had to go get "girl stuff"—a euphemism he instantly understood. They split up, agreeing to meet back at the meat section in a few minutes for Kyinkyinga, take two.

She browsed the tampon section, marveling as always at why little cardboard tubes and cylindrical cotton wads cost ten bucks a box. It was highway robbery. Making a selection, she proceeded down the aisle . . . only to run into Josh.

His hair was mussed-up in its usual rock-star way, not like hers, which looked like she'd stuck her finger in an electrical socket—twice. The truth was, even under the too-bright fluorescent lights of Shop Smart, he looked great. Even better than she remembered. He was with another kid, a guy Saskia vaguely remembered from school.

Instantly, she wished she were somewhere else, anywhere, even back in the car listening to her father. Could anything be worse than running into your crush while holding a jumbo-size box of Tampax? Saskia grimaced. *Not crush*, she told herself. *Ex-crush*. She wasn't Adrienne, after all, flitting between two boys, one living and one dead. No, Cornelius was the only one she was interested in.

"What's up?" Josh said, smiling at her.

"Nothing. Just shopping with my dad." Saskia positioned the tampons behind her back and glanced at the other boy.

"You guys know each other?" asked Josh. He was standing close to her, uncomfortably close. "This is Benny. He's our year."

She nodded in shy recognition.

"What have you been doing with yourself?" Josh went on.

"Not much. Seeing friends, mostly. Paige and Adrienne and Lila . . ."

She realized, suddenly, that Josh was wearing the same T-shirt as *that night*. The discovery made her heart quiver. *Stop, Saskia, stop*. "What about you? Keeping busy?" Her voice seemed to be coming from someone else, the sound of it foreign to her ears. With Josh mere inches away, she felt strangely insubstantial, like dandelion fluff in the wind.

"Shoot—nothing, really. Playing music. Benny on drums, me on guitar. We've started a band. We still need a bass player, though. Know anyone?"

She shook her head.

"You play anything?"

For the first time in her life, Saskia wished she'd indulged her mother and taken piano lessons. Again she shook her head.

"Can you sing?"

"Not unless you want your audience to wear earplugs."

Josh laughed. "You should come by sometime. We're at his house—in the garage—every night, practicing."

"Trying to rack up as many noise complaints as we can," Benny added.

Saskia smiled.

"You said you hang out with Adrienne?" asked Benny. "How's she doing?"

She realized with a start that Benny was Benjamin. *The* Benjamin. Adrienne's Benjamin.

Ding, ding, ding.

"She's fine."

"I haven't seen her for a while. She got mad about something I did—it was stupid."

"You mean, when you guys went for ice cream?"

He looked surprised that she knew. "No, after that. We were hiking. In Sleeping Giant State Park—you know it? She got mad 'cause I took my dog off his leash and he ran away."

Saskia couldn't believe they'd gone out again. Benjamin seemed to sense her surprise.

"I wanted to talk to her. I wanted to make sure everything's cool, even if we're not gonna be together."

"Yeah, I get it."

"You guys pretty close?" he asked her.

"I'd say so," she replied cautiously.

"When you see her, can you tell her to hit me up? I need to talk to her about one other thing." He looked nervous and insecure, like he was the one holding a bright pink box of tampons.

"Yeah, okay."

Silently, the three of them looked at one another. She waited, hoping Josh would reissue his invitation and tell her where the heck Benjamin's garage was. Then again, maybe he didn't want her to visit. Maybe it had just been something to say, a way to be polite. She tried to catch his eye, but he seemed distracted. She could never hold his attention for long.

"Well, I gotta get going," she said, before he could.

"Yeah, us, too," replied Josh.

"It was good to meet you," Benny said, sticking out his hand. She clasped it firmly, like her dad had taught her to do long ago.

Josh nodded a goodbye—it seemed to Saskia a half-hearted gesture. She gave him, in return, a half smile. Before she knew it, he and Benjamin were trudging away. She continued to feel strange, like she was only partly there. Maybe because Josh had taken her self-esteem with him. She looked at the box of tampons and thought quite seriously about hurling it at his head.

A flood of feelings rose up in her. Excitement, disappointment, desire, anger. She was surprised by how strong those feelings were. The run-in colored her mood for the rest of the day. Even so, she was glad it had happened. Glad because it made her appreciate Cornelius even more. Cornelius, who never ignored her or confused her. Cornelius, who never let her down.

Saskia

Saskia stood in front of a run-down house. Beside her, Cornelius gripped two heavy leather satchels in his hands. Saskia wasn't sure what they contained, nor was she sure where she was. It was probably a neighborhood on the fringes of Philadelphia, judging from the dingy, weatherworn houses and buildings. They looked similar to the ones she'd seen on previous occasions with Cornelius. She glanced around. Piles of ashes and animal droppings fouled the street. A mangy dog yelped, and an unseen baby cried. Passersby looked somber, grime and worry etched on their faces as they trudged down the street. Even the children seemed to carry a burden: shoulders slumped, eyes on the ground. Saskia glanced at her clean white blouse, which had been part of her old school chorus uniform, and felt guilty.

"Who lives here?" she asked, nodding at the door. It was unpainted, the wood warped and splintery.

"A woman I met yesterday. She asked me to do her a favor."

Saskia wondered what kind of favor but decided not to ask. She would find out soon enough. Unthinkingly, she scratched at a Band-Aid on her finger, which covered the healing blister. Lately, the wound had started to itch like crazy.

"What happened to your finger?" Cornelius asked. He set down the satchels and took her hand gently.

Saskia shrugged. She didn't want to tell him the truth for a lot of different reasons. "I burned it on the stove," she lied, repeating what she'd told her dad.

"Does it ail you?" he asked worriedly.

Saskia hesitated. "I'm ailed—a little." Cornelius smiled amusedly, causing Saskia to question her word choice. "Whatever. I'm fine now," she said defensively.

But he continued to stare at her finger with an expression she'd seen before, back when he'd first spotted the Velcro on her sneakers.

"It's called a Band-Aid," she said.

"The object covering the burn?"

She nodded. He investigated it with great care, as if the Band-Aid were an astonishing technological breakthrough, or an unsolved mystery.

"It's doesn't match," she muttered. "I mean, it's way paler than my skin."

They hadn't talked about this difference between them. She wasn't sure she wanted to.

Cornelius shook his head. "I am only wondering how it stays in place?"

She laughed, a little relieved. "It's sticky."

"Sticky?" He continued to stare at the Band-Aid with such studious fascination that Saskia peeled it off and offered it to him.

"I couldn't," he said.

"Too gross?"

"Not at all. But you need it." He looked pointedly at her still-ugly wound.

"I'd rather let it heal on its own now."

At that, he cupped his hand, and she placed the soiled Band-Aid into his palm. His eyes glowed with genuine gratitude, as if she'd gifted him a rare gem. The absurdity made her laugh again. He carefully tucked the Band-Aid into his pocket and smiled at her.

Resuming a serious expression, he knocked on the door. At first, there was no sound from the inside, and then Saskia could make out faint footsteps. He knocked again. On the first floor, someone moved aside a stained oilcloth from a window and peeked out. Saskia only caught a glimpse of a woman with a pale, narrow face and sad-looking eyes.

A moment later, the woman opened the door.

"Mrs. Rothschild," Cornelius said, bowing slightly.

"Mr. Cornelius," she replied politely. Up close Saskia could see that it wasn't just the woman's eyes that were sad. Her whole body conveyed a sense of deep sorrow, even devastation. Saskia saw it in the pitiful stoop of her back, in her pigeon-toed stance, in the fine pink veins threading the whites of her eyes.

"I'm so sorry for your loss," he said.

"It was very kind of you to come," Mrs. Rothschild said. "I didn't know if you would."

"I gave you my word."

"Yes, but when there is no money on the table, sometimes words are forgotten."

Cornelius shook his head. "Money means nothing in this case. Losing a child—there's no greater sorrow."

Fresh tears sprang to the woman's eyes. Cornelius handed her a clean handkerchief from his pocket.

"My boy fought hard, but it was too much, the fevers and chills," Mrs. Rothschild said, wiping her eyes. "And then the coughing—terrible coughing. When blood came up, I knew it was the end. God was calling him."

"Yes, and now he is beside the Almighty Father in heaven," Cornelius reassured her.

"It's a better place than here," Mrs. Rothschild said, her eyes flickering toward the street.

"That it is."

"But I didn't want him to go—not so soon. He was only seven. Maybe I'm selfish." She closed her eyes, obviously trying to suppress a fresh round of tears. When she opened them again, she seemed to notice Saskia for the first time.

"My assistant," Cornelius said as the woman appraised her. "I hope you don't mind her presence."

Mrs. Rothschild took Saskia in from bottom to top, starting with her modern flats and ending with her wild black hair. Saskia was aware of how extraordinary she must look: a Black girl in strange clothes accompanying a prominent and well-respected white businessman. Their pairing was bizarre, even scandalous. But the woman was clearly too steeped in grief to give the matter much thought. She opened the door and stepped aside, gesturing for them to come in. Saskia went in first, followed by Cornelius, who hoisted the satchels.

The inside of the apartment was as bleak as the exterior. The front room where they entered was small, low-ceilinged, and sparsely furnished. Saskia saw three mismatched chairs and a scuffed table. On top of it sat a basket of rags, a Bible, and a few potatoes riddled with eyes. She spied a little cast-iron cooking stove surrounded by ashes. Beside it was an open sack of flour. Some of the flour had spilled onto the floor, mingling with mud tracked in from the streets. Out of the corner of her eye, Saskia saw something small—a mouse, a cockroach?—scurry across the floor, disappearing into a hole in the wall.

"He's in the other room," Mrs. Rothschild said. "I laid him on the bed. He was so light by the end . . ."

Saskia felt tiny hairs prick up on the back of her neck. She didn't want to step into the other room. Nevertheless, Mrs. Rothschild led them through a narrow doorway.

It turned out her tenement consisted of two rooms: the room where they'd entered, and this one—a tiny space for sleeping. With no windows or ventilation, it was even less pleasant than the front room. Worse, it stank of sickness.

Through the shadows, Saskia made out crumbling plaster walls and a mattress on the ground. The dead boy lay upon it. His eyes were open, but they were vacant, hollow. His clothes were stained with blood, vomit, bits of straw and god knew what else. She shuddered.

"Do you have other children?" Cornelius asked.

"Two older girls." Mrs. Rothschild sniffed. "They ran off last year. Lord knows what became of them."

"And your husband?"

"He ran off, too."

Cornelius nodded, as if her story were a common one. Saskia realized with a jolt that it probably was. "So you are alone, then?" he asked.

Mrs. Rothschild narrowed her eyes. Sensing her discomfort, he took out an envelope from his pocket and tried to hand it to her.

"Here is a little something. It's not much, but it may help you for a month or two, till you get back on your feet."

Her hesitation turned into surprise. "Oh, I couldn't, sir. You've been too kind already."

Cornelius pressed the envelope into her hand. She paused a moment, and then her fingers closed over it gratefully.

"We'll need more light to make the photograph," Cornelius observed, glancing around the room.

"Then we'll need to move him," Saskia said.

"I'll carry him into the other room."

Saskia watched, her heart pounding, as Cornelius ever so gently lifted the boy like a rag doll from the mattress and brought him into the front room. He set the boy down into a chair and arranged his limbs so that he appeared to be sitting at the table. It was the most macabre thing she'd ever seen.

"Does he have other clothes?" Cornelius asked.

Mrs. Rothschild shook her head, ashamed.

"No matter," he replied, carefully picking straw off the boy's clothes and out of his hair. His head kept lolling forward. Cornelius tried several times to prop it up, but it wouldn't stay. Finally, he unwound the white scarf from around his own neck. He tied it securely around the boy's neck, then looped and knotted it around the back of the chair, forcing the boy's head to stay up.

Saskia had read a little about postmortem photography in researching daguerreotypes. She remembered that extreme measures were often taken to make the dead appear alive and animated. On the Internet, she'd seen pictures of iron headrests fitted to the backs of chairs and other tools that looked like medieval torture devices. They'd struck her as gruesome, but she supposed they were simply part of Victorian culture.

Cornelius took a step back and observed the boy. The child's pallor was gray-blue, his eyes the color of water. But this was the best he was going to look. Time was the enemy now, Saskia realized.

"There isn't much light here, neither," Mrs. Rothschild observed, her own pallor unnaturally white.

"I brought some small lamps," Cornelius replied. "Maybe they'll be enough."

"I haven't any whale oil."

"I brought that, too."

Saskia watched Cornelius open the satchels and remove their contents. Along with the lamps and oil, he'd also brought a camera, tripod, and other photographic equipment. For several moments, he stared thoughtfully at the boy and the room itself. Then he went about lighting the lamps and arranging them in different ways. He set up the camera and showed Saskia how to adjust the focus. The camera had a "slide-box design," Cornelius explained. The lens was located in the front box. A second, smaller box was placed into the back of that one. By sliding the rear box forward and back, Saskia could control the focus.

"You will take the picture," Cornelius said.

"Me?"

"You're my assistant, aren't you?"

Saskia stared at him incredulously.

"Now," he said, "when I give the signal, remove the lens cap. That will start the exposure." He looked around the room again. "I just hope the light is sufficient."

"What's the signal?" she asked.

He snapped his fingers.

"Okay."

"You'll do fine."

She gave him an uneasy smile.

During that interval, Saskia was quiet. She knew it would be fine to talk, even to move around, as long as she didn't enter the camera's frame. But a stillness had descended upon the room. Everyone appeared deep in their own thoughts. Saskia's heart went out to Mrs. Rothschild. Here she was, watching her dead son being photographed for the last time, and probably for the first time, too, when only a little while ago he'd been playing, running, talking, laughing. Doing everything a little boy should.

When Cornelius snapped his fingers, she was relieved to put the cap back on the lens. Carefully, he carried the boy back to the mattress and laid him down. Cornelius crossed the boy's arms over his chest, then pulled down his eyelids and placed coins on them to keep them in place.

"The cart will be coming soon," Mrs. Rothschild whispered.

Saskia's stomach lurched. She wished there were something she could do, something she could say. But she knew nothing would ease this woman's pain.

"The photograph will be ready in a few days," Cornelius told Mrs. Rothschild. "I'll bring it by."

"I'm much obliged. I don't have another way of remembering him."

Cornelius nodded. Saskia realized he must have heard that phrase often. She helped him gather the equipment and put it back into the satchels. More and more, she felt as if she really were his assistant, or even his collaborator.

After they bid the woman goodbye, they walked back to his photography studio on the northeast corner of Eighth Street and Lodge Alley. On the way, she praised him for helping the woman.

"I wasn't lying," he said. "Money is of no consequence when the life of a child is involved."

"How many children do you have?" she asked hesitantly. She knew over the course of his life he would have many.

"Three. And I can't imagine losing any of them."

The mention of his family filled Saskia with jealousy, guilt, and an uneasiness she couldn't escape. Though she'd never admit it aloud, it was increasingly hard for her to bear the thought that he belonged to someone else, that he could never be hers. Next to her father, Cornelius was the kindest man she'd ever met. The fact that he'd offer his services for free to a mourning mother spoke volumes about his character.

"You did a good job," he told her as he flung one of the satchels over his shoulder.

She shrugged. "It was nothing."

"It's not easy to remain composed in such situations. Sometimes I want to weep," he admitted.

She nodded. "How do you not?"

"I dig my fingernails into my palm." She put her hand over her mouth when he showed her the angry red indentations in his skin. "Then I try to remind myself that I'm doing the right thing. I firmly believe all of human morality can be distilled into three rules."

"Which are?"

He ticked them off on his fingers. "Be kind to others. Be kind to yourself. And never allow others to deter you from your chosen path."

Saskia stored this away in her mind in the same place where she stored his other advice. Sometimes he was a fount of wisdom. "Do you ever break your own rules?"

He smiled sheepishly. "All the time. But one can keep trying."

CHAPTER FIFTEEN

About an hour before Saskia was due to leave for Paige's house, the home phone rang. Saskia and her father looked at each other in surprise. Since the move to Coventon, the home phone hadn't made a peep. Saskia thought of it as a fossil: old, dusty, and useless.

"Aren't you going to answer that?" she asked her father.

"Anyone I need to talk to has my cell," he replied.

"Then why do we have a home phone?"

"Sentimental value?"

Saskia rolled her eyes and picked it up.

"Hello?" a boy's voice said. For a breathless moment, she thought it was Josh.

"Hi," she said hopefully.

"Is this Saskia?"

"Yes."

"Uh, I don't know if you remember me. It's Benny. From Shop Smart?"

"Oh yeah, Benny. Sure, I remember." She hoped her disappointment wouldn't come through in her voice.

"So, uh, do you have a minute? I wanted to ask you something."

"Sure," she repeated. "Can you wait a sec?" She put her hand over the mouthpiece and tried to stretch the spiral cord into another room.

Her father shook his head and mouthed, *Don't bother. I'm going for a jog.* The back door closed behind him.

"So," Benny said, "did you have a chance to talk to Adrienne?"

"Um, it hasn't even been twenty-four hours since you asked."

"Yeah, I know. Sorry. I shouldn't be bothering you."

"No, it's okay." Saskia considered asking about the band, then thought better of it. She didn't want to look desperate. "Are you worried about her or something?"

"Can you tell?"

"Yeah. You seem . . . anxious."

"Kind of." He paused. " Listen, I wonder if you could give me some advice—on Adrienne?"

"What kind of advice?"

"I know she's seeing some other dude . . ."

"And?"

"He's older, right? In the army or something? She said he just came back from a tour."

"Benny, I can't go behind her back," Saskia warned.

"But you must have some details."

"None that I feel comfortable giving out."

"I just want *something*. Something helpful. It doesn't even have to be on this dude."

"I don't understand."

He sighed. "Listen, I want to win her back, but I don't know how. I was hoping you could lead me in the right direction."

Saskia wasn't sure if Benny was a die-hard romantic, a stalker, or both. "If you're looking for tips on love, I'm the wrong person to ask," she said.

Just ask your friend Josh.

"Adrienne and me . . . we used to be close, but not anymore," Benny said. "She's so distant now. I can never get ahold of her, and even when I do, she's all spacey. Do you think there's something going on with her? Could she be using?"

"Again, I don't feel right talking about this with you."

"Understandable." When he sighed again, Saskia started to feel sorry for him.

"Maybe it's time to move on," she suggested.

"I've tried! But every time I have this voice inside me saying, 'Just take one more shot. Plead your case.' Sometimes I wait outside her house, hoping she'll come out so I can talk to her. But she barely goes anywhere. Tell me, how is she seeing someone if she never leaves her house? Unless they're Skyping or sexting . . ." His voice trailed off in disgust.

"You know that saying: if you love someone, set them free. If they come back, they're—"

"Screw that saying!"

"Maybe it *is* overrated," she admitted.

"Saskia, please. Look, I've never begged in my life, but I'm begging you to help me. She listens to her friends. Maybe you could change her mind?"

"No offense, but I don't know if you can compete with this other guy. He's seen things we haven't, done things we'll never do. He's—in a whole different league."

"He can't be perfect," Benny complained.

Saskia hesitated to discourage him again. She didn't want to be cruel. Plus, he seemed intense. She wondered if further dejection might push him over the edge.

On the other hand, if she wanted to stay in the Mercury Boys Club, she couldn't be his ally.

"Benny, I can't make any promises, but I'll try to put in a good word for you."

"Really? Oh, that would be great . . ."

"Just please don't get your hopes up."

'Cause they're bound to come crashing down, she thought, saying a brisk goodbye and hanging up the phone.

At the sisters' house, Saskia didn't know whom to tell about Benny's phone call, if anyone. She had the feeling that sharing would only get her—or more likely, Adrienne—in big trouble. She really didn't want the drama. The healing blister on her finger reminded her that she'd had too much of that.

Everybody at the Sampras residence seemed to be in good spirits, Paige especially. She announced she had a surprise—something special. In the den, on the usual pieces of plush furniture, the girls sat up straight and attentive.

"Close your eyes," Paige instructed, "and don't peek."

Saskia heard the sound of footsteps and then something large and heavy being dragged across the floor. Beside her, Adrienne wiggled giddily.

"Okay, you can open them," said Paige.

There, in the middle of the room, stood an enormous old trunk. It was so big, one of the girls could easily have fit inside. The trunk had rusty, ornate buckles and fasteners and tattered leather handles. The initials MBC were painted on the side in chipped white paint.

It was a steamer trunk, Paige said. She explained that in the olden days, steamer trunks were a common kind of luggage. This one was made of steel and wood—the former rusted into a rich brown patina, the latter worn smooth by age and handling.

"Where'd you get it?" asked Adrienne, her eyes alight.

"eBay," Paige replied. "When Sara Beth and I saw the initials, we knew we had to have it."

"It's amazing," Lila said, running her fingers over the wood, which was smooth and glossy with tung oil. "Must have been expensive."

Paige flipped her hair and gave Lila a withering look. "It was worth the price."

"What are we supposed to do with it?" asked Adrienne.

"That brings me to the second part of the surprise."

"Paige and I went a little crazy on eBay," added Sara Beth. "We kept finding new things."

"Necessities," said Paige.

The sisters unsnapped the buckles and lifted the heavy lid. It groaned on ancient hinges.

"Voilà!" Paige said. Both she and her sister beamed.

Peering into the trunk, Saskia saw heaps and heaps of old clothes. They looked fragile and discolored, items you'd find in a museum or historical society. An odor of decay and dust filled the air.

"These are our period clothes," Paige informed them, "for when we meet our Forever Boyfriends. Everything here's real. We couldn't find many things from the 1800s, but most of this stuff's a hundred years old."

Paige took out the pieces one by one. She laid them carefully on the floor. Kneeling, the girls examined them up close.

"The drama club would go nuts if they saw these!" Adrienne said. She sounded as if she were swooning.

Saskia studied whalebone corsets, layered lace petticoats, buckled shoes, bonnets, bustles, fancy hats, parasols, dresses with cinched waists and puffed sleeves, and eyelet summer frocks, once white, now ivory as an elephant's tusk. She thought uncomfortably about the ladies who'd once worn these clothes. Women who were now only moldering bones in the ground.

Saskia hoped these women had living relatives who knew their stories. Knew enough to miss them. She thought about Lila's dragonfly parable, and wondered if the women who'd owned these fine things were still out there somewhere in the ether, like the Mercury Boys. Saskia shivered at the thought. More and more she felt like the line between the living and the dead was dissolving.

"Careful. It's delicate," Paige warned as Adrienne lifted up a fancy cream dress, all frothy lace and delicate appliqué. The bodice was cut low, and a train at the back was long enough to skim the floor. Something about the gown's eerie beauty sent another shiver down Saskia's spine. She realized it was a wedding dress.

"I love this one," Adrienne exclaimed.

"It's beautiful, isn't it?" Paige said.

"Totally. I wish girls dressed like this now."

"You can. In fact, you *should*."

"But it reeks!"

"Mothballs. You'll get over it."

"Is there any way to get rid of the smell?"

"Try hanging it outside for a day," Sara Beth suggested, "and letting it air out."

Adrienne held the dress against her body to see if it would fit.

"Go ahead, try it on," Paige said.

"Are your parents home?" Adrienne asked.

"Are they ever?"

Adrienne giggled and shimmied out of her clothes. In her bra and panties, she lifted the gown gingerly over her head. Paige helped her straighten it out and fasten a row of hooks and eyes on the back. In an instant Adrienne was transformed into a ghostly gothic bride, the fabric an even sharper contrast to her fiery red hair than her pallid skin. The train accentuated her height, making her seem regal, an ethereal beauty.

Before she knew it, Saskia was digging through the trunk. She wanted the same metamorphosis, this kind of transformation. But even the largest dresses looked too small. She didn't bother to try them on. Embarrassed, she dug deeper, until her hands skimmed the bottom of the trunk. One of them brushed something small and hard. A tarnished medal.

"Paige?" she asked, dangling the trinket.

"Ooh, you found it."

"Found what?"

"Surprise number three."

Saskia studied it: a round silver medal attached to a ribbon with faded stripes of blue, yellow, red, white, and green. On one side of the medal was the face of a young Queen Victoria. On the reverse Saskia made out a palm tree in the background, and a shield and cannon in the foreground. Emblazoned across the bottom was the word *CHINA*.

"It's from the Royal Navy. You know, the British equivalent of our Navy," Paige said, glancing at the medal as she, too, began changing into an ancient gown. "It's Sam's. When I visited him last night, he gave it to me. I have to tell you something: he enlisted."

"He joined the Royal Navy?!"

"Yeah, that's why he got the pin. It was given to all the men who fought in the Second China War."

"What?"

"The Second China War," Paige repeated. "I looked it up. It was also called the Second Opium War. I guess between 1857 and 1860, British and French militaries fought against China."

"Why the heck would Sam want to fight against China?"

Paige bit her bottom lip fretfully. "So . . . he wasn't accepted as Lord Tennyson's protégé. Someone else got picked. Not only that, but Tennyson wrote a letter to Sam saying that he thought Sam's talent was mediocre. *At best.*"

"Oh my god."

"Yeah, I know. Sam was devastated. *Beyond* devastated. I told him Tennyson's opinion isn't everything. Who cares what that old geezer thinks? But that didn't make him feel any better."

"So what happens now?" Saskia asked.

"He leaves soon. Tomorrow or the next day. For China! And he told me he doesn't want to see anybody—even me—when he sets sail. He said he needs time to 'grieve.'"

"He's taking it hard, huh?"

"Very."

"Do you know when he'll be back?"

"No idea. I don't even know *if* he'll be back." Paige's voice quavered. "A lot of British men were wounded. Some were killed." She blinked away a tear. "That's why he gave me his medal. To remember him. You know, just in case."

Saskia helped button the back of Paige's bodice. She worried the ancient velvet buttons would break from the pressure of her fingertips. "I hope this doesn't sound bad, but our Forever Boyfriends have already passed away, right? So maybe we don't need to worry about *how* they died. Maybe it doesn't matter."

Paige mulled that over. "Maybe. Maybe not. Either way, I'm terrified for him."

"These relationships are so complicated," Saskia lamented. "I wish our guys came with instructions."

"I know," Paige said. "They *are* complicated. And yours is probably the most complicated of all."

"What do you mean?"

"Just that . . . you know." Paige turned around and met Saskia's gaze. "On top of everything else, your Forever Boyfriend was married."

"Well, I'm not sure that's such a big deal."

"Wasn't he married for a really long time?"

"Yeah."

"And wasn't he married *with* children?"

Saskia didn't like the accusatory tone that had seeped into Paige's voice. "He and I—we're just friends."

"Come on, Saskia . . ."

"No! We just talk. Nothing else."

"But you've admitted you like him."

Saskia bristled. She felt even more annoyed when she realized the other girls were listening in on their conversation. "I guess I do. But I know he's off-limits."

"I just wonder why you picked him, that's all. Why pick someone who's taken?"

"Because I liked *Cornelius*."

Paige shrugged. "Well, if you're fine with it . . ."

On the defensive, Saskia changed the subject. She nodded toward the pin. "So how did you bring that back, anyway?"

"Sam gave it to me, like I told you. When I woke up, it was in my bed."

"I tried to take something home once. It didn't work." She told Paige about the newspaper Cornelius had bought her. "What did you do differently?"

"Maybe I'm just luckier."

In that moment, a tiny part of Saskia wanted to slap the superior smile off Paige's face. The intensity of that desire seeped into her quickly and dangerously, like water pouring through a hole in a boat, threatening a capsize. She loved Paige, but if Saskia were being a hundred percent truthful, she resented Paige, too. Everything came so easy to her. She could buy anything she wanted, have any guy in the world, and was beautiful on top of it. Even now, in an elaborate Victorian dress that would have looked ridiculous on anyone else, Paige seemed to Saskia like a glamorous extra from the movie *A Room with a View*.

"Congratulations," she told Paige, struggling to suppress her simmering annoyance. "If Sam gave you that, he must really care."

"He even used the *L* word."

"He did?"

"Yeah. Second time I've ever heard it. The first was from Josh, of course."

Saskia almost flinched. "Did you say it back—to Sam?"

"No way. He has to work for it."

At that, Paige departed to help her sister button up a dress, leaving Saskia to her own thoughts.

Saskia found herself clutching the medal so hard that Queen Victoria's face imprinted itself on her palm. Pensively, she stared at her indented flesh. Paige had touched a nerve. A raw nerve. Even if nothing physical had happened with Cornelius, Saskia knew their relationship wasn't really platonic. She didn't think of him as a friend. And she didn't go to see him because of friendship.

In all honesty, deep down, she *did* feel dirty about the relationship. Cornelius's wife wouldn't have approved of his spending so much time with another woman, just as Saskia's father never approved of Saskia's mother spending time with Ralph, claiming she was his "professional mentor." Comparing the two situations made Saskia queasy.

She brightened a little when Sara Beth turned on music. She watched Paige and Adrienne clasp each other's hands with mock seriousness and dance to a waltz. They moved about the room like whirling tops. Suddenly, Saskia remembered one of her SAT prep words: *anachronism. A person or thing that belongs to another time.* That was exactly how Paige and Adrienne looked—like people who had stepped out of history.

At the end of the song, Paige slipped on the train of Adrienne's dress. Adrienne grabbed her to keep her from falling, but both girls tumbled to the floor, giggling. When they made no effort to get back up, Sara Beth knelt down and handed them pretty red drinks in martini glasses.

"Cosmos?" asked Paige. "You read my mind."

"Don't I always?"

Sara Beth handed Saskia one of the glasses, too. She had heard of cosmopolitans before but until now had never seen one. Yet one more new experience, care of the Sampras sisters . . . As she sipped the drink, the sour kick of lime on her tongue, the music went from classical to pop, the volume turned up so loud the room vibrated.

Saskia moved her head to the beat, and then Lila got her dancing. It felt good to let go, to toss her hair, throw up her hands, and forget herself in the music. Soon, she and Lila leaped onto a coffee table, then a couch, then an ottoman. Jumping around for the hell of it, like hyper little kids, flying and free.

Paige handed her another drink. Saskia swallowed it in one go, feeling invincible. She spun in a circle, faster and faster, her unruly curls flying around her face. Even when she stopped, the room kept spinning, 'round and 'round, a never-ending carousel. She collapsed in a fit of laughter, watching the girls from the floor. They seemed larger than life, prancing around in their glamorous dresses from bygone eras, faces glistening.

Paige suggested the pool. Saskia thought it was the best idea she'd ever heard. The girls doffed their clothes—even Saskia, who'd drunk enough to finally stop body-shaming herself—and trekked out the back door. In a wild pack, they dashed to the edge of the pool and leaped in, bobbing to the surface one by one. Saskia felt a little dizzy, and her ears rang. Paige engaged her in a splash fight, but Saskia found the spray in her eyes disorienting.

"Stop!" she cried angrily.

"Are you mad at me, Sask? Don't be. I mentioned Cornelius's family because you're better than that. Better than *him*."

At that, Paige flipped over and kicked her way to the other side of the pool.

Saskia watched her disappear, then disappeared, too, air bub-
bling out of her lungs, body feeling lead heavy. She let herself sink
to the bottom and linger there, mesmerized by the mosaic scene
on the floor. Jeweled glass in shades of violet, turquoise, cerulean,
and emerald. There were creatures in the mosaic she had never
noticed before. Winged creatures, birds or butterflies. Or were
they dragonflies? Saskia couldn't tell; her eyes were stinging from
the chlorine.

The creatures started to stir. To dance. Drink had clouded her
mind, and now water was filling her mouth. Still, she traced a pair
of wings with her fingertip over and over, until her eyes closed, until
the water streamed down her throat. She tried to cough, but choked
instead.

A spasm seized her, violent and eruptive. Suddenly she felt terrified. Which way was up? Why was her body fighting itself? Who
had left her here, confused and alone?

These were the questions raging through her mind when Lila
raced down to get her in the nick of time, grabbing her arm and
forcefully yanking her to the surface.

The next morning Saskia clambered out of bed, drank about a gallon of water, and promptly threw up on her own feet. Wincing,
she touched her spinning head. She had a vague memory of Lila
unlocking the front door for her late at night and putting her to
bed. Saskia made a mental note to thank Lila later.

She called out for her dad, at once wanting his help and thankful
that he wasn't home to see her in such a state. Hastily, she wiped
up the mess, washed off her feet, and stumbled toward the kitchen.
She saw a Post-it from him on the counter; his shift had started
even before she'd arrived home last night. He'd reminded her to eat
breakfast and left a list of chores for her to do.

"Great," she muttered.

She poured a glass of orange juice and drank it down fast. Big
mistake. More puke on the floor, but at least she missed her feet this

time. Drained of energy, feeling like roadkill, she dragged herself back to bed.

Two hours later, she woke up again. Her head still ached, but at least it wasn't spinning anymore. She fetched a Tylenol and took a sip of water. Cautiously, she drank more, hoping to feel alive again.

She checked her cell phone, expecting to see a concerned text from Lila or maybe Paige, but finding one from Adrienne instead.

A: checking in. u were a lil out of it yesterday

S: no kidding. had a few too many

A: like 20 to many

S: Ha!

A: ugh. been there

S: did u know OJ = terrible for hangover?

A: 😔 could have told u that!

S: how are u?

A: um, not great.

S: ???

A: u really want to know?

S: U can't decide between e and b?

A: Haha. got me. 1 needs constant care, 1 cares for me. 1 is a man, 1 a boy. 1 gone (dead), 1 alive. 1 thinks i'm an angel, 1 thinks i'm a mess. i could go on . . .

S: ok, I get it. who do you like more? maybe that's a stupid question

A: no its not

A: i care about both

S: 1 more than the other?

A: hard to say

S: well benny cares about you a lot. that's clear

A: he's always been protective. sometimes overprotective!

S: intense is better than uninterested

A: u think so?

S: definitely

A: do u think paige would be mad if she knew i still can't decide?

S: royally. so don't tell her

A: i won't. will u?

S: never! cross my

A: thx, girl. catch you later. momz on my back to look at college apps. she doesn't no I don't want to go

S: gotcha. good luck

A: i'll need it!

S: bye

A: feel better

Sara Beth

Sara Beth was back in the Crystal Palace, watching her Mercury Boy try to work his magic. He and the old woman with the expensive brooch were too far away for her to hear their conversation. But Sara Beth could understand a lot from their body language. The old woman stiffened when he approached. Soon, though, she seemed to relax. As the man bowed deeply, the woman smiled. She tilted her head almost coquettishly when he kissed her extended hand. Sara Beth wondered what he'd said.

The duo talked for several minutes. Sara Beth strained her eyes but dared not move closer.

Finally, the woman took something out of her purse and handed it to him. They discussed something for a while longer before parting ways. Sara Beth watched the woman hobble off. As for her Mercury Boy, he positively swaggered as he returned to her. He tipped his hat, his eyes sparkling again like stars in an inky sky. Then he *surreptitiously* revealed a handful of money.

"How did you do it?" She gasped. He was holding fifty-dollar bills. A half dozen of them. How much would that be in the mid-1800s? A fortune, she realized. "What did you say to her?"

"That she knew my parents. That I remembered her fondly from my youth."

She scoffed.

"We grew up in the same place," he continued. "New Bedford, Massachusetts. It's a rich town."

"Why do I have a feeling you grew up somewhere else?"

"Baltimore."

Sara Beth shook her head.

"I told her that my father had been employed by her husband, Mr. Rodman, a whaling merchant."

"Naturally."

"He changed my family's fortune, Mr. Rodman did. Thanks to him, I was the first man in my family to go to college. And now I am studying to become a doctor."

"But you're having trouble paying for it," Sara Beth said.

"Like I said, miss," her Mercury Boy said, "you are unusually astute."

"And you're unusually manipulative."

"So I've been told."

"And she just gave you the money—simple as that?"

"Her own son is a failure. A misfit. He's had every advantage, every opportunity, and he's squandered them."

"The prodigal son."

"I, on the other hand, am committed to the welfare of others. And she supports that."

"Seriously, she believed all that?" Sara Beth demanded.

"Why wouldn't she?"

"Well, she wasn't born yesterday. More like the Stone Age."

"We are all innocent at our core."

She laughed. "Innocent is the last thing you are."

"You learn quickly."

"Learn?" she said, taken aback by his condescension. "I could teach *you* a few things."

He balked. "Is that so?"

"You're not the only one who can trick people. I've been doing it my whole life."

Again, that sparkle in his eye. It would be hard, she realized, not to fall for his charm. "If that's so," he said, "then—how did you put it?—'show me what you've got.'"

"Fine," she said, extending her hand to shake on it.

He took her hand as he'd taken Mrs. Rodman's, bending down to kiss her fingers.

"Just so you know," she warned, "I've never lost a bet."

"I have little doubt of that."

"I don't know your name.

"Mack."

"I'm Gillian."

They sized each other up. Sara Beth realized he was probably lying, too.

Then she left abruptly, having spotted her mark. He had the same qualities as the sucker Mack had chosen: old age, fancy clothing, the gleam of precious metal on his person. She knew what to do, but she was aware of a disadvantage. Her outfit. That would put him off—it would make an unseemly first impression. She'd have to compensate for it somehow.

She arrived dramatically, fainting right in front of him. She crumpled tragically, yet elegantly to the floor and tried not to move a muscle. He emitted a sound halfway between a squeak and a cry. She could hear him bending down, the old hinges of his knees creaking at the effort. She felt his old hand, dry and crepe-y, on her forehead. She sensed him leaning over her. Was he listening to her breathing? Was he searching for a heartbeat?

After a minute Sara Beth came to, pretending to be groggy. Her eyelids fluttered open. His face was directly over hers, inches away. It would have been an intimate moment if not for the people who had amassed around them, loitering with concern and curiosity. She wished they would go away. It would be easier to get this done without an audience. She looked into his face and for a split second saw the youthful man he had been once, before old age had settled over him like a tattered quilt. His eyes still keen and adroit. His hair, though white, still thick. If she squinted, she could erase the deep lines and liver spots on his face.

In that same second, she realized she would be the same way, eventually. Old. Weakened by time. Robbed of her looks.

And then she realized with a wallop, that Mack—though long gone in one realm—was immortal in this one. Like a prehistoric insect preserved in amber. Always the impishly charming scamp in the daguerreotype. This realization doubled her resolve to win whatever game they were playing.

Sara Beth knew what she had to do. She and Paige had played this role before, many times and for many reasons. The key was making the right impression: vulnerable, but not needy; grateful, but not indebted; alluring, but not provocative. She had to make an unspoken promise—the promise of her body, even if she had no intention of making good on it.

She clasped the old man's hand and pressed it to her chest. "Thank you," she whispered, her eyes wide and appreciative. "Sir, would you mind helping me up?"

"Careful, my dear. You've had quite a fall," he replied, giving her his hand. She pulled herself up slowly, careful not to tug very hard on the man, who was too frail to rely on. Pretending to feel dizzy, she clung to him just for a moment, enough time for him to feel the shape of her body.

"Can you stand on your own?" he asked, attempting to brace her with his feeble arms.

"I . . . I don't know. I think so," she murmured, her hands gliding over the corded edges of his silk waistcoat.

He held her in place until she found her footing, her eyes on his the whole time. When she assured him that she could stand on her own, a look of accomplishment, of something like pride, shone on his face.

"Thank you," she said. "You're such a gentleman."

"Are you sure you're well?"

"I'll be fine. I just felt so faint, and this place is so warm."

"It's the windows," the old man said, motioning to the glass walls. "Too many windows. An architectural vanity." He shook his head. "I feel a little faint myself."

"But you're so strong," she insisted.

"You must rest, young lady. Do you have someone who can help you home?"

She shook her head. "I'm by myself, but I'll be fine. I feel much better already."

He looked at her doubtfully.

"Really," she assured him. The people who had gathered were

losing interest in this bit of drama. They scattered one by one, to
Sara Beth's relief. Soon she and the man were alone.

"Are you sure?"

"Yes. But thank you. I won't forget your kindness."

"I think I should help you home."

She shook her head and gave him a last smile before inserting
herself into the crowd once again. When she returned to Mack,
who had watched the whole thing from a distance, she smiled tri-
umphantly. She pulled at the bottom of her shirt, wishing it would
stretch enough to hide the bulge in her pocket.

Mack caught a glimpse of a wallet. "Did he *give* that to you?"
he asked.

"Of course not."

"Impressive."

"I told you."

Before she knew it, he had grabbed her hand. He yanked her
through the huge main room, swiftly guiding her around clusters of
people. Mack seemed to know the building by heart, and they made
their way to the nearest exit in record time.

"Hurry," she heard him say, "before he finds out." Her flip-flops,
completely inadequate for running, kept slipping. She allowed herself to be pulled along, laughing, delirious, her face flushed, the beat
of adrenaline in her veins.

Soon they were outside, the sun hanging lower than when she'd
entered. She couldn't stop laughing even when he kept pulling her
across Forty-Second Street, zigzagging around a horse-drawn carriage. The horse neighed in annoyance and reared up its front legs,
spraying dust into the air.

He led her to the same building she'd noticed earlier—the one that
was shaped like a needle. Unbelievably, the crowds were even thicker
here, bodies packed so tight that she could smell sweat, barber's soap,
and hair oil. Those odors, combined with the earthy tang of dung
and dirt, contrasted deeply with the smells of modern New York:
roasting peanuts, diesel exhaust, a hundred ethnic foods wafting
through bad ventilation systems, the occasional rancid blast of urine.

Inside the narrow building, Mack drew her in front of him, shielding her from view with his taller, broader body. "This is the tallest building in New York," he told her as they waited in line. For what? She wasn't sure. "I've been told that when you're in trouble, you should always seek higher ground."

"What's this place called?"

"Latting Observatory."

It turned out that they were waiting in line for stairs. Steadily, they followed a slow flow of people up a series of winding staircases. Though she was in good shape, Sara Beth found herself exhausted, less from exertion than from being in such cramped quarters. Still, she was grateful for the congestion. In this airless, jam-packed space, not many people noticed—or cared about—her clothing. When at last she and Mack arrived on a landing, she thought they were done.

But Mack pulled on her hand again. "Let's go higher," he said.

"How much higher?"

"All the way to the top."

She stared at him doubtfully.

"Higher ground is safer, remember?" he said.

She wasn't so sure, but she complied reluctantly.

For the rest of their ascent, Mack was right behind her, so close they were like nestled spoons. Higher and higher they climbed, the staircases seeming to her never-ending, until at last they reached the final landing. It could accommodate only a dozen people or so. She and Mack jockeyed for a coveted position in front of a window. From there, Sara Beth peered through an affixed telescope. She could see for miles. New York in the nineteenth century was a serene expanse of green and brown and blue.

"Queens, New Jersey, Staten Island—you can see it all from here," Mack said knowledgeably, as though he'd been here a hundred times. And perhaps he had. Perhaps his work required frequent retreats to higher ground.

"Do you think we're safe?" she asked.

"I think so."

"How long do we need to stay?"

"Long enough."

For the first time, she counted the bills in the wallet. Almost four hundred dollars. The second small fortune of the day. Mack whistled. "You picked the right gull," he quipped.

They stared out the window awhile longer. The sky was turning an arresting collage of oranges and pinks and purples. Sara Beth was mesmerized, glued to the view. She almost didn't notice a man in uniform appear, announcing that the building would be closing soon.

"May I walk you home?" Mack asked her as they headed for the stairs.

She again pulled at the hem of her shirt. "It's late," she hedged. The truth was, she didn't want him following her.

"Can I see you again, at least?"

"Maybe we can arrange that."

"When?"

"I'll find you."

In the empty stairwell, Mack tried to put his arms around her, but she took a step back. "I never thought I'd meet you," he said admiringly.

"What do you mean?"

"My female equivalent."

She couldn't help but think of his photo. *A daguerreotype is a mirror with a memory*, Saskia had said. Sara Beth wished she could tell him this somehow. But she knew he'd never believe it. She could hardly believe it herself.

She could tell he wanted to kiss her, but that would have to wait. They had plenty of time. And besides, she liked seeing him like this, hesitant and nervous, so different from the cocky rascal in the portrait.

They descended the last flight quickly, and then she left him abruptly. Left him to wonder. Walking down Forty-Second Street, she savored the balance of weight in her pockets: the old man's wallet in one, her Mercury Boy's fat roll of bills in the other.

CHAPTER SIXTEEN

After a couple more weeks, Saskia's tattoo had almost healed. The letters were now clear and crisp on raised skin. She shared the finished product with the other girls. Adrienne went a step further and posted hers on social media, a direct violation of rule number seven.

Stupid girl, Saskia thought. But a part of her could relate. She could understand why Adrienne would want to show off. Saskia, too, was proud of the club and its unique secrets. It was better than any club at school, better than the college sororities she'd heard about. Better, even, than most of her favorite old movies.

There was no question the club was dangerous, too, but wasn't that part of its allure? The danger was what filled Saskia with a rush of euphoria, like balancing on a precarious high wire between two cliffs, one for the living, the other for the dead, and who knew what was in the chasm in between if she lost her balance and fell?

On a hot July day, Saskia told Lila she didn't need a ride to the sisters' house for that night's meeting; Paige was picking her up. She didn't mention that she needed to talk to Paige in private.

In the shiny-slick Mercedes, she admitted to Paige how she'd swallowed a drop of mercury, how it had made her scared, so scared she couldn't even fall asleep. She tried to laugh off the experience, but Paige quickly saw through her façade.

"Look, I started taking a drop every night, and I'm fine. Sara

Beth, too. You have to loosen up, girlfriend!" said Paige. "You know what? Lots of famous people took mercury for years, back when it was used in medicine."

"Yeah, Lila told me Lincoln took it."

"See?"

"But it may have contributed to his depression."

"There's no way to prove that. Besides, you're not depressed, right?"

Saskia had to admit she wasn't.

"So don't worry. I wouldn't steer you wrong. You know I think of you like a second sister, right?" Paige asked.

Saskia felt touched. "Me, too," she said shyly.

"I wanted to say," Paige continued, "if you don't already know, that I would never intentionally hurt you."

"Of course not," Saskia replied, a little confused.

"And I always have your best interests at heart."

"This is beginning to scare me . . . Is something wrong?"

"No! It's just that tonight's meeting might be a little different, and I don't want you to get freaked out."

"Different how?"

"Different, like, we all need to put our cards on the table."

"What does that mean?" Saskia asked.

"We need to be honest with each other, but also with ourselves. No matter what the consequences."

"I don't get it . . ."

"You will," Paige assured her. Affectionately, she took a lock of Saskia's crazy-curly hair, pulled it straight, and let it snap back into a coil.

Saskia's mind danced with questions, but before she could decide which one to ask, Paige floored the gas pedal, and suddenly they were flying. Saskia wanted to close her eyes, but she couldn't; she could only clench her hands into tight fists and squeal in freaked-out delight as the car whizzed past eighty, then ninety; roaring down the quiet residential streets of Coventon; ignoring stop signs, yield signs, and honking cars; zooming so fast it felt like a rocket ship, until suddenly Saskia realized they were on the sisters' street, the houses larger than houses had any right to be.

The Mercedes finally slowed, gradually, gradually, until it crawled, and Paige effortlessly turned into her driveway, flipping her perfect hair and saying, "See? Everything's in control."

The girls sat in their usual circle on the warm, damp ground under the giant tree. Saskia noticed *FOREVER BOYFRIENDS FOREVER!* carved into the bark of the trunk. She wondered which of the sisters had done it.

Though her friends talked amiably, Saskia could see Paige's mood had changed since their daring car ride. She had the same expression as when she'd written the pledge and rules—contemplative eyes, flattened lips. The air around her felt electrically charged, as if filled with positive ions, which Saskia had learned in chemistry were often corrosive, abrasive, and toxic, contrary to their name.

When Paige said the meeting was about to start, even her body language seemed different—amplified and a bit contrived, like she was performing for a hidden camera. Saskia looked around uneasily, but of course she saw nothing unusual, just the cascading canopy of branches and leaves.

"Adrienne," Paige said sharply. Adrienne looked as if she were expecting to be rebuked. "From now on, you'll be taking the minutes of each of our meetings for posterity."

"Posterity?" Adrienne asked weakly.

"Posterity—yes, future generations. We need notes—a factual record—of each meeting, so that those who come after us know everything that happened."

"She means the Mercury Boys Club might last longer than we do," said Sara Beth somberly.

Goose bumps rose on Saskia's skin.

Paige handed Adrienne an expensive-looking leather notebook with gold-leaf pages and the Sampras name embossed on the front. Saskia thought again of the engraved shaker and wondered just how many of the family's belongings sported their name. Were the Samprases driven by arrogance and egotism, or did they simply believe, like Paige did, that certain things might outlive them?

Adrienne took the notebook gingerly. "I'm not sure what to write . . ." she said.

"Our story," said Paige tartly. "Starting from today on."

But maybe Adrienne shared Saskia's sense of foreboding, for she shot up suddenly, brushing an invisible insect or spiderweb from her arm. "I'm so sick of these creepy-crawlies! Can't we go inside?"

"No," replied Paige. "The 'rents might come home early. I don't want them to hear us."

"Where are they tonight?" Lila asked.

"The movies."

"A double feature, we hope," said Sara Beth.

Paige nodded. "A few months ago, they saw four movies in a row. We didn't see them all night."

"Everything in excess," Sara Beth added, smiling ruefully. "But they could also cut out after five minutes. You never know with them."

Paige sighed. "Let's get going, just in case. Since all members of the Mercury Boys Club are in attendance, I hereby call this meeting to order. First item on the agenda: our new clothes. Everybody happy with them? Any comments, questions?"

Saskia shook her head, unwilling to admit to the group that all the clothes were too small; she had found nothing that would fit. Nor would she admit that she was still wearing her old chorus uniform to bed. The outfit was at least three years old and wouldn't have been considered fashionable in any era. But at least she wasn't wearing shorts anymore. She'd privately asked Adrienne to help her find something more suitable. Maybe the drama club had something in its costume closet.

Paige continued, "Nothing? Okay, then, next order of business: membership. I think we need to talk about whether the club is accepting new members."

Adrienne raised her pen. "I like the club the way it is," she said.

"But new members would bring new ideas," replied Sara Beth. "Otherwise, it's the same old, same old. Not that I don't love you guys, but come on—this'll get boring."

"But new members could also leak secrets," said Lila. "And they'll need daguerreotypes. I can't take any more from work. Marlene's been on my case."

"Do you think Rich told her?" asked Sara Beth.

"No, but still, I think she suspects."

"How do you know?"

Lila shrugged. "It's just a feeling."

"So no more daguerreotypes from the college?" asked Paige.

"No," Lila said firmly.

"Well, if we don't have more daguerreotypes, I guess that answers our question, but we might as well take a vote. All in favor of new members, raise your hands."

The only hand that went up was Sara Beth's.

"Add that to the minutes, please," Paige instructed Adrienne.

As Adrienne scrawled, Saskia glanced at her writing. She was struck by the number of spelling mistakes. She was also struck by the hearts Adrienne used to dot her *i*'s. She thought girls stopped doing that in the third grade.

"Next on the docket," said Paige briskly, "is a rumor we need to clear up."

"What rumor?" asked Saskia

"Is it bad?" asked Adrienne.

"It's not good," Paige replied.

"What's it about?"

"You."

Startled, Adrienne put down the pen.

"I hear that you've been talking to Benjamin *again*," Paige said.

Adrienne took an audible breath but maintained her composure.

"Is it true?" Paige prodded.

Saskia shifted uncomfortably. The wolfish look in Paige's eye was exactly the reason she hadn't told her about Benjamin's phone call. It was becoming quite clear that there were many sides of Paige, some more kind and generous than others.

"Kind of," Adrienne murmured.

"'Kind of'? So you've spoken with him since your date?"

Hands trembling, Adrienne fiddled with a piece of her hair.

"Listen, there's nothing wrong with communication. It all depends on what you say. For example, Josh called me last week. He wanted to go out. But I told him straight up, it's not happening."

Sara Beth looked at her sister and nodded.

Saskia dug her nails through the damp soil, thankful that no one was paying attention to her. Any mention of Josh still made her heart race and her face flush with guilt, especially when she was around Paige.

"That's what I told Benny," Adrienne insisted. "That it's not gonna work."

Paige eyed her skeptically.

"It's not my fault that he keeps calling," Adrienne said. "It's like he won't give up."

"You have to make him give up."

"And how am I supposed to do that?"

"Tell him you have zero interest. That your new man is *the one.*"

"I have . . ."

"Really? I find that hard to believe. Especially since you and Benny were making out in the park last night."

Adrienne blinked rapidly. "I . . . that was just . . ."

"Just what?"

"I don't know how it happened," she murmured. "I mean, I love Emery, I really do. But during the day, I don't know, sometimes I doubt what's happening. I know I shouldn't, but I do. I start to think it's all in my head: Nurse Reynolds, the wounded soldiers, everything. I . . . I panic. That's why I called Benny last night. I was freaking out. I—I made a bad decision." Hands still trembling, Adrienne picked up the pen again and began to doodle. Saskia figured she was trying to avoid eye contact with Paige.

"That's inexcusable," said Sara Beth.

"Unconscionable," added Paige.

Suddenly Saskia couldn't sit quiet any longer. This time it wasn't a matter of choosing sides—Paige's or Adrienne's. She just couldn't stand by and watch someone get picked part.

"I disagree," she said. "I think Adrienne's just confused. We all get confused, right?"

Adrienne looked at her gratefully.

"No, Saskia," said Paige sharply. "We do not *all get confused.*"

"Really?" Saskia asked, "You've never once made a mistake?"

"Don't be childish," Paige snapped. "There's a difference between making a mistake and deliberately breaking a rule you've agreed to follow for the rest of your life."

Adrienne applied so much pressure to the pen that the nib ripped right though the paper. "Are you going to kick me out of the club, Paige?"

"She doesn't have the authority to do that," said Lila, giving Paige a stern look. "We make decisions as a group."

"Yes, but our decisions must reflect the pledge and the rules," Paige reminded her. "The fact is, Adrienne broke rule number thirteen. Which means if she wants to stay, she has to be punished."

"I do—I do want to stay," Adrienne blubbered.

"Then you have to accept the punishment we decide."

"Paige . . ." Saskia said.

"What?" Paige demanded.

"Come on. She doesn't deserve to be punished."

"Did you or did you not agree to the club's official rules of membership?" Paige asked.

"You know I did," replied Saskia.

"Then *you* are as accountable as Adrienne is. Rule number twelve. 'MBC members must support their club sisters and help them remain HONEST.'"

Saskia shook her head and glanced at Lila. "A simple apology from Adrienne would be enough punishment for me," she said.

"For me, too," agreed Lila.

Paige sighed. "Listen, we can't let her off that easy—for Emery's sake. It wouldn't be right."

"I agree with my sister," said Sara Beth. "The rules are the rules. They're there for a reason."

Saskia felt a rising dread. She didn't want Adrienne to suffer. Especially when she felt partly responsible. No matter what the girls had signed or agreed to, getting punished for a minor lapse in judgment didn't seem fair. They were teenagers, after all. And no teenager on the planet didn't regret *something*. Plus, the girls' relationships with the Mercury Boys were strange, confusing, and ambiguous. There was no road map for a club involving dead people—it was uncharted territory. No wonder Adrienne had messed up.

And there was something else that nagged at Saskia: the fact that the Sampras sisters had so much power, and yet shared less than the other girls. Lila and Adrienne had confided in Saskia about their complicated love lives. Saskia had confided in Lila about—well—everything. But Paige and Sara Beth hardly ever revealed their innermost feelings, despite having so much control of the club.

It didn't seem fair. Saskia wanted to say this, about how, regardless of the official rules, the girls needed to allow one another to be vulnerable without fear of judgment or retribution. But one look at Paige's stern face, and Saskia's resolve faltered.

And then the opportunity was lost.

"Fine, I accept it," Adrienne said. "I accept the punishment."

Paige led the way through the branches toward the front of the house. The girls followed warily, Saskia bringing up the rear. Adrienne was directly in front of her. Saskia wanted to reassure her or grab her hand and run away. But she walked obediently in the line Paige had created until they reached the fountain. Water gurgled down the long hair and bulbous breasts of the mermaid, who up close looked obscene with her outlandish, Barbie-like proportions.

"The punishment involves Meryl Streep?" Lila asked disbelievingly.

Paige nodded.

"What is it?"

"Adrienne will dunk her head in the basin," said Paige, pointing. "And keep it there for sixty seconds."

Adrienne's eyes widened. "That's too long," she sputtered. "I can hold my breath for two minutes in the pool, no problem."

"But you're a swimmer!"

"You'll survive."

"It takes three minutes to die," added Sara Beth.

"This is a terrible idea," said Lila. Paige gave her a steely look.

"Lila's right," said Saskia. "It's excessive. We need to think of something else."

Avoiding Paige's eyes, she dipped her fingers into the basin. The water was surprisingly cold for such a warm night. Nervously, she looked toward the road, then toward the neighboring houses, which were set some distance away. She wondered if anyone was watching them. She couldn't help but hope someone—an adult—would inquire about what they were doing and tell them to stop.

"I'm not surprised you keep disagreeing with me, Saskia," said Paige.

Saskia looked at her curiously.

"'Benny cares about you a lot. That's clear,'" Paige said, repeating one of the texts Saskia had written to Adrienne.

"'Intense is better than uninterested,'" added Sara Beth sarcastically.

Adrienne cupped her hand over her mouth. "Saskia, I didn't show them. Honest!"

Saskia gawked at Paige. "Where did you read that?" she demanded.

"On your phone—obviously."

"You know my password?" Saskia asked incredulously.

"It's easy to figure out just about anything if you pay attention—and as you can see, I have to," Paige retorted snarkily.

"You shouldn't have been looking at her phone," Lila hissed. "That's an invasion of privacy."

"Tell me which is worse—a minor invasion of privacy or Saskia going against the rules and endangering Adrienne's relationship with her Mercury Boy?"

"But that's Saskia's personal property," Lila argued.

Saskia put her hand on Lila's arm. "It's okay, Lila. I can speak for myself."

"If you insist," her friend said with a shrug.

Saskia wasn't sure why the night had taken such a dark turn, or why Paige was so pissed off, but she wanted to turn things around. If only everyone would calm down and be rational.

"When I talked with Adrienne, I was trying to be fair. I was trying to understand Benny's perspective as much as Emery's," Saskia said, resisting the urge to chew on her fingernails.

"Trying to be fair, okay," muttered Paige cynically. "So you believe in fairness?"

"Of course."

"Good. Then you won't mind taking your share of the punishment."

Saskia blinked hard. She had a feeling that the situation was going to deteriorate no matter what she said.

"Snooping is nowhere near as bad as breaking rule number twelve, Saskia. Or rule number thirteen, Adrienne," Paige replied coolly.

"We can't just overlook what you've done," added Sara Beth.

Paige nodded. "Sadly, Saskia will get the same punishment as Adrienne: one minute underwater."

"Oh, come on!" said Lila incredulously.

"It's not a bad punishment," Paige replied, "all things considered."

"It's ridiculous, is what it is."

"What do you think Emery would suggest if he could have seen Adrienne last night?" Sara Beth asked.

Adrienne, who'd been quiet, suddenly raised her hand. "I'm okay with one minute," she said. "I guess I deserve it."

"You do," Paige agreed.

"I'm . . . speechless," Lila spat, turning to Saskia with a stunned expression. "Are we in a *Black Mirror* episode or something?"

The word "mirror" stirred something in Saskia. With an ardent pang, she remembered the phrase "mirror with a memory," and then thought of Cornelius.

For the first time, she considered how Cornelius might feel if she were to betray him in some vital way, as Adrienne had betrayed Emery. It pained her to think of disappointing him. She realized that while she and the other girls had a doorway to the past, Cornelius and the other Mercury Boys didn't have a window to the future. They couldn't see events in the modern world, never mind react to them—everything after their deaths was beyond their control. Their sheer powerlessness struck Saskia as cruel.

"Lila, why don't you keep time?" Paige suggested, disrupting Saskia's thoughts. "Adrienne and Saskia should keep their heads underwater for sixty seconds—no more, no less."

"No way," Lila replied. "Saskia, Adrienne, let's get outta here. This has gone too far."

"If you leave, you can't be a member of the club again—ever," Paige said matter-of-factly.

"I don't care," Lila scoffed.

"I do," Saskia said softly.

"What?"

"I did sign the contract," Saskia reminded Lila. "And I did break a rule."

"Saskia, don't be stupid."

"I'm not being stupid. I'm trying to make good on a promise." She looked Paige in the eye. "I don't think you should have gone through my phone, but that doesn't excuse what I did. The boys deserve better."

"Are you listening to yourself?" demanded Lila. "You're . . . brainwashed."

"And you're overprotective," Saskia snapped, surprised by her own harshness. "I can make my own decisions."

Lila twitched with anger. She opened her mouth to stay something, stopped, and then tried again. "Okay, Miss Self-Sufficient. Since you can take care of yourself, find your own ride home."

"Come on, Lila, don't overreact."

"Overreact?" Lila repeated in disbelief. "Seriously? You think I'm overreacting when you're about to drown yourself?"

"Lila . . ."

But Lila was already striding furiously across the sisters' immaculate lawn.

"Well, that makes things easier," said Sara Beth said flatly.

"Okay, enough already," said Paige. "Let's get this over with. Adrienne, you're up first. Saskia, you keep time. Sara Beth, you and I will do the heavy lifting."

As if on autopilot, Saskia lifted her hands to catch the stopwatch Paige tossed to her. She had accepted the punishment, but the last thing she wanted to do was keep time. If anything, she wanted to rewind time—to go back to when the girls were jumping around the house without a care. How had things changed so quickly?

Saskia stomach sank as she watched the sisters take each of Adrienne's arms. They marched her toward the basin. Adrienne went willingly. Saskia heard a sharp splash, and then Adrienne was under. The sisters murmured to themselves, the muscles of their arms and backs visible through their skimpy summer clothes. Four hands gripped Adrienne's body.

"Start the clock, Saskia," Paige said.

Her fingers fumbling, Saskia pressed the button on the top of the watch. She counted aloud as the seconds passed.

"Seven, eight, nine . . ."

One eye on the stopwatch, the other on Adrienne, Saskia grew increasingly queasy—and alarmed. At first Adrienne seemed calm. Dead calm, Saskia thought somberly. But at the thirty-second mark, she began to struggle against the sisters' grasp. The back of her head pushed up, hair afloat like pieces of orange seaweed. Unyielding, Paige and Sara Beth shoved her back down.

"Forty-one, forty-two, forty-three . . ."

Now Adrienne was fully resisting, knuckles white, fingernails clawing at the edge of the rough stone basin, making a sound like sandpaper. Saskia gritted her teeth. Adrienne surfaced, with time only to sputter and rasp before the sisters plunged her head back into the water.

"Stop it!" Saskia screamed.

Punishment was one thing, death something else entirely. Feeling overpowered and overwhelmed, she grabbed Sara Beth's arm and tugged hard.

"Hey, get off!" Sara Beth scolded, kicking Saskia in the shin.

"You're hurting her!" Saskia replied.

"She'll be fine," Paige assured her, her shoulder and arm muscles tensed. Despite all Adrienne's flailing and the sisters' consequently wet clothes, Paige's voice was calm. "We're almost done."

At a loss, Saskia stared at the clock and willed it to move faster. The harder she concentrated, though, the slower the seconds seemed to pass. At long last, the minute was up.

"Let her go!" Saskia called out, scared that it was too late.

The sisters immediately released their hold on Adrienne, who lifted her head slowly, like it was too heavy to support. She tried to stand erect, wobbled, and collapsed. On the ground, she lay in a rag doll heap next to the fountain. Her eyes were open, but they were glassy, inscrutable. Wet hair stuck to her cheeks and forehead. Her lips were the color of unbaked clay.

"Is she all right?" Saskia heard herself whisper.

Paige knelt beside Adrienne and gently cupped her chin. "It's over now, Adrienne. You did it."

"She—she doesn't look good," Saskia said, kneeling, too. She stroked Adrienne's face.

"She'll be okay."

Feeling a little woozy herself, Saskia allowed herself to believe this. She took one of Adrienne's hands, which was cold despite the summer heat. Such a thin hand, the skin so translucent Saskia swore she could see bones and sinew, blood running through blue-green veins.

"Question," Adrienne mumbled weakly.

"What is it?" Paige asked, leaning in.

"Am I still in the club?"

"Of course you are," Paige said, smoothing back Adrienne's hair from her forehead. Saskia struggled to reconcile Paige's sudden gentleness with her behavior only seconds before.

"How do you feel, Adrienne?" Saskia asked. She didn't think she'd ever forget the way Adrienne's orange hair had floated limply atop the water, or the way she'd struggled so hard to surface, only to be shoved back down again.

Adrienne licked her pale lips. "Glad that it's over," she said, attempting to smile, but grimacing instead.

"See?" Paige said, gazing at Saskia. "She's fine, just like I'd told you."

Saskia stared at her, remembering the things she'd said in the car.

I wouldn't steer you wrong.

You know I think of you like a second sister, right?

I always have your best interests at heart.

Was all that really true? Was what Adrienne had just gone through a rough but ultimately fair penalty for her misconduct?

Looking at Paige's face, which in the twilight looked strangely luminous, like an angel's, her eyes shining with not just conviction, but also tenderness and compassion, Saskia was inclined to believe Paige knew best.

"Your turn now," Paige told her.

Underwater, Saskia kept her eyes open. The water, which looked clear from above, was murky below, a snowstorm, a fog. The harder she looked, the less she saw. She blinked and tried to think of something, anything, other than how her lungs were already screaming for air. Soon her heartbeat became a roar in her ears. Images, blurry as the water, skittered through her mind. Her mother braiding thick black hair. Cornelius scrawling one of his ideas on paper with a fountain pen. Heather slipping a note through a slat in her locker. Her father rubbing shaving cream on his face.

Saskia wanted to call to him; she was desperate, but water plugged her mouth and ran thickly down her throat, just as it had in the pool. Now she understood how Adrienne had felt: how quickly acceptance gave rise to panic. Her whole body was shrieking for oxygen. She tried to surface. But the sisters wouldn't let her. They kept pushing her down into that cloudy, muddled world. It didn't matter that she kicked and bucked. It didn't matter that she could die.

"Saskia?" The voice sounded like sonar, like a faint frequency passing through water. "Saskia, wake up."

When she opened her eyes, she wasn't sure where she was. She felt like a dingy piece of flotsam washed ashore. She tried to ask, but when she opened her mouth, water trickled out. She began to cough.

"You made it," she heard a girl say.

After a time Saskia felt herself being dragged and lifted. Someone pulled off her shirt and unsnapped her bra. She tried to resist but was too tired. Eventually, she felt the soft pile of a rug against her back, the weight of a blanket over her body. Someone slipped a pillow beneath her head.

"If they come back, just say she's sick," Saskia heard a voice say matter-of-factly.

"Right, she's got the flu," said another with equal briskness.

"Not in the summer!"

"Okay, fine. Food poisoning."

Saskia understood now. She understood everything. She was lying down in the Sampras den, the sisters on either side of her. Paige was urging her to sit up, to sip chamomile tea. Saskia obeyed, but the fetid taste of stale water remained on her tongue.

"I threw her clothes in the dryer," said Sara Beth.

"When they're ready, let's take her home," Paige replied. "The sooner, the better."

"What if her dad's there?"

"She'll be okay by then. It didn't take Adrienne long."

"I'm fine," answered Saskia, though they weren't addressing her.

She wasn't fine—her throat hurt, and her head felt clogged. She was embarrassed by how weak and infantile she was, naked on the floor.

"Hey, you're back," Paige cheered, her voice suddenly bright and animated. She put her hand against Saskia's cheek. "You had us scared."

"Yeah," she answered, sitting up and taking the cup of tea Paige offered her. Her hand was unsteady, and hot liquid dripped down her wrist.

"You took it harder than we thought," Paige said.

Saskia took another sip of tea, then set down the cup. It had felt weirdly heavy in her hand, and she was pretty sure she would have dropped it if she'd held it any longer. As Sara Beth and Paige crowded close, Saskia longed to go home and rest in her own bed, in her own house, alone. She didn't like being the object of their attention; their solicitousness felt too much like pity.

"Can I go home now?" she murmured.

"Of course," Paige assured her.

For better or worse, Saskia's father wasn't at home when the three girls arrived. Sara Beth and Paige followed her into the house and up the stairs. Paige walked behind her. "Just in case you get dizzy," she said. Sara Beth turned down her sheets and teased something about a bedtime story. Saskia smiled weakly.

When she was nestled under the covers, Paige kissed her on the forehead like a mother would. Her lips felt warm and soft. "See you soon, brave girl," she said. "You did a great job."

"Yeah, you were a champ," added Sara Beth.

"Thanks," Saskia replied groggily.

"We'll lock the door on our way out," said Paige. "Want us to do anything else?"

Saskia shook her head.

"All right. Good night, then. Love you."

"Love you, too," Saskia replied, as if on autopilot.

When they'd gone, she tried to shut her eyes, to shut off her mind. But now that she was finally alone in her own house, the events of the night lay heavy on her mind. She tried to process what had happened, but she felt confused by conflicting emotions: relief, anger, satisfaction, resentment, thankfulness, doubt. *Go to sleep*, she told herself. Yet her mind insisted on consciousness, and her thoughts bent in odd directions. She reflected on dripping-wet hair, heavy stone breasts, dull eyes, strong hands, furtive whispers too quiet to hear. She wondered if the sisters were truly safeguarding the club or if they had an ulterior motive, then felt guilty for doubting them. After all, they had cared enough to take her home and put her safely to bed. And Paige thought of her like a second sister—didn't she?

Minutes passed. Then hours. Still her thoughts and feelings continued to whir like a blender in her head. Exasperated, she sat up and threw off her sheets. She knew she needed to do something drastic, or she would never rest. She thought briefly about the baggie of pills, but dismissed the idea when she remembered her father's lecture in the car.

Creeping out of bed, she found the mercury, tipped a drop into the palm of her hand, and licked it off before she could talk herself out of it. *Water silver, quick silver, hydrargyrum. People have given it many names through the ages,* Cornelius had said once. Whatever mercury's name, and whatever its capabilities or dangers, she was grateful for it, and the daguerreotype, too. When at last she saw Cornelius, she sighed with relief.

Finally, an escape.

Adrienne

"Man alive! Where have you been?" Nurse Reynolds exclaimed, soapy hands on her hips.

Adrienne blinked and found herself outside the front of the barn. She felt disconcerted and a little queasy. It was usually like this when she arrived at the field hospital. Like she'd been dropped from an airplane.

"You can't come and go as you please. Here one day, gone the next!" she heard Nurse Reynolds say. "The men depend on you. I do, too, frankly."

Still trying to get her bearings, Adrienne looked tentatively at the barn door, relieved to see that the rancid pile of limbs finally had been carted away. It had been rotting and festering there for what felt like an eternity.

"Sorry!" Adrienne replied, and she meant it. If she could spend all day at the field hospital, she would. But sometimes in her bedroom in the modern world, she just couldn't fall asleep. Even when she handled the mercury for a half hour, rubbing it between her palms like lotion. Even when she swallowed a few drops, along with more than a few sleeping pills.

"Your young man—Emery—he's been asking for you," the nurse said, her annoyance having waned. Lately, she'd seemed more willing to turn a blind eye to the affection between the two young people.

Nurse Reynolds had even given up quoting Dorothea Dix, superintendent of all wartime nurses. "Nurse Dix expects your hair to be combed back," she used to repeat to Adrienne ad nauseum. "And for land's sake, don't you own a single dress with a high neck and long sleeves?"

Adrienne knew that since her arrival only two men had died, and both had been hopeless cases to begin with. The other men were healing. Some were even flourishing. This hadn't happened in the course of Nurse Reynolds's tenure. It must be clear to her that Adrienne's presence and suggestions were the reason for this improvement.

"Thanks. I'll go check on him," Adrienne said, hustling into the barn.

When she saw Emery, he was sitting up. He looked good—healthy, like the boy in the daguerreotype. The only difference was that his gaze was more contemplative now.

"Good day, Nurse Arch!"

"Good day."

"I've been hoping you'd appear."

She smiled shyly.

"It's the oddest thing," he said, pointing at his stump, "but I can still feel it. It's like my arm is still there."

Adrienne nodded and sat on the edge of his cot. Another soldier, who'd lost his leg, had said the same thing. "Miss Reynolds calls them phantom limbs," she explained. "Even though you lost your arm, your mind hasn't erased the memory of it yet."

He looked away from his missing arm and took her hand. "I missed you."

She was too startled to respond.

"Where do you go?" he asked.

"Why does everyone keep asking me that?"

"Because you just disappear."

"Every girl has her secrets."

That made him laugh. "All I know is, everything is better when you're here. See how I was worried about my 'phantom limb'? As soon as you explained it to me, my worry vanished. The same when I told you I feared I'd never swim again or swing an ax. You assured me I would. You're the only person who makes me feel like life is still worth the trouble—especially without my brother."

Adrienne looked down, not wanting him to see how moved and humbled she was. She wasn't used to this kind of praise. Or any praise, really.

"I'm starting to write again, too." Emery motioned to a cedar pencil and a couple scraps of rough paper lying under his cot. "My left hand's getting better. But it's still weak. Would you help me write a letter?"

Adrienne glanced at the other men in the barn. No one seemed to need her urgent attention, and Nurse Reynolds was still here. "Okay," she agreed. She could spare a few minutes before changing sheets and bandages. For Emery, she could always spare time. "Who's it for?" she asked.

"A young lady."

"Oh?"

"Her name's Mollie."

"Who is she?"

"If you wouldn't mind, I'd just like you to write the letter."

"Fine," Adrienne replied.

Emery cleared his throat.

My dear Molly,

As Adrienne wrote, he corrected her. "Mollie ends with an *ie*." "Fine," she said again, this time more sharply.

I write in the hope that this letter finds you in good health and good spirits. It's been months, surely, since I last had the opportunity to write. But trust in the fact that you have remaned in my mind and heart these many weeks.

Adrienne wrote slowly. She began to feel very worried.

Though I still support President Lincoln and our Goverment, this war has been bloodyer than I ever could have imagined. It takes lives indiscrimanately, and leaves the living to stew in the grief. I have lost so many of my friends, I dare not count. Every night I am racked by guilt—why has God taken my comrades in arms, but not me? I have no answer.

By now, Mollie, you have probably heard that we have lost dear Harry, too. My only solice is that my brave brother died quickly. I don't think he experienced but a few moments' pain. I am grateful that he is now peaceful and safe in Our Heavenly Father's kingdom.

As for me, the Union says I am no longer fit to fight. I lost my arm, you see. Mollie, as I lay here ailing, I think about returning to you, and to all the promises we made to one another.

"I'm not sure I want to write this anymore," Adrienne said abruptly, setting down the pencil. She'd summited a mountain of anxiety. There was nowhere else to go but down.

"Please—I'm coming to the end."

"No."

Emery looked her in the eye. "Miss Arch, I *need* you to finish." He said this with such insistence that Adrienne found herself resuming her task, albeit reluctantly.

For two years we talked about changing our situation in life. And never once did I question our decision to unite as man and wife once the war ended. Yet battle has changed me. It has changed everything. And I fear the lives we used to live, and the dreams we used to have, have been shelled to the point of annihilation.

I am no longer the man you knew. It wouldn't be fair to pretend other wise. And as a changed man, I must now change my course. I realize I am destined, by the great hand of providence, to love another. I see in her all the hope I feared was lost. This revalation may pain you, and I am sincerely sorry for that. It was never my intention to bring you anything but happiness.

May God ever bless you.

Farewell—

Emery

"So you're dumping her?" Adrienne ventured, her head spinning. "This fiancée I didn't even know you had?" She wavered between shock, anger, and relief.

"If 'dumping' means what I think it means," Emery replied.

"And the girl—it's me?"

"Who else would it be?" He smiled tentatively. "I know I can't ask now, not in these conditions. Not as I am. But will you consider later when I'm able?"

"Will I consider what?"

"Marriage, of course."

She gaped at him. "Are you for real?"

"Are you?"

She took a deep breath. "Listen, Emery, I need to tell you something."

"Your answer, I hope?"

"It turns out there's a lot I don't know about you. And, well, there's a lot you don't know about me, too."

"I know everything I need to."

"No, not everything."

Emery put his hand to her face. His thumb brushed her cheek. "Tell me whatever you want, but my mind is made up."

"We'll see about that," Adrienne said evenly.

CHAPTER SEVENTEEN

S: lila, I'm sorry. i f'ed up
S: I shouldn't have yelled at u. it was stupid. i was stupid
S: i know you're 😡, but can u pls write me back
S: i need to talk to u
S: pleaze!
S: come on . . . I'll wash your  /buy u French fries/baby-sit your 1,000,000 siblings?
S: just as long as we're good
S: are we?
S: Lila?

Many hours later, Lila finally replied.

L: i don't know if I can be your friend anymore
L: sorry, but it's true

Saskia's stomach sank. Lila was a matter-of-fact person; she wouldn't write something she didn't mean. Still, Saskia had to try. She had to believe there was still a chance to save their friendship. The alternative was too heartbreaking to consider.

S: lila! i didn't mean it. honest

L: yeah u did

S: ok so maybe I kinda meant it—at the time. but I know u were just trying to be a good friend. i blew it

Minutes passed. Saskia's stomachache got worse. She figured Lila was done with her. If she were to put herself in Lila's place, she'd be done with herself, too. Lila was always going out of her way to help her, and how had Saskia repaid that? By being selfish and ungrateful. She stared at her cell phone, wondering if there was any way, any way at all, to redeem herself.

L: maybe I'll take the car wash

L: the buick does need a bath

Saskia grinned. She texted faster than she'd ever texted before.

S: have sponge + soap; will travel 😊

L: so . . . how did it go??? the punishment with meryl streep

S: i'm alive

L: you're loco. so's adrienne. u 2 will do anything the sisters say

S: maybe. but this time it wasn't about them

L: come on

S: it was about cornelius. i wouldn't want to betray him. and I realized I kind of had. by proxy. By telling A. it was OK to keep seeing B.

L: u didn't do anything wrong

S: yeah i did

L: loco

S: wouldn't u take a punishment for Cassie?

L: punishments do not = loyalty/love

S: maybe they do

L: maybe don't pick up what the sisters put down

S: they're just passionate about the mbc. esp paige

L: passionate's NOT the word I'd use

S: I get u don't like her
L: i don't understand her. but she's your friend. I don't want u to have to choose between us
S: thanks. u r the best. the best friend I have
L: you back
S: so you forgive me?
L: yeah, but u still owe me a favor
S: besides beautifying the buick?
L: buick = already beautiful. I have a new plan — stay tuned

The location, Saskia soon found out, was the Howard and Alice Steerkemp Daguerreotypes Collection. She was back there with Lila. Like old times, Rich eyed them warily.

"How are you, Rich?" Lila asked.

"Pretty good," he replied, pushing his black glasses up the bridge of his nose self-consciously.

"Anything new?"

"Whelp, no . . . except Veronica died."

"Oh no! How?"

"Not sure. Old age, maybe. She was sixteen or seventeen."

"I'm so sorry." Lila turned to Saskia and explained, "Veronica was his pet snake."

"Oh," said Saskia. "Sorry to hear that, Rich."

His downcast eyes betrayed sadness, but he waved her off. "No big deal—she was just a snake."

"Are you gonna get another one?" asked Lila. "Sorry. That wasn't a very sensitive question. She only just died."

"It's all right. And the answer is, I don't know. I got Veronica when an old roommate left her behind. I didn't even want her. I wasn't a *reptile guy*. But, you know, I got used to having her around. I guess you get used to anything after seventeen years."

"True."

"Hey, I do have some good news, though," Rich said, suddenly more chipper.

"What?"

"I put in that application . . . for the Master of Library Science program."

"Whoa! Good for you, Rich!"

"It'll be good *if* I get in . . ."

"You will."

He shrugged, but he seemed proud, too, like Lila's opinion meant something.

"Rich, we need to go into the archives again," she told him quietly.

Agitation snuffed out his brief, flickering gladness. "Lila, one of these days, I'm telling you, you're gonna get hoisted by your own petard."

"What does that even mean?" she asked, giggling.

"No idea, but it can't be good."

She stopped laughing when she met his serious gaze.

"Listen," he said, "Marlene didn't get the raise she was up for. Now she's on the warpath. She's actively *searching* for victims."

"Has she mentioned any of the daguerreotypes we borrowed?"

"I'm amused you're still using the word *borrowed*."

"Look, I know I've been a pain, but we just need to go in one more time."

Rich sighed, looking like he wanted to say more, then gave up and waved them through.

They entered the Collection room and ventured into the adjoining workshop. Saskia hadn't been there for a while, and she realized now that she'd missed the place. All the chemicals and old-fashioned photography tools, the rickety tripods and ancient cameras, they made Cornelius seem closer to her somehow.

Lila had given her a short list of items to look for. On a shelf above the sink, Saskia reached for a vial of mercury and a jar of crystal iodine.

Then, suddenly, she sensed the presence of someone behind her.

"Lila?" she asked, wheeling around.

But it was Rich, still wearing a serious expression. Guiltily, she put the vial and jar back on the shelf.

"What is it, Rich?" Lila asked, scurrying over.

"Hey," he said, fidgeting. "I didn't want to scare you, but I've got to come clean: Marlene is on to you."

"How do you know? What'd she say?" Lila was fiddling with an old tripod, but Saskia could tell she was trying to hide her concern.

"She said she noticed some of the daguerreotypes are missing. She asked me if I knew anything."

Lila locked eyes with Rich.

"I said no one other than staff has been in here," he continued.

"Oh god. Thank you, Rich."

Saskia couldn't quite read his expression, but she thought it teetered somewhere between irritation, affection, and avuncular concern. "Look, now that Marlene knows something's off, you've *really* gotta stop."

"I know, but she has no proof it's me," Lila argued.

"She doesn't need proof. All she needs is reasonable doubt. Watch as many *Law & Order* reruns as I have, and you'll know."

"We have a huge archive of daguerreotypes. Maybe a few just got misplaced . . ."

Rich crossed his arms over his chest. Saskia figured he was trying to appear defiant and imposing, but he looked uncomfortable instead. "Listen up, both of you," he said in a strict schoolteacher's tone. "You keep doing what you're doing, and sooner or later, you're gonna get caught. It's inevitable. And then everything you hope to do, everything you hope to achieve—it'll be gone. You'll be like freight trains going over a cliff."

He made a swooping motion with his hand.

"I know you're trying to keep us out of trouble, Rich," Lila replied. "And I know Marlene means business. But we really are going to stop . . . soon."

"Soon?" he asked bleakly. "I'm not used to giving advice, but you two need it. I'd give anything to be where you are now—sixteen, your whole lives in front of you. You still have time to do anything. Be anything. But you keep making trouble, and there's gonna be a chain reaction. Things will go from good to bad, bad to worse. Eventually, you could end up like me—living in your mother's basement and mourning a dead snake."

"Oh, come on! Your life's not so bad," Lila replied. But knowing what she did about Rich, Saskia wasn't so sure. "And as for us, we'll be fine—we've got it figured out. Marlene's intimidating, but she's not *that* intimidating."

"Are we talking about the same Marlene? Genghis Khan Marlene?"

"I just said we'll be fine—and we will."

"I feel like I'm talking to a wall."

"No, just a teenager."

"Same difference," Rich griped, rubbing his shiny scalp. He looked tired and exasperated. His attempt to sway them seemed to have taken a toll, Saskia observed.

When he left dejectedly a few moments later, she looked at Lila with apprehension. "You sure we've got this figured out?"

Lila held up a leg that had broken off the tripod. "Do I look like I have it figured it out? I just needed to get him off our backs."

"But a part of me agrees with him, Lila. I should quit coming here."

"And I should quit bringing you. But we can't leave now. I've started something, and I'm gonna finish it."

Saskia knew Lila well enough to realize that once she'd made up her mind, there was no stopping her. There was really nothing Saskia could do except help Lila comb the room for more supplies—all the supplies they'd need to make a daguerreotype of themselves.

Lila swore that she'd watched enough YouTube tutorials to understand the process. Saskia went along with it because a) she owed Lila a favor, b) she was intrigued by the prospect, and c) because she'd already done so many bizarre things this summer that one more wasn't going to make much of a difference.

Lila laid out the steps they needed to take. She and Saskia worked slowly and carefully, double-checking their steps. Saskia was pretty sure they'd mess up anyway. Making a first daguerreotype, she believed, was probably like making the first pancake. It was

bound to be bad—the image would be blurry or, way worse, she
and Lila would manage to poison themselves.

Lila had more faith. Maybe it was bingeing all those YouTube
videos, or maybe she was preternaturally confident. Whatever it
was, Lila didn't second-guess herself. She proceeded self-assuredly.
Diligently, too. It was Lila who did most of the work, meticulously
polishing the silver-coated copper plate for almost an hour, until its
mirror finish was pristine.

When she was through, it was time to make the plate light sensitive. In a bathroom-sized dark room adjoining the workshop,
the girls donned rubber gloves—a modern convenience Cornelius
hadn't had. Lila brandished iodine monochloride and bromine
monochloride. "Proceed with caution," she warned. "These chemicals can cause birth defects, DNA damage, and cancer."

"Wonderful," muttered Saskia.

"Dealing with this stuff, those early photographers must have
died young," theorized Lila.

"Not Cornelius. He lived a long time." Saskia felt a surge of
longing just saying his name. She wondered, with increasing shame,
if he ever felt the same.

When the plate was sensitized, she helped Lila put it in the plate
holder. Then they secured the holder inside the camera, which was
worrisomely brittle. Nothing like the shiny new model Cornelius
owned. Then again, in the 1800s, the camera Saskia and Lila were
using had probably been pristine.

Finally, the girls were ready to take a picture of themselves. Cornelius's photography studio had sported the brightest lamps from
his shop, perfectly arranged at optimal angles for the best shot. But
here, the girls had to make do with mediocre LED tube lights flickering on the ceiling. Still, Saskia wasn't without hope. She'd never
forget that haunting incident in which Cornelius had photographed
the dead boy in dim light. She and Lila would just have to make it
work.

"Ready?" Lila asked, voice quavering.

"I think so."

"I forgot how long we have to hold still."

"Five minutes," Saskia confirmed.

The girls stood side by side, their backs pressed against a wall.

"Are you going to smile?" asked Lila.

"No. Are you?"

"Nah. Let's look mean and badass."

Saskia laughed. "Okay, then."

"Anyone from the future who picks us should know what they're getting themselves into."

"Mean and badass it is," Saskia agreed. "You ready?"

"Ready."

"Here we go . . ."

Saskia ran over to the camera, now mounted on the precarious tripod, and removed the lens. Then she bolted back and repositioned herself beside Lila. The girls put their hands on their hips—Saskia aware of a subtle pressure on her MBC tattoo—and stared at the camera like they meant business.

It was hard to stay still, even harder not to blink. Five minutes suddenly felt like an eternity, but the girls were committed. They knew they had to be statue still, or all their work would be in vain.

When the time was finally up, Saskia inhaled deeply and hustled to put the lens back on.

"Do you think it worked?" asked Lila, barely able to contain her excitement.

It occurred to Saskia that this was the very first time she'd ever seen Lila exuberant.

"Yeah," Saskia replied, surprised by her own answer. "I think we may have pulled it off."

By and by, an image began to appear. It was only a vague, shadowy outline at first. The girls put the plate back over the lamp and waited several more minutes. When they checked again, they were shocked to see a perfect rendering of themselves.

"No way," murmured Lila.

Saskia couldn't take her eyes off the final product, either. Far from being the first pancake, the daguerreotype was sharp and focused. More than that, the girls looked strong, brazen, and bold.

"We nailed badass," said Saskia.

For some reason, the picture made her feel like the temporal and physical distance between Cornelius and her had decreased. She supposed that was because she had created the very thing that gave her access to him. His daguerreotype was a type of portal. And now she'd made a potential portal of her own.

"Do you really think someone from the future will bring us back?" she asked Lila. She had a hunch her friend was wondering the same thing.

"I don't know. I hope so. It's our only shot at immortality."

"You really think that?"

"Well, I told you before I don't believe in all that Catholic stuff. I don't think our spirits are gonna rise to heaven and we'll spend all eternity with the Father, Son, and Holy Spirit or some other patriarchal BS. That's imaginary. But this daguerreotype—it's real."

"Say we get lucky and someone picks us," Saskia said. "What if we don't like them? What if they don't like us?"

"I'm willing to take that risk."

Saskia wasn't sure she was. "Don't you think the gravestones might be right—that people really are meant to rest in peace?"

"Was Cornelius meant to rest in peace?"

Saskia was taken aback. "No!"

"Thought so."

A little flustered, Saskia looked again at the daguerreotype. "So . . . where are we supposed to put this?"

"Where else? In the collection, along with the rest of the daguerreotypes."

"And Marlene? She could find it."

"She won't."

"Even if she doesn't, the chance of someone finding our

daguerreotype in the future—and figuring out what to do with it, with the mercury and all—is practically zero."

"Well, we'll give them a little help."

"What do you mean?"

"I made instructions." Lila reached into her pocket and took out a folded piece of paper. "This explains the whole process."

Saskia's eyes widened.

"We can't leave everything to fate," Lila said matter-of-factly.

"Lila Defensor, that's ballsy."

"Well, we are badasses, aren't we?"

Saskia paused to think. She realized this was her last chance to change her mind before the daguerreotype was stored away, maybe forever. "Are we gonna tell the others?" she asked apprehensively.

Lila gave her a withering look.

"Okay. Guess that answers my question."

Back at Saskia's house, Lila put on an apron and rummaged through the freezer. She took out a packet of chicken breasts and a bag of chopped vegetables and thawed them under running water. Then she found a big pan and began sautéing the vegetables in olive oil, ginger, and garlic. A delicious aroma soon filled the air. She fried the chicken in a separate pan and tossed everything together.

Then Lila served Saskia the best meal she'd had since coming to Coventon.

"Can you live here?" Saskia asked, swallowing a bite.

Lila laughed. "Make sure you save some for your dad. He's way skinny."

"I wish I could cook like you."

"It comes from having a hundred siblings. From age six on, I was my mom's sous chef."

"I can barely pour a bowl of cereal," Saskia replied.

"So what do you guys eat?"

"Well, my dad recently attempted Ghanaian shish kabobs. *Again.* He used so much cayenne pepper, my tongue's still on fire."

Lila laughed again, but Saskia was more pensive. She had a serious question she'd been meaning to ask. "Lila, do you ever think that maybe, I don't know, we're fooling ourselves? That—and please don't be mad at me—we could be making this up, Cornelius and Cassie, without even knowing it?"

"Sometimes," she admitted, sighing. "Sometimes I feel like we're in a play. Did you ever read *The Crucible*?"

"The one about the Salem witches?"

Lila nodded. "Yeah, that's the one. The thing is, those girls weren't real witches. They had an illness. Hysteria. Mass hysteria."

"What's that?"

"It's when a bunch of people, usually girls, who all live in the same place start behaving strangely, but for no apparent reason."

"Strangely like how?"

"Can be anything. Fits. Crying. Numbness. Blindness. Believing your dreams are real."

Saskia felt a rising dread.

"Hysteria still happens," Lila continued. "A few years ago it happened in this town in New York State. I read about it. All these girls started twitching. Having random fits. Hysterical episodes, they're called. Even now, nobody knows why. Maybe it somehow spread from person to person, like yawns. Or maybe something in the environment caused it. Some kind of toxin . . ."

"Like from a chemical plant?" Saskia suggested.

"Like Arrivo? Yeah, exactly. Pollution can have psychological effects—it's been proven. But it could be something else. Something simpler, something common. Like screwed-up families. The girls in that town had a lot of problems: money problems, divorce, absent parents. That got me thinking how all of us in the club kind of have family problems, too."

Saskia thought about that—about her own selfish mother, the Sampras sisters' parents living like they were wild college kids, Lila and Adrienne having no fathers—or at least none worth mentioning. Some of what Lila was saying was hard to hear, but Saskia knew it was a conversation they had to have.

"Nobody really understands hysteria," Lila pointed out, "its roots, or how it spreads. Could be that some girls give it to each other like a virus. Could be some girls fake their symptoms. Or maybe, unconsciously, they mimic each other."

"So it's possible that we're all crazy?"

Lila shook her head. "I wouldn't say that. Psychiatrists don't use the word *crazy* because, like, what's normal? I just meant we might all be influencing each other without being aware of it. During the day, yeah, sometimes I think we might be imagining our Forever Boyfriends—and Girlfriend—without really knowing it." She paused, her expression hardening. "But at night, I know we aren't. I know what's happening is real. Because Cassie's too good to make up."

Saskia thought again about Lila's dragonfly story, wondering for the millionth time where the line between life and death was. Did the girls in the club walk it every time they visited their Mercury Boys? What about the line between sanity and madness? Were they walking that line, too?

Suddenly someone unlocked the door. Saskia was so on edge she jumped out of her chair. But it was only her father coming home from work.

When he entered the kitchen, his face lit up, and he followed his nose to the pan. "Did you girls make this?"

"Lila did," said Saskia, hoping he didn't notice how tense she was.

"I made enough for you," Lila added.

Saskia's father stared at her with unabashed gratefulness. "If this tastes half as good as it smells, I'm gonna be in heaven."

"It tastes even better than it smells," Saskia assured him.

He stabbed a piece of chicken with a fork and chewed thoughtfully. Then he stabbed another piece, and another. "You don't have to answer this right away," he said to Lila, "but can you live here?"

Lila burst out laughing. Saskia joined her, but inside she was still reeling. The conversation about hysteria had thrown her for a loop. Broken families, witches, toxins, mimicry—it was a lot to take in. She needed time to think, to let it settle.

Her father spooned the remainder of the food into a dish and took a seat with them. He and Lila chatted amiably about things to do in and around Coventon. From time to time, Saskia nodded or smiled appropriately. But really, she felt separate, adrift in her thoughts. Barely tethered to the real world.

Before his shift the next day, Saskia's father reminded her to call her mother. Again. Saskia gave the obligatory nod, though she had no intention of following through. She had enough on her mind without adding her mother to the mix.

Besides, Saskia reasoned, nothing good ever came of communicating with her mother. Inevitably, Saskia hung up the phone feeling hurt, angry, or disappointed. The last time they'd talked, her mother had said, "It's time to move on, Saskia. Onward and upward!" The declaration had made Saskia feel small and pathetic, like she and her father were failing to climb to the upper rungs of her mother's metaphorical ladder. But Ralph, improbably, had reached the very top.

Saskia had wondered then, like she wondered now, why her mother considered Ralph so valuable. So precious, like a rare specimen. She spoke of him like an equal. But he wasn't. Mathematically, he was half her mother's age and had only a quarter of her brains and education. As for charisma, Saskia gave him a big fat zero.

Saskia was sure her mother was aware of his deficiencies. She must know they made a strange pair—a middle-aged Black woman and a young white man. They looked less like girlfriend and boyfriend than teacher and student. Or even mother and son. Secretly, Saskia wondered if people ever stopped them on the street and mentioned adoption, the way they had stopped her father when Saskia was a little girl.

I just wanted to tell you, sir, that you're a good man. A good man to adopt a child like that, misguided strangers would sometimes say.

She's mine, her father would reply. He'd always been calm and polite.

Of course she is.

She's mine genetically.

Saskia remembered how embarrassed and confused those people had been. Sometimes they'd even been defensive, as if her father had played a trick on them. But he'd always kept his cool. If he'd been annoyed and disgusted—and Saskia was sure he had—he'd never showed it, at least in front of her.

Was her mother as tactful when it came to questions about Ralph? Saskia doubted it. Unlike her father, her mother didn't suffer fools. She probably told them to book a ticket back to whatever antebellum plantation they'd come from. Better yet, take a mule. Then they could bond with another jackass.

Saskia smiled. Sometimes thinking about her mother made her furious. Other times it made her nostalgic for the stability she'd once had in Arizona, before the affair. She remembered all the good times she'd had with her parents, all those happily regular moments she'd taken for granted.

But inevitably, she also remembered how it had all gone wrong, and her nostalgia felt like a lie.

When her father left, Saskia tossed her cell phone onto the couch. It lay there, forgotten, until Lila called. As soon as Lila said, "Hey," Saskia knew something else was up. Her friend's voice sounded different, brittle.

"What's going on?"

"Something bad happened," Lila replied.

"What?"

"Marlene found out."

"No . . ."

"Yes."

"Christ! What happened?"

Lila exhaled audibly. "It started when I got to the library this morning. I knew something wasn't right. Marlene and everyone in my department were in the Collection room. Even Rich was there, and he's always up front.

"I heard Marlene call my name. When I walked in, she looked like a bomb about to detonate. I mean, she was *red*. The other people—they seemed upset, too, except Rich. He looked at me and put his finger to his lips, like to warn me.

"Then Marlene said, 'I used to *suspect* someone was stealing from our holdings. Now I know.' All these terrible thoughts started rushing through my head—how I was gonna get fired, and lose my scholarship, and have a criminal record. And my mother—she was gonna have a nervous breakdown. 'Cause I'm supposed to be the good one, the responsible one . . .

"Marlene was staring at me. Staring me *down*. I was on the verge of admitting everything. But then Rich stood up. Sask, he told them *he* did it."

"What?!"

"He took the fall."

"Oh my god . . ." Saskia said.

"He told this story—this whopper of a lie. Maybe he'd planned it, or maybe he made it up on the spot; I don't know. He said he needed money. He said he was planning on selling the daguerreotypes on eBay. Some bullshit like that. And Marlene bought it."

"What did she do?"

"What do you think?" Lila retorted. "She went berserk! She started yelling about how she'd trusted him, how he should be ashamed of himself. She was like, 'I treated you like family, and you betrayed me.' It was like a scene from a movie—a *bad* movie."

"Did she fire him?"

"No."

"No?!"

"No—because then I told everyone the truth."

"Oh, Lila."

"Well, *most* of the truth. Not about Cornelius, or Cassie, or any of that. Just about how I'd been borrowing the daguerreotypes. I told them Rich was trying to take the fall—that he was being protective of me, but that he had *nothing* to do with it."

"Wow," was all Saskia could muster.

Lila started sniffling. "So I'm the one who got fired, Sask. Crap, I have no idea what I'm gonna do."

Saskia could hear Lila choking up. She could picture her face: splotchy, wet with tears, crestfallen. She felt like throwing up.

"Marlene told me to leave immediately," Lila continued, voice quavering. "She threatened to call the police."

"You got out of there, right?"

"Yeah, I booked it out. I wanted to hug Rich—he looked like he was gonna cry. But I didn't dare in front of Marlene."

"I'm so sorry, Lila," Saskia said. "This all started with me. It wouldn't have happened if I hadn't asked for Cornelius's daguerreotype in the first place. What if I go to the library and talk to Marlene, admit that the whole thing was *my* fault? Tell her I put you in a terrible position, which is the truth?"

"No. You can't do that."

"Why not?"

"Well, for one thing," Lila said, "it wouldn't help. Marlene knows I allowed you in—nothing you can say would change that."

"What if I wrote her a letter?"

"Still wouldn't work."

"Okay, fine. But there must be something I can do to help," Saskia said desperately.

"I don't think so, Saskia. And listen, I don't blame you for all this. Like my mother says, I made my bed, and now I have to lie in it."

Saskia's face burned with shame, regret, and remorse. She wanted so much to make things right, but it was too late, like Lila said. The damage was irreparable.

"Hey," Saskia said. "Do you wanna come over? How about I make you dinner for once? You could sleep over . . . We'll eat huge amounts of popcorn and binge-watch some dumb show . . ."

"I don't know. Right now I just need to be alone—to process everything."

"Okay, I understand. Lila?"

"Yeah?"

"You're the bravest person I know."

Lila snorted. "What are you talking about?"

"You saved Rich—you took the fall without thinking twice. And you've had my back more times than I can count. You're just—fearless . . ."

"It's okay, Saskia. You don't have to flatter me."

"I'm *not*. I'm telling you the truth. Because I don't want you to doubt how special you are—not now, not ever."

Lila was quiet for a while. Saskia waited a little nervously, her eyes moist. At length, Lila started to giggle. "So are you trying to say I'm a *badass*?" she asked.

"Uh . . . yeah. That's exactly what I mean," Saskia replied, cracking a smile. "And I have photographic evidence to prove it."

Saskia

Cornelius was taking Saskia somewhere new. Though her curiosity was piqued, he wouldn't let her guess their destination. So she tried to focus on the journey. They were in a part of Philadelphia she'd never seen—a cosmopolitan area of the city. Gleaming white marble buildings were the norm here. Elsewhere the streets were uneven and riddled with mudholes, but here they were smooth and paved. The pair strolled along a sidewalk made of handsome red brick, laid out diagonally. The bricks were wet, not from rain, but from a recent scrubbing. Fire hydrants were on many corners, and clearly utilized.

Here and there, Saskia noticed open areas filled with wildlife: birds, chipmunks, scampering squirrels, even a deer. These rural spaces, teeming with flora and fauna, felt like tranquil reprieves from the rest of the city. That must have been their intended purpose.

Eventually, Cornelius led her down a narrow street, which in turn led to a narrow alley. He stopped abruptly in front of a nondescript doorway. After fishing for a key in his vest pocket, he unlocked the door. It creaked as they entered. Saskia's eyes struggled to adjust to the dark interior. Meanwhile, Cornelius began to light lamps—no doubt merchandise from his shop. As more corners of the space were illuminated, she could see that this was no ordinary place.

She walked around the vast room slowly, her fingers grazing all matter of machines, gadgets, contraptions, and contrivances. She had to watch her step as she walked. If she'd thought his office at the lighting store was cluttered, this place was ten times worse. It had everything an inventor might want or need: tools and worktables, pipes and pegs, clamps and wires, bolts, screws, every conceivable form of hardware. A nook for woodworking, a corner for metalworking.

She noticed that many of the actual items from his patent papers, diagrams, and drawings were here. Some of these inventions were complete. Some were still in development. He showed her a chicken deboner, automatic baby burper, lightning strike forecaster, chin fat diminisher, no-hands teakettle, automated chimney sweeper, and carrier pigeon wallet. When Saskia giggled, he laughed, too—clearly well aware of how absurd many of his creations were.

"How much time do you spend here?" she asked.

"Every spare minute. Well, every spare minute that I'm not at the lighting store, making daguerreotypes, tending to my children, or doing Harriet's bidding."

"Harriet—your wife."

He nodded.

"You never talk about her."

"Do you want me to?"

Saskia felt her face flush.

"I took you here," Cornelius said, "because it's very important to me. It's my refuge. I've never shown it to anyone else."

Saskia felt honored. At the same time, she felt supremely uneasy. It wasn't hard to see that she and Cornelius were getting closer, probably too close. She felt more and more like they were walking toward the edge of an inevitable cliff. Soon there would be only two options: backtrack or jump, hand in hand.

"Why?"

"Don't you know?" he asked softly. "Because I trust you implicitly. Because you seem to understand me. Because from the first second I saw you, I've been fascinated."

Saskia, suddenly light-headed, took a step back. "I don't know if you should have said that."

"I already did."

"Careful. You could mess everything up."

"I'd like to think we're separate from everything—and everyone," he replied.

"I don't know about that."

"Saskia, we don't really know the shape of space and time. There's no conclusive evidence, only theories. Maybe the linear version of time we learned—the steady running of a clock—is just an illusion. Maybe there are multiple versions of this life."

"Like parallel universes?" she asked.

"Yes! It's difficult to fathom, but we cannot rule out the possibility of many, many realities. Alternate versions of our lives coexisting but never overlapping and interacting."

"You really think there are thousands of copies of both of us, living other lives?" she asked dubiously.

"Perhaps. And not just thousands, but billions, trillions, untold numbers. Infinite variations of us living every conceivable scenario."

She shook her head. "And there's also a possibility that this is the *only* life we've got, and I managed to slip back into the course of it."

"That's possible, too."

"Or maybe all those versions of reality *do* overlap. And people could find out. Lives could change."

"Or maybe they couldn't."

"Maybe this isn't happening at all," she whispered. "I still wonder . . ."

"I don't," he said firmly. "For all my tinkering and inventing, there is no way I could have created this. You're far superior to anything I could have conceived of on my own."

Saskia was reminded of what Lila had said about Cassie.

He took another step toward her, and this time she didn't step back. He leaned down and kissed her tenderly. It was the best kiss she'd ever had. Perfect.

And yet, when it was over, guilt engulfed her like a tidal wave. Maybe Cornelius was right: maybe they were separate. Untouchable. But maybe they weren't. At this very moment, he was cheating on his wife. And Saskia was the other woman.

"Saskia?" he asked.

She recognized the confusion and earnestness on his face; she knew she wore the same expression. And yet she also knew, some-how, that whatever their relationship was—and whatever it could be—there was one boundary she could not cross. Would not cross.

Why not a single guy?

If you're fine with it . . .

"I'm not," she said suddenly.

"You're not what?"

"I'm not fine with it. With any of it. You have to think about your children."

"But I . . ."

"Your children. They should be your priority, not me."

"I never said . . ."

"This can't work. I shouldn't be here. You shouldn't have brought me here. We've made so many mistakes. I should know."

Cornelius grabbed her arm, but she snatched it back and stared at him with stony finality. Her heart seized. She knew what she had to do, but that didn't make it any easier, any easier at all. She dashed toward the nondescript door, feeling like at any second her skin might burst open and reveal all the sharp edges and broken pieces underneath.

CHAPTER EIGHTEEN

S askia felt depressed and prickly when the doorbell rang. With a carton of Ben & Jerry's Phish Food in one hand and a spoon in the other, she also felt like a real-life stereotype. All she had to do now was cut her hair and spend too much on retail therapy, and she'd be a breakup poster child.

Expecting to see Lila, she wasn't worried how she looked. So what if her best friend saw her wearing a chocolate-stained T-shirt and pajama bottoms at three in the afternoon? So what if she spontaneously started crying every five minutes? Lila would understand.

But when Saskia looked out the peephole and saw Adrienne standing there, she was taken aback. Adrienne had never even been to her house before.

"Just a second," Saskia said from behind the door, frantically trying to smooth down her frizzed-out hair. She didn't feel like talking to anyone except Lila. She wanted to crawl back into her bed and hide under the covers.

"It's me, Adrienne," Adrienne yelled back.

"I know," Saskia said when she finally opened the door. She glanced around outside, half-thinking she'd see Sara Beth or Paige lurking in the bushes. But all she saw was Adrienne's red bike parked on her front lawn. "You know how I knew it was you? When I looked out the peephole, all I could see were your shoulders."

"I've heard that before," Adrienne joked.

Despite her jovial tone, Saskia could see that Adrienne's eyes were troubled. Secretly, she was glad. She didn't think she could do lighthearted banter right now.

"Come on in," she said, guiding Adrienne to the kitchen. "What's up? Did I forget a Mercury Boys Club meeting or something?"

"No. At least I don't think so. I just had some spare time and thought I'd say hey."

"Oh. Cool. Do you want something to drink? Or a snack? I'd offer you ice cream," Saskia said, shaking the carton, "but you're a little late."

Adrienne smiled sympathetically. "You just have to go for it sometimes."

Saskia nodded, not sure if she wanted to open up to Adrienne about her last encounter with Cornelius. Rehashing the story would only make her more miserable. Yet before long she found herself telling Adrienne the tale, every last detail.

"Oh, man, that sucks," Adrienne said. "I'm so sorry."

"It's okay," Saskia said stoically.

But it was a lie, and Adrienne knew it. "You'll get over it soon. I know you will," she replied, lying, too.

"You can tell the others if you want," Saskia said. "I'm not looking forward to sharing the news."

"Okay—I'll let them know," Adrienne replied.

"Hey, let's talk about something else now, okay?" Saskia willed herself not to cry. "How are *you*?"

Adrienne wrinkled her nose, which seemed to Saskia to be sprinkled with more freckles than ever. "Well, unfortunately, the same as you. Crappy."

"Oh my god, don't tell me you broke up with Emery?"

"Oh no, it's not that bad. But it's close."

"So what happened?"

"I'm still . . . what's the word, when you go back and forth?"

"Waffling?"

"Yeah, I'm still waffling."

"You still can't decide between Emery and Ben?"

Adrienne shook her head. "And obviously I can't tell anyone else in the club after what happened. I'm so sorry, Saskia. That's the main reason I'm here. I want to apologize for getting you involved. I was so stupid. If I'd known you'd get punished, too, I never would have said anything."

"I'm all right," Saskia replied with a carefree wave of her hand. She sounded more benevolent than she felt. "What's done is done."

"So you forgive me?"

"Yeah, of course. There's nothing to forgive." Saskia stared at the floor. The dirty linoleum needed a good mopping. The thought depressed her even more. It was like the whole world was soiled and ugly. "Which way are you leaning?" she asked Adrienne.

"Between the boys? Are you sure you want to know? I don't want to get you in trouble again."

"This time there's no evidence," Saskia joked, but her voice had an edge.

Adrienne gathered her red hair into a bun, securing it with a lime-green elastic she took off her wrist. "Promise you won't tell Paige?" she asked nervously.

Saskia kicked a crumb with the toe of her sock. "Uh . . . what am I, masochistic?"

Adrienne looked at her curiously.

"Of course I won't tell Paige," she clarified.

"Okay," said Adrienne. "So the truth is, I think I might want . . . Benny."

"Wow, really?"

"Yeah. But it's, like, fifty-one to forty-nine percent, so it's not like I'm definite or anything."

"Is it because you can be around Benny anytime, and Emery's, well, far away?"

"Exactly. Plus, Benny and I have known each other for years. We understand each other. I still don't totally know Emery, you know? And he doesn't totally know me, either. I worry we don't have enough in common . . ."

"Well, let's face it—he is from *another century*."

"I mean, I probably *love* Emery more than Benny. And I'm more attracted to him. But it's hard to imagine living my whole life with him. How do I explain, like, Wi-Fi, or cable TV, or air-conditioning? What about my driving test or studying for the SATs? What about the stupid *prom*? He won't get any of that stuff."

"I guess not," Saskia conceded. She noticed that a muscle under Adrienne's left eye kept twitching. Saskia wondered if it was a side effect of the mercury or if Adrienne was just stressed out.

"What do *you* think I should do?" Adrienne asked.

"God, I don't know." Saskia really didn't.

"Please, I need your advice."

"Why *my* advice?"

"I don't know who else to talk to," Adrienne conceded. "And I . . . I think you understand my problem better than anyone else."

Saskia knew what she should say, what Paige would want her to say—that Emery was the obvious choice. The only choice, according to club rules. But she couldn't force herself to speak the words. Because she honestly didn't believe them.

"If you can't decide, maybe just leave it to chance," she said carefully.

"What do you mean?"

"I mean, you don't have to figure it out this second. Maybe you should take a step back, and see where fate leads you."

"Where fate leads me," Adrienne repeated, as if weighing the value of the words.

"That does sound a little cringy," Saskia admitted.

Adrienne giggled. "Well, it's not like I have any better ideas."

"So you think you'll wait?"

"I guess so," she said.

Saskia nodded. "Good. So now that we kind of resolved your problem, can I ask you something? Something serious?"

"Sure—anything."

"Would you go with me to buy more ice cream?"

. . .

"It's Rich," Lila whispered to Saskia after answering her cell phone.

They were in Saskia's room, where Saskia's sputtering window air conditioner provided welcome relief from the day's insane heat. The temperature was projected to reach a hundred degrees. Saskia thought it was already there—and then some. She'd been sprawled out on the floor, but sat up quickly and scooted closer to Lila, who nervously put her phone on speaker.

"Hi," she said tentatively.

"Hey, kid. How are you?" Rich replied.

Saskia could tell that Lila was grateful to hear his voice. Though it had been only a short time since the firing, Lila had said that life already felt drastically different. She missed the paycheck, the archive, the comforting repetition of her work, and of course her conversations with Rich.

"Miserable," Lila admitted. "You?"

"I've been better."

"How's *Marlene*?"

"Killing puppies. Eating babies. The usual."

Lila giggled. Rich cleared his throat. "I convinced her that she shouldn't, you know, lodge an official complaint—or worse, file charges," he said.

"She was gonna file charges?"

"She was thinking about it."

"That's hard-core."

"It's Marlene—what do you expect?" Rich retorted. "I told her you're going through some bad stuff—which honestly seems to be the case—and she calmed down a little. I mean, don't get me wrong, she's still pissed. But now at least she's not cursing and hurling stuff around her office anymore."

"Thanks, Rich. I owe you. And I guess I am going through 'some bad stuff.' It's a weird time."

"I gathered that. Ever think about talking to someone? Like, a counselor or therapist?"

"Sometimes," Lila admitted.

"I mean, you must believe in therapy. Isn't that what you're gonna be—a psychiatrist?"

"Yeah."

"And not that you need my advice," he continued, "but I gotta say one more thing. Those friends of yours—especially the blonde and her sister—I'm not sure they're a great influence. In fact, I'm pretty sure they're a terrible one. Maybe you should think about that, too—who you want your friends to be."

Saskia exhaled, feeling guilty all over again, but Lila gave her a reassuring smile. "You've got a point," she told Rich, then added shyly, "I miss hanging out with you. You were the best part of the job."

"Well, turns out I'm not gonna be here much longer, either."

"What?! Don't tell me Marlene fired you, too."

"Nah," said Rich. "I gave her my two weeks' notice. 'Member that library science program I applied for? I got in."

"Oh my god. That's so great! I'm so happy for you!"

"Thanks, kid. It's crazy to think I'm gonna be a student again. But I figure it's never too late to make a fresh start, right?"

"Right."

"And listen—there's one other thing I wanted to tell you. I talked to a buddy who works at Yale—in the psychology department, of all places. He says they're looking for a part-time administrative assistant. The pay's not great, but the job's in your wheelhouse. He thinks he could get you an interview . . ."

"Holy crap, Rich!" Lila exclaimed.

"Hey, hey, don't get all excited yet. It's only an interview. No guarantees."

"Yeah, I understand. But still, thank you . . . for everything."

"I'll text you the info. I hope it works out."

"I'll bring my A-game," she promised.

"And I'll try to survive my last two weeks with Satan. Wish me luck."

• • •

A few days later, Lila came to Saskia's house to cook another meal.

As she bent over a simmering pot of spaghetti sauce, wooden spoon in hand, Lila revealed there was new fallout from her library firing. "My scholarship to Western Connecticut State's off the table," she muttered, stirring the sauce so vigorously Saskia was sure it would splatter the walls.

"Damn, that sucks."

"Tell me about it. And what's worse is, my mother's been praying on her rosary. *Nonstop.* I haven't even seen that rosary since was I was in elementary school and my dad left."

For what felt like the millionth time, Saskia wished she hadn't asked Lila for so many favors, that she hadn't caused this domino effect of problems by insisting on taking the Cornelius daguerreotype. In her darkest moments, sometimes she even regretted meeting Cornelius in the first place.

"At least you have a shot at that Yale job," she said, trying to stay positive for Lila's sake.

"I don't know. The interview went well, but I can't assume they liked me as much as I liked them."

"Have some faith. I'm sure you made a great impression."

"You really think so?"

"Of course!"

Just then, Saskia's phone beeped. The sound startled both girls. It was a text from Paige about that night's MBC meeting. Saskia read it aloud.

> P: change in location. we're not gonna meet under the tree,
> but at the end of whallen ave.

"Whallen Ave.—that's where Arrivo is," Lila said, pursing her lips.

Concerned, Saskia texted back.

S: Arrivo? why?

P: you'll see it'll be a surprise

"I've never really liked Paige's surprises," Lila muttered, stirring the sauce harder than ever.

Later on, as the two drove slowly down Whallen Avenue, Saskia had to admit she agreed with Lila. It was an ugly street, frankly, pitted and pockmarked, with acres of weeds, wild brambles, and straggly trees on either side. Saskia was surprised by how close Whallen was to her own street—much closer than she'd thought. After what Lila had said about the connection between pollution and mental illness, it wasn't a comforting thought.

Saskia rolled down the window and instantly regretted it. The air that poured in reminded her of chem class. She wrinkled her nose and gazed at garbage along the roadside: beer bottles, crumpled newspapers, fast-food wrappers, soda cans. A white plastic bag, the kind you used to get at grocery stores, blew past like an amorphous ghost. As Saskia watched it disappear, she wondered uncomfortably if she even belonged in the Mercury Boys Club anymore.

She'd confirmed what had happened between her and Cornelius after Adrienne had told the other girls. She'd been worried about their reactions; after all, she'd technically broken rule number eleven: *If an MBC member wants to break up with her Forever Boyfriend, she must seek permission from the club.* But the girls had been understanding and consoling—even Paige.

Still, now that Saskia didn't have a Forever Boyfriend, she wasn't sure of her place in the club. Did she have to get another Forever Boyfriend to stay? She wasn't ready for that—and in fact, she wasn't sure she'd ever be ready. All she was sure about was that she didn't want to lose her new friends and Cornelius all in the same week. She was already half depressed because of the breakup; she didn't want to spiral down any more.

As she and Lila neared the end of the road, the plant loomed like a hulking metal beast. A postapocalyptic fright. It was an enormous structure with huge, weather-beaten storage tanks and a couple dozen sky-high smokestacks. The latter furiously pumped chemical clouds into the night; Saskia was surprised she had never spotted those gloomy puffs of smog from her house. Within the plant, ladders and scaffolding rose to various decks and bunkers, some several stories high. All around machines were at work, noisy machines with wheel cranks, belching pipes, screeching valves, and gurgling boilers.

Lila parked in front of a chain-link fence that stretched so far Saskia figured it must encircle all of Arrivo. The sisters' car sat nearby, but there was no sign of them or Adrienne. Saskia texted Paige.

S: Where are you?

Unsure of what to do, Saskia and Lila walked the perimeter of the fence. Every fifteen feet or so, they read a new and alarming sign: DANGER. DO NOT ENTER. HAZARDOUS CHEMICALS. KEEP OUT. AUTHORIZED PERSONNEL ONLY. PELIGRO: ALMACENAMIENTO DE SUSTANCIAS QUÍMICAS.

Saskia was scared even to breathe. She felt like she should be wearing a hazmat suit and gas mask. She texted Paige again. No response.

When she and Lila had gone a few hundred feet, they spotted a way in. One of the fence gates was ajar. Two thick locks lay open on the ground.

"Did the sisters do that?" asked Saskia, kicking one of the open locks with the toe of her sneaker.

"Probably."

"Which one knows how to pick locks?"

"I'd put my money on Sara Beth," said Lila. "Bet she's learned all kinds of tricks from her pickpocket boyfriend."

They entered cautiously and looked around. The plant was only partly lit, and visibility was poor.

"Should we yell for them?" Saskia whispered.

Lila shook her head. Saskia knew what she was thinking: that someone else might be listening—a workman, a cop, maybe someone worse. Her eyes darted back and forth. Trudging forward, she worried a shadow might come to life, jump out, and grab her. Arrivo would be a great place for a horror movie—or a murder.

The girls passed a heaping pile of scrap metal, an area grimly marked CHEMICAL BURIAL GROUND, and storage tanks that reminded Saskia of oversized steel coffins. To her left, a tarp-lined holding pool of rust-colored liquid looked like something out of an especially creepy Edward Gorey book. When she spotted what appeared to be a dead animal floating in the middle, she started to feel dizzy.

Putting her hand on Lila's shoulder, Saskia tried to steady herself. She noticed Lila was gazing upward. "Do you think a storm's coming?" Lila asked, pointing.

Saskia shrugged. The sky was so smothered by air pollution that it was hard to tell. "Where are they?" she murmured, checking her phone again.

A few minutes later, the girls heard a whistle, almost lost in the whir and wheeze of machinery. It seemed to be coming from one of the metal decks in the heart of the structure. Lila whistled back.

"Up here!" someone called.

Squinting, Saskia could just make out the inky silhouettes of three people deep in the labyrinth of scaffolding. The sisters and Adrienne. They looked like flies caught in a rusty metal web.

"Come on up!" It was Paige. She sounded strangely chipper, given the setting.

Saskia looked at Lila. "Is she serious?"

"You know the answer to that," Lila replied grimly.

With a sigh, Saskia took hold of a ladder. Loose paint chips stuck to her sweaty palms. Some made paper cut–thin scratches in her skin. Still light-headed, she ascended. She looked down exactly once and vowed not to do it again.

"Keep going," urged Lila, who was right behind her.

One rickety ladder led to the next. Saskia tried to ignore how the metal creaked and groaned under her weight. She wondered if the structure had been inspected recently, if it had *ever* been inspected. She remembered the movie *Vertigo*, starring the ever-charming Jimmy Stewart, who had talked a terrified Kim Novak into climbing the steep steps of a very tall bell tower. And how Kim Novak had climbed those many steps, even knowing that it wasn't going to end well—that *she* wasn't going to end well.

Finally, not a moment too soon, Saskia made it to the platform where the girls were standing. The sisters grabbed her hands and helped pull her up. Lila soon joined them.

Paige gave each of them a hug. Saskia tried to smile, but it came out contorted.

"Are you okay?" Paige asked her. "Post-Cornelius, I mean?" She squeezed Saskia's hand.

"Yeah, I guess. Well, not really."

"It can't be easy."

Saskia shook her head. "It's weird to just sleep at night, knowing I won't see him."

"I can relate."

"How are you dealing with Sam gone?"

"I spend all my time trying not to think about him, but thinking about him, anyway."

"Yeah, I know all about that."

"Paige," Lila interjected, "why didn't you guys wait for us at the fence? And why are we *here*?"

Paige laughed. "I thought we needed some adventure. The Mercury Boys Club is all about trying new things, right?" From her pocket, she pulled out a jangling ring of keys. "The Arrivo master set. I talked someone into giving them to me."

Saskia recalled how easy it had been for the sisters to trick that smarmy tattoo artist, Jimmy. They'd probably used the same technique on some sucker at Arrivo.

"So the MBC meeting's officially here?" Lila asked dubiously.

Paige glanced at her sister. "We thought it would be fun."

"Hmm . . . I'd use a different word."

"Terrifying," said Adrienne with a shiver.

"Or suicidal," said Lila.

"I kinda like this place," Sara Beth retorted, looking around. The whites of her eyes glinted within rings of smoky black shadow. "It's very Tim Burton."

Saskia vaguely recognized the name. She believed Tim Burton was a director. Still, since 99 percent of the movies she watched were at least fifty years old, she had no idea what he'd made. She began to sway, still feeling off-balance, and decided to sit down. She poked her fingers through the open gaps in the metal mesh floor. It was all too easy to imagine the structure groaning, straining, collapsing. Everyone falling. She wondered if they could survive such a thing. She wondered what would happen if they didn't.

Rule #15: MBC members will meet body and soul with their Forever Boyfriends in death!!!

"We're all together, and that's what matters—not the place," said Paige, settling down beside Saskia. "Are you ready to get started?"

The others nodded and sat down, too. Once Adrienne took attendance, her pen fluttering over the official notebook, Lila revealed to the others that she'd been fired from the library at Western Connecticut State. Now, she confirmed, the girls officially lacked access to the daguerreotypes and mercury.

"So much bad news," complained Adrienne. "Sam gone. Lila out of a job. Saskia and Cornelius breaking up. It sucks."

There came a moment of silence, each girl lost in her own head. Then Paige said, "I'm afraid I've got more bad news."

Saskia's first thought was that Paige had new information on Samuel. Maybe he'd been hurt since joining the Royal Navy. Maybe his ship had gone down. Maybe, god forbid, he'd died. Was that how Samuel Pendleton had lost his life—drowning at sea? And if so, would Paige ever be able to visit him again, or was this the end?

Saskia's mind spun. There was still so much about the Mercury Boys they didn't understand.

She was still considering the possibilities when Paige looked at her curiously. "What's going on, Sask? You look preoccupied."

"Sorry."

"Thinking about Cornelius?" Paige asked gently.

Saskia looked away. If she started talking about Cornelius, chances were she'd start crying—and that was the last thing she wanted to do.

"It's okay," Paige assured her. "You don't have to talk . . ."

"Thanks," Saskia murmured.

"But I'm sorry to say the bad news does have to do with you."

Saskia wasn't sure if she'd heard correctly. "What?"

"Yeah, I'm sorry, it does," Paige confirmed. She had the courteous but firm voice of a flight attendant telling someone to put on her seat belt. "Why don't you tell us about your last conversation with Adrienne?"

Goddamn.

Saskia ran her fingernails over the rough mesh. She felt a jab of pain when one of them snapped off.

"You went through a lot at the fountain, didn't you?" continued Paige.

Saskia refused to say anything.

"You weren't afraid to admit you'd messed up, and you accepted your punishment. As your friend, I was really proud of you. I didn't think you'd break rule number twelve again. So I was really surprised when you did."

Saskia studied Adrienne. She turned evasively and tucked her legs underneath her body, as if trying to look smaller. It was an impossible task for such an Amazonian girl.

Why would you want to look smaller, Adrienne? Because you're feeling guilty?

Saskia knew in an instant what had happened, how Adrienne had shown up at her house the other day not because she needed advice, but because she'd wanted to trick Saskia into breaking yet another club rule. And Saskia had. As soon as she'd suggested that Adrienne "leave things to fate" instead of urging her to focus on Emery, Saskia had broken her promise. And Adrienne had probably wasted no time in telling that to Paige.

Savagely, Saskia tore off the rest of her broken nail with her teeth and tasted blood. She'd learned that the sisters could be difficult and even calculating at times, but she never would have guessed sweet, simple Adrienne could be.

Adrienne stared at her and mouthed, *I'm sorry*, but Saskia wasn't in a forgiving mood.

"Why—why set me up?" she demanded. "I was trying to *help* you."

"I asked her to," Paige interjected. "It's my job to make sure we're following the rules. And I had a feeling, even after the last punishment, that you weren't complying, Saskia."

"God, talk about backhanded," Lila groaned. "Paige, you're, like, the textbook definition of toxic."

"She's not," Sara Beth said defensively. "She's tested me, too— her own sister! She's just being protective of our guys—and the club in general."

"I'm sorry, Saskia," Adrienne repeated. "I really am."

"Stop apologizing," Paige scolded. "Saskia's the one who should be sorry. Right now I would do anything to see Samuel. I would swim across the ocean if I thought I'd find him. And here you are, Saskia, telling Adrienne it's okay to choose Benny over Emery."

"That's not what I said," Saskia protested.

"It's what you implied," said Paige. "Did you not say, 'leave it to fate'? That's like telling her to roll the dice or pick a card. What you didn't do was stand up for her Mercury Boy."

Pick a card—like Josh asked me to do?

"I was just trying to be a good friend," Saskia replied.

"A good friend—or a good member of this club?"

"Are they mutually exclusive?"

"In this case, yes."

"Paige," interjected Lila, "stop acting all high and mighty. You're not innocent, either. You and Adrienne basically set her up."

"Look, it's not like Saskia did only one thing wrong," Paige said, clearly irritated. "When she broke up with Cornelius, she didn't ask permission from the group. I know she had to do it—or thought she had to, but she still broke rule number eleven."

The metallic tang of blood stayed in Saskia's mouth. She hated being called out. Picked on. Scapegoated. What had happened to Paige thinking of her like a second sister? What had happened to the special bond Saskia could've sworn they'd had?

"Saskia broke two rules," continued Paige. "The bottom line is, if she wants to continue being in the MBC, she has to do another punishment. And look, I'm not trying to be mean, even though I know you think I am, Saskia. I'm just trying to keep us accountable. Maybe someday you'll see it's for the best."

See it's for the best. Where had Saskia heard that before? Oh yes, her mother had said it when she'd tried to convince Saskia that breaking up their family to be with a thoroughly mediocre twenty-something was the best option for everybody.

Sure . . .

The thought of her mother tossing her to the side like a pair of jeans that would never fit again walloped Saskia. Maybe it was because she was still reeling from her breakup with Cornelius. Or maybe it was the distinct possibility that she'd fallen out of Paige's good graces forever—if she'd even been there to start with. Maybe it was even the memory of a wild-eyed Kim Novak plunging many stories to her death—exactly like the audience knew she would. Whatever the cause, Saskia began to sniffle and then to sob, which was—second to falling—the last thing she wanted to be doing.

She wondered if there was something inside her, something in that metallic blood of hers, that was inherently repellent and unlovable. There had to be. Why else did the women in her life always cast her away? Her own mother. Heather. All those other girls in Arizona who Saskia had thought she'd be friends with forever. And now Paige and Adrienne and probably Sara Beth, too. Maybe even Lila would abandon her, too, eventually. All those people had decided that Saskia wasn't worth the trouble.

They couldn't all be wrong.

"The punishment won't be any harder than the first," she heard Paige say.

"Not harder than almost drowning?" said Lila. "Wow, Paige, you're so charitable." She faced Saskia. "You wanna jet? I'm kinda over this soap opera."

"I'm assuming that means you're over your girlfriend, then, too," said Paige.

Lila glared at her.

"I don't know why you keep it such a big secret," Paige continued. "You're gay. So what? Where's the scandal? This is the twenty-first century, not the Middle Ages."

"I like to keep my private life private. And I don't like when people get all up in my business."

"Get all up in your business?" Paige repeated amusedly. "If you're trying to sound tough, Lila, it's not working."

"What I'm *trying* to do is get you to back off."

"Don't get all triggered! All I did was pay attention. The truth's not hard to see. And by the way, I'm happy for you. You found love. It should be something you *want* to share with the group."

Lila bristled. "I have to do things in my own time."

"Okay, I can understand that. But we have to be open with each other. If we keep secrets like we've been doing"—Paige looked pointedly at Saskia—"this club's gonna implode."

Though the mesh floor was still holding up, Saskia felt herself sinking. Sinking back to the place she'd been when her mother had packed her bags, when Heather had ghosted her, when Josh had ditched her in front of Ethan's house. A place she seemed to return to again and again, though it was the last place she wanted to be.

"I'll do it," Saskia heard herself say.

"Sask, no. Let's just get out of here," Lila said. "It's not worth it."

"I'll do it," she repeated.

Because if I don't, then I'll be alone. And I can't bear that—not now, not again.

"You will?" Paige asked.

"Yes."

"Attagirl," Paige replied.

Sara Beth was the first down the ladder, followed by her sister, and then Adrienne. Saskia watched them scramble down effortlessly, their long, coltish limbs seemingly made for the job, and wondered if the descent would be easier for her. It wasn't. The volume turned up on her vertigo. Her head spun. The world heaved. She clutched the rusted rungs for dear life. A few feet below, Lila voiced encouragement. It was just enough to get her down, step by step, in slow motion.

Back on firm ground, she wiped away the tears that clung stubbornly to her cheeks. She sucked at her still-bleeding finger and blanched as Paige approached, trying to brace herself for whatever Paige had to say. But it was hard for Saskia to steel herself when all the fight had left her.

Paige came close, uncomfortably close, and stared at Saskia with wide, beseeching eyes. Then she dug into her pocket and produced something. The medal. Samuel's medal.

She must carry it with her everywhere, Saskia thought. *She must sleep with it tucked under her pillow.*

"Here, I want you to have this."

Saskia was too dumbstruck to react.

"Go on, put out your hand," said Paige.

"But—I couldn't. It's yours."

"Wanna know why I'm giving it to you?"

Saskia shook her head.

"It's because I can tell you think I'm being too hard on you. And maybe you're right. Maybe I am. But that's because I hold you to a higher standard. Higher than the other girls, but don't tell them that—especially not Sara Beth."

Still, Saskia couldn't speak.

"And I hold you to a higher standard," Paige continued, "because you're important to me. More important than you know. Sometimes I think that if there's one friend I want to have forever—one friend who's smart and cool and funny, who sees through all this petty high school BS—it's you."

Saskia struggled to hold back tears. She didn't want to cry again. She couldn't. But it was as if Paige had applied a balm to all her hurt, ragged edges. Saskia hadn't realized how desperately she'd needed reassurance and validation.

The next thing she knew, Paige was taking her hand and pressing the medal into her palm.

"But—it's so important to you," Saskia sputtered.

"You're more important."

Saskia felt its weight in her hand. She marveled at the serenity of Queen Victoria's face. She thought about how lately the club was both the best and worst aspect of her life, and how its seesaw effect was getting harder and harder to endure.

"After I do this, the punishment," she asked, closing her fingers around the medal, "do you think we can go back to the beginning? To when we first discovered how to visit our Forever Boyfriends and things were . . . easier?"

Better? Happier? Saner?

"That's exactly what I want, too," Paige replied.

Saskia trudged to where the others were waiting beside the holding pool. It was shallow and large. Up close, the color of the liquid reminded her of orange Jell-O. She could only imagine what kind of chemicals had combined to create such an unnatural shade. Dozens of dead flies dotted the surface, their diaphanous wings stained tangerine. And then there was the carcass in the middle, a gruesome clump of dingy, matted fur that was better left unidentified.

Saskia noticed that the water was even with the top of the containment tarp. There had been runoff, if the wet ground around the periphery of the pool was any indication. She thought again about her conversation with Lila on hysteria and how there could be environmental triggers. She wondered what kind of secrets scientists would find if they ever bothered to test the soil and water around Coventon.

Her thoughts were interrupted by grunts of exertion. The sisters were dragging a long two-by-four toward the pool. Saskia didn't know where'd they found it, but here it was. With Adrienne's help, they hoisted it upright, one end arrowed at the sky, then let it fall with a booming clatter across the pool. The two-by-four extended past either end of the containment tarp. Liquid lapped against the bottom.

"Saskia, maybe you've already guessed the punishment," Paige said. "You have to walk across this beam."

"You can do this, Saskia," said Adrienne, her voice full of forced cheer. "I know you can."

Paige nodded. "It's way easier than the fountain punishment. Concentrate, keep your balance, and you'll be done in no time."

"Unless I fall in," Saskia said.

"You won't."

Saskia took a deep breath, then regretted it. The air around the pool smelled wretched, like burnt plastic, wet dog, and stale beer all mixed together. She was pretty sure it was as toxic as it was nauseating.

"It's not too late," whispered Lila from beside her. "Are you sure you want to do this?"

"Yeah," Saskia whispered back, her jaw clenched. She thought back to better times, to when she had been as drunk on the club as she'd been on the sisters' booze.

Lila gave her a boost onto the plank. For several seconds Saskia clung to her hand. "Just let me make sure it's stable," she said. "Feels kinda shaky."

When she took her first step, she knew she'd been right to distrust the board: it was rickety. She looked back at Paige, who nodded encouragingly. Moving slowly, Saskia shuffled along, arms raised for balance. She'd taken two gymnastics lessons in second grade, then quit because she'd hated wearing a leotard. Now she wished she could throttle her second-grade self.

With every inch of progress, her stomach lurched. She imagined falling into the tangerine murk. She imagined it entering her mouth, her nostrils. She imagined it eating like acid through her innards. She tried to glance again at Paige, but tottered, a little to the left, even more to the right. Gritting her teeth, she regained her balance just in time.

Finally she reached the midway point. She was now inches away from the dead animal. A possum, Saskia saw. Its eyes were gone. Eaten or dissolved. It would be the perfect prop for a Stephen King movie. Propelled by fear, she moved faster. Adrenaline pumping, she lifted her gaze and fixed it on a point in the distance.

Look at where you're going, not where you might fall.

One foot over the next, body straight, head high, she literally ran the rest of the way. When she jumped off the end, she said a Hail Mary in her head.

"You did it!" gushed Paige, rushing over. Adrienne and Sara Beth were a half step behind, followed by Lila, faces beaming, arms outstretched to hug her. Saskia let herself be enveloped in the dubious safety of their arms.

Adrienne

The gauzy green dress was, frankly, completely inappropriate. But Adrienne didn't care because all she saw was the way she looked in it, as reflected in Emery's appreciative eyes. She hitched up the skirt a few inches. Even though the field hospital grounds were far cleaner now, they were still no place for fancy clothes. Her dress would be filthy in no time.

She fingered the brooch, which sat in the cleavage she'd tried to create with one of the awful corsets Paige and Sara Beth had bought. The brooch was impressive; the cleavage, not so much. Adrienne smiled, remembering how the girls had erupted into laughter the first time they'd tried on those corsets, which fit like straitjackets. The girls had paraded around the sisters' house like a bunch of nineteenth-century floozies, whiskey in hand. The funniest part, though, was that those corsets weren't nearly as bad as what Victorian women had really worn: pantalettes, chemises, petticoats, camisoles. So many clothes Adrienne figured it must have taken them an hour to get dressed every day.

As Emery had promised, there was a carriage waiting on the outskirts of the field.

It was small and shabby with a couple of old, tired-looking horses tethered to the front. Even so, when she looked at it, Adrienne felt like Cinderella bound for the ball.

Emery smiled at her. "Ready?" he asked, extending his hand.

Adrienne's own smile was more restrained. She still wasn't sure she was doing the right thing. The pills, the Nyquil, the half-bottle of mercury she'd swallowed—the combination was more than she'd ever taken before. The mercury alone was probably enough to put her over the edge.

Soon, if not already, she'd lose control. The mercury and the drugs would take over, and then fate would decide. Fate would lead her, like Saskia had said. Fate would determine if Adrienne rode away with Emery into a new future, never again waking up to the present, or if she'd see Benjamin again.

"Ready," she answered, forcing a smile. She tried to ignore the fact that her vision was going blurry at the edges.

"Good. Everything is prepared."

It was true. Their bags were packed. The horses had drunk. Emery had been offered a job with the printer he had apprenticed with before the war. It wouldn't be much money, but he assured Adrienne it would be enough. She took his hand and placed one foot cautiously on the folding step of the carriage.

But she was suddenly shaky. She couldn't trust her legs. They were starting to capsize. And what was that new feeling in her mouth? It was awful—a hundred needles simultaneously pierced her tongue.

"Careful now, sweetheart," she heard Emery say, catching her mid-fall. Her eyes were open, but he, too, had gone blurry. "No need to be nervous. You're going to love your new life."

CHAPTER NINETEEN

Lila and Saskia reached the tree and crawled through its dangling branches, which shifted back into place with uncanny precision. A dozen votives flickered on the soft earth. The sisters were already there, sitting on the ground. They looked like beautiful ghosts in their period clothes: delicate lawn dresses adorned with eyelet embroidery and yards of lace trim. Saskia remembered the dresses from the trunk. Their color reminded her of tea, of the patina that yellowed many of the daguerreotypes in the library.

Though the dresses were modest—long-hemmed and high-collared, bits of skin peeked out. Saskia saw a calf, a forearm, a flash of thigh. She hadn't realized how tan the sisters had become. The summer sun had made them almost as dark as she was.

"Thanks for coming to the meeting," Paige said, watching the flame of a candle. "Now Adrienne's the only one we're missing."

"She's probably running late," Sara Beth said.

"Should we wait?" asked Saskia.

Paige glanced at her phone. "Nah, let's just get started. I'll fill her in later so that she can update the minutes."

As soon as Paige called the meeting to order, Sara Beth reached her hand behind her back and pulled out a bottle. "Since our last meeting was not exactly easy, I thought we needed a boost," she said, grinning. "This is fifty-year-old Glen Grant Single Malt

Whisky. It's worth at least a grand. Our dad's been saving it, but his loss is our gain."

Saskia gasped. "A grand? You can't open that . . ."

"Oh, I can, and I will."

Paige winked at Saskia. "We have to finish it, too . . . and bury the bottle. Get rid of the evidence, if you know what I mean."

"Let's just hope it doesn't taste like horse piss," Sara Beth joked.

Paige distributed a stack of Dixie cups—uncharacteristically lowbrow for the Sampras family—and Sara Beth poured. Saskia took a small sip. Giddily, nervously, she wondered how much money was sliding down her throat.

"To the club," Paige said, lifting her cup above her head.

"Hear, hear!" cheered Sara Beth.

"Adrienne's gonna regret missing this," Saskia said, taking a slug. She liked the way the whiskey slid down hot and spicy, wending a warm path through her body. Pretty soon she felt different, relaxed, like maybe the club really was going to be easier from here on in. Sara Beth refilled her cup.

"Hope this helps me sleep tonight," Paige remarked from beside her.

"Why?" asked Saskia.

"Oh my god, I've had terrible insomnia lately."

"Even with your mom's Restoril?"

"Oh, forget about that. I've taken so much I've built up a tolerance."

"What about the other pills?"

"The baggie? That's like popping M&M's for me now. They don't do *anything*. For Sara Beth, either. Do they work for you?"

"I don't really use them," Saskia admitted.

"What do you do when you can't sleep?"

"I just . . . don't sleep."

"I wish there was an easier way," Paige said. Saskia noticed a subtle spread of freckles on the bridge of her nose, probably from the summer sun. They made her beauty a little more relatable.

"I could try to find a dealer, but I don't trust them," Paige continued. "How do you know what you're getting is legit? Safe?"

Saskia nodded in agreement, not that she had any experience with drug dealers.

"Hey, Sask, isn't your father a doctor?" Sara Beth asked, inserting herself into the conversation.

"A nurse." Saskia felt a shred of shame and hated herself for it.

"But he works in the hospital, right?"

"Yeah . . ."

"Couldn't he, like, help us out?"

"What do you mean?" she asked cautiously. "Like, help us steal medicine?"

Paige stared at her, all long lashes and cornflower-blue eyes. "God no! Nothing like that. That could get him fired. I just thought if your dad's in the hospital, then he must be around meds a lot. Maybe you could visit him. Maybe see what's around. If something good's in reach, and no one's looking, you know . . ."

Saskia shook her head. "I don't think so."

Paige nodded understandingly. "Fair enough. But at least think about it—maybe for the future. Some of that prescription stuff would save us a lot of sleepless nights."

"Okay, I will," Saskia said, although she knew she wouldn't. She wouldn't risk her father's new job—not even for Paige.

"Thanks," Paige said, bumping her shoulder against Saskia's affectionately. "Even one bottle would help. We could cut the pills in half, make them last. This could be a one-time thing—until we come up with a better plan."

"Sure . . ."

Saskia went to take another sip from her cup, but it was empty. Hadn't Sara Beth just filled it up? She must have already drunk two of those little cups—or was it three? Enough that she felt like she could melt into a warm puddle. Enough that her head was spinning a little, and this time it had nothing to do with vertigo. Enough that she had to pee. She muttered something about needing the bathroom. Lila, who had abstained from drinking as usual, watched her go with a vague look of concern.

Saskia slipped through the branches, across the yard, and inside the Sampras house. After the heat of the whiskey, the cool blast of AC felt refreshing.

She found the nearest bathroom—she wasn't sure how many there were in the house, but she'd been in at least four. This one, like the others, was massive, expensive-looking, and a little garish, with floor-to-ceiling Spanish tiles, shiny bronze hardware, a tub as big as a toolshed, and cascading tropical plants. The air smelled like the foil-wrapped, triple-milled French soaps that were heaped in a basket on the sink console. She felt indulgent as she locked the door behind her.

She lingered after she was finished, fingering a tower of cloud-soft towels in a closet. They were all perfectly folded and blindingly white. The towels in Saskia's house, by contrast, were a hodge-podge of colors, styles, and sizes. The only things they had in common were stains and threadbare edges.

Saskia splashed cold water on her face, selected a towel from the closet, and held it to her wet skin. It was then that she heard the voices. Unfamiliar voices. A man and a woman. Her first thought was that they belonged to burglars. But wouldn't burglars whisper? These voices were loud and animated.

Saskia realized with a start that Mr. and Mrs. Sampras must be home. Was it possible? The sisters' parents were like elusive legends: unicorns or yetis.

She had to investigate. Opening the door quietly, she tiptoed in the direction of the conversation. It was coming from the kitchen. As she got closer, she realized that Mrs. Sampras sounded very much like Sara Beth. Saskia wondered if she looked like her, too.

She crept to the archway leading to the kitchen and pressed herself against a wall, careful not to make a sound. Much as she wanted to see the parents, she wasn't sure *she* wanted to be seen.

"The realtor?" Mrs. Sampras said. "She said five hundred K. I think that's a little high for the Cape, don't you? It's not like it's the Hamptons. But, honey, we could lowball."

"I don't understand why we can't rent," Mr. Sampras complained.

"You know I can't stand the idea of other people's houses. Other people's things. Other people's *beds*."

"We can't buy a house in every single place we vacation."

"Not every single one. Just this one," Mrs. Sampras countered.

"Sure, you say that *now*."

Saskia heard the clink of a cup hitting a saucer. A slurp of coffee or tea. The rustle of a magazine.

"Todd, while I remember, do you know where my grandfather's collection is?"

"Isn't it usually in your dresser?" Mr. Sampras asked.

"Yes, but it's not there."

"You must've moved it."

"I never touched it," Mrs. Sampras said. "I think the housekeeper took it—the one we fired."

"Out of everything in this house, why on earth would she take your grandfather's junk?"

"It's not junk! I was watching *Antiques Roadshow*—it's a very interesting show, by the way—and I was thinking maybe I should have his things appraised."

"Don't bother."

"I wouldn't mind knowing what they're worth."

"I'll tell you what they're worth," Mr. Sampras said. "Nada."

"You're impossible."

"Come on, what's in there?"

"A pendant, *and* part of his uniform, *and* some letters. War memorabilia is very hot right now."

"Listen to you."

"Listen to *Antiques Roadshow*! Anyway, it's not like I'm going to sell anything. I'm just—curious."

Again, the rustle of paper. A loud sip. "Alexis, did you get the brioche rolls? The good ones?"

"They're in the pantry."

Seconds passed. Saskia heard nothing but her own breath, in and out. Faster and faster. Her body still felt overheated—was it the whiskey or her nerves?

"Not to encourage you," Mr. Sampras said, "but I may have seen your grandfather's things in Paige's room a while ago. An old medal was on her desk. It has a striped ribbon, right?"

"What would Paige want with my grandfather's stuff?"

"She mentioned she's reading about it."

In Saskia's head, the pieces were beginning to snap together. And the picture they were forming was beyond disturbing.

"Well, now, that's a new interest," Mrs. Sampras said.

"She's already read every book in this house and most of what's in the town library. What do you expect?"

"Maybe she saw *Antiques Roadshow*. Like mother, like daughter."

They both giggled, and then Mrs. Sampras unconvincingly complained, "Hey—stop that!"

"You've got some time . . . I don't take long."

Saskia found their lilting laughter grotesque. Infuriating. Here she was, feeling like she'd been punched in the gut, and there they were—acting like, well, teenagers. She was glad her back was to a wall; there was a serious chance her legs would give out from under her.

The medal—Samuel's medal—was no token of his love. He hadn't given it to Paige in a dream. He hadn't given it to her at all. It was simply a Sampras family heirloom, something that had been kicking around the house. The ironic thing was that the "lost" medal was, right now, in Saskia's pocket. She'd put it there when she'd dressed in the morning, thinking it was lucky, a talisman, a totem, a sign of a friend's devotion.

Chewing on a fingernail, Saskia wished to god she'd listened to her instincts. She'd had her doubts about the medal's authenticity from the beginning. She remembered how she hadn't been able to bring Cornelius's newspaper from the past to the present. Why should Paige's experience have been any different?

The suspicious medal was one thread, but now that Saskia had pulled it, Paige's whole story started to unravel. If she'd lied about the medal, then chances were she'd lied about other things, too. Her "dates" with Samuel, their conversations and adventures, had they all been invented? And her participation in the Mercury Boys Club? Indeed, her founding of the club?

Was it all a sick, elaborate joke?

Her legs still threatening to give out, Saskia retraced her steps out of the house and toward the giant tree. She didn't know if Mr. and Mrs. Sampras heard her exit, and she didn't care. She no longer wanted to see what they looked like. In light of what she'd learned, everything related to Paige was different now. Tainted and distorted. Even the tree—their sacred meeting place—looked ugly, mocking, monstrous.

Saskia rustled through the branches. Adrienne was still missing, but the other girls were just as she'd left them. And yet, at the same time, completely different. She took the medal out of her pocket and hurled it at Paige, narrowly missing her head.

"What the hell, Saskia!" Paige cried.

"I overheard your parents," Saskia hissed, glaring. "They were talking about a war medal. How it belonged to your grandfather . . ."

She continued to feel unsteady, like the ground beneath her couldn't be trusted, like it was as suspect as the mesh floor she'd sat upon at Arrivo.

Paige stared at her without a hint of guilt. "Oh—that. Well, yes, he does have a medal. But it's different. It's just a coincidence that there are two. You didn't have to go ballistic; I could have explained."

How easily lies flew off her tongue! It was a talent, truly. Or an illness. Looking back, Saskia remembered how effortlessly Paige had deceived Rich, Jimmy, and how many others? Was Saskia just one more notch on her belt?

"Come on, Paige. Give it up. I *know*."

Paige glanced at Sara Beth, whose smirk confirmed Saskia's worst fears. Paige didn't have to confess. The truth was written in her sister's mischievous expression.

"What's going on?" Lila asked.

"It's a lie," Saskia told her. "All of it. Everything she said about Samuel. She just invented it."

Lila flinched. Her face turned a sickly shade. Meanwhile, Paige extended her arms in an idle stretch. Swimmer's arms, long and toned, inches longer than the sleeves of her dress. She had the audacity to yawn.

"I prefer to think of it as a game, not a lie," she said. Hearing this, Sara Beth let loose a low whistle.

Saskia's insides felt molten all of a sudden, like an internal volcano about to spew. "Why?" she asked, barely getting the word out.

"Why?" Paige repeated. "I'll show you." She lifted the hem of the gossamer lawn dress, pulling it all the way up to her waist. She was wearing underpants that matched her flesh, underpants so tiny and sheer she might as well have been naked. Saskia averted her eyes. All these weeks, and still she wasn't used to the sisters' utter lack of inhibition.

Boldly, Paige held her pose until Saskia looked. There, in tiny letters below Paige's hip bone, were not the letters MBC, but rather JM. Saskia felt the hot feeling climb up her throat. It singed her tongue until she was speechless.

JM.

Josh McClane. Oh god.

"I think Jimmy did a good job. He should have, considering the special bonus he thought he was gonna get from us," said Paige. "He had no idea what JM stood for, but I made something up."

"You always do," said Sara Beth admiringly.

"Thanks, Sis," Paige said, blowing her a kiss.

"All of this," Saskia whispered, still struggling to find her voice, "because of *Josh?*"

"Because you're a sneaky little slut," sneered Paige, suddenly contemptuous. "A sneaky little slut who should consider herself lucky. Usually Sara Beth and I aren't so forgiving."

The smile on Sara Beth's face now appeared dangerous to Saskia: reckless, vicious, lupine. "Paige is right. Other girls who've bothered us have learned *never* to do it again."

"Bet you didn't know my sister was kicked out of her last two schools," added Paige, her voice spiked with pride. "'Aggression and severe behavioral problems'—it's on her record."

Even if Paige was lying about that, too, it didn't matter. Goose bumps prickled Saskia's skin, every one of them a red alert. Clearly the sisters were no passive Victorian ladies. They were formidable enemies, cunning, strong, and unrelenting.

Saskia considered Lila, feisty but tiny, and realized that Paige and Sara Beth would easily win in a fight if it were two against two. Was that what was about to happen? Or would it be worse?

"God, this is crazy," she said, looking Paige in the eye. "We could have fixed this at the very beginning. I wouldn't have even talked to Josh if I'd known you guys were together. I didn't mean to do anything wrong."

Paige laughed gaily. "You didn't *mean* to. I see. You didn't mean to flirt with my boyfriend at Ethan's party. Or to throw yourself at him. Or fool around in an empty room with him. No, of course not. I'm *so sorry* for thinking you had."

"I was going to explain," Saskia protested. "I really was. I just . . . couldn't."

"No, just like you couldn't resist stealing someone else's boyfriend."

"I didn't think you were with him anymore," she repeated coldly.

"You know what I think, Saskia? I think it wouldn't have mattered to you. Not one bit. Even if Josh and I were attached at the hip, you still would have made a move. Because that's just the kind of person you are. Someone so insecure and pathetic that you'll do whatever it takes to feel better about yourself. To feel wanted. You'll break friendships—you'll break *people*—just to feel loved for one night."

Saskia winced. Paige's assessment hit too close to home.

Paige continued, "Thank god Adrienne was at that party and keeping an eye on Josh for me, or else I'd never have known."

"Did Adrienne know all of this?" Saskia asked her, her voice porcelain-brittle. "The lies?"

"Are you kidding? Adrienne's loyal, but she can barely spell her own name."

"Bless her dumb little heart," added Sara Beth.

"Then why put her through it?" asked Lila angrily.

"The more players, the better the game," answered Paige.

"Why do you keep calling it that? A game?" Saskia demanded. Her fists were clenched so hard her hands ached.

Paige looked at her sister. "You want to do the honors?"

"Sure," Sara Beth said cheerfully, as if agreeing to lead another toast. "The purpose of our little project, Saskia, was to make you suffer. I wanted an all-out assault. But my sister is more ambitious. She wanted something unique, something big and memorable. And she figured out what. Actually, *you* gave her the idea. You and your photo of Cornelius. All Paige and I had to do was pretend to believe your weird little secret. It's crazy how fast you fell for our stories, the club, the rules. Everything. You lapped it up."

"And licked the bowl clean," added Paige.

"But you missed the red flags," Sara Beth continued. "Samuel's not even Paige's type. He's basic and vanilla. With about as much charm as a dirty Kleenex. My sister likes guys like Harry Styles— know anyone like that?"

Saskia turned away from Sara Beth's antagonistic glare, almost as ashamed as she was furious. She thought back to the first time she'd been in the Sampras house. How she'd marveled at the huge wall of books in the den. *Paige's books*, Sara Beth had said. *She's read every one. Twice.* Back then, Saskia should have realized Paige was a girl who loved stories. A girl with an unbridled imagination.

Saskia had vastly underestimated her.

Hell hath no fury like a woman scorned. Was that a line from one of Saskia's classic movies? Or was it just an old saying? Either way, it was evidently true.

"My sister's got mad creative skills, doesn't she?" said Sara Beth admiringly. "Me? I'm the straitlaced, boring one. I may have gotten kicked out of school, but I've never done drugs, smoked cigarettes, or gotten a tattoo. And I never would."

Saskia could tell Lila was trying to hold it together. But her friend's face looked like it was about to cave in on itself. Paige noticed, too.

"Don't take it so hard, Lila," Paige said. "I know you and I didn't always get along, but hey, at least this summer was entertaining, right?"

"I feel sorry for you," Lila spat. "You're beyond help."

"Depraved," added Saskia.

"Aw, don't be bitter, Sask. All we did was make you pay your dues," Paige said.

"And toy with you a little bit," added Sara Beth.

"Like a cat toys with a mouse."

"Until it's dead."

"Or so mangled it wishes it were dead."

At that, the sisters dissolved into giggles. Saskia realized she would never know what made them tick. And she didn't want to know.

"I have to admit," Paige said, "Sara Beth and I didn't think it would go this far. That was a bonus. Just like Lila and Adrienne were bonuses. I wasn't sure what to do with them at first, but then everything just fell into place like it was meant to be. It was all pretty perfect."

"Except for the ending," said Sara Beth.

"Yeah. That didn't work out so well."

Saskia blanched. She knew now that Paige and Sara Beth were capable of unbridled cruelty, and that she and Lila would be in grave danger as long as they remained anywhere near the sisters. Paige smiled at her with mock sympathy. "So . . . you're wondering about the ending, right? Well, you and I just talked about stealing meds from the hospital? That was going to be the grand finale. The coup de grâce. The clincher. I'd talk you into it, and you'd get caught. I'd make sure of that. I'd make sure to implicate your dad, too. He'd get fired. Your whole family would fall apart."

"But wait," said Sara Beth, tapping her finger on her chin in a caricature of profound reflection. "Didn't that already happen?"

As an uncontainable rage coursed through her, Saskia lunged forward. She wanted to claw at the sisters' faces, to rake out their eyes, but Lila held her back.

"You're pathetic—both of you," Lila snarled, struggling to keep a firm grip on Saskia.

"Say what you want and think what you want," Paige retorted calmly, "but this whole thing from day one was a war as much as a game. And we won." She turned toward her sister. "Damn, that's a good line. Wished I'd used it for one of the Mercury Boys."

"Oh well. Missed opportunity," said Sara Beth. "Those boys don't need any more lines. It's the end of the road for them."

"I'll miss them, though," Paige said wistfully. "Believe it or not, I'll miss you, too, Saskia. We vibed in our own weird way, don't you think? We could have been real friends under different circumstances."

She was still gazing frankly at Saskia when she reached for one of the candles on the ground. For a few moments, she just stared at it, like the day she came up with the initiation. Saskia thought she'd blow it out—one last bit of drama.

Instead Paige held the flame to a nearby branch. After a couple of seconds, it caught fire. Bold and bright, the flame grew quickly, dancing from branch to branch, dry leaf to dry leaf. It spread swiftly, climbing stealthily in a dozen directions, toward the trunk, even over the girls' heads. Smoke and heat filled the air faster than Saskia could react.

The sisters began to make their way out. One of them—was it Sara Beth or Paige?—kicked Lila in the ribs. Hard. Saskia's panic ratcheted up as her friend, now winded, choked and coughed. Saskia knew she had to think fast. Lila wasn't moving. She scrabbled toward her and realized that the fire was creeping close to a section of branches directly behind her friend. If Saskia didn't reach Lila soon, the whole section would kindle and incinerate them both. But as smoke swirled, Saskia's eyes watered so much she couldn't see.

Her broken fingernails scratching earth, her knees bleeding, she crawled faster in Lila's direction, remembering suddenly how Lila had saved her in the pool. Her brave friend. She heard Lila coughing, a battle to breathe that might not be won, and scuttled toward the sound, finally finding a wrist, something to grab on to.

Saskia tugged with all her might. The fire was encroaching, but she persevered, pulling and dragging her friend through a rough veil of branches. And then, suddenly, they were out. Safe—if safe were possible on the Sampras property.

Catching her breath and blinking away tears and soot, Saskia clambered to her feet and forced Lila to stand, too. Together they fled as the fire engulfed the tree and its secrets, turning everything to ash.

CHAPTER TWENTY

They didn't stop moving until they'd made it to Lila's car. From there, they could still see the fire. Smoke billowed, rising higher than the roof of the house in huge, distressing plumes. Saskia heard yelling—the parents' voices. Mrs. Sampras, clearly distraught, shouted to her husband to call 911. Mr. Sampras yelled back, "Keep your distance, goddamnit! It's coming close to the house!"

"Where are the girls?!" Mrs. Sampras screamed.

Saskia and Lila didn't wait to find out. Lila hadn't recovered, but she nevertheless started the car with shaking hands.

They drove like hellions, the wail of fire engines rushing past as they sped in the opposite direction. Lila pressed hard on the gas until the car shook, while Saskia tried to calm down. Her head reeled. She was bruised and scratched. She felt like she'd swallowed a burning torch, but if Lila could concentrate enough to drive, she could manage, too. Still, she couldn't calm her mind. All she could think about was the mind-boggling extent of the sisters' trickery.

"We have to tell Adrienne," she said.

"That's where I'm going," Lila rasped.

Neither knew what else to say. The fire had shocked them into silence. In her head, Saskia went over everything the sisters had revealed. There were so many levels to their deceit. She tried to find her way back to the beginning. What was the very first lie Paige had told her?

She looked at Lila, whose brow was furrowed, whose own arms and hands were scratched from the branches. She wondered if Lila was wondering the same thing.

When they arrived at Adrienne's apartment, not a single light was on inside. Nevertheless, Lila parked, and the two girls got out. They went so far as to knock on the front door, though it was clear no one was home.

"They've been gone since early this morning," someone said. Startled, the girls wheeled around. An older woman, not quite a senior, but not middle-aged, either, appraised them from the foot of the driveway. Her face was concerned. "Are you a friend of the girl? Adrienne?" she asked.

Saskia nodded.

"I saw an ambulance here at dawn."

Saskia and Lila glanced at each other anxiously.

"Do you know why?" Lila asked.

"No, but they took the girl out on a stretcher. She didn't seem to be moving."

"Oh my god," Saskia heard herself say.

"Did they take her to Yale New Haven Hospital?" Lila asked.

"I don't know. I wish I did, dear. I'm prayin' for the girl. Seems like a nice kid."

Back in the car, Lila turned on the ignition. She touched her grandmother's dragonfly. Watching her, Saskia got a terrible feeling.

"Do you think Adrienne . . . did something?" she asked.

Lila didn't reply. She just gunned the engine.

They drove straight to the emergency room, where they were told Adrienne was in the Pediatric Intensive Care Unit. Yale New Haven Hospital was large and confusing, laid out mazelike across several city blocks. Lila cursed the one-way streets as they got back into the car and struggled to find the right building. Finally Saskia spotted it.

Inside, they hurried to the reception desk in the lobby and inquired about their friend. The woman asked if they were family.

Saskia shook her head. "Friends."

"Good friends," Lila added.

The woman studied the girls with a frown. Saskia realized they must look like hell between the scratches, dirt, and soot. "How old are you?"

"Sixteen," Saskia replied, regretting the answer when Lila nudged her with an elbow.

"I'm sorry, but anyone under eighteen has to be accompanied by an adult."

"We really need to see her."

The woman seemed to soften a bit. "Your friend's mother is with her. If she comes out, maybe she'll agree to escort one of you."

"One of us?" Lila asked, coughing.

"Only two visitors allowed at a time."

"Ma'am, please, can you tell us why she's here? What happened to her?"

"I'm sorry, but I can't release that information."

Saskia and Lila looked at each other helplessly, and then back at the woman. "Can we wait here, at least?" asked Saskia.

"As long as you like, but visiting hours end at nine."

Resigned, the girls settled in beige vinyl chairs. Saskia stared at the walls, at bad still lifes illuminated by the glow of sconces, at magazines fanned out on the tabletop in front of her. She reached for one blindly and flipped through the pages. She didn't read a single word.

Suddenly it occurred to her that her father was here. Not precisely here—but somewhere in the hospital. Knowing that he was nearby should have comforted her a little. Instead, it made her more nervous. What if they happened to run into each other? What would she say? How would she explain when she herself didn't know what had happened?

After a while, Lila got up and fetched two cups of water from a cooler in the corner. Saskia thanked her and gulped hers down. She hadn't realized how parched she was.

There was nothing left to do but wait, and wait some more. They sat for upward of two hours before Adrienne's mom swept past suddenly. She moved so fast, they almost missed her. Saskia had met Mrs. Arch once before, but she swore she looked older now. There was more white in her strawberry-blond hair, which hung limply around her tired face.

"Mrs. Arch," Lila called, standing up. Saskia got up, too.

Adrienne's mother stopped in her tracks and turned around. For a moment she looked distracted, even lost. Then she seemed to realize who they were, and her demeanor changed—for the worse.

Lila and Saskia approached cautiously.

"I'm so sorry," Saskia began. "We heard Adrienne's here. What happened? Can we help?"

"Are you Paige?" Mrs. Arch asked bluntly.

"No, I'm Saskia—and that's Lila."

"Oh yes, we've met. Now I remember."

From the tone of her voice, it was clear the memory wasn't a pleasant one. Saskia's hands went clammy. She wasn't sure she could take another showdown.

"We were hoping to see Adrienne," Lila said. "We've been so worried about her."

Mrs. Arch didn't look convinced. "Have you?"

"Yes. Of course."

"Tell me, were you also worried about her the night she came home catatonic, with soaking-wet hair? What were you girls doing to her?"

Wracked with guilt, Saskia looked down at her feet.

"How about the time when she threw up a stomach full of pills?"

"Mrs. Arch, please," Lila pleaded. "We know we haven't always done the right thing. But you have to believe us—we care about Adrienne."

"Very much," Saskia added.

"We just want to be here for her."

"I think you've done quite enough," Mrs. Arch sniped.

Saskia wilted under her glare.

"And don't expect sympathy," she continued. "You're not innocent. I don't know what happened, but I think you do."

"No, we don't know," Lila protested.

"Spare me! She shares everything with you girls! I hear the name
Paige five hundred times a day. You *do* know. Adrienne couldn't
have done this on her own. She's an innocent girl. A good girl. This
morning I found her with blood coming out of her mouth! Her
organs were shutting down. And she was in excruciating pain—did
you know that?"

"No," Lila whispered.

"Now she's in a medical coma," Mrs. Arch said, almost to herself. "Oh Lord, how could this happen?"

She put her face in her hands and started to cry. Saskia wanted
to comfort her somehow, but didn't dare try. It was a good thing,
because when Mrs. Arch lifted her head, she was even more livid.

"My daughter wouldn't take so much as an Advil until she met
you girls!"

Hastily, she opened her purse and fumbled through it. Saskia
half thought she'd pull out a gun and aim it at them. Instead,
she unearthed the daguerreotype of Emery. "What is this?" she
demanded.

Saskia looked at Lila uncertainly.

"What is it?" Mrs. Arch repeated, more loudly this time.

"Emery," Saskia said.

"He's Adrienne's boyfriend," Lila added quietly.

"What? This photograph has to be a hundred years old."

More than that, actually.

"It's—hard to explain," said Lila.

"And what do you mean, 'boyfriend'? Her boyfriend is Benjamin."

Again, Saskia glanced at Lila. She had no idea how to explain,
or where to start. Maybe it was better to say nothing. Information
on the Mercury Boys Club wouldn't help Mrs. Arch feel better.
It might even make her feel worse. Because no matter how you
distilled the story, it ended the same way: Adrienne had behaved

recklessly. Maybe she'd tried to kill herself on purpose to be with Emery. Or maybe it had been a terrible accident.

Either way, she was in a coma because of her involvement in the club. Saskia felt a guilt so acute she wanted to curl up in a fetal position.

"Adrienne was happy—*normal*—before she joined that group of yours. But when I found her, she was wearing a ratty old dress. She looked like a witch! Is that what you're teaching her to be? What are you, Wiccans? Satanists? Members of some other weird cult?" Mrs. Arch's voice was increasingly frantic. The woman at reception eyed them with concern. She stood up, phone in her hand. Saskia wondered if she'd call security.

"I don't know why you picked my daughter to bully," Mrs. Arch continued. "But I can promise you, when she gets better, you will *never* see her again!"

Grabbing Lila's sleeve, Saskia started to back away. Mrs. Arch glowered at them as they retreated.

On their way out of the hospital, both girls lost it, crying, leaning on each other. Today felt like the longest day of Saskia's life, and it wasn't even over yet.

"What's gonna happen?" she whispered when they were back in the Buick.

Lila shook her head. "Whatever's going on with Adrienne—it sounds bad. Real bad."

She started the engine, but idled on the street. Neither of them knew where to go. "At least it wasn't Paige who put her in the hospital."

Saskia shook her head. "But in a way, it was."

In a way, they'd all put her there. They all shared some responsibility in Adrienne's undoing. But Saskia didn't say this aloud. She figured Lila already knew.

CHAPTER TWENTY-ONE

After that, Saskia didn't have any more contact with Mrs. Arch. She didn't dare. It was Benjamin who gave her updates. Saskia couldn't have anticipated that they would call each other daily, their conversations polite and stilted at first, then more personal. She admitted that she'd quarreled with Adrienne. She admitted feeling guilty and ashamed. When she told him she wished she could do everything over again, only differently, he said she was being too hard on herself. He'd known Adrienne a long time, and she'd always been high-strung, impulsive, and prone to depression.

Saskia couldn't have guessed that she and Benjamin would bond in their common concern and even become friends. Who could have guessed that any of this would happen?

He visited Adrienne every day, sometimes twice a day. He probably knew as much about Adrienne's state as Mrs. Arch. It was Benjamin who told Saskia when Adrienne finally opened her eyes and when she squeezed his hand. Days after that, Saskia learned that Adrienne had spoken, only a few words, but the doctors were encouraged. They'd assumed she wouldn't pull through; they'd even warned Mrs. Arch to expect the worst. But day by day, Adrienne proved them wrong. She was fighting, and she was getting better.

When Adrienne was finally well enough to leave the hospital and begin treatment that would help with her neurological damage, her mom opted to take her to an out-of-state facility. To take Adrienne "somewhere safer," Benjamin told Saskia.

Days passed into weeks. But time didn't absolve Saskia of her guilt. She and Lila drove by Adrienne's apartment and saw a "for rent" sign. Once again, all the lights were off inside. There was an eerie stillness about the place, a sense of suspended animation.

If Adrienne never fully recovered, if she lost her coordination, or faculties, or memory, Saskia knew that she, Lila, Paige, and Sara Beth were to blame. It was a burden that they'd have to carry forever, a burden they deserved. Saskia felt a heaviness in her heart that hadn't been there before. But she knew that it wasn't nearly as bad as the price Adrienne had paid.

School was right around the corner. It was impossible for Saskia to believe classes were about to start. She was in no way ready. The summer had turned her world upside down and inside out. And yet life went on.

When her bus came on the first day of school, Saskia wondered if she'd ever make peace with all that had happened—Adrienne nearly dying, the sisters' lies, the end of certain friendships and her relationship with Cornelius. She didn't know how long it would take to feel normal again, and to some extent, it didn't matter. If nothing else, Adrienne's close call had made her more patient—and thankful. When she woke up in the morning, she was grateful just to be there, to have more time.

She relied on her father during those difficult days. He didn't know all that Saskia had been through, but he knew she needed him. He called and texted a dozen times a day.

> Just checking in. How's it going? Let's plan to eat dinner together at 6 at the diner.

Saskia realized she'd spent so much time griping about her mother, she hadn't given her father his due. He was a tremendous parent.

As she got deeper into her senior year, he got serious about studying for the MCAT. No more *Gilmore Girls* or cigarettes. Now whenever Saskia saw her father, he was taking practice exams or reviewing biology, physics, and biochemistry. Sometimes they studied together in the kitchen, sitting on either end of the table in silence.

On the morning of the test, Saskia made her father breakfast: eggs, toast, sliced tomatoes, and a big glass of lemonade.

"The taste and scent of lemons are supposed to improve mental acuity," she told him. "I read that in the news somewhere."

"Not sure that's science, but I'll take it," he replied, chugging down the glass.

To his immense surprise, her father scored well—in the ninetieth percentile. Now he had ammunition to get into medical school. A top medical school, even. Preferably Yale, so they wouldn't have to move again. He had never expected such a positive outcome.

But there was a hitch.

"I don't know how we'll pay for it," he said, scratching his head.

"We'll find a way," Saskia replied, meaning it.

As for Lila, Saskia still saw her every day. She still counted her as her best friend. Lila had been accepted for the Yale position, and now Saskia was starting to job-search, too. Only this time, she was serious about it. After all, she'd promised to help out her father, and she had to start saving for her own college tuition.

She would have preferred never to think about Paige and Sara Beth again. But she did. Every day. They hadn't gotten hurt in the fire—she'd read that in the news. The flames had spread to the Sampras house, but it had suffered only cosmetic damage. The firefighters had done their job quickly. Saskia admitted to being disappointed. If the house had burned down, then maybe the Sampras family would have moved out of Coventon. Maybe Saskia would never run into the sisters again.

Knowing they were still in town, Saskia and Lila at first went to great lengths to avoid them. They didn't go within a mile of the sisters' neighborhood and steered clear of their hangouts. Even so, Saskia imagined what she'd say and do when she met the sisters again—which was bound to happen eventually.

It was a huge relief when she didn't see Paige on the first day of school. Turned out she'd decided at the last minute to transfer to Sara Beth's school in Hartford.

"She told Josh there was nothing left to do at Coventon High," Benjamin said. "Whatever the hell that means."

Saskia knew exactly what it meant. The sisters were bored. They wanted adventure. Fresh meat. New blood.

"They're still together, you know. Josh and Paige," Benjamin said. "I would've thought they'd have broken up, with Paige at a different school, but I guess they're trying to make it work."

"What about you and Adrienne? Do you think you'll try to make it work?"

"I don't know. Honestly? All I want is for her to get better."

Saskia nodded, thinking that she and the other members of the Mercury Boys Club had been wrong to dismiss boys like Benjamin so easily. He was an upstanding person, moral and principled. In fact, he could have taught some of the Mercury Boys a thing or two.

CHAPTER TWENTY-TWO

Saskia's first semester as a senior lacked summer's excitement. In fact, it was downright boring at times, but that was just fine with her. She pushed herself and took multiple AP courses. She joined the yearbook committee. She even started Coventon High's very first film society. So far there were only a few members, Lila included, but Saskia was pretty sure more would join when she screened the first movie, her favorite Bette Davis flick: *Deception*. It was only appropriate.

She should have felt like her life was getting back on track. But after such a tumultuous summer, she was still on edge. There was always a feeling at the back of her mind that another bombshell was about to drop.

Then one morning, only a few seconds after she awoke, her father handed her his cell phone. "It's your mother. And this time she's got you."

Saskia sighed, too tired to put up her defenses. "Fine," she grumbled.

"Be nice."

"I'm always nice."

"Sure you are."

She put the phone to her ear and shooed him away. "Hi, Mom," she said.

"Thank god! I thought we'd never speak again!" Her mother's joke was laced with accusation.

"I'm here," Saskia replied dryly.

"It's been a long time—a very long time. *My* mother used to have a rule: she and I had to speak at least once a week, and that's when I was here, and she was in Ghana. You and I live in the same country. Don't you think we could do better?"

Saskia braced herself. Whenever her mother invoked Saskia's dead grandmother, the conversation usually went south.

"So how have you been?" her mother asked. "The whole summer's passed, and I barely know anything that happened. Did you meet any nice kids? Did you have a job? What's that town of yours like?"

Here they were again—the machine-gun questions. Bang, bang, bang! By now Saskia should have been used to them, but they always seemed to pelt her in the gut.

"Your father told me you have a friend named Lila," her mother continued. "Tell me about her. I'd love to learn about your new life."

"What do you want to know?"

"Well, *anything*, frankly."

"Everything's fine," Saskia said. "Everything's normal." The lies rolled out with surprising ease. Maybe she'd learned it from the sisters. She realized it was simpler to deceive her mother when she didn't have to look at her face. Her mother's searching brown eyes could root out just about anything. Thank god they were two time zones away.

"Saskia, a few details, please. I haven't spoken to you in an eternity. I don't even know what you mean when you say things are 'normal.'"

"I mean that they're good, Mom. I have this friend, Lila, like you said, and we hang out. School started, so I'm super busy. In fact, I should probably go, or I'll miss the bus."

"I think you can spare a couple more minutes for your mother."

"Well, if you want me to be late . . ."

"What books have you read? Have you tried that SAT prep app I texted you about? And how is your father? Is he *handling* things?"

Saskia took a breath and decided to adopt her mother's tactics. It was the only way she'd survive this conversation. "Mom, what about you? How's work? Any interesting new clients? How did that big DUI case go—the one with the politician? Did you win it?"

"Oh, we lost that one. He's going to jail. It was disappointing; we put in hundreds of hours."

"But he was a jerk, wasn't he?"

"Most of them are, dear."

There came a silence. Saskia searched her mind for a question, any question, but couldn't find one fast enough.

"Saskia, there is some news I want to share with you. I wish I could tell you in person, but I don't want to wait any longer."

"What is it?" A sense of dread spread through Saskia's body. She'd barely come to terms with her mother's last news: Ralph.

"After a lot of consideration, I've decided to have another baby."

Saskia just about keeled over. She felt like her mother had walloped her. "Is that even, like, possible?"

"Of course it's possible."

"Aren't you a little *old*?"

Her mother laughed uncomfortably. "I *feel* young. Besides, with technology nowadays, it doesn't matter how old you are."

"Um, it kind of does, Mom."

"Saskia, it's not like I'm a hundred!" Her mother was clearly surprised by Saskia's lack of enthusiasm. "I'm not going into this lightly, believe me. I know there are risks. But it's something I'm ready for." The finality of her tone made Saskia blanch.

"If that's what you want . . ."

"It is. And honestly, Saskia, I thought you'd be more supportive. You used to want a little brother or sister, remember?"

"That was a long time ago."

"It wasn't that long ago."

"Well, things are different now. *Really* different."

"You sound so—so jaded. No sixteen-year-old should sound like that. Are you trying to move forward like we talked about?"

"I *am* trying. I've been trying. It's been hard, Mom."

"I know."

Do you?

"There's another reason for my call. It's not just the baby I wanted to discuss."

Seriously . . . there's more?

"What I want you to know is, I want you back," her mother said. "Saskia, I want you to come and live with me."

Saskia tried to swallow, but there was no saliva left in her mouth. "I like being here with Dad."

"I understand that, but . . . well . . . the thing is, I need you."

Saskia wasn't sure whether to laugh or cry. Could this be it? The moment she'd been waiting for? Was her mother finally making her secret, innermost dream come true?

Saskia waited, praying her mother would give the speech that Saskia herself had scripted.

"I miss you. I'm so sorry. I realize now that you're my everything. I know I messed up, but it's not too late. Let's be together—you and I and your father. Let's be a family again. I promise I'll be a better person. And I'll get rid of Ralph. Can you forgive me?"

"I don't know, Mom," Saskia replied uneasily, waiting for the speech to come.

"Will you at least think about it?"

"I . . . I guess I can."

"Because when Ralph and I have the baby, we'll need help with childcare. I'll take a couple of weeks off, like I did with you. But then I have to go back to work full-time. I'd hate to hire a nanny. They're so expensive, and you can't trust them. Not a hundred percent, like family. I was thinking you could help out. Then you could spend a lot of time with your new sibling and really bond. Wouldn't that be nice?"

But after that first sentence, the rest of her mother's words sounded like static. Saskia's heart sank. Was that really all she was to her mother? A prospective babysitter?

"We'd use daycare while you're in school, of course," her mother continued. "But then you could watch the baby from three o'clock until Ralph and I get home—around six. He's working a temp job now, Ralph. Sometimes he gets home later than I do! But it's good for him—he's taking on more responsibility. Showing more initiative. I wouldn't be surprised if they hire him full-time."

Her mother paused. She was waiting for an answer. But the only thing Saskia could do was fight against a deluge of anguish and anger.

"Saskia?"

"I don't want to talk about it."

Her mother sighed. Lawyers weren't fond of noncompliance. They liked clear, crisp answers: yes or no. "Ralph and I need to start planning."

"That has nothing to do with me."

"Saskia, have you heard anything I've said? I'm asking you to help me. I'm asking you to come back to Arizona and be a part of this family."

"I already have a family. Dad."

"No, what you have with your father is an experiment. And I don't think it's going to end well."

Saskia shook her head, too riled up to respond.

Her mother read her silence. Correctly, for once. "Maybe you need to think this over," she soft-pedaled her suggestion. "Why don't we check in with each other in a couple days? I think by then you'll see the benefits."

Saskia let these words go in one ear and out the other. After hearing "experiment," she knew her mother had nothing worthwhile to say.

"Saskia, are you listening to me?"

"I don't want to talk in a couple days," she replied.

"Fine. A week."

"Not in a week, either."

"I hate to say it, but you're being selfish. You need to think about other people besides yourself."

Now that's the pot calling the kettle black.

Saskia clenched her father's phone so hard she wondered if it would crack. "I'll call you when I'm ready."

"Do you have any idea when that will be?"

"No clue. And if I were you," Saskia said, "I wouldn't hold my breath."

At that, she hung up the phone and tossed it aside. She felt as jittery as if she'd drunk a gallon of Coke. Moments later, she got up and went into the kitchen. Her fingers shook as she drank a glass of water.

Her father walked in but, seeing the look on her face, put up his hands. "Bad?" he asked.

"Awful."

"Want to talk about it?"

She shook her head, set the glass down, and went to the closet where the washer and dryer were stacked. She found one of her father's many clean white T-shirts inside the dryer, then returned to her room. She hadn't "made" any clothes for a long time, but she suddenly felt the desire. No, the need. Her emotions were causing such havoc inside her body she had to find some way to release them.

With a box of markers, she wrote word after word across the white cotton.

Defector.

Vigilante.

Subversion.

Mutiny.

Renegade.

Revolutionary.

Today, the day that she'd finally stood up to her mother, she couldn't wear her usual drab clothes. She needed a change. A new uniform for a new life.

Soon her white T-shirt was a helter-skelter hodgepodge of words. Different sizes, different colors, running in different directions. But they all delivered the same message.

When she ran out of space, she put on the shirt and stared at herself in the mirror. The last time she'd worn something brightly colored was the night she'd met Josh at the party. She'd been self-conscious, timid, and insecure then. Easy prey.

Not anymore.

"Benny, can I go to band rehearsal with you sometime?" Saskia asked him one day on the phone.

"You mean, at Josh's?"

"Yeah."

"Sure, I guess. Didn't know you were into our band."

"I just want to stop by," she said.

"Yeah, fine. That works."

When she asked Benny for directions, she didn't have any butterflies in her stomach. She was different now: a girl on mission. Lila volunteered to drive her, but warned her to be careful. "Don't regress and get a crush on Josh again."

"Are you kidding me? Give me some credit. Besides, this isn't even about Josh."

"I think I know what you're gonna do," Lila said. "And I probably should tell you not to. But hell . . . good luck."

When Saskia arrived, Josh's garage was open, and the boys were warming up. At least, she thought they were warming up. She hoped that whatever grating noise coming out of their instruments wasn't supposed to be music.

Benjamin put down his drumsticks and gave her a wave.

Josh flicked his hair out of his face, adjusted his guitar strap, and eyed her in surprise. "Hey! Saskia Brown, good to see you."

"I came to audition."

"Really?"

"Nah." She smiled shyly.

"Yeah, well, welcome anyway. The other guy, Frankie, should be here soon. You're welcome to stay and listen to us rehearse."

"Actually, I kinda wanted to talk to you about something."

His hair had fallen over his face again, so Saskia couldn't be sure if he was nervous or not. Interestingly, she felt perfectly at ease.

"Here?" he asked.

"It's private."

Josh nodded and said he was taking a five-minute break. Then he and Saskia walked around back to a fenced garden. Fall blooms, asters and black-eyed Susans, drooped in the cool air. Muck and wet orange leaves clung to the soles of Saskia's shoes.

"So what's up?" he asked.

"You probably know that Paige and I were pretty good friends this summer," she said, letting the statement dangle.

"Yeah, she mentioned that. But she also said you guys had a falling-out."

"Did she say why?"

He shrugged. "Not really."

"It was 'cause of a boy."

She watched Josh kick a clod of dirt with his sneaker. "It wasn't me, was it?"

"Um, don't take this the wrong way, but definitely *not*."

Even with hair in his face, Saskia could see his cheeks flush. "Yeah, that's cool. I get it."

"This guy, he's not someone you know. He's older—in college. And he lives in England."

"How'd you guys meet him?"

"Well, his poetry is very . . . memorable. It's been compared to Thoreau's. I think he and Paige connected over that."

"Over poetry? Huh. So, what, they found each other on social media or something?"

"They met in person."

"In England?" he asked incredulously.

Saskia nodded. "They've met a bunch of times in secret. Their relationship's been on the down-low for months. His name's Sam.

They're really into each other. This summer he was all Paige talked about. I guess I'm telling you because I'd want to know if I were being cheated on."

Josh exhaled audibly. "Are you sure?"

"Very. Paige's obsessed with him. Sam's introduced her to all his friends. He gave her, like, a valuable family heirloom. The whole situation's very . . . dramatic."

Josh suddenly crouched down. She wondered if he was feeling light-headed.

"Look, I don't like being a snitch," she continued, "but I also don't like when guys are suckered. It's not a good look."

"I just . . . I can't believe it."

"Believe it," she said, then took out her phone and showed him some texts from the summer.

> P: all I can say is sam's PERFECT. i'm blown away
> S: what happened?!
> P: what didn't happen? i feel like i've known him for years & we only just met. Can't stop thinking about him. maybe I'm under a spell?
> S: maybe. tell me more
> P: tell u everything tonight. Every juicy detail
> S: how juicy
> P: u won't be disappointed. I'm falling fast.

Josh got a queasy look. She touched his shoulder lightly. "I hate that she's been keeping this a secret from you. But you should know . . . her relationship with this guy—Sam—it's serious. I mean, she even wrote, like, a marriage contract. Swearing she'd *die* for him."

"What?"

"I know. Crazy, right?"

"I—I don't know what to say."

"You should talk to her. Demand the truth—the whole story— from the beginning."

"Where would she even start?" he asked bitterly.

"Probably Mirror Lake."

"Mirror Lake?"

"Paige said that's where things first heated up." Saskia gazed at him with as much solemnness and commiseration as she could muster. "One word for you, Josh. Skinny dipping."

He sighed. "That's two words," he muttered.

"Does it matter?"

"Yeah, you're right. Hey, um, thanks for telling me. I guess. I mean, I'm not sure how to react to this."

"It's okay—I've been there. Paige has a habit of messing with people's minds."

"I guess we have that in common," he agreed. His eyes flashed to hers, and he offered a sad smile. "Hey, you wanna stay? Maybe hang out after we rehearse?"

Saskia held his gaze for a moment, then shook her head. "Nah. It's too late for that."

They talked about it all the time, Saskia and Lila. What should become of the Mercury Boys Club. Adrienne was no longer in the picture, and Lila and Saskia promised themselves they wouldn't reach out to her. Maybe someday Adrienne would contact them, but that was her decision to make. They would just have to wait and see.

As for Paige and Sara Beth, they had mercifully stayed away. And Saskia had let go of Cornelius. Everything had changed. It only made sense that the club change, too. In fact, it only made sense that it end—that was what Saskia and Lila were thinking. No more mercury. No more pills. No more dangerous pranks, health scares, and backbiting.

And now, no more Cassie.

"She broke up with you," Saskia asked in disbelief.

"I broke up with her."

"It's because you're in love with me again, aren't you," Saskia deadpanned.

"Shut up. I broke up with her because it's too much—it's just all been too much."

Lila didn't have to elaborate. Saskia knew exactly what she meant.

"And for your information, my crush on you is ancient history," Lila informed her. "I have my eye on a hot little number in my study hall. She always sits at the same table as me. Every Tuesday and Thursday. It means something, right?"

"What do I look like—some kind of love expert?"

Lila rolled her eyes. "Speaking of love, is anyone on your radar?"

"Last night I had a date with a king-size Kit Kat. Does that count?"

"It depends. What were you wearing?"

Saskia giggled, but even with Lila, her best friend, she didn't admit that she was often lonely, and that she often thought about Cornelius far too much. Still, she knew she couldn't have him—not in that way. She wouldn't put another family through what she'd been through. And besides, she'd finally returned Cornelius's daguerreotype to the library. She'd mailed it back to the library, care of Marlene.

The thought of it sitting there alone in the archives saddened her, but some things must be done.

"I have an idea," said Lila.

"You do? What?"

"We have these darn tattoos, right? Let's make another club—with the same initials. A club that doesn't involve lying, injury, trespassing, arson, and poison."

"So something like the Mad Barbaric Cowboys?"

"Not exactly what I had in mind, but I like the creativity."

"More Boiled Cabbage?"

"No. But an A for effort."

"Merry British Cyclones?"

"That's a big nope. It appears we're failing."

"'But failure is merely a necessary catalyst, propelling us ever closer to success.'"

"What?"

"Nothing," said Saskia wistfully, shaking her head.

"I see this may take a while, so how about this? I'll come over, help your dad not ruin his weekly Kyinkyinga, and then we come up with a club we'd *actually want to join.*"

"I like it, Defensor. Good plan."

As the girls walked toward Lila's Buick, which had accrued a few more dents and dings since the summer, Saskia realized with a jolt that she was feeling, well, like herself. Like the Saskia she'd been before moving to Coventon, someone who was secure, confident, and comfortable in her own skin. It had been a long time since she'd felt this way. Too long.

Rifling through her backpack, she found a Sharpie and added a few more words to the assortment scribbled on her T-shirt.

MILESTONES/MISTAKES
ENEMIES/FRIENDS
HOPE/REDEMPTION
THE JOURNEY

ACKNOWLEDGMENTS

We writers like to complain about toiling alone, but the truth is that our books would not be half as good—or even possible—without the wisdom, hard work, support, and professional expertise of many others. There are many people who made invaluable contributions to *Mercury Boys* and who helped transform a glimmer of an idea into a full-fledged reality. My deepest thanks to my crackerjack literary agent, Marly Rusoff, who is as resourceful as she is smart. My early editor, Dan Ehrenhaft, championed this novel from the get-go and offered insights that were always sound and often transformational. I was doubly lucky to work with ace Soho Team members Rachel Kowal and Alexa Wejko, who guided this novel to the finish line. Thanks to other talented members at the press, especially Bronwen Hruska, Janine Agro, Rudy Martinez, and Steven Tran. Loving gratitude also goes to my family, especially Basil, Niki, Alexie, Anna, Ravi, Maggie and Rick Wetzel, and my parents, Radha and Sue Prasad. Friends new and old, including John and Theresa, Erin, Trina, Mayumi, Neela, Steve, Audrey, Donna, Katie, Deb, Lee Anne, Colette, Emily, Michelle, Amy, Jennifer and David have all been lodestars to me in so many ways. Thank you.

Finally, I consulted numerous resources for this book, including but not limited to *Quicksilver: A History of the Use, Lore and Effects of Mercury* by Richard M. Swiderski; *Cased Images & Tintypes*

KwigGuide: A Guide to Identifying and Dating Daguerreotypes, Ambrotypes, and Tintypes by Gary W. Clark; "A Very Good Specimen of the Daguerreotype" by Marian S. Carson; *Pennsylvania: History of a Commonwealth* by Randall M. Miller and William Pencak; *Robert Cornelius: Portraits from the Dawn of Photography* by William Stapp; and the clever, funny, and diverting Tumblr account *My Daguerreotype Boyfriend* curated by Michelle Legro.